AQUALENE

High Adventure to Clean Energy

PAUL K BROWN

D1451217

Dedication

*In honor of the many
forward-thinking engineers
and scientists advancing
clean energy independence.*

One

Somebody wanted him dead.

Awareness of the shadowy assault crept over him while he lay in Seattle's lower downtown section. Beneath his sprawling body the greasy damp asphalt chilled his bones. One eye blinked under a smear of blood and rain dribbling down his forehead. His mind slowly began clearing away the remnants of lost consciousness. The crumbling alley way came into focus.

Someone had clobbered the 31 year-old mineralogist, and whatever blows he'd been lucky to survive wouldn't be the last attempt on his life. He knew he must move on from where he lay, perfectly still, listening, waiting … for what?

Who had tried to kill Adam Harlow?

Insubordination was the culprit that'd put him on the streets. That he knew. After six years with Chemtx Corporation, a local firm in the business of developing hydrogen cell technology for public & private transportation applications, questions had turned into confrontation. Adam could sit back and watch no longer his labors to develop safe reliable components get shelved away by the paper-pushing clowns upstairs. What sort of business model hacks up its quality-control department … only to scrape up a few more cents of bottom-line profits?

No, it wouldn't be long now. Frank Chamberlain and his boardroom cronies would be run out of town. Reports of the company's first wrongful death case had already made headlines. An inferior fuel cell, designed and marketed by the firm, had exploded under the hood of a hydrogen-electric car on a New Jersey turnpike.

Now, inside two months without work, Adam had learned to adapt. Had adjusted to the worst of urban street life deep in the heart of town. In a world of desperation, perpetual hunger and putrid stenches, he was leaner, tougher. Attempted muggings and assorted back-alley threats had been a string of traumatic awakenings since departing a secure office life. Beggars demanding food, cash, cigarettes, liquor were now an

1

integral part of daily life. One which Adam Harlow reluctantly had come to accept as reality.

Hard living had changed him. Made him stronger, more resilient. In bad times full employment is always a luxury. It was something else to walk in another man's shoes. Adam was less a stranger to the streets. To survive is to adapt, and if one could not adapt, one expired to make room for those who could adapt.

Local jobs offerings had mostly dried up, leaving nothing to be found on Craigslist and other local publications. Personal effects of all sorts were piled high on sidewalks. Guarded and sold at bargain-basement prices, evictees all over town unloaded anything and everything that was no longer a necessity. Domestic creatures of every sort ran free, seeking the same dry places and discarded food sources accessed by the homeless. Excess living in America had come to a bitter end for much of the middle class. And God knows where else. No jobs translated into raw survival for man, woman, and child.

Now somebody wanted him dead. And for good reason, given certain developments transpiring inside his dingy underground lab in recent weeks.

Adam propped himself up on one elbow and gingerly slid a hand inside his jacket. He was surprised to find his wallet intact. The quarters and some folded ones he kept in a worn leather pouch for amiable beggars were untouched. Who was after his blood and not his money?

During the past year with a monthly paycheck, nearly half his salary had gone to helping his mother steer out of a pending foreclosure while shoring up hospital debts she'd been saddled with since a botched hip replacement. Now, in a matter of weeks the bank threatened to take her little house away. Force her to camp in the woods as others near her did.

Mom had relied on a few neighbors back in rural Dakota who'd promised to help.

But everyone had problems of their own. Promises were not what they used to be. Not anymore.

Having little cash left in reserve, Adam had resolved to vacate his over-priced downstairs studio apartment in a rundown section of Seattle's Fremont neighborhood; once a trendy locale for affluent twenty and thirty somethings until the city suburb had fallen into decay, in tandem with hard times. Months before getting the axe at Chemtx he'd been strong-armed for cash three times on the city bus; while daytime burglaries cleaned him out too many times to bother the cops about it. The evening before moving out he was held up at gun-point before leaving a Fremont Arco station. Armed thugs jacked his early model Saab with one goal in mind: Suck out his six-gallon fuel ration, which sold quickly on the black market for three, four, maybe five times what he'd paid at the pump.

Times were tough, making theft a way of life for the innovative and the desperate.

Gingerly, Adam examined what he found to be a superficial head wound. His hair was matted where he'd shed some blood that night. He surveyed the alley with due caution from where he lay. Detecting nobody lingering about he staggered to his feet. An unmarked delivery truck stood several feet off to his left. Its hazard lights flashed yet he saw no sign of the driver. Gray light penetrated drizzling skies, suggesting Adam had been out cold for several hours. Beyond the surrounding brick walls he recognized the tops of neighboring buildings. He was within two blocks of his original destination. The bustle of foot traffic some twenty yards beyond the dumpster where he steadied himself brought mild relief. In the denser sections of town daylight hours were reasonably safe. After dark was another matter.

If nothing else, downtown living had eliminated the long bus commutes and other assorted dangers where police presence had become non-existent. In the heart of town Adam could hang on. For he'd seen worse among those he considered friendly faces, many with whom he elicited comradery and traded meager assistance. On the street generosity is remembered and reciprocated in the smallest of notions. In the lab Adam had invoked his most frugal cash-saving survival skills. Reminiscent of his college days, he'd resorted to watered down soups, potatoes, rice, and noodles. Cheap carbohydrates.

He was hungry now and longed for a single egg in boiled ramen. He would warm it over from a leftover batch prepared yesterday in a tiny microwave oven adjacent to his narrow cot situated in a dusty corner of his underground lab.

Renee DeLong—a woman he knew little about, except that she was a significant player inside NASA—had recruited him among others around the country to help resurrect a lost fuel formula. The federal government had been developing a highly volatile liquid alternative to the nation's failing gasoline supplies. Labeled *Aqualene*, its properties were highly complex, derived of a specific blend of largely ignored but readily available minerals whose elements when correctly and precisely processed could rapidly extract the hydrogen from salt water. Through a potent but stable fusion sequence, an incredible burst of heat and explosive energy could be generated. Clean heat, many times more powerful than fossil-based fuels. A rather remarkable substance of a subtle blue tint when balanced perfectly, as DeLong had described it. Before concluding their interview, she'd insisted this was the answer to the world's economic woes. America would lead a crusade to clean energy!

An accident at some secret lab, in a location she did not reveal to him, had interrupted the data-collection sequence. Whatever data NASA had been tracking had been lost instantaneously to an uncontrollable fire. Clues of the formula's makeup now remained sketchy, according to DeLong. While an inferior specimen from earlier tests was available to Adam for analysis, it lacked the potency necessary for widespread manufacture. The higher grade had to be found and duplicated. And for that, a handsome reward was to be offered.

A labor of love, she had confessed while outlining the non-salaried assignment. A dangerous undertaking with a handsome reward for whoever could turn up the right data.

And now the value of such a purse was bearing out truth. Someone had taken a lethal whack at him in the middle of the night. Most likely for purposes of leveraging the unimaginable gains *Aqualene* would yield as a precious commodity.

4

He was dealing with something he knew little about, yet it was Adam to embrace such ventures. Since childhood he'd been a fool for long-shot tasks, challenges yielding lofty results, big returns. Presently his doubts were adding up, and fast. The minerals cited by NASA to construct *Aqualene* were largely unfamiliar to the average mineralogist. There would be other scientific unknowns, anomalies, obstacles ... and with no financial backing to carry him. The bank account he'd watched erode away was all but depleted.

Logistics presented their own issues.

"Absolutely NO Internet transmissions!" DeLong had firmly stipulated; a matter of security. This meant travel. Given the state of fuel supplies, travel was now a major undertaking in America. Its cost was prohibitive and its procurement cumbersome.

So here he was pitted against all odds. Contracted work that paid nada ... until he could hand-deliver definitive results to NASA's Jet Propulsion Labs in Pasadena. All the while glancing over his shoulder for the next assault. If nothing tangible ever came of his toils, he'd reasoned, NASA's brainchild might keep him off the cold damp streets until summer. He would move forward. Even at the risk of failing.

Memory of his plight in the pre-dawn hours drifted back into his aching skull. A vehicle, silent, unseen, had pulled up onto the sidewalk. A powerful arm, extending from the window, wielded a blunt instrument of some sort and had struck Adam from behind. He'd stumbled, fallen, and then somehow managed to get up and run in a dead sprint. The spins overtook him within a block or two. Desperately he'd searched the shadows for cover, finally dropping to the pavement in a notch between the slimy brickwork and a soiled dumpster. It was there, concealed from the side streets, Adam Harlow had been fortunate to lay unconscious.

If someone wanted him dead they'd be searching for him, or perhaps monitoring his every move. So, where ... or when would they strike next?

Swaying over his feet he moved blindly toward a rusted drainpipe protruding from the brick wall. Enough water dribbled from it to rinse his face clean. Gingerly, he raked the half-dried blood from his hair. He'd been lucky. A more careful probe to his head told him the gash was superficial; the result of being a moving target. His aches would pass with some nourishment. He longed for sleep, a luxury he'd not enjoyed for days.

Hundreds of minds were on the *Project*. Many inside clean, safe, warm government labs. Positions filled by tenured scientists. Meanwhile, Adam Harlow had been working from a five-pound bag of lunar & earth bound minerals, along with a diluted sample of the formula. Working inside a dingy space beneath the streets of Seattle's condemned historic underground section. DeLong had pulled some strings with the city, arranging for him to occupy the unseen spot disguised as a tectonic monitoring station for the U.S. Geological Survey.

The rain water from the pipe helped to clear his mind. Adam Harlow was eager to get back to his lab. Wary of trouble ahead and behind him, he made his way to Sonny's Place, a small lunch café off First Avenue near the bottom of Yesler Way. It was there Adam could access the basement lab, through a back door behind the café's kitchen.

Rounding the corner, he found a handwritten sign taped to the café's front door. *CLOSED*. Adam tried the knob. It turned under his hand. He stepped inside and pulled it gently shut, pausing long enough to glance at a clock on the wall to his right. Almost noon! What the hell was happening? The joint was dark, stone silent?

"Over here, Mr. Harlow." The voice came from a dimly lit corner to his left. Sonny's tone conveyed the imperative rather than his usual sing-song greeting. "I want you to talk with Detective Fischer … now, sit down, my friend."

Adam paused long enough to scan a stretch of police ribbon cordoning off the kitchen entrance to the Underground. Had the cops come to inspect? Shut him down?

He pulled off his jacket and slid into a chair across from the detective.

His mind raced for clues. A fire in the kitchen? Nothing smelled burnt. A robbery? A restaurant was as likely a place as any to make off with some quick easy cash. The thought of a

6

holdup crossed Adam's mind, yet the restaurant owner failed to display signs of personal trauma.

The possibilities were countless. Times were tough and crimes of the desperate nature occurred daily, all over town.

Fischer looked Adam up and down methodically, noting the broad shoulders outlining a slender but powerful frame and muscular forearms. Adam's wire-rimmed lenses gave his brown eyes an unassuming, gentle appearance.

"Okay, tell me ... what's going on here?" Adam looked first to Sonny and then to the plain-clothes cop.

Fischer delivered a slight nod over to Sonny.

"About ten this morning ... two men show up," he began. "And they start demanding entry to the underground corridor. So I ask 'em: 'Who you guys looking for?' They wouldn't give a name. One of 'em, a tough bruiser of sorts, he says he needs to speak with a technician in a laboratory run by the Geological Survey."

Adam waited for Fischer's interjection. Nothing.

"Next thing I know they're forcin' their way past me and headed downstairs. That's when I called the police."

Fischer raised a finger and drew in a breath between taut jaws. Slowly he phrased his first question: "Do you know *what* they were looking for, Mr. Harlow?"

Sonny locked an expectant gaze toward Adam, his curiosity heightened.

Adam's mind raced for any explanation. Anything to satisfy Fischer ... without getting into details. He'd been ordered to keep the *Project* under his hat. The wrong people would be snooping around to learn what they weren't supposed to know. The lab was under some degree of automated surveillance, a level of security of which DeLong had expressed serious doubts. The underground section had been largely barricaded by the city. For decades only one or two access routes had remained open for employees working the steam tunnels.

Adam had permitted himself to recruit a few others to handle some of the repetitive testing. The operation was piecemeal and part-time. He'd rationalized help in light of improving his odds of discovery. Having only two qualified assistants beat going about it solo.

One was Moi Song, a Chinese exchange student who helped write computer algorithms. She'd been working upstairs part-time for Sonny while she studied coding at the University of Washington, three or four miles away. They'd gotten acquainted in the café and he'd offered her a few extra hours a week to develop a computer search model. Hiring strangers carried some risks. He'd known that. On the other hand, finding nothing of *Aqualene* was guaranteed failure.

Adam's thoughts returned to the detective's question, still undecided about his answer.

Like a hole in the head, he needed the cops and the media profiling him for running an undisclosed research operation in a condemned historic section of 19th century Seattle. A confession could jail him for handling classified data, if not conspiring to reconstruct a highly combustible substance beneath metropolitan streets. Weeks … or months might pass before the police department could verify Adam's legitimate connection to NASA's recovery project.

Fischer leaned forward. "Mr. Harlow, tell me, what is the nature of your business downstairs?"

"It's all really quite tedious and mundane," Adam paused, his eyes scanning the vacant restaurant again. "I analyze soil samples, some of which contain sedimentary compounds embedding highly intricate molecular structures, indicative of regional tectonic shifts." Brilliant, he thought, how it all just rolled off his tongue. And in some round-about way, it was true.

More importantly, Fischer seemed to be buying it. He'd shrugged a shoulder and begun tapping on his electronic tablet.

Adam and Dr. Heinrich Mann, a professor of Atmospheric Sciences on loan from the University of Wurzburg in Germany, had shared data on NASA's venture two weeks earlier. That was hours before Mann deployed for a post aboard the International Space Station. The two conceded the lost secrets of *Aqualene* would take tens of thousands of trials to arrive at the exact molecular structure that had mysteriously vanished from NASA's test equipment late last year. Mann had agreed to stay in touch and was eager to hear what news Adam could offer on any progress he was making. Mann promised to do what he could from ISS to decipher more details about the minerals.

Adam's mouth became dry. His chest tightened. What had occurred down in his lab to invite a police investigation? Before he could prepare himself for more technical Q & A, Fischer was on the prowl with a new question.

"Mr. Harlow, tell me ... how well did you know Mr. Kabib?"

Adam blinked. A knot grew deep in his throat as he played back the detective's question in his head. He then sprang suddenly to his feet. "What do you mean: How well *did* I know Mr. Kabib?"

After meeting the middle-aged chemist from Cairo in the steam tunnels where he worked for the city's maintenance, Adam had hired Gamil Kabib six hours a week to help run the algorithms that Moi had programmed into Adam's laptop. He'd been very efficient, testing and evaluating NASA's stash of minerals. Mr. Kabib had been scheduled to come in early that morning, after pulling a late shift at the steam plant a half mile north of the lab. Before Kabib's arrival, Adam had gone out for fresh air and to fetch a midnight snack.

With reserved horror, Adam Harlow began to piece together the puzzle.

The detective's jaw stiffened. His brows furrowed and tracked Adam carefully. "Mr. Harlow, sit down." Deep lines on his face twisted and he spoke slowly, mindful that Adam understand his every word. "Mr. Kabib was *murdered* earlier this morning."

Shaking his head, Adam sat stunned. A jumble of emotions boiled up inside him. "What the— how the devil... No, no this can't–"

Fischer patiently sipped a water bottle and gave Adam time to unravel in his wooden chair. He studied the young man, a lean and muscular mix of Native and Anglo stock. Methodically, gracefully, as if he were following some ancient rite, Adam Harlow mourned his loss and gradually collected his wits.

9

"I was hoping you could offer us clues, Mr. Harlow."
Fischer was ready to move on with business. "I suspect these
characters didn't have the time to find whatever the hell they
were after. Evidence suggests Mr. Kabib startled one or both in
the underground corridor, not far outside your laboratory."

Adam gulped and stared past Fischer toward the kitchen.
Haunted by Gamil's last goodbye, he clenched a fist. "Any
chance they're still down there?"

"Strange thing," Fischer said, studying Adam. "They split
up and ran in opposite directions. The killer took off
somewhere up the line toward the steam plant."

"And the other one? Is he still loose?"

"My partner found the accomplice lying in the alley with
a slug in his hip ... from the same firearm that was used on Mr.
Kabib." The detective peered at his tablet. "Richardson's the
name, Thomas Richardson. Sound familiar?"

Half listening, Adam mumbled the name aloud. "I...I
don't know anyone by that name. Is the bastard local?"

"He was carrying a Texas driver's license. I suspect the
two were hired by a bounty organization. That may explain
why one shot the other. Richardson and his partner were
looking for something important. Extremely valuable, worth
killing another man for."

Adam coughed. "Look, I need to get into my lab."

"No dice. Not unless I escort you down there, but only for
a minute or two. You're likely to muck up the evidence we
need to nail these guys."

Adam turned to Sonny. "What about your employees?"

"They're okay," he replied. "I sent 'em home for the day.
Miss Song is waiting to hear from you." Sonny handed Adam
a napkin with a telephone number scribbled on it.

Adam breathed easier. At least one from his lab was out of
harm's way. Fischer made a note of her Chinese first name,
rhyming it aloud with *soy*, then closed his notebook and led
Adam down the decayed set of wooden stairs into the dimly lit
corridor.

Once down below, Adam detected the smell the sulfur
lingering in the musty cavernous air. Fischer hadn't taken ten
steps when he halted and pointed to the dirt path ahead of

10

them. "I suspect the two were busting up the place when Mr. Kabib came through. My partner found his body over there." His flashlight flicked over a spot several yards beyond the lab's entrance.

Adam felt a sudden urge to vomit, unable to ignore the traces of Gamil's blood stains on the ground. A swirl of confusing odors entered his nostrils. Burnt gunpowder, blood, and something else; odd smelling, unfamiliar.

Keenly aware of the latter, Adam probed for more answers. "Any evidence of a struggle?"

"Not yet. Only that Kabib somehow got in their way." Fischer wagged his finger toward the ground. "That, Mr. Harlow, leads me to wonder about the circumstances. There's little physical evidence to suggest a premeditated motive. Unless, the gunman had somehow mistaken him for ...."

A mix of anger and fear swelled up in Adam. Gamil had been doing what he could under hard-luck circumstances to feed his wife and two kids. Such a tragedy as this was unforgivable! Adam fought to push thoughts of revenge aside and stared over Fischer's light beam at a pile of printouts scattered on the earthen floor. The binder he and Gamil had used to keep notes about *Aqualene* was open and lying on the workbench. Some of its pages were bent and tattered. Others were missing, along with his laptop.

Fischer pulled out a business card. "We've taken pictures and fingerprint samples. Soon as I hear back from my tech in Forensics, I'll notify you." He looked down at the narrow army cot. "For now, I suggest you find another place to lay your head." Fischer reached out toward a small messy workbench and poked a pencil he'd drawn from a coat pocket at some open containers. "Anything hazardous here?"

Adam paused. "Dangerous?"

"You know what I mean: toxic chemicals, acids, flammables ... hazardous!"

Adam shrugged. He saw little he could deem valuable of his research, unaware that earlier the detectives had spooned into a plastic bag some small quantity of a blue foamy substance that had spilled over the workbench into the dirt. Some variation of Thorium had been detected in the mix; a distance sister to Uranium. Oddly it hadn't been labeled as Thorium but the material he'd analyzed showed identical properties. Resolving to add no more to the conversation, Adam let silence fall between them.

Fischer spoke finally. "Look, I'll need to get a HAZMAT team in here as soon as we're finished with the investigation. Anything you want back will have to be claimed at the downtown precinct with this here receipt."

Before leaving, the detective dusted more fingerprints and repeated orders that Adam stay out of the lab. Fair advice, considering the odds Richardson's partner was apt to return, and would kill anyone who got in his way.

Two

Inside his corner suite atop the Power Building in downtown LA, 63-year-old Rodney Panach lit up a cigar and watched the smoke curl into the air between his desk and three wall screens. It was here where he agonized over the declining market indexes, the worst having been for six straight weeks.

Two decades into the millennium he'd possessed the power and influence that likened him to the great W. C. Durant of the 1920s. For several profitable years Panach controlled much of Wall Street and remained at the helm of the largest petroleum conglomerate in the world. This meant navigating a post oil-boon era. Fracking produced little more than a million barrels a day, a tenth of its peak at 10.4 million barrels three years earlier. Furthermore, the volume of crude oil trading was down to a third of what the stock had traded nine months ago. The long & short? Oil prices were skyrocketing and supplies were plummeting. Speculators could agree on one thing: the only certainty about oil was that its future was absolutely *uncertain.*

The deepening lines on Panach's face attested to the fact he had labored to take Admiral Petroleum a few steps out of the woods, by short-selling a cache of hedge funds against the price of foreign crude—a significant loss to his American-based empire. Tens of billions of inflated U.S. dollars had electronically changed hands and been sent to bulging offshore accounts before OPEC's emergency energy summit in Paris had reconvened on its third day. Media not yet controlled by Panach had missed Admiral's move to bolster its cash holdings while stockholders talked about a major reorganization of the industry to prepare for harder times. Panach controlled enough of America's foremost media organizations to deceive the public en mass. A well-oiled public relations machine, news agencies simply reported the sell-off as a goodwill gesture at a time when investors were hungry to rebuild battered portfolios.

Admiral's assets, heavy in once lucrative Venezuelan and Mexican oil stock, had begun to slide while leaking into the hands of eager investors clamoring on false rumors that oil futures might rebound. But economic revival would rely too heavily on an unlikely surge in refined fuel products. Admiral Petroleum's layer of cash-rich insulation wouldn't hold for long. Logging the Sierras for biomass had been tabled, but its political fallout had quickly strained regional relations, despite the California governor's effort to campaign for an aggressive harvest. The company desperately needed something groundbreaking. A game-changing venture through which to channel idle capital and reverse diminishing returns.

It was time to procure a fuel product with the comparable input-to-output energy that gasoline had been during its profitable years. A renewable energy source that could make a resounding splash across imploding energy markets around the world.

He gazed at his father's portrait on the wall. He'd been a self-determined magnate whose use of commercial satellite technology—made available to him by wireless media moguls ruling Mexico's economy ten years earlier—had tipped Admiral off to unexplored oil reserves lying beneath exhausted ranch lands covering America's interior. Before his death, Father had succeeded in buying the family empire another lucrative decade. With conservation on the rise and easy-to-extract oil all but depleted, high-profit refined fuel sales were drawing down. The company's modus operandi had to be restructured entirely.

Every facet of the world's economy had revolved around oil for a full century. Now, with supplies in jeopardy, every corner of commerce was in shambles. Time and patience were running out on crude oil and tar sands that had become far more costly to extract, and could no longer be easily billed to the local community from which they were taken. Folks out there wanted jobs but had increasingly rejected the responsibilities that come with security. What gives, these days?

He poured himself a brandy. The liquor helped dull the phantom pains that constantly shot through his lower back before fading into his permanently paralyzed thighs. Every day it seemed to take more and more of his preferred poison to numb his agony. He eyed the screen to his right where a color-coded graphic displaying active worldwide oil exploration confirmed that regions across all latitudes and longitudes had fallen dramatically in three troubling years. Shaking his head with a grumble he knocked back the drink.

The usual stress of the day's market news hung in the afternoon air. Volatility, regulated barrel prices, and diminishing profit margins were pushing tensions in the office. Once upon a time in his late twenties, Rodney Panach had taken over the firm's daily operations under the diminishing tutelage of his father, ten years following a boating accident that killed Rodney's twin brother.

Now, forty some years later Rodney enjoyed control of energy markets on a global scale, but with a diminishing supply of the black gold. Clinging to a majority market share had become a shrewd undertaking. Manipulating the price of oil within a sizable margin was no longer possible. The cycle began with internal pressure on the Federal Reserve to report favorable corporate earnings and employment statistics in the energy sector to encourage domestic spending, which in turn ramped up demands on shipping in time for barrel price hikes.

For decades profits hinged more on legislated drilling restrictions. Between corporate bail outs, stimulus packages, federal tax cuts, and windfall profits, the company enjoyed dry ground amidst a deluge of mega bankruptcies, factory closures, and raging inflation. Today that sizable margin had shrunk to a thin red line as gasoline markets lay in shambles, yielding an energy return to energy investment in the neighborhood of three to one—a pitiful output compared to the standard seven or eight to one in previous years.

Declining supplies of petroleum product could no longer be tolerated.

A village idiot knew there were increasingly more ways the energy shortage could benefit the adept opportunist, even if it meant engaging one's industry brethren. In terms of capital and political affluence, Admiral dwarfed its archrivals. Montech Energy Corporation, a distant second based in Toronto, exercised its own ambitions to emerge as a leader in natural gas exploration. As others in the industry did, Montech's CEO relished its vendetta against Panach that stretched back five years when his company surrendered a mammoth settlement to Admiral's subsidiary, Arctic Mining Ventures. A disputed and highly speculative land deal between the two companies had sat embroiled in litigation. Eventually the golden goose turned sour and the huge swath of oil-rich territory fell into the hands of the Canadian government on a grandfathered homesteader's claim dating back to the 1890s. This national gem was immediately traded away to Admiral under parliamentary pressures to abandon a popular deforestation moratorium, and ramp up exploration. The tradeoff? A handsome cash-out to cover back-interest payments on a string of Canadian bond defaults. Since then, people wearing big shoes inside Montech pledged to bring Admiral to its knees.

Panach's eyes narrowed on the middle screen again. The Energy Department's announcement of a setback in its own research on mineral synthesis rolled across the bottom of the stock exchange's monitor. It was seeking any formula in which energy return significantly exceeded energy investment. He took a long draw on his cigar. The warmth of liquor settled deep inside his gut. This hype over revolutionary science comes and goes with the tides. It was imperative that he not allow new technologies to strip away the wealth of an entrenched oil man.

Alternative energy sources had been around for many years, but always made up tiny percentages of the pie. Would Admiral be left in the dark ages while newer, cleaner alternatives marched forward? Would petroleum be supplanted by hydrogen? By electricity? The sound of his whispered thoughts made him wince. It was absurd but the words rankled. They stuck like barbs in his mind, and he could not rid himself of the dire consequences should he not change course.

The executive secretary's voice interrupted his thoughts.

"Sir, line *two* is holding. The representative from the Cuban Children's Fund wishes to—."

"Forward it to our bleeding hearts in Washington, Miss Lopez. I've no time for charity today."

"Sir, it's regarding Admiral's agreement to rebuild three schools damaged by our strip mining division."

16

"Mining operations down there have been less than profitable, Miss Lopez. Now, how long must I wait for those recruitment files?"

Ms. Lopez knew better than to press for humanity at the office. It was said her boss was, at one time, many years ago, sympathetic to the needy. Having grown up less than a mile from the slums of Caracas and befriending a number of talented boys across the tracks before moving to the U.S., young Rodney had appealed to his father to help fund a new soccer stadium as part of an inner-city football federation. With oil money supporting the project, some members took their game to dizzy heights. Those with brilliant athletic careers eventually returned to the Panach clan to pay tribute.

In the midst of his own rising stardom as a formidable center-forward, a boating accident while drinking with his brother left one dead and the other paralyzed. Rodney's end game was the loss of both legs.

Watching many of his friends and rivals from the federation come around, served more to agitate than to comfort him. The health enjoyed by ordinary people, he'd lost forever. Even with the best of prosthetic technology financially accessible to his family, lower spinal damage prevented Rodney from smoothly propelling himself on artificial limbs, eventually resigning physical mobility to a wheelchair.

Sarah was an efficient Latino woman working in perpetual fear of losing her visa, hired on the recommendation of a Venezuelan banker and personal friend to Panach. Inside three months, she had mastered the daily demands of coordinating executive air travel, fielding media agents, booking speeches at energy conferences, and directing communications all the way down to squeezing appointments with doctors, caterers, and a barber into Panach's calendar. Professionally trained to serve elites, Lopez could produce more in two hours than others could in a whole day.

"Here you are, sir," she announced, scurrying into his office suite. Hovering cautiously at one corner of his desk, she still clutched a stack of manila file folders in both hands. Like most people in the company, Sarah avoided looking directly down at her boss, pretending the empty pant legs flopped over

17

the edge of his wheelchair weren't completely vacant of flesh and bone. She'd been satisfied with his abbreviated story of the boating accident that had left him a double amputee at the knee and caused the death of his brother many years ago. There was never a reason to bother him for details. A plus in her favor.

"Well?" Panach growled, waiting for Sarah to hand over the files.

Raising one of them, she swallowed hard. "I'm afraid one of our candidates has taken a position elsewhere."

Panach raised a menacing gaze and took sordid pleasure in watching his secretary squirm. She dared to glance back at him nervously, repulsed by the fat fleshy cheeks and his steamy breath saturated of hard liquor. His strong set jaw pulsated with prosecution and his tone dripped with belligerence whenever he spoke.

"Don't tell me someone rejected my offer for interview?"

"Um, yes sir. He had accepted something else by the time I could reach him." Sarah's voice shook as she delivered the news, which she considered rather trivial with all the candidates piling on her desk. But instinct as well as common sense told her not to question it further. "A federal government project, I believe."

"Okay, I get the picture, Miss Lopez." Panach glared at Sarah past a pair of bifocals he used for close reading. "Put the files down here and get me my pain meds."

Sarah gathered her composure and slid the stack onto the desk then backed away toward the door, her words dribbling out in Spanish-English. "Si ... yes, of course, sir, right away."

Panach rifled through the printed stack with haste, in search of one name. After Sarah had come with his meds and left him in private he was gulping another brandy.

Clayton Beard's voice came over the office link, a call originating from inside Admiral's branch office in Dallas. Panach cut into him with a vengeance.

"What kind of idiot are you, ordering Sands and Richardson to shoot their way into that Seattle laboratory? How can this company collect proprietary data or conduct useful surveillance if we're stirring up law enforcement?"

18

Beard choked on his words. "Sir, I confess it was hasty of me to send Richardson. But he's turned up nothing at those state-run refineries in Anchorage. I thought we could depend on him to—"

"Hell with what you thought!" Panach roared. "We cannot afford to assassinate some of our best prospective hires. Dead bodies don't do us any good right now."

Beard changed the subject and waved a knuckle full of torn pages in front of his video monitor.

"Sir, did you take a look at my attachment? It's got—"

"High hopes at best." The pain meds had begun to show a calming effect on Panach. He opened the applicant's profile and placed it under a document camera on his desk. The contents appeared on the screen he was using for the conference call. "Adam Harlow, age 31, single, a few credits away from a degree at University of Minnesota, worked for a Seattle startup until he got fired some months back." Raking the stubble over his chin, he paused. "Never finished school, huh?"

"Yup. Pulled out a quarter short of a mineral sciences degree."

"What's the use in hiring this guy? He's a goddam dropout."

For a moment Beard's glossy forehead dropped off Panach's monitor. After pulling up some notes he reappeared. "It does get better, sir."

"Give it to me, then."

"Turns out he's registered with the feds to work on one of them inside fast-track technical initiatives. NASA business."

Panach drew a lungful of smoke from the imported cigar drooping off his lips. "It's time for a little more digging inside the Energy Department."

"Rosen?" Beard inquired while attempting to hide a shot of whiskey off camera. "He's kinda fucked things up for us a time or two, hasn't he, sir?"

"No more than some others on my payroll."

"Yessir ... but can we really trust that guy on *this* one?"

"I'll deal with Rosen. What else did you dig up on Mr. Harlow: ambitions, personal history ... women?"

19

"Outspoken on environmental shit. Votes independent, seen as a menace to big industry, a noisy opponent to GMO food production, fired for insubordination ... consumer advocate." Beard paused. "This one's off the trail if you asked me. The sort of pilgrim we try to screen out, sir."

"I'll make that call. Go on. What about a girl?"

"Chinese national hangs around the lab ... chick on a student visa. Works in a café nearby. Don't know if there's any romantic attachment. Been showin' up there couple days a week. Business or pleasure ... not sure."

"Nice. What about family?"

"Mother's on a small parcel in the Dakota hills, livin' on the edge of bankruptcy." "His father?"

"His old man's dead. Was a tree hugger and a rabble-rouser. Worked for Dakota's land management office. Sided with the Indians over any environmental fights they could pick whenever Progress came to town. Blocked two of our own strip mine ventures.

Panach nodded. "Yeah sure, I remember him. Our boys took the wind out of his sails. That was some time ago."

"Ten years, sir. Adam pulled out of school to bury his dad."

"Arson, wasn't it?" Panach recounted with a gleam in his eye.

"Yup."

"Justice always goes to the highest bidder. Any fallout still blowing around?"

"Nope. Our PR department sewed the case up nicely. Had the local fire chief blame it on a faulty oven. She's tight as a rusted oil drum, sir."

"Keep it that way." Panach finished eyeballing the document Beard was holding on the video screen. "It seems I owe Mr. Harlow a favor for his hardships. He may also have something that belongs to me."

"Sir, what about the girl?"

"We'll arrange a little reception for her later. In the meantime, Harlow is to keep his mind on his work. Give him some distance but keep him under watch."

Panach cut the conference link and returned to glaring at the wall-screen. The price per barrel on imported crude had gained over a dollar since Wednesday, settling at $461—a steal compared to where domestic crude was trading.

Regardless of a rising price index, government caps on retail gasoline would stay put until the next Energy Summit. Could Admiral hold out that long?

Three

Getting out of town occupied Adam's mind in the hour since walking out of Sonny's café.

Jumping on a flight back home to see his mother however was out of the question. Not only could he be tracked at the airport, he'd never get authorized to fly on such short notice. The airlines had trimmed their schedules down to comply with fuel rationing. An automated email from Seattle Police reported the Saab had been recovered and impounded, yet ponying up the $350 fee to collect it was out of the question. And there'd be costly repairs to make it roadworthy, according to the clerk when he'd identified the car over the phone. Train service was booked two months out.

Greyhound? Crowded as it was said to be, even with extra coaches running, there was Greyhound. Fuel shortages had riders flooding to ground transportation. It was the best choice for leaving Seattle without going far. His destination would be within the state. Adam managed to arrange a bus to Bellingham the next day and needed a place for the night before traveling north. A buddy he hadn't seen since college operated on small farm up north. The perfect refuge while deciding his next move.

Upon gathering physical evidence against Richardson and his partner, Fischer had hauled a few tools and a hammer off to forensics. Toiletries, a change of clothes, and a pair of overalls he'd inherited from his dad were all Adam was allowed to remove from the lab.

Later that afternoon Moi waited at her car outside the Pioneer Building, near the café. The Toyota was rusted through at the fenders. A damaged passenger door and a blown out muffler was evidence of her humbled existence as a university student. Riding in the passenger seat meant prying the door open and then holding it closed while she drove a few miles to her apartment.

He'd explained his situation over the phone and she'd generously offered her sofa for the night. In exchange Adam had insisted on helping with whatever needed fixing there.

22

From previous conversations he knew Moi lived alone and had not seen her family for three years. The Chinese government had conscripted her from a pool of students excelling in mathematics. After further evaluation she was inducted into a rigorous school in Beijing. Without going into much detail, she had described her plans to return home last summer but was ordered by an emergency commission to complete her studies in the United States on a special research visa under time-limited tutelage of the consulate general. This had brought her to Seattle where she was placed in a master's program at the University of Washington.

In China's capital her family struggled with the painful changes that come with a failing economy. Public transportation had been severely curtailed and millions were hurled into unemployment, forcing young people to migrate to swaths of vacated farmland hundreds of miles from upscale cosmopolitan city centers. A letter from her sister had arrived through the consulate's office, reporting their mother had fallen ill. What's more, Moi's father had remained quiet about his official duties in China's government affairs. Then one day he failed to return home from a business trip.

Moi had little choice but to acquire the traits of a survivor. She suspected Beijing was monitoring phone calls to her mother. And there was the diminished prospect of earning her H-1V credential from the U.S. immigration service, permitting her to stay and work for a high tech American firm. Jobs were tight for outsiders, even those with connections. Many foreigners were forced to leave in mass unless it was determined they could contribute significantly to the U.S. economy.

Moi pulled away from the curb. A local jazz station turned to its afternoon news report on the car's radio.

"In Top-of-the-Hour News, Thursday, February 11th Department of Transportation officials this week postponed the lifting of a national ban on hydrogen car production over allegations the vehicles remain unsafe following a recent string of fatal explosions on major U.S. highways.

Today, hundreds more people died outside Yemen's capital in the wake of renewed attacks on Western-run oil refineries.

23

The country's defense ministry has confirmed the presence of radioactive fallout in the region, and believes the detonated device to be similar to those smuggled from plutonium plants outside of Tehran last month.

Tensions between United Auto Workers and General Motors escalated into violence as talks broke down late last night over the company's plans to close its flagship Chevrolet Division next month. Federal mediation is expected to resume later this week.

Lengthy food lines around the country indicate higher unemployment while stocks on Wall Street slid further in heavy trading since the opening bell today, with energy and manufacturing sectors leading the free-fall for a seventh consecutive week.

Retail gasoline prices edged higher on Wednesday, topping the national average at seventeen dollars, forty-two cents per gallon.

Rain changing to—"

Adam breathed a dismal sigh. Picking up on his mood, Moi switched off the radio. The world's news wasn't getting any prettier. In sight were no signs of economic recovery. His thoughts returned to NASA and *Aqualene*. What had Gamil accomplished that day in the lab before his death? Had he managed to catalog any useful data? Or had his death been entirely in vain?

Adam cringed at the thought of Gamil's death. He had to know more of what was accomplished in the time he'd left the lab. They'd made some connections together on two key minerals. Had the rest of the puzzle come together before the brutal attack? Unless he went back to recover the files and the notes he and Gamil kept hidden in the lab, he'd never know.

His thoughts drifted in Moi's direction. Her beauty was unmistakable. He'd stolen many glances of her in the café, appreciating the way her high cheekbones framed her delicate nose and full lips. Her quiet-but-determined spirit had attracted him the day he'd moved into the lab. Now, sitting next to her, alone in the car, Adam wondered if she knew how he felt. Did he know himself?

Seeing Moi at the café and then inviting her into the lab, things had been somehow different.

*****

Earlier that afternoon, Europa—NASA's contracted hybrid space shuttle under Boeing management—took off from a runway in the Mojave Desert. In less than an hour docking operations at the reconfigured International Space Station were completed.

The nuclear powered spacecraft had reached its maximum ascension speed in less than seventeen minutes. Dr. Heinrich Mann enjoyed little time to marvel at Earth's departing topography. Details of the living planet had quickly shrunk into patches of brown and green carpeting, outlined by its vast blue-green oceans.

Inside the circular galley aboard the station, Mission Director Skip Halverson reviewed safety procedures, exercise schedules, meal preparations, and bunk assignments. Sleeping quarters, the exercise floor, and the station's galley were situated in specially designed modules that rotated to simulate an eighty-two percent gravity factor of Earth. Each of four sleeping modules accommodated three crewmembers. Heinrich would share sleeping quarters with his assigned intern, Greg Walker.

Greg was a tall fair-skinned African American youth from Denver who'd won the internship aboard ISS under a grant supported by a major software company who'd established the Kids-in-Space program. His scholarship came as a reward for honors in calculus and physics. In the final round of qualification, Greg had secured his spot aboard the station when he delivered a compelling speech to the United Nations assembly, proposing to reroute polar melts onto vast tundra depressions in an effort to capture pure drinking water while minimizing the impact of coastline flooding.

During preflight training Heinrich and Greg quickly bonded on their common values and beliefs about Earth's climate trends. Mann agreed to become Greg's designated mentor throughout the nine-week mission. The third man in their module was Dr. Truett Thompson, the station's on-duty life-support technician and resident optical & radio astronomer. He had spent his early years of research at New Mexico's Big Array, interpreting and cataloging radio signals from deep space.

A graying but fit man in his sixties, Thompson spoke honestly and shared his theories with anyone who would listen. He was renowned for his discovery of planetary bodies in other solar systems by tracking wobbling movements of stars orbited by unseen masses. Despite his fascination with detecting Earth-like planets, he openly conceded that manned missions beyond the moon were a waste of taxpayer money.

Crewmembers soon dispersed throughout the four main work modules that had been completed two years ago. In the galley, sipping a sealed container of coffee, Thompson was busy educating Greg on his own theories of Venus's formation—the oddball in our solar system that rotates on its axis in the opposite direction of other bodies, only once on its annual trip around the sun.

Thompson rotated a finger around his fist. "This behavior suggests Venus may have formed much slower, and so it wasn't thrown into the same spin as the other planets. In fact, I have evidence that suggests our sister planet began taking shape somewhere—"

Heinrich stepped inside the galley and smiled at Greg. "I'm glad to see you and Dr. Thompson are getting acquainted. He's got some crazy notions … but that is, my friend, an important prerequisite for cohabitating in orbit."

Greg smiled, swiveling side to side in his chair. "I'll bet you didn't know Venus is the alien sister in our solar system."

Thompson's eyes widened. "Ah yes. A clever way to put it, young man."

"This fellow's no dummy," Heinrich added, clasping his hands together and becoming drawn into the topic. "He'll be Harvard material when we're finished with him."

Thompson nodded. "Young man, you drop by my lab anytime. It's that-a-way, into the next module." He pointed a finger through the airlock before cutting into a dissertation on why volcanic matter from Venus could be found on Earth's moon. His technical babble shot miles over Greg's head, and before long the two professors were lost in their own orbit, rattling off complex formulas and validating one another's theories on foreign elements in the solar system.

Halverson showed up in the airlock.

"Dr. Mann, my staff in the medical bay is ready. Would you escort Greg up there for his orientation shift?"

Heinrich looked over at Greg and chuckled. "Think of our days up here in terms of a big cherry pie. Time gets sliced up into sweet little pieces. One third of it is dark, the rest of the time this string of beer cans is exposed to direct solar energy. A guy could get badly baked up here if not for the insulation they stuffed in these walls."

The station's central computer controlled a combination of window shading and module lighting. Put into retrograde orbit, the platform circled Earth every 1.3 hours at an adjusted altitude of 197 miles. For approximately fifty minutes of each cycle, the station is exposed to the sun's full radiation before slipping behind Earth's horizon into darkness. During darkened periods, sensors activate artificial lighting. Then power down as the station reenters phases of direct sunlight. Lighting transitions provide a natural break for the crew working in the research modules, some of which rotate to simulate gravity, while others remain static in order to conduct experiments requiring zero gravity.

Through the linkway, on the way to the medical bay, Greg grimaced. "Cutting up dead things wasn't my best subject."

"Relax," Heinrich laughed. "Mundane lab work, my friend. The ultimate form of out-sourcing to pay your room and board up here."

By 2019 the World Health Organization had accumulated a daunting backlog of drug and treatment testing. Much of it was connected to highly potent viruses that had broken out in Asia and Europe. All station crewmembers were expected to participate, putting in shifts of biological and viral experiments inside a specially designed work module that maintained zero gravity conditions at all times.

Greg and Heinrich showed up outside the central hub where a vertical hatchway leads crewmembers up into the medical bay. Connected to the main hub, a series of zero gravity labs remain stationary while the rest of the station platform rotates. The medical bay serves as the central axis that stabilizes the platform, much like the body of a spinning gyroscope.

From the hatchway Heinrich pointed out the sensors along a column of flexible joints connecting the hub and medical lab. These sensors monitor rotational speeds. "From here we enter a vertical causeway. As you can see, it appears to be rotating— like one of those fun houses that plays havoc on your senses."

Slightly pale, Greg shrugged. "The trip up here took care of that."

Heinrich gripped a handlebar inside the causeway. "This is one of those environments preflight can't quite prepare you for."

"A parallel dimension … without the gravity," Greg chuckled, hoping a sci-fi reference would calm his nerves.

"Good one," Heinrich insisted. He climbed up into the turning drum and gestured Greg to follow. "I didn't realize you were into science fiction."

"Only the required stuff they assign in English class. A bit weird, much of it is."

Hanging on guide grips outside the hatchway leading into the medical bay, the two were greeted by Halverson who attached his clipboard to a tether and instructed Greg to put on a pair of magnetic slippers, gloves and a mask. Greg sat down at the workstation and watched Heinrich strap him into the chair while the director stepped away.

A minute later Halverson was at Greg's side. "You'll be working with our resident biologist. Someone will return for you in time for your assigned exercise shift."

Four

Scaling the heavens over the Pacific, darkness quickly blanketed the station.

Heinrich spent most of his shift programming chemical and infrared sensors. Using a robotic arm, he configured the tethered devices and then successfully deployed each sensor outside the service module. This allowed him to begin mapping ozone sectors over Central and South America—a process that would take up to three weeks to complete if orbiting debris did no damage to the equipment.

Heinrich sat down and pulled up an e-mail attachment he'd received from Adam two days earlier. It listed a description of three specific minerals he and his assistant in Seattle had catalogued from NASA's rock samples. Pulling up his computer's Identification-Scan Log, he accessed a database capable of listing every substance known to the human race. The unique quality of this index allowed it to provide real-time updated information from all scientific research efforts on Earth and in space.

NASA had kept a low profile, but it was evident that hundreds of new and remarkable substances had been discovered in the past three years. Most of this data was becoming more accessible to researchers aboard the International Space Station and completed the ultimate step in linking the world's scientific community together.

Heinrich pulled up a short profile on the first substance Adam had identified in his e-mail as Armalcolite-F40. It had a low toxicity—less than 5%; transparent in color; and its mass to water was about +2%. That was everything the screen offered on the mineral. Heinrich requested a *general portfolio* in hopes of discovering the common and alternate uses of the substance, including a map disclosing its mining locations and its abundance value.

He punched it in. The screen suddenly flashed: RESTRICTED ACCESS!

It made no sense for *mined* elements to have a restricted classification. He'd seen many technical data sites come up as restricted, but the only mining restrictions had appeared on radioactive ore such as Uranium 235, and a few regulated metals taken for chemical warfare.

Heinrich Mann entered his military identification number. With that he expected to access layers of restricted sites. After muting the audio, he searched for the Armalcolite portfolio data again. The screen lit up with blinking text:

ACCESS DENIED
HIGHLY RESTRICTED CONTENT

Heinrich looked around the module to see if the others had noticed. Going to a restricted site would break protocols and create suspicion. Under new restrictions from International Security charters, the scientific community had become more obligated to follow security protocols governing activities aboard the space station. Military content often included materials that ran counter to the ambitions of privately funded research and were therefore considered off limits. Moreover, breaching security clearances invited criminal prosecution and jail time. Civil researchers found themselves looking over their shoulder more often than ever before. A dysfunctional fear had descended on the scientific community, fears reminiscent of Cold War era politics.

Denied access for Armalcolite-F40 had only heightened Heinrich's curiosity. Could this be something else, relabeled to keep snooping eyes off-limits? Was there some other reason the government was hiding this material? He now wondered about the other two substances. Pulling up their profiles, he noted the basic physical nature of each. Neither one indicated unusual properties. Both had similar masses. One was mildly toxic, the other completely neutral. One appeared milky white while the other was a deep blue.

Heinrich requested a general portfolio on one substance, and then the other. On both counts his inquiries yielded restrictions and access denials. Glancing out a nearby port window, the sunlight glowed beyond the approaching horizon. A few minutes later the module's lights dimmed off.

Heinrich carefully wrote down the names of each substance, followed by a jumble of mathematical coding to form names—all out of his professional reach. These were obviously labels that had something to do with the molecular makeup of uncharted elements. His limited knowledge of geophysics served as a sure barrier to getting the details.

He got up from the monitor to stretch away the aches that had invaded his knees and ankles. His face felt flush and heavy from the gravity differential on board the station.

Behind him, still working at his terminal, was Dr. Shinichi Tanaka, an inorganic chemist trained in astrophysics at Tusukuba University in Japan. He was the only scientist who had opted to stay on board the station for three consecutive intervals, rather than return home on sabbatical. Labeled a prodigy in courses of *particle analysis*, Tanaka was considered a devoted slave to his work and therefore was the most qualified on board to provide specific knowledge of these minerals.

Heinrich mentally reviewed his approach. Again, he pondered the risk of speaking off the topics that were outlined in the current mission aboard the station. Finally, his words came in a flurry of casual speak that seemed to fit well with the break crewmembers were taking during the change in light cycle.

"Pardon me, Doctor? What do you make of these three substances?"

Heinrich handed him the printout, feeling like a freshman intern addressing a senior professor. Tanaka slid a pair of bifocals down over his nose and read the text with thoughtful examination. Heinrich waited patiently for an informed response.

Tanaka's fascination with chemistry began at middle school in his hometown of Sendai, a moderate-size city north of Tokyo. He was said to have memorized and recited the entire Periodical Chart by the end of his first week in class. By his second year in high school he had designed a lightweight hydrogen cell for automobiles that was later adopted by two major automakers for mass production. Tanaka's privilege to

31

enter Tsukuba's doctorate program in applied chemistry had become a foregone conclusion.

Aboard the station he spent most of his energy on vulcanizing synthetic materials to be used in manufacturing artificial body organs, particularly kidneys and liver. Yet his expertise didn't end there. He was also instrumental in the development of prototype propulsion engines that were capable of regenerating themselves for longer distance space travel.

After reading the entire document, Tanaka began scribbling figures on a notepad. Occasionally he referred to a chart at his workstation peppered in a confusing mosaic of incomprehensible Chinese and Japanese characters. Heinrich's eyes gazed helplessly over the script, fueling his professional desire to know more.

Finally, Tanaka mumbled something as he swiveled around in his chair. He confirmed the names of each substance and pointed to one with a ballpoint pen. Though his English intonation was awkward, Tanaka's technical description hit the mark.

"This one is a derivative of *rhodium463-C9*," he asserted over his lenses. "At one time it was considered a pigment-based substance containing a key ingredient for treating metals for exposure in highly corrosive environments. However, its C9 component recently urged mineralogists to reclassify it as a powerful, yet stable catalyst."

Heinrich noted the detail. "What about its origin, can you tell me where it came from?"

Tanaka peered closer at the coding, his gaze holding longer than it had before. Finally he pulled off his eyeglasses. "The profiles I've seen state that traces of C-9 specimens were gathered and analyzed by Apollo astronauts visiting the moon, decades ago. Though still unconfirmed, this same mineral is thought to exist in some of Earth's deepest canyons. I do not know how much truth that bears," Tanaka added, his tone hinting irritation. "One can surmise the answers will be found on the network by those entitled to proper security clearances."

"Yes, of course, Doctor." Heinrich glanced back at his notes. "And the two others?"

Tanaka pursed his lips. His finger paused on the scroll pad. Carefully he propped his lenses back on his nose.

"These two are simple carbon-based compounds, coded as *ceria-480-LD8* and *hadrit-480-CS12*. The LD8 is common bedrock. As for CS12, it is cataloged as highly restricted content."

"Do you know the reason?" Heinrich asked.

"Of course I do," Tanaka snorted. "It is common knowledge among most qualified geologists. Its carbon component, CS12, is a close relative of Uranium. Organically formed in sedimentary pockets, a process similar to bacteria-produced methanol."

"I've never heard of it," Heinrich confessed. "Excavated on Earth, I presume."

Tanaka shook his head. "It may be that no one is supposed to know that information. The documents reveal nothing of the mineral's inventory or location."

"You're saying, it's not available on the network ... anywhere?"

Tanaka's voice was suddenly flat and conclusive, as if he wanted no record of this conversation. Shaking his head, he delivered a curt reply: "Not anytime soon. CS12 was re-classified two years ago ... a *need-to-know* status. Likely for NSA coding."

Tanaka had promptly brought the subject to a close when Halverson showed up with a binder containing lab results on infrared photography of ozone sectors over Central America. He handed the data to Heinrich and reminded the two doctors of revisions in the exercise schedule. Halverson disappeared down the linkway.

Dr. Mann thanked the professor and stepped away, feeling apprehensive for bringing up the matter in the first place. Other scientists aboard ISS had recently been admonished for discussing classified material that had once been open sourced within scientific and industrial domains. Things were different today, with a number of newly discovered elements in the solar system receiving a reclassification by tight-lipped defense advocates. Was it just about military defense? Or were there other motives for camouflaging certain substances? NASA had

33

a vested interest to protect its secrets for simple reasons of liability, as the Agency was, more today than ever, expected to answer to its defense counterparts. Still, a discerning mind must always look for clearer answers, beyond the superficial layers that so often hide the larger view.

Pausing outside the medical bay, Heinrich poked his head inside. Greg was busy looking into two different microscopes and jotting down figures on a notepad. Heinrich said nothing, but continued on to the sleeping quarters where he gazed into a private pantry stocked with beverages for rehydrating the body at scheduled intervals. He ran his fingers along the bottom edge of the upper cupboard and found the button to release the lock. A variety of juices in gravity-free dispensers were lined up in neat little rows on the shelf. He pulled out a Dr. Pepper that had been treated for partial-gravity environments and sat down, replaying Tanaka's comments in his head.

A low-level radioisotope, excavated from a celestial body foreign to Earth's atmosphere.

It made sense to reclassify and restrict a newly discovered mineral akin to Uranium. But how had Tanaka obtained so much about the substance? Had the restrictions gone into effect sometime after he'd learned the details? Or did Tanaka enjoy privileged access to the network others could not? It was true the Japanese had established a cozier partnership with the American military in response to North Korea's nuclear ambitions, but a role in defense business was too far removed from Tanaka's stature in medical research.

The high fructose drink triggered an appetite, urging Heinrich back into the pantry. He warmed up a chicken casserole and consumed it in four bites before returning to his workstation. Earth's blue horizon, viewed from a port window in his module, moved him as he watched its dark hue fade to blackness. The station's orbit would take the crew around to the dark side of the planet in a few minutes. The usual delay of the lighting system would send crew members into the galley for a snack. Others would opt for a stretch break in the exercise module.

The Kevlar window in his module grew dark enough to hint at the next lighting transition. Dr. Tanaka was the last one to leave. The others in adjacent labs were stretching and chattering along the linkway toward the galley. The aroma of coffee and soups hung in the re-oxygenated air that was pumped throughout the station. Heinrich craned his neck to see Tanaka disappear down the linkway.

His mind made up, Heinrich would resort to some tricks he had picked up and refined years ago in college. Aboard the station he'd hack into the main network computer to override its restricted zones. Timing things correctly would give him about four minutes along and unseen at the terminal. Any longer and the exposure could end his career if the wrong person were to return from the galley. Now any success depended entirely on his memory of the network's inner security codes.

The brightness of his terminal guided him through the dark, back to his workstation where he noted the time on the digital readout and began punching in a general access code for military personnel. Immediately a new screen prompted him to choose between Military Intelligence, Reconnaissance, and General Operations. He could get further into the system through General Operations; an area that led him initially into civilian services. From there he accessed the Homeland Security link, taking him to *Mining* via a national parks security window.

Glancing at the time, Heinrich entered his military ID and accessed a map displaying the location of parks and mines secured under military jurisdiction. He clicked on *mining security* and got a screen with links to dozens of North American quarries and mining installations.

At the bottom of the screen appeared a link labeled *Secured Minerals*. This was it! A backdoor to restricted substances. U.S. Geological Survey personnel needed access to this sort of information, so personnel restrictions hadn't taken effect, he hoped. Oddly, the government maintained a ten to fifteen day window between military restrictions and civilian restrictions on the network. From a security standpoint, it seemed to make more sense the other way around. At the moment there was little point in filing a complaint.

Two minutes had passed. Time would quickly run out. Heinrich entered his Federal Employee's access code and clicked on a tab labeled LIBRARY. The screen flashed the way it always did when the system crashed and restarted. Holding a breath, his pulse quickened. More seconds slipped away as the network labored over its decision to grant him access to the technical library. Finally the screen turned green and the bold-lettered title *Library of Known Substances* appeared.

Laughter echoed from the galley. Heinrich's nostrils flared as a breath of relief rushed out of his lungs. He gambled on another minute or two, and quickly entered the names of the three elements he'd discussed with Tanaka. One at a time, each file displayed itself across the screen. Two of the substances were remotely akin to rare alloys, found deep in Earth's crust. The third, Armalcolite-F40, had no record of existing on Earth. Silently, he applauded Adam for deciphering this mineral from the rocks given to him by NASA. The online document mentioned nothing about atomic properties, but its molecular structure was incredibly complex. This helped to explain why NASA hadn't been able to pin down the missing data required to completely recreate *Aqualene*.

Heinrich scanned through the profiles, glancing under the sections labeled: *Known Locations*. According to the file, the minerals had been excavated from basalt deposits of limited hydrous exposure. Strangely, all locations had been deleted. A link cross-referencing hadrit-480-CS12 suggested properties similar to Earth's mantle, still inaccessible to human exploration, substantiating Tanaka's claim the quarry had to come from another planet.

As he logged off the network, Heinrich realized how close Adam had come to uncovering the formula's secret properties. There had to be some way of piecing together three incredibly sophisticated elements to simulate *Aqualene*'s original molecular structure. But at the moment, that was the lesser of two worries.

Considering the e-mail Adam had sent about his lab assistant's death, as well as a string of other related homicides around the nation, Heinrich was certain that a powerful group was operating at a very high cost to interfere, destroy, or perhaps gain possession of *Aqualene*'s formula.

If things were left up to chance, Adam Harlow's life was in grave danger.

Five

Hours before dawn Adam awoke in cold sweat.

On the sofa in Moi's apartment he blinked until the opaque features of the dimly lit room came into view. Across from him below a poster of Disneyland on the wall, Moi slept silently over a foldout futon bed. The light of a gray winter moon illuminated a ribbon of her breast through the open flannel shirt she slept in. A chilly draft from a fractured window frame cooled Adam's face, urging him to sit up and examine the anxieties that had stirred him so suddenly to consciousness.

An urgent text message was waiting on his phone next to the pillow. Heinrich had fully identified the minerals and then proceeded to tell him to get out of town.

Adam loaded the details into a hidden folder he kept in his phone. There would be time to get back to them later. As for getting out of town, he had taken care of business that afternoon by telephoning Dell Jackson, an old high school buddy who for the past several years had worked a small raspberry farm in northern Washington near the Canadian border. Formally an apprentice machinist at Boeing until a string of lay-offs hit the Seattle-based plants; he purchased the twenty-six acre plot on a foreclosure deal and transplanted his life in the morning shadows of Mount Baker. Isolated from friends, Dell had issued an open invitation of which Adam had never bothered to accept until now. Over the phone Dell promised to be waiting for him at the Bellingham bus station on Friday.

Adam's thoughts shifted back to what had awakened him. He pressed to dig deeper into his memory. Some provocative glimpse of optimism had triggered an alarm inside his head. The ingredients for something extraordinary began to clear, like silt settling at the bottom of a mud puddle.

"I've got to go back into the lab," he whispered to Moi across the room.

Her cheeks twitched.

Adam jumped to his feet. His voice rose with exhilaration. "The answer to one very complex question … is still in the lab."

Moi suppressed a yawn and gazed back at him. "What do you mean?"

"My lab, the formula is there in the lab."

She shot him a bewildered look. "Are you sure? The formula is there?"

"Yes. I've got a strange hunch the algorithm you wrote generated the working formula." Then Adam let go of a long breath. He watched Moi's eyes glow in the reflection of a nightlight attached to the wall between them. "I knew we were getting close. It must have happened in the short time I was out."

Moi's eyes flashed suddenly. Her broken English echoed off the low plaster ceiling of her apartment. "Mr. Kabib. Could he discover lost formula?"

"Yes, exactly! You see Gamil was the last to work there … so I must get the vials to analyze his results."

"Vials?" Moi looked confused.

"The minerals we debased in the lab, they are in a set of vials. Before the detective took me down there, he had cut the electrical power, fearful of combustibles starting a fire. I didn't see much. Only what his flashlight beam passed over. I can recall a faintly familiar odor, which had escaped me at the time—the one I noticed weeks ago when I agreed to take on their project.

"Gamil had instructions to leave the vials in a wooden box, one I keep stowed beneath the workbench. Time probably had gotten away from him. He must've exited the lab in a hurry for his other job. He left before having time to run a full analysis."

"That is when he ran into two bad men?"

"Yes." The same knot grew in Adam's throat and for a moment he could not speak. "Such a waste," he uttered finally.

"No!" she exclaimed. "Your friend, he die with honor." She jumped up and clutched Adam's wrist. "Tomorrow I drive you to police. We ask to get your box from the lab."

"Not a chance." Adam's hands began to shake nervously. I got up and paced the room. "I have plans to catch the early

39

bus out of town. It leaves in five hours. I must get those vials tonight. Right now. Please let me use your car."

Moi's eyes flashed as she anchored herself against the front door. "It is too dangerous. I won't let you. Not over my dead brother."

Adam smiled and let go a mild chuckle. "You mean body. Not over my dead *body* is the correct expression."

Eluding his interjections, Moi thrust out her chin in defiance. "Okay, maybe I not know English … but you not go to the jail tonight."

"A risk I'll have to take," Adam insisted. "Everything depends on the contents of that box." His palm opened before her. "The keys. May I have them, please?"

Moi glared back at him. Her eyes filled with determination. "Then I go too."

The drive down to Seattle's Pioneer Square was silent. Both were mentally engaged in the de facto crime they were about to commit. Adam wondered if the box would still be there for the taking, heedless of the legal ramifications. Moi worked to disguise her fears of being arrested and then discharged from the university. She would likely be deported directly back to Mainland China where her government would levy a harsh punishment upon her family. Dishonor has its consequences.

She pulled the Toyota up near the bottom of Yesler Street in a vacant bus zone and cut the motor. Along the sidewalk were tents ruffling in a gentle but cold wind. More could be seen under the street lamps up First Avenue for several blocks. Posted signs reminded the homeless to be off the sidewalks by 7am in the morning. Nine on Sundays.

They sat in the car, squinting through the bare branches of trees that cast skeleton gray shadows over cobblestones outside the Klondike Cafe. Finally, Adam got out of the car and peered at the museum across the street. It was no longer occupied and its front windows were boarded up. Adam had found a discarded tour map in the storefront next to the old barbershop. He remembered an alternate entrance to the underground through the back of the museum.

40

Moi followed Adam across the street where he was pointing to a side stairwell that led to a locked door. He felt his heart sink at the sight of a large padlock securing the door. Beneath her, in the stairwell he leaned against the cold cement wall to think.

"We need to cut it, somehow," he whispered.

Moi didn't answer. He turned toward her, ready and willing to consider a different approach. Anything. But she had disappeared.

In a panic, he spun around and ascended the steps up to the street level. In the shadows of a malfunctioning streetlamp, Moi was kneeling at the base of the building near the corner just inside the alley behind them. He watched with baited breath as she tugged at a spot where two sections of window framing were splintered and coming apart.

"What the ...?"

Moi lowered herself and curled her fingers underneath the slats. She lifted the boards out toward her and smiled at him. "You go in first. I follow behind."

In the beam of the miniature LED flashlight she aimed at the window's ledge, Adam wriggled through the opening. After swiveling his feet around he dropped five or six feet to a basement floor. There he watched her squeeze through the opening, then guided her toes to the wooden planks.

Adam renewed his bearings by looking up through a side window at an adjacent brick building to the north. From the map he remembered the access point to the underground corridor was slightly west, toward the water. Ten to twelve feet below the street level they were soon hustling along a sunken dirt corridor that took them east again, angling past dilapidated storefronts that were on the verge of caving in at the slightest disturbance.

The first obstacle showed up somewhere beneath First Avenue. There, street drain-off had filled a depression zone, leaving only a narrow margin of dry ground on one side. Walking around it posed another serious hazard. They would have to pass dangerously close to a leaning bulkhead, colonized by dozens of long-tailed rats. "I suggest we wade through the water." He reached back for Moi's hand and submerged one shoe into the water. She followed without complaint. Three steps took them halfway across the muddied water until it was at their knees. Carefully, he took another two steps when Adam slipped suddenly under the water. Beneath him his feet searched wildly for something to stand on. Blinded in the muck his head finally surfaced. His ears cleared not a moment too soon to hear a voice ring out.

"Here, grab to this!"

Adam thrashed in the mud and darkness, twisting his body around in the direction of Moi's call. Wiping the foul smelling silt from his eyes, he glimpsed her standing almost directly over him. The shadows cast from the flashlight sticking up from the mud revealed a long rotten timber in her hands. It swung over his head as she counter-balanced herself with a free hand that clutched a rusted pipe jutting out from a tangle of debris. The stench of decomposing building materials filled his nostrils. It was hard to imagine they once supported the lower part of the wood planked roads built above the sound's daily tides.

Adam gripped what he could of the timber and hoisted himself to a muddy embankment upon where Moi stood. He shook off what he could of his annoyances and assayed the situation. There had to be an alternative to this monkey business!

He reminded himself they were wallowing around in a long-ago condemned level of Seattle's past. Slipping past the rickety bulkhead was no doubt risky. Any misstep or disturbance could cause a cave-in. The cavern's lid—a grid of rotten timbers miraculously supporting corroded steel planks above them—was simply out of reach. At the same time, asking Moi to swim through the murky pond was hardly a desired option.

Once more Adam surveyed the bulkhead. He was running out of ideas. Presently he considered back tracking to the old building. They could always explore another route. He estimated they were less than a block from the point at which a bend in the underground path would lead them north into a fork that passed next to the Klondike Cafe. From there his lab would be steps away.

Adam was wringing water from his flannel shirt when he noticed Moi squatting a few yards behind him in shallow water. She had propped the flashlight against remnants of a broken straight-back chair turned upside down on the muddy bank. Its light cast an eerie silhouette of her slender figure crouching over the black pool. Both her arms were fully submerged, the water lapping up to her shoulders.

Adam panicked. What the hell had pulled her into the water, inches from drowning?

"You okay?" he gasped, suddenly navigating the strewn debris between them. She'd given no reply and that worried him.

Quickly Adam waded through knee-deep water to where she appeared completely immobile. In the shadows of the flashlight Moi's eyes remained fixed on something beneath the water's surface. Her arms twisted and labored patiently.

Adam adjusted his footing next to her. Without a word, Moi calmly drew her shoulders up and stood in the faint light, panting. What began as a faint gurgling sound beneath them grew into a powerful whoosh.

Adam steadied himself and gaped at what he saw happening around his legs.

Instantly currents of cloudy water swirled around their knees. The waterline fell to expose their ankles in no time at all. The hole between Moi's muddy sneakers drew eddies of swirling black water. The earthen depression seemed to rise up around them.

Though sticky, the newly exposed ground was easily passable. The bend in the corridor took them north just as he'd expected it would. A minute later they were wringing themselves out at the dusty entrance of the lab.

With haste, Adam ducked under the yellow police tape stretched across the lab's entrance. He stepped inside and pulled a blanket from a box against the wall, handing it to Moi who'd elected to remain just outside the doorway.

Standing inside the lab, Adam was again reminded of the murder. Another man had given his life ... and for what? A dreadful waste, it was, for all parties. Adam grappled with himself as he surveyed the work area. The physical space and the odors of his lab somehow redirected him back to the task at hand. He was there for *Aqualene*, whatever was left of Gamil's last labors. He owed that much to the family!

Moi projected the light over his head now, following his hand that guided her beam to the workbench. There, Adam rifled through the binder where he had made his notes. Watching the page sequencing, he confirmed his worst suspicions. Some of the pages were missing—those which described *Aqualene* and its purpose. Other missing pages contained an incomplete portion of the mineral properties that were fundamental to the formula. These were duplicate hardcopies of a selected portion of the data he'd stored on the flash drive. Whoever had taken them possessed only half of the puzzle.

He shoved the binder under his arm as his shadow moved toward the rusted iron safe. Behind the loose brick in the wall he expected to find the hidden drive capsule. But when Moi's light found him again, the brick was lying in the dust beneath the safe. He pointed out the niche in the wall to Moi, urging her flashlight beam over to it.

"Dammit!" The capsule was gone! Gamil obviously had no time to reinsert the data drive and replace the brick when he was overcome by the intruders. Had there been time to clear the memory on the laptop, a procedure all three agreed to do after each upload?

Again and again Adam looked over the cavity in the wall. Had his hard-earned data fallen into the wrong hands? If Richardson had been the one to take it, the capsule was likely to be in police hands. The other scenario—in which Richardson's partner had taken it—was unthinkable.

His thoughts drifted back to threats against his own life. Who had clobbered him the night before? Was someone trying to prevent him from accessing the formula? What if Gamil made a discovery that Adam could run with? If he had, who else knew about it? Was someone watching him, waiting for the right opportunity to finish what they'd started?

"Let's get out of here," Adam whispered as he stooped to pick up a wad of dry clothing. The wooden box of vials was on the lowest shelf of the workbench, hidden from view. In his trembling hands he balanced them and stepped into the corridor. His hands full, he handed the notebook off to Moi. She smiled and clutched it tightly in her arms.

Moi had stood behind him, ready to follow him out, when a powerful light suddenly blinded them. The beam, originating a good distance in the opposite direction of the cafe, bobbed and flickered. Behind it the sound of heavy footsteps was trotting closer, but the light was twenty, maybe thirty yards short of the intersecting corridor they had used to approach the lab.

Adam turned his face away from the light. Giving his eyes time to readjust to the darkness ate up crucial seconds. Moi shut off her light and slipped behind a leaning timber. In one swift instant she scrambled down the corridor and cut a hard left, uttering something fearfully in her native tongue.

Adam spun around to follow, taking the same route from which they had come. He pushed his legs to a full sprint to make the bend. Angling downward, he entered the muddied depression that appeared under threads of light from a street lamp bleeding through overhead skylights installed in the sidewalks after the Great Seattle Fire. Much of the water had drained away, exposing the rusted culvert Moi had cleverly unearthed minutes earlier.

With no trace of her, other than a sneaker stuck in the mud near the opening of the drain hole, Adam searched the shadows of the archway leading toward the museum. Behind him the light carried by the intruders became visible again. By the rhythm of the footsteps there had to be two, maybe three large men in pursuit.

He bent down and scooped up Moi's sneaker before continuing on.

At the museum's entrance he ducked into the splintered remnants of a small coatroom, the space where he and Moi had crawled in through the damaged window. He spotted something on the floor that brought him some relief. In the light of a street lamp, a footprint of mud on the wood plank proved Moi had found her way back and climbed through the window. She'd be waiting right outside for him.

45

Adam ripped a slat from the planking at his feet and wedged open the splintered windowpane. This allowed him to push the box of vials through first and then shimmy up the brickwork and out. The outside air was cool and crisp.

Rounding the corner onto Yesler, Adam felt a rush of accomplishment. Chilled in his wet clothes, he anticipated reuniting in her warm car. But Moi was nowhere in sight! Neither was the Toyota.

Adam searched up and down First Avenue. A dozen barrel-fires were burning along First Avenue. His eyes swept up Yesler Way. One block east he spotted a parked taxi cab, its vacancy sign glowing. It was the only occupied car for blocks.

What had become of Moi? Why hadn't she waited for him? Was she in some kind of danger? Who had she encountered while climbing through the window into the alley?

Adam adjusted his grip on the wooden box and wheeled up Yesler toward the cab. Vigilant of trouble coming from behind, he climbed into the back seat, reciting her address to the driver. "Step on it, would you."

In the minutes it took to get to Beacon Hill Adam replayed in his mind what had transpired. Something allowed him to feel relieved that Moi had kept moving under such frightening circumstances. She had probably seen the cabby sitting yards from her car, and realized it safer to split up. Quick thinking had allowed her to escape, and now Adam felt eager to reunite with her, having possession of the vials.

On the other hand, what if she had something else in mind? After all, she had his notebook. It contained some valuable data, but wasn't complete. Why had she left without him?

The taxi pulled up in front of the old Victorian house where Moi rented her room. Adam paid the man and got out, glancing around for her car. But there was no sign of the Toyota. Adam knocked gently, but there was no answer. The door swung open under his hand, revealing darkness inside. He remembered her locking the door before they'd left for the lab. Adam grew increasingly puzzled at the circumstances. Yes, she had locked the door on the way out. Had Moi returned?

Was she waiting inside? Or had someone else entered? If so, was Moi's life in danger?

"What do you want?"

The bark of an old woman came from above. She was peering from an upstairs window. Adam stepped into a sliver of light cast from the street.

"Pardon me, ma'am. I've got to speak with Miss Song," Adam tried to keep his voice to a whisper.

"Ain't none of my business what you and her do," she replied, "but do you mind coming back at a decent hour?"

Offering no chance for an answer, she yanked the window shut.

Adam turned his attention back to Moi's apartment door and cautiously stepped inside. The place was silent. Nothing he could see in the dim light from outside had been disturbed. He knelt down and ran his fingers over the carpet inside beyond the doorway. No trace of mud or moisture. He was almost sure Moi hadn't returned.

So he would wait for her.

After several minutes the same worried feeling poked at him again. Had she sensed danger down on Yesler and driven around the block, fully intent on returning for him? Or did she go to a friend's house, to seek privacy, refuge? There was no way to know, he reasoned. One thing was clear: She had fled the scene, if for no other purpose, to confuse their pursuers. The fact that the Toyota was gone when he climbed out of the window would have to serve as a comforting clue that she had escaped unharmed.

Unless there was reason to believe otherwise.

Six

Later that morning in Los Angeles, Panach rolled off the elevator and paused at his secretary's desk.

Sarah Lopez squared her shoulders and took a deep breath as she faced her boss, peeling a slip of paper from her notepad. "Good morning, sir. A Mr. Jim Rosen telephoned late yesterday, two hours after you left the building."

Panach smiled. "Rosen, huh, calling from DC?"

"Yes, I believe so," she answered. "He requested that you call back right away. I tried to forward the call to your—"

Panach wheeled around to the side of her desk to snatch the message out of her hand before propelling himself down the hall to his office suite.

Ties with Rosen went back almost twenty years when the two had crossed paths at a congressional energy conference in DC. Working as a petroleum reserves analyst in the Department of Energy, Rosen had been on a drunk the night Panach overheard him bragging at a table full of Department of Interior officials about the energy secretary publishing bogus figures on drilling enforcement quotas. Carelessly, the fool had dropped a handful of corporate names—powerful individuals who routinely skimmed profits from federal oil trusts. By the time Rosen sobered up the next morning, he'd been officially inducted into Admiral's intelligence network. Playing him an audio recording of the evening's events, Panach laid out the ground rules and threatened to expose Rosen if he refused to fulfill company demands for government information.

Inside his office suite, Panach growled into the speakerphone and met eyes with Jim Rosen through the video link. "You called with something important yesterday. What is it?"

"I've stumbled onto something that might interest you."

"Let's have it. Speak up."

"One of my people came across a report of some unidentifiable material plucked from a crime scene by police

48

yesterday. One of those red flags my eyes are trained to pick up on in this business."

"Okay. Where?"

"Seattle."

"Oh?" Things were getting interesting. "Keep talking. Give me a name."

"Hold on, I'll take a look." Rosen peered into a nearby screen at his desk "Got it! Fella by the name of Harlow ... Adam Harlow. Could be nothing, but maybe we ought to run some tests."

Just the break Panach needed. Beard's idiot henchman had blundered in the right direction this time. "Don't let me down, Jimmy boy. You send me the lab results ASAP. There'll be a little something in it for you."

Rosen's face was beaming through the monitor. "I've got a friend over at Seattle PD who can get her hands on more of the same stuff. I'll have it in our DC labs this afternoon."

"You've done well, Rosen. Very well."

Panach cut the line and poured himself brandy.

*****

All points considered, Rosen figured he could pull twenty-five grand out of Panach on this one single favor. He was hungry and needed to pay off some debt.

One hundred times that sum amounted to peanuts when stacked up to the numbers the oil man was known to gamble on inside information. Cheap federal land deals and exclusive drilling permits had always commanded big money to fellow colleagues savvy enough to assist Admiral in crowding out unwanted competition. Rosen could feel it in his bones. A decent assignment would yield some much-needed cash to bills his wife had accumulated on overpriced antique furniture and clothes she could never get into. Consequently, Rosen knew Panach would muscle him into compromises that further exploited his security privileges inside the Energy Department. Opportunities came with risks.

The phone buzzed again. Bingo. The screen at his desk notified Rosen the call originated from a government trunk line in Seattle. A woman working in the logistics section was speaking. Her voice cracked and sputtered from the speakerphone inside his office.

"Hello, uh … Mr. Rosen?"

Immediately he scooped up the receiver to ensure absolute privacy.

"You're late, Sims," Rosen snapped into the mouthpiece. "Do you have it?"

"Sir, about that substance you requested … uh, it was not found on the premises."

Rosen's throat swelled. He sat frozen, his palms suddenly wet and sticky. Finally, he mustered a sobering breath, trying to calm himself. His words spilled out in short comprehensible bits.

"Ms. Sims, can you tell me *why* the substance is not on the premises?"

"Apparently, sir, there was a break in during the night. Someone has removed it."

With agony, Rosen's heart dropped into the generous belly that poured over his belt. It was all he could do to inject the last of his composure into sensible words. "So you're telling me someone violated the crime scene and took all traces of the substance?"

"Yes, sir. An officer was called out to poke around. He found nothing. The brass is trying to keep a lid on it. They claim this is a homicide investigation, yet someone apparently slipped inside to take the containers you described."

Rosen's heart sank. "This is a goddam tragedy, to say the least. Telephone me at once if you hear anything … anything at all."

As he hung up, Rosen considered his next move with Admiral. He risked losing everything. No doubt, Panach would take full pleasure in dangling him from a very thin string. Beads of sweat dribbled over his receding hairline and collected in the deep crevices that ran between his eyes and chin. Rosen debated who to contact first, his lawyer or a funeral director.

Seven

Adam had stayed awake for almost an hour after changing into dry clothes and worrying about Moi.

Now he awakened on the sofa just before 9:00. Still Moi had not returned. This worried him until he reminded himself that she had, more than likely sought refuge with a girlfriend. It was embarrassing enough that she'd been seen in soiled wet clothes. Now he realized he wouldn't hear from her until later that morning, perhaps after he'd traveled a hundred miles north toward Bellingham.

The clothes he'd hung up over a baseboard heater were now dry, and the first northbound bus was leaving from downtown within forty minutes. After checking his notes in the computer file he kept in his phone, Adam packed a change of clothes he pulled from the box of personal belongings Moi had agreed to store for him in the apartment. Adam sealed the last of three acid-resistant plastic bags containing the compounds he'd extracted from the box of vials. He stuffed each one into the breast pockets of his jacket.

Uniformed security officers were still inspecting the bus's undercarriage when Adam walked into the station. Inside, a line of passengers was herded through metal detectors at the far end of the station lobby. The operation seemed crude in comparison to airport procedures, but the number of security officials scrutinizing the crowd seemed quite adequate in preventing a foreign invasion. Several minutes past the scheduled departure time he boarded the bus.

From front to back, Adam made a quick evaluating glance at the seated passengers. His survival now depended on personal vigilance. He rechecked up and down the aisle again, cautiously searching for faces that could kill another man in cold blood. The bus pulled away from the station.

Three and a half hours later, the bus pulled up in the rain outside a single story cinderblock building splattered by layers of incomprehensible graffiti. Adam didn't see Dell among the dozens of people behind a roped-off greeting area. He waited for the attendant to finish raking baggage from the belly of the bus and leaned over to pull his from the pile when an imposing hand gripped him on the shoulder from behind.

Adam spun around to defend himself, his elbow at eye level ready to strike.

"You're still tough as ever!" Dell chuckled, shoving his hand into Adam's. Rainwater dripped down his wiry beard onto the pea-green slicker that draped over his stout frame. "Could use more meat on them bones of yours."

Adam shook his hand with vigor. "Look man, thanks for putting me up in such short notice."

"I can use the company. Gets mighty lonely out in these parts."

Dell escorted Adam over to his pickup parked down the street. It was an older rig, the kind to be found rusting behind a caved-in barn along a rural highway. Dell had restored it to a bright red with a glossy blue top glistening in the faint afternoon sun. Fixing old trucks kept Dell busy during the bleak winter months.

Adam pulled open the door and marveled at the truck's interior. The shiny black dashboard shimmered against all its chrome knobs. Spanning door to door, the cloth bench seat still had that playful bounce that gave old pickups their place on the country music dial.

Dell climbed into the driver's seat and slapped the steering wheel. "Guess you never met Buford before."

"Buford?" Adam asked as he tossed the baggage in the back and jumped in. He saw no cat or dog—any pet that might be called *Buford*.

"Ford truck with a Buick motor," Dell grinned as he pulled out onto a local highway.

"Clever." Adam cracked open his wing-window. "I'll bet you've got some steamy memories packed away in this old tank. I'd love to hear them all, but I probably won't be around that long."

Dell shot Adam an expectant look. "How long you gonna stay?"

"A couple of days, I hope. Depends on when I can get on a flight to Pasadena."

"What's your hurry, city boy?"

"Another long story," Adam replied. "I've got to get down to NASA's Propulsion Labs."

"Wow, the Propulsion Labs! I never expected you'd hit it this big, Harlow. When do they want you?"

"Soon as I get cleared for a seat on a plane."

Dell sucked in a thin stream of air and shrugged. "Sorry to break the bad news ... but getting a flight from out here could take some time. A neighbor of mine put in for a flight to Kansas City to bury his deceased brother. Took three weeks before the FAA drew his name. The guy done missed the whole funeral."

Adam began to wonder if requesting flight authorization so far out of town had been a wise choice. On the other hand, he wouldn't have been too smart hanging around Seattle's underground either.

The truck rumbled east on a tree lined, two-lane highway. Dell caught him up on old times during the twenty-minute drive as the wipers skated over the glass in opposite directions. A mile or two after turning onto a winding gravel drive Dell's log cabin came into view.

As the truck pulled up Dell shut off the engine. "I remember you as a fish eater," he said, slamming the door of the truck.

"Sure, back in the day when I could afford it ... before salmon hit forty dollars a pound."

The two walked through mid-winter shadows that blanketed remnants of snow patches melting over brown sod in front of the weathered cabin. Leafless cottonwoods arched over a small creek that meandered behind a painted white barn. The scene conjured up images of growing up back in rural South Dakota, adding in the fragrance of rain-soaked cedars.

Dell stopped on the rickety porch and kicked a loose board back into place. "I saved my last sockeye for our dinner tonight," he chuckled. "This one came to me from an old fella who knows where to row out into the bay. Just sits there, then when nobody's around he drops his line and reels 'em in. Once or twice a year he'll bring me a live one. I've got one in a ten gallon tank out in the barn."

After lunch Adam stood up from the table and looked over the antiques hanging on the knotty-pine walls between photos of the raspberry fields taken in summer. "You never told me; how was last year's raspberry crop?"

Dell delivered him a lurid smile. "My best crop in the eight years. Sad thing is most of it ended up in jars. I lost my shirt *and* pants on that crop."

Adam couldn't believe his ears. Considering the price of fruit he'd been paying in Seattle, he expected Dell to be raking in record profits and driving a new Porsche, at least a Cadillac.

Dell sighed. "Things haven't changed much out here for us farmers. We still get pennies on the dollar...then tack on the cost of freight to get your product to market. Everything's gone darn near through the roof."

Adam looked back to size up the truck. "Buford looks up to the job. Can't you truck it yourself?"

"Look, I've been through the math, backwards and forwards. On my ration of fuel—throw in some homemade ethanol from the growers association—the old girl still don't make it."

By the look in Dell's eyes, hopelessness had turned sourly desperate.

Adam grinned despite it all. "Look, I fell into something huge," he confessed. Briefly he explained the details of NASA's fuel formula, hidden in sealed bags he began pulling out of his jacket. "With these, I believe I can duplicate this fuel they call *Aqualene.*"

"That explains your trip down to Pasadena."

Adam nodded. "What I've got here actually belongs to NASA."

"That's one hell of a big secret for one fella to be carrying around. You being followed?"

"Don't know. But I can understand perfectly if you'd rather I didn't stay the night. I could check in at a motel in Bellingham and find my way back to Seattle."

Dell let go one of his hearty laughs. "Won't have such a thing ... not when you figure in all them wild ideas we'd toss around back at school. Dreams don't just evaporate with hard times."

Some of Adam's worries left him. "Can't argue there."

Dell sat down in a chair at the kitchen table. "I may have followed my dad's footsteps into busting sod, but I ain't lost passion for science and adventure."

"Okay, but don't say I never warned you."

"Not a word," Dell replied flatly. "How do we get started?"

Adam began clearing a space on the kitchen floor. He rattled off a list of items they could expect to find around the place, and sent Dell scrounging for jars and an old iron skillet. Putting their minds together, they soon modified a condensing unit from a dead refrigerator rotting behind the barn.

Adam had worked a good part of the afternoon when he spied the final component they needed to finish the apparatus. An antique copper teapot hung over a windowsill off the kitchen. It was the perfect size for the chamber to attach to the condensing line. "I'll replace it someday," Adam insisted. "Ought to be more of these beauties on eBay."

Dell cradled the pot with sentimental hands as he wiped a layer of dust off and set it carefully down on the floor. "That belonged to my great grandmother," he said, letting go of a gust of air through his nostrils. Adam cringed over his own audacity to ask for it. But Dell brightened. "Consider one vintage memory of my grandmother our little contribution to science."

After heating up the minerals he had squeezed from the plastic bags, Adam carefully worked the ingredients into a malleable compound. He settled on a 3-part combination in careful proportions he could derive from memory of the few notes he'd made before leaving Gamil alone in the lab. Two hours passed after the compound reached its target temperature, yet nothing resembling Renee's blue juice trickled through the end of the condensing unit.

Adam double-checked the equipment while Dell stoked the fire. During their night vigil both silently took turns staring at the bottom of the small glass bottle, but it remained dry.

The next morning Adam sat down to breakfast Dell had cooked up over the woodstove. His eyes were barely open enough to see the fire crackling at the stone hearth across the room. He'd spent half the night lying awake wondering how he was going to get a plane bound for Southern California. Flights departing from the community airport in Bellingham were booked, especially those few carriers serving the west coast. Getting FAA authorization to fly created just one more obstacle to making it to the Propulsion Labs.

Weekly automated e-mails from NASA had advised Adam to document any significant findings about the fuel's composition, including an efficiency rating—a definitive statement that outlined his interpretation of *Aqualene* and its combustibility. This final stage of Gamil's discovery remained to be fulfilled, which made Adam a little nervous. He needed to test the blue fluid that still failed to appear from the spiral of condensing coils spread out over the cabin floor.

The landscape of Adam's dilemma soon changed.

At daybreak a message arrived. It was from NASA, congratulating a Clarence Riggs from Phoenix for delivering a recovered version of the formula. The news struck Adam like a hammer. Painfully he read on to find that additional stipends were available. Up to ten thousand dollars would be paid to those who could submit findings of a similar quality. This was said to provide useful cross references to existing variables. For Adam the stipend wouldn't come close to paying his mother's delinquent mortgage … let alone sustain him for another three months.

In the form of a lousy post script, the email instructed him to show up at a site in Los Angeles where secondary support data would be collected and evaluated before it was sent to the Propulsion Labs. It was here that one or two candidates might be recruited for full-time employment with a leading energy research firm. Such news was slightly less than bleak.

An interview with top-level executives, pending flight authorization out of Seattle-Tacoma International Airport, awaited his acceptance. NASA officials urged the recipients to consider this option as a gesture of appreciation for their efforts.

Though he was more curious than interested, this was a reasonable, second-to-last break for Adam under the present economic circumstances. Staring at his handy work sprawled

56

out over the cabin's floor, he punched in his reply. By the time the second message arrived with flight information for a Monday morning departure, Dell was standing in the kitchen drying his hair with a towel.

"You look like the doctor just drew blood. What's up?"

"Someone beat me to the punch. Some clown in Arizona made it to I got an interview, Monday at 11:00am."

Adam explained to Dell the site where the interviews were to be held was at the old Arco Towers in the downtown business district of Los Angeles. It now belonged to one of the nation's major oil concerns. According to the message, it had been renamed.

The Power Building served as the company's west coast headquarters, under a contract with the defense department.

"Wait a minute. I thought you were supposed to report to the Propulsion Labs," Dell remarked under the towel.

"Looks like things have changed ... ever since Riggs got there first."

"Maybe. But I bet you're one of the few in the country to have the complete formula. Why not play your hand in both places? It's worth the extra hassle, if you ask me."

Dell did have a point there. By using the Internet during his flight, Adam decided to map out plans to catch a bus or taxi to Pasadena directly after the job interview and personally deliver his sample of the formula along with the digital file containing his notes. This would allow ample time to return to Admiral for subsequent formalities ... on the condition the company was generous enough to offer him a position. The transition between the job interview and the Labs would be dicey and require some clever footwork. Why had the notion of working for mega oil interests failed to dampen the rush of landing steady work?

When you're hungry you do whatever's necessary to survive, he reminded himself.

Eight

Adam was eager to get back to the condensing unit.

Time passed tediously as the two dismantled and repaired the jumble of lines and valves. Sure enough, a hairline crack had prevented the system from reaching the proper pressure. Adam used an acetylene torch from Dell's tool shed to heat the tubing and braise a number of suspected areas. By sundown the unit was ready to go. The night before, Adam had slept scarcely three hours. The excitement of bringing all his patience, not to mention the tragic loss of Gamil, and Moi's disappearance to a conclusive end somehow revived Adam.

Over the cabin's wood stove and the additional heat of Dell's acetylene torch, Adam reheated the blended minerals and worked them into a consistency that soon met his satisfaction. The evening dragged on until shy of midnight. That's when the first drop of blue formula dripped from the condensing unit. Both watched from armchairs, taking turns fueling the fire between dozes. To avoid nodding off on his shift, Adam spent his minutes thinking about Moi. Was she safe tonight, where ever she'd gone? Where *had* she gone? Was she in danger? Did she wonder the same about him?

By the light of dawn there were no messages. Yet the condenser had produced maybe two precious milliliters of the formula. Was it enough needed to make *Aqualene*? According to Renee DeLong, one could make a significant quantity when mixed down with saltwater. Adam recalled the meager drops DeLong had mixed with a can of saltwater before running a chainsaw engine for several minutes. "No emissions," she'd said while he'd sat marveling its properties.

Dell was gazing curiously at the emerald substance that had dribbled into a small vial while Adam ran some calculations. In a matter of minutes he determined the tiny ration could yield a significant quantity of the fuel, once they'd mixed it down with saltwater. It would produce more than enough burnable fuel to convince NASA he'd struck gold!

Carefully he documented the measured ingredients and the ratios he'd used earlier while combining them, saving carefully selected bits of the data in his thumb drive. Using molecular cross-references sent by Heinrich Mann, Adam confirmed that *Aqualene* was the product of a combination of three distinct minerals whose facts and mining locations were deliberately kept obscure. And though Renee never got around to explaining exactly where the government acquired the minerals, their molecular structures suggested they were from a stratum of planetary crust of which he was unfamiliar.

Sunday morning Dell sat in his easy chair glaring at NFL replays on Internet TV. The Redskins had just lost the ball to Miami in blowing snow on Washington's own field. To the average fan the event would have been little more than circumstance. But at the farmer's grange, Dell had lamented earlier, he'd thrown his heart and wallet into the game, betting handsomely on the Redskins with decent odds of securing a win on their own turf.

Adam stepped out of the bathroom, pulling a borrowed sweatshirt over his head. The sight of Dell fussing over game highlights two months past amused him. He took a long look at the blue formula they had collected in the bottom of the glass jar. "I'll need to get on the road tonight...after we test this stuff to see if it's got the kick I'm looking for."

"Buford's your best bet," Dell grunted across the room, punching off the remote. He fancied any opportunity to take her out despite a persistent lack of fuel. "Like us sports fans, she'll drink just 'bout anything you pour down her."

"Perfect. But I'm not ready to pour something unproven into that beautiful old truck of yours. We need something simple, light duty ... like, say, a lawnmower."

"Not mine. It's in pieces. Got a busted flywheel."

Adam scratched his chin and turned a full circle, his eyes panning the room for ideas, anything that would suggest..."You still got that old Honda I sold you before we left college?"

"Settin' out yonder in the barn."

Adam glanced at the blue fluid and lit off a grin. "That's money! Let's try it."

Dell slowly rose to his feet. "You sure bout this? It's been seven years since you almost killed yourself on that thing. Now ya wanna do it again?"

Adam slapped the jawbone doctors had rebuilt the night of his motorcycle accident. "I'll take my chances."

Dell cocked his head with doubt and hunted for an extra raincoat. "Weather report's predictin' drizzle today. Round here that translates to mud."

Silence came between them as the two walked across the yard. Inside the barn Dell pulled away old farm implements to reveal a dusty gray tarp. The motorcycle beneath it was caked in a layer of dried mud. Immediately the machine brought back mixed memories.

"You really *are* a junk collector," Adam declared, disguising a covert yearning to climb on the old Honda.

Dell shrugged. "I've kept her round for errands; herdin' some sheep I once had on the property ... and the chance I catch one of them low-budget mid-life crises."

Adam kicked at the front tire. "Looks like your crisis ended before it ever started."

"Postponed a bit, I reckon."

Adam walked the bike to the center of the earthen floor. Dell stood back to cast further doubts. "She ain't run for two, three years."

Adam squeezed at both tires, then circled around to the front of the bike and knelt down to get a closer look at the 350cc engine. The deep scrapes across the engine's aluminum casing brought back ample memories of the horrible scene that sent him to the hospital for a week. Maybe, just maybe, the machine had one more life. The bike would provide him a quick efficiency test. Performance feedback ... and leave plenty of his homemade sample for my judgment day at NASA.

Dell twisted the gas cap off and sniffed for fumes. "She's dryer than camel's piss in the Sahara."

"Perfect," Adam grunted as he got to work scraping gunk from the carburetor float bowls. "Just what I need for an accurate assessment."

"You really itchin' to ride that thing again, ain't you?"

"Well, I might … if you put some air in the tires."

Dell grabbed a hand pump leaning against the back wall and inflated both tires, voicing his doubts they'd hold it for long. "Okay, now what?"

"I'm going to need some saltwater, as much as you can get."

"How bout a cup of saline solution? I've got some in a first aid kit I keep in the truck."

Adam paused. He got suddenly to his feet. "How about the water that fish came in."

"Dell beamed. He pointed toward the back wall. "Must be at least three, four gallons in that big white bucket. Li'l dirty but good-n-salty."

"It'll have to do," Adam declared. "I'll need some clean jars."

Dell trotted off to the cabin. Adam pulled out his phone and pecked out a quick message to Moi. He was flying for LA early the next morning and wanted her to know his whereabouts. He requested a reply again, hoping she had forgiven him of the awful experience he'd put her through in the muddy underground.

A cold rain was slapping at the roof of the barn when Dell returned from the cabin.

"Everything okay?"

Adam drew in a breath, shoving the device into his pocket. "I had hoped to hear back from a good friend by now."

"Sounds kinda important."

"She's a Chinese exchange student. Helped me in the lab before we had to get out in a hurry."

Dell cracked a smile. "Someone to smooth you out a little?"

"Well, maybe," Adam admitted, a bit flushed.

Dell fixed his eyes back on the Honda. "Well then, let's not dawdle."

As if the rain clouds had parted, a definite glow returned to Adam's face. "Fill me a jar full of that saltwater."

After dispensing two drops of the blue fluid into the jar, Adam passed it to Dell, who immediately began to grin with astonishment as the glass heated up in his palms.

61

"Give it a couple more seconds," Adam instructed as he began scratching a test line near the bottom of the fuel tank.

With an appraising eye, Dell watched him pour barely a cup of *Aqualene* into the motorcycle's tank, up to the line for a benchmark. "You'll be lucky to get off the property with that dribble."

Adam just smiled. He replaced the bike's filler cap. Pouring off some of the blue formula into the bottom of a second jar, he set it on the shelf alongside several cans and unmarked containers.

Dell watched with curiosity. "What's that gonna do, kill the rats?"

"This small amount will serve as a storage experiment, measuring shelf life and evaporation rates. I'll check on it when I make another trip later this year."

The chatter of lightly falling rain had ceased. Adam pushed the motorcycle outside the barn. Large residual water drops rolled off the cottonwood branches above them, making a deep thud as they collided into Buford's hood, two or three at a time. Adam pulled on the scraped up orange helmet that hung from the handlebars. His heart quickened with anticipation to hear the Honda roar to life. The tattered saddle wheezed and squeaked as he bounced the rear springs up and down. Adam glided his fingers over the peeling handgrips. Right away he sensed a familiar touch to the steering. The weight of the Honda between his legs invoked memories of push-start skids down the street in front of his apartment six blocks from the college campus in Minnesota—the result of the bike's kick-starter gear busting off by its previous owner.

Dell stepped out of the barn and stood in the mud. "You ready?"

"All systems go!" Adam surveyed the property a final time and suggested a trail of well-packed woodchips that led down toward a stretch of creek. With the ground this damp, it was the best surface for getting traction to the rear tire during a compression start.

Adam wheeled the bike into position. Dell angled around to grasp the back of the bike, then gave Adam a shove down

62

the path. Adam maneuvered between overgrown laurels and let out the clutch. The rear tire skidded and fishtailed to a stop.

"Doesn't sound right," Dell hollered to Adam as he puffed back up the trail. "Try second gear!"

Dell dug his boots into the mud to put more speed under the bike the second time. Adam released the clutch. The engine began pumping and sucking air until its compression dragged the Honda to a despairing halt. The test looked like it was destined for failure until an errant pop from the tailpipe echoed through the cottonwoods. The engine coughed once, twice, then, with a guttural roar began reciting rhythms of better days.

Dell waved his arms and shouted over the rumbling motor: "That there tank'll run dry in a minute or two. You'd better get going."

"I'll take her out to the highway and back. Back in a few."

Adam pointed the Honda westward and started down the gravel track. Easing through the gears he remembered the several hooks and blind turns on the way in, and how easy it would be to take a wrong turn only to get lost and then run out of fuel. By third gear the smoothness of the two-cylinder engine surprised him. In fact, he couldn't remember the engine ever running this strong. By fourth gear the cold air was pushing against his cheeks. Weaving the bike right and left served as a test of its maneuverability over crunching rocks. The knobs on the tires had worn down badly over the years, causing the bike to slip around beneath him. The danger of drifting into a perilous slide persuaded him to back off the throttle.

The first hairpin turn came up fast, taking him out of sight of Dell's property. The pattern repeated itself, making Adam feel like he was driving over a giant snake slithering through a Northwest forest. He downshifted to make the second turn without running off the trail into dense brush. The damp greenery that flanked the road afforded him a glance at Mt. Baker in the distance to his right. From the other side came the sudden roar of motocross engines, erupting through a grassy field. Adam stopped and watched two big dirt bikes wheel up over a firmly packed ridge and then drop deftly onto the road.

Both pulled up on either side of him, closer than he liked. One of them began shouting over their engines. "Don't see many riders round here this time of year. You alone out here?"

Adam nodded. "Just out for a little practice run."

They killed their motors and looked the Honda over. One let go of a boyish laugh and shot a disgusted look at the other. "I was hoping for something with a little more guts, like a Ducati or a Kawasaki. A *dirt* bike, not a—"

Adam's blood pressure surged. Who was he to turn down a challenge dripping with insults?

"A dirt bike, huh!"

"Yeah. How 'bout a race to the bridge?" the younger one suggested, pointing into the woods. "That-a-way, bout three miles."

Adam had heard enough of their spiked egos. Without so much as a nod he throttled the two cylinders, spraying gravel in a wide arc and let the Honda lurch into the underbrush toward a wall of cedars. Shifting up with a flick of his wrist gave him the acceleration he needed to pull ahead of their huge knobby tires. He knew poor traction would be his nemesis in this playful sprint to where he wasn't quite sure.

Standing high on the pegs, Adam let the Honda bound into a low marshy depression. Instinct told him to penetrate the cedars and search for any path that dropped down into the ravine falling off to his left. Within fifty yards the trail faded and the foliage thickened. But his hunch to keep traversing the hillside proved wise when the roar of both bikes suddenly sped up behind him. Something of a trail reappeared. He'd begun to savor the exhilaration of a good cat & mouse game.

Here were a couple of country punks, probably with stolen gasoline and nothing better to do, who needed a good whooping.

Why not? Adam thought. After all, the Honda was running like a champ. Not only was the test in the fuel tank, but it was also in the way the machine purred as Adam shot deeper amongst the trees. Beneath him the engine wound up and sung like a kamikaze going vertical. Every now and then the rear tire broke loose its tenuous grip of the ground, which now deteriorated into a smelly swath of brown muck.

The other bikes, suspended generously over fresh rubber, screamed after him and rode his tail. Each began jockeying for a chance to skirt around him and take the lead. Boys, you'll have to earn it, Adam mused to himself.

He squinted through a line of drooping branches that beat at his elbows, each one biting like angry fire ants as they tore at the raincoat Dell had lent him. Stinging pain slithered up to his shoulders.

Adam had accepted the bikers' challenge, one that he would finish in triumph.

The trail circled now, breaking the Honda into a small clearing that descended to the bottom of the ravine—a good two miles to the bridge, he estimated. Shifting up and throttling a little more of NASA's miracle juice into the two pounding cylinders, Adam widened the gap between his muddied back and the two riders, ripping through a litter of dead foliage.

Their huge, over-bored engines whining at top speed, gained lost momentum and roared up alongside Adam. One had the notion to play dirty and cut him off inside the base of the trough. This cat and mouse game persisted without success for another mile, the Honda responding loyal and true. Ahead the prized destination—a steep embankment leading to the bridge—appeared beyond a series of mud traps that forced him to downshift and pray the worn tires could dig him out of the slimy bogs that skirted an eroded streambed. Suddenly the Honda rolled onto hard flat ground—the sort of terrain that fancy big bikes could turn on a nickel ... and leave the rider some change.

With astounding acceleration the two tightened the gap with a menacing vengeance. But their rally against the Honda and a few ounces of *Aqualene* had come too late on the open stretch.

Dripping with indignation their obscenities amused Adam as he shifted up and stood on the pegs. A hundred yards of sand and riverbank now separated him from the base of a steep embankment. The Honda's rusted power plant beneath him drove the speedometer's slender red needle past the top of its fogged dial. Instantly the bike shot up a hard packed berm and hurled through the air like a missile. Adam pulled up on the handlebars and locked his knees around the fuel tank. Everything about the flight felt good. But his sloping trajectory suddenly began to spell disaster in a world where gravity always trumps velocity.

Yards under his wind-milling front tire, a thicket of wild blackberry bushes threatened to snag him into ruthless thorns. In the likes of a crippled navy plane, approaching its carrier's burning deck on one engine, Adam fought for distance. Awaiting him was a clay-packed ridge that seemed hopelessly out of reach.

Rolling his shoulders back, he postured for a rear-wheel touchdown. Then gunned the engine for torque to the rear tire, a popular stunt to lessen frontal impact.

The move was a stroke of brilliance.

Underneath him the ground was solid enough, giving the Honda's rubber something to grab as the bike surged for higher ground. Fishtailing violently the rear tire crested the ravine. Adam pulled up onto a plank of blessed concrete, cut left and rolled to a stop, letting the motor spool down to a loping idle. A vacant strip of roadway filled his sights—shiny wet asphalt ran for a quarter mile before disappearing into a misted turn that would lead him back to Dell's gravel drive. The ravine beneath him was oddly quiet—his opponents unavailable for comment.

When Adam pulled up to the porch Dell ambled over to the bike to inspect the idling motor. "Get lost out there? Been over ten minutes." He twisted off the fuel tank's filler cap and peered down inside. "You dog! You topped off up the road somewhere, didn't ya?"

"No, I swear, I didn't!" Adam protested. The accusation suddenly amused him. There would be plenty more of that where he was going. Adam peered into the tank, seeing his reflection off the remaining quantity of fuel. He remembered what Dell had said about a farmer's ration of fuel. "Look man, this proves Buford can make it to Seattle … and back! Will you take me?"

Dell was grinning ear to ear. "You *know* I will."

"Good. We'll leave in the morning. Meanwhile, you help me make up three gallons of two-hundred proof, tonight.

Nine

Sunday, about 3:00pm, Pacific Time, Heinrich analyzed the latest pictures of Earth's atmospheric grid.

The regions having the highest levels of hydrocarbon emissions were centered over Mexico. This was indicated on the map in heavy splotches of red. The disappointing data drained what was left of his energy. Heinrich sighed and began to set up for an automated sweep that would take hundreds of readings and record them into a statistics file.

The other scientist involved in ozone mapping had gone to the upper deck for exercise. Heinrich was usually the last one to log out. It was his habit to go back over his data a last at the end of his shift, leaving the workstation with a head full of statistics to digest on his downtime.

Before closing out his last screen—the human resources menu that listed him as a staff member with the International Ozone Repair Initiative, and an active volunteer at New Mexico's SETI institute—Heinrich found himself looking at a blinking icon he'd failed to recognize earlier. It appeared at the top corner of his screen and identified itself as an instant message that had to be opened as a coded attachment, under a SETI user's password. Probably an error in one of the self-monitoring programs, he reasoned. Pesky glitches came up all the time.

He glanced back at the screen, anticipating self-repair to dissolve the flashing icon. But it remained, inciting in him a new level of curiosity. Taking a sip of his coffee, he opened a dialogue box linked to the icon.

Heinrich's jaw dropped.

The panel lit up in bright red letters: *Level Four Distress*. He turned toward the linkway to alert someone, but something stopped him. His fingers raced over the keyboard. A locator's field popped up. It read: *Moon Surface*.

This had to be a computer-generated message, contrived by one of several probes drifting somewhere between Earth and the asteroid belt. A lot of older units out there were either dead or malfunctioning.

"A distress signal from an unmanned machine? Impossible," he whispered. Communications between probes and landers took place through a series of highly secured satellite links that corresponded directly with NASA centers in Arizona and Houston.

Heinrich inquired for details and waited. After a short delay, a text message filled his screen.

DISTRESS UM-331
THE CREW ABOARD VASHON IS IN DANGER.
SCRAMBLED IGNITION CODES PREVENT OUR
ATTEMPTED LIFTOFF. LOST CONTACT WITH
GROUND CONTROL. REQUESTING ALTERNATE
LINK TO EUROPA COMMAND.
SCC DELONG

Heinrich narrowed his eyes and glanced back at the field showing the origin of the message. Oddly, Vashon showed up as a robotic probe, a spacecraft that didn't support life. Landing probes were too small and carried no means for life support, only electronic equipment.

Again Heinrich stared at the text, this time through a pair of reading glasses he kept at his workstation. Suddenly the profiles of three astronauts zipped across the bottom of the screen. A line of digitized frequencies followed.

Heinrich clicked back to the first screen where the message had shown up. Just then Skip Halverson appeared in the entrance to the linkway. "Doctor, you're late for exercise."

But Heinrich gestured him over to the monitor. "What do you make of this?"

Halverson sighed, then leaned toward the screen. He scanned the text and shook his head. "Nothing of this nature in *my* log. Consider it bogus."

"On what grounds?"

"A manned spacecraft on the moon? Not in the works for another two, maybe three years. Those clowns in the medical lab are pulling your leg."

"Of course," Heinrich chuckled with a slap to his knee. He glanced at his watch and apologized to the station's director for his tardiness. Halverson disappeared down the linkway.

The notion of a moon mission was totally possible, given Apollo's history. But for economic reasons, NASA had delayed plans to set up a lunar base. Heinrich stared back at the message screen. He pondered the dilemma for a long moment. Before logging off, he needed to verify the message's authenticity on his own.

Dr. Tanaka would know something about a lunar landing mission. But then, the professor was a purist, a traditional thinker. He'd never been keen on sharing information if it could be procured from its properly assigned source.

Tactics in hand, Heinrich stepped into the next module to poke his head behind Tanaka's partition.

"Doctor, tell me, what is the nature of the next manned mission to the moon?" Heinrich asked. He waited and watched a contorted little squint in Tanaka's eyes telegraph his reply.

Tanaka bobbed his head and released a breath filled with sheer annoyance. "Might you be referring to the *Liberty Mission*? Everyone up here knows the project was grounded indefinitely on the basis of congressional funding caps. Do you not read the newspapers these days, doctor?"

The man's snide remarks began to grind on Heinrich's nerves. But he decided to bury his indignation and press on. "What do you know about mechanicals on the lunar surface?"

"Negative," Tanaka answered with an agitated sigh. "Far too expensive when you consider what the government pays to keep us up here."

"You're sure?"

Tanaka snorted. "Perhaps, doctor, you have contrived a precarious link between reality and fantasy."

"Must be the recycled air up here."

"Or possibly you are missing mandatory fitness sessions." Tanaka pursed his lips cynically, jotted something into his log, and exited the service module.

Returning to his own terminal, Heinrich continued to puzzle.

Backing up to the origin field, he reread its print: *Vashon Mission, Lunar Surface*. It made sense that a big gun like Tanaka was totally convinced a landing mission was out of the question. But why was the message forwarded only to his terminal. The icon hadn't shown up on Tanaka's screen.

Maybe Halverson was right. Someone on board was playing a joke on the big German guy from SETI—an amusing target for receiving a mysterious message from deep space. Realizing he'd played into this too far, Heinrich grinned at his monitor. Two can play this game. *"MAJOR TOM TO GROUND CONTROL, I'M LIVING IN A—"*

Instantly his fingers halted and his attention returned to the sender's location in a corner of the screen highlighted in a blue sidebar. How could he have failed to notice it? Heinrich stared at the signal locator, startled at what he saw.

The message did not originate *inside* the space station. A visual display showed the real-time location of every research craft, probe, and transport vehicle beyond Earth's atmosphere.

To verify authenticity, he found two probes on Mars, both put there two years earlier for data collection in preparation for a manned landing. But the fuel shortage and all of its effects had frozen the lofty endeavor approved by Congress.

Heinrich zoomed in closer, squinting to make out an icon representing a moving spacecraft. Strangely, a Europa vehicle was orbiting the moon. The enlargement allowed him to trace the craft's path backwards on the electronic map. The Europa craft had made dozens of close lunar orbits.

"Impossible," he muttered.

In front of his eyes, a tiny dot was blinking on the surface of the moon. Could this be the so-called Vashon Mission? Were three humans stranded inside a spacecraft so top secret, Skip Halverson and Dr. Tanaka knew nothing of the mission's existence?

Heinrich pondered the magnitude of his discovery. He had wandered deep inside government files, far beyond the scope of his work aboard the station. If this wasn't a malfunction, he had discovered a secret program of no business to civilian scientists. This had to be a big military job.

Just then, Greg appeared in the airlock. "Halverson's checking everyone's blood pressure in the exercise bay, and he's asking for you, Doctor."

"Okay, okay. Tell him I'm on my way."

Greg's words faded away and Heinrich resumed staring into the monitor. Next thing, Greg was standing there at his side.

"What's up, man?"

Heinrich's hand shot up. "You'd better not get involved. Not with any of this."

But it was too late. Greg had locked a narrow gaze on the screen. At this point Heinrich was again preoccupied with the text as they read the distress message again, silently. Greg finished and turned to his mentor. "Some sort of joke, huh."

"Who's to know?" Heinrich choked. "Whatever it is, we can't go blabbing about this. Not just yet … with all the stiff laws governing civilian research these days."

"So, now what? I mean, uh, we can't just stand here!" Greg protested in a hoarse whisper.

Heinrich considered things carefully. "First I must contact this fellow," he said while pointing to the name *Stan Rockwell* on the screen. "He's with Europa Command. There's another problem, however. According to this display, his spacecraft is leaving the moon's orbit and returning to Earth … as we speak."

Greg gave a puzzled look and glanced back down at the electronic map on the screen. It didn't make sense. Why would Rockwell return to Earth without the others? Heinrich broke the silence, answering Greg's unanswered question: "It's quite possible Rockwell is having some kinda technical issue." But his words were laced with doubt. "No pilot would abandon three comrades, unless he had a darn good reason."

"You mean like if all three were dead?"

"Absolutely."

Greg cocked his head and rested on one elbow. "This other commander dude—the one sitting on the moon—how long has he been stranded?"

"Guy? No. It's a woman. I read the bios."

Greg raised his eyebrows in astonishment.

72

"Don't look so surprised. Some of our best pioneers have been women. The space corps is full of them."

Greg nodded. "Okay, let me get things straight. This lady and her crew are stuck on the moon. So why doesn't she just contact Rockwell herself?"

"Excellent question, young man. DeLong indicated they lost contact with NASA days ago. Indeed, a strange occurrence to lose communications with Rockwell, then turn around and contact us a quarter of a million miles away."

Greg sat down at the terminal. "I still say Rockwell would have to believe they're all dead *before* heading back to Earth. You remember in training how they told us our body vital signs are monitored and sent back to Earth on a separate frequency?"

"I'm with you so far. Go on."

"Wouldn't NASA receive that data about astronauts on the moon?"

"Yes, of course. At that distance the data would be delayed by only seconds. Maybe you've got something, Greg!" Heinrich's eyes widened as he raked at the stubble on his chin. "All the crew's vitals must have blanked out ... along with their radio communications. Unlikely but possible!"

"NASA thinks the mission's over," Greg added. "So what's the use in Rockwell doing cartwheels around the moon?"

"That's a harsh way to put it," Heinrich remarked, "but I'm afraid your theory holds water. Rockwell must have gotten the official word from someone higher up the chain of command. Some mucky-muck inside NASA has scrubbed the mission!"

"Either that or ... Rockwell's up to something criminal."

"I doubt that one, Greg." Heinrich stretched with a deep yawn and turned toward the light down the linkway. "Look, I've got to send a short reply to Vashon and acknowledge their message. Then I'll copy these communication codes into my cell phone. To keep this quiet, we'll transmit everything from my bunk."

Expectations hung in Greg's tone. "What'll we do about Rockwell?"

73

"Be patient. Nothing can be done until I drop back into the network and find the codes for contacting him. In the meanwhile you'd better keep your mouth shut ... now that I've broken security protocols and both of us have viewed highly classified material. We'll camp out in the observatory a little longer, until Thompson returns."

With little more than twenty minutes, Heinrich and Greg hunched in front of the astronomer's terminal. Heinrich closed his eyes and rubbed at his temples. One of his migraines was setting in. He reached out and slid his military identification card into the side of the terminal. A minute hadn't passed before they were staring inside NASA's restricted section.

"Wow, you've got the touch," Greg whispered between little jets of breath.

Through his reading glasses the text became blurred and heavy. Heinrich kept scrolling and clicking deeper through the maze of windows until he arrived at the archives base file. Sure enough, there were additions to what he saw only minutes ago.

"You're going to have to read it to me, Greg. I'll be lucky to keep my eyes open with this headache."

Greg craned his neck and leaned over the glowing plasma. In the darkened lab he began reading:

"396 million samplings of the two dormant volatiles produce a scatter plot that indicates a positive correspondence between active and inactive catalysts. Mining of Rhodium463-C9 and the ceria480-LD8 on Earth buried in igneous mantle could yield rich deposits directly beneath Pliocene strata."

"What the hell does all that mean?" Greg whispered.

"Too much to go into it right now, son. But it's all beginning to make sense," Heinrich mumbled. "This isn't your run-of-the-mill techno-bureaucrat working at NASA."

"Then who writes this shit?"

"Scientists and cutting-edge engineering teams draft these reports. Still, this could have come from only a few minds. From there, with its content highly classified, only a handful of the highest brass are authorized to lay eyes on it."

"Jeez, that's me," Greg whispered with outstretched hands over his head.

"Promise me none of it will leave this room."

Greg kept his right hand up and smiled. His eye caught more text zipping across the lower part of the screen. He squinted and began chopping through it in a hush while Heinrich massaged his throbbing temples:

"Additional sampling and analysis of the lunar soil indicates an optimum mix of acids and toxins to accelerate the formation of elements in C9 in tandem with LD8—two minerals melted on impact to create simultaneous catalytic reactions. Both minerals—identical to similar references presumed to exist on Earth—are present in a shallow field just below the lunar crust."

Greg had barely finished when the text suddenly disappeared. Heinrich smashed a fist down over his knee. "Christ all mighty! This is downloading from the moon, in real time! That proves someone aboard Vashon is sending these reports. It might explain why the commander's mission is in peril. And why NASA isn't doing anything to help."

Greg shrugged. "Somewhere you've lost me."

"A mole! There's a mole," Heinrich snapped, "skimming it off the system as fast as it goes in."

"You mean like a computer virus?"

"Worse. I'm talking about human vermin, the kind that goes to prison for selling off huge government secrets."

"No shit! Like hawking sophisticated technology to the enemy?"

"I didn't know you kids bothered to read the news these days."

"I don't. Facebook's full of this shit."

Heinrich sat up with an introspective stare, then turned back to the screen.

"Look here," he said, referring to a tab revealing the presence of someone accessing the site. "This guy probably works inside the government."

"He's one of us?"

"Except he's not on our side."

75

Greg shifted directions. "We got into the system, so who else in the country can do it?"

"That's what scares the hell out of me," Heinrich sighed. "Half the federal government's got some kind of security clearance. Tragically, this transmission is getting dumped into a hidden sub-file and probably won't be seen by legitimate NASA people for days, if ever. Somebody or some group is diverting this data so they can glean off the mission's technology."

Greg's thoughts caught up with Heinrich. "A black hole file?"

"Exactly. And damn hard to trace. That's why killing off the inventor becomes a necessary step in this dirty business. Imagine Vashon's crew returning to Earth and telling their story of how our own planet's crust may contain the minerals needed to manufacture gasoline's ultimate replacement. Governments and alternative energy firms around the world could begin producing it in a matter of months, and put the oil giants out of business for good."

Greg was astonished. "You mean three astronauts sitting on the moon have the answer to the gasoline shortage?"

Heinrich nodded grimly. "Yes, but only part of it."

Ten

Due to flight delays in Europe, representatives from Beijing had to arrive a day late into Washington DC. The two-nation partnership was set to convene in strict secrecy, an emergency summit unlike any other.

Presently, Arab-based petroleum shipments had been devastated, running less than fifty percent of peak production, achieved a few years earlier. With the demand for gasoline expected to only grow, the United States and China were willing to risk hundreds of billions in a space-based mining venture. The very root of their objective had been to send qualified scientists to the moon, extract several tons of the minerals, and return safely to Earth. The secrecy of the project had grown out of the political repercussions of hurling these nations into unforgivable debt as a result of financing the controversial mission.

That afternoon, the President of the United States positioned himself at a round table set up for high-level conferences in a briefing room adjacent to the Oval Office. Armed with his war cabinet—a term he used privately to refer to China's delegates and NASA's top officials—Kirkpatrick was fighting a battle against total economic collapse.

Everyone sat down. President Kirkpatrick adjusted his mic and called the meeting to order.

"Utmost secrecy must be observed … until we can systematically begin producing *Aqualene* for world markets. I am privileged to announce the finish-work on three manufacturing plants in the U.S. is near completion. Only a few key details are to be worked out, depending on how aggressive research moves forward. As we have agreed, it is imperative that this coalition lay out a balanced infrastructure that will serve the entire world within two years—a dangerously narrow margin when we consider existing petroleum reserves."

The Chinese delegate, Shen Zhang had replaced Beijing's energy minister, following calls for a firmer stance from Chinese hardliners opposing the weighted formula used to determine Chinese funding of the mining project. Zhang, a skeptic and a conservative, had pushed for an opt-out clause, not to mention Chinese inspection privileges at sensitive sites in the United States, during the drafting phases of the pact. This had incited a flare-up among NASA officials who flatly refused Chinese demands, followed by recommendations Beijing consider bowing out.

But during a heated debate inside the Communist party over the economic consequences of leaving the coalition, China's premier promised a softer approach by installing a new pair of advisors to accommodate Zhang with orders to focus on the outcome of the Project in terms of long-term economic benefits.

After outlining a host of government incentives designed to bolster public cooperation, Kirkpatrick called on Zhang to highlight technical and economic progress his nation was making toward production of *Aqualene* on Chinese soil. Less than an hour later the partnership concluded its formal reports, opening the meeting to discussion. The task of fielding questions specific to the Project began with Zhang speaking through an interpreter.

"Please summarize the security risks and interventions at the handling facilities in the Pacific, Mr. President?"

Kirkpatrick waited for the interpreter's signal and responded.

"Our naval base on Johnston Island has been completely retrofitted. Each side of this pact can rest assured of its utmost integrity to secure Vashon's first shipment of minerals, in the most covert of operations."

The female advisor accompanying Zhang raised a gloved palm and began speaking with near-perfect English. "Sir, please confirm the estimated quantity of fuel that potentially could be produced with the minerals excavated and returned to Earth at this time."

Kirkpatrick turned to an aide on his left who promptly began poking at the keys of a laptop. Around the table, sparkling water fizzed inside fine crystal during the short interval. The aide stood up to speak. "Our best estimates indicate enough fuel for thirty-two months, given present consumption rates. This provides us a reasonable window to negotiate rebuilding damaged refineries in the Middle East, thus restoring ancillary oil trade around the world."

"Much danger lies in American optimism!" the Chinese delegate blurted out. Her statement raised eyebrows and pulled NASA's administrators closer to the table. "Mr. Kirkpatrick, would you update our esteemed delegation on the fate of the Vashon astronauts, and whether or not their second shipment will be arriving back to Earth?"

A synchronized twisting of necks put the room's faces back toward Kirkpatrick who took a gulp of water and nervously shuffled documents in front of him. Tense silence hit a high point and a White House aide shot to her feet and promptly refilled the water glass. The president cleared his throat and tactfully thanked NASA's man for bringing up the question, which segued well for the president. Spontaneity of tabling difficult questions had always been the task of choice for Kirkpatrick. He preferred handling questions over delivering long-winded oratories whenever getting down to the meat of a critical issue—a trait that proved successful to him during his presidential debates.

"As each of you know, Vashon's crew has been on the surface of the moon for over three weeks now, making their scheduled liftoff date significantly overdue. Responding to communication glitches and a propulsion failure, NASA engineers have been on the matter day and night."

Kirkpatrick went on to disclose this concern as the chief purpose of their meeting in Washington. His eyes dropped to NASA's hourly reports now trembling between his fingers.

"I'm afraid we've come to a decision to abandon this mission."

Anxiety turned into mumbling amongst the Chinese. The president leaned over his elbows, forming a steeple with his fingers, then drew a long breath. He braced for repercussions of delaying the inevitable. The buzz soon faded and delegates returned their attention as Kirkpatrick went on.

"Commander DeLong is renowned as a competent scientist and physics engineer. Everything had progressed on target for a flawless mission. Then we lost communications minutes before liftoff. NASA engineers fear the landing craft may have been overcome by a combination of radiation and structural damage that led to mechanical failure in the life-support power unit."

Painfully, Kirkpatrick watched his Chinese partners grimace over the tragedy. Zhang shook his head and spoke in hushed whispers. His interpreter turned to the president.

"Mr. Kirkpatrick, at what hour do you propose the Europa spacecraft leave the crew marooned and return to Earth?"

"Europa's esteemed Commander, Stan Rockwell has exhausted all means to re-establish contact with Vashon. Therefore, I suggest the order be transmitted immediately."

"Is there not a thing that can be done, sir?" asked Zhang's advisor.

"We've done everything we can. Late last night NASA ordered Europa, for the safety of its crew, to prepare a return to Earth."

Kirkpatrick felt as though he were addressing his nation in the throes of declaring nuclear war. A bad case of nerves had dried his mouth, prompting him to sip water and helplessly observe the effects of losing Vashon. The Chinese whispered between themselves—some in their native tongue. The room suddenly erupted into pandemonium.

Kirkpatrick could do no more than to take the podium and rap his gavel.

"Let us reconvene tomorrow at 10:00 am, sharp."

*****

A quarter mile beneath the ground in an unpopulated valley in northeast Arizona, transmissions between NASA and Vashon were processed via a secondary-relay defense satellite.

It took an inconvenient twelve and a half minutes for a high-level official to pass through identification screening, viral scans, and coded authorization before entering NASA's command center where mission communications took place. The master link—off limits to civilian personnel—doubled as one of the Pentagon's top surveillance posts. Interfacing silicon-powered sensors, the system monitored the movements and communication activities among seven rogue nations conspiring to topple Western oil interests grounded in central and southwest Asia.

The three-star general assigned to coordinate communications with Vashon yearned to light up a cigarette as he waited impatiently to be put through to a secured audio channel. In a moment he would be chatting with Colonel Striker, a stiff-lipped Pentagon lifer whose lean, leathery face attested to forty-eight years of profiling and scrutinizing enemies of American Intelligence. Now at the twilight of a shadowy career, cloaked in NSA secrecy, Striker maintained satellite reconnaissance systems while living aboard the International Space Station. Purpose: Interpret suspicious transmissions and relay military data to the Defense Department.

Spy duty in space lacked the glory of his former post in the roughest quarters of Baghdad. There, he'd won accolades for profiling extremists and intercepting their bombing schemes, engineered by risky elements. But after stiff reprimands for publicly referring to Iraqis as *neo barbarians*, and then drafting a CIA plot to reform Middle East order by staging a military coup in Tehran to protect Saudi oil interests, William Striker had interpreted his demotion as a casualty of gutless foreign policy. The transfer, in his opinion, translated into minimal contact with a new order of brass that was paralyzed by bungled wartime surveillance operations and shell-shocked by an over-sanctioned chain of command. "Security of a nation," he'd stated in the presence of a G-20 membership, "supersedes the luxury of debating policy that advocates petty human rights."

When Striker's voice came over the audio speaker, there was no time for internal shoptalk. The general's call—a stretch from routine matters of validating coordinates and details linking Iran's atomic energy ambitions with international bomb trafficking—consisted of a directive from NASA to troubleshoot a glitch in its long-range communications satellite. He quickly briefed the colonel on failed radio transmissions aboard an unspecified spacecraft, informing him that engineers had exhausted all possibilities of technical malfunctions on the ground.

From his private cabin aboard ISS, Striker assured the general he would look into the matter and run a battery of tests on satellite relays—a procedure that no longer required a spacewalk.

Eleven

Greg's mind raced as he hurried down the linkway, past the research modules.

All were quiet. The airlock leading into his sleeping quarters was ajar. Except for a panel of tiny control lights above each of the three bunks, the module was completely dark.

He moved toward Heinrich's bunk and retracted the slider. "Did you send the—"

Greg choked with horror. Under a bead of florescent light that glowed whenever the bunk's slider was drawn back, the doctor's face appeared lifeless, pale. His cheek was rigid to the touch, like cold modeling clay.

Fright melted into nausea. He knelt down and took a breath. Closing his eyes, he waited for a transformation of sound reasoning to fall over him.

The nose was the most logical body point to confirm whether a person was alive ... or dead. Yet his own breaths did little to calm the trembling knuckles he placed over Heinrich's nostrils. With painful concentration his sense of touch strengthened with anticipation that a wisp of warm air would come from the mortal doctor.

Nothing.

The passage of endless seconds steadied his hand. Nausea receded. Finally a thin sheet of warm air brushed over his knuckles. Greg watched Heinrich's chest rise slowly under the fluorescent light. His buttons crested and then fell again.

Greg clutched Heinrich by the shoulder, prodding him to wake up, but failed. He found himself unsteady again; fearful that something horrible was happening. He got to his feet. The cabin smelled of some odd medical odor. Okay, Heinrich was alive, but obviously under some drug!

Inches above his head was a lighted panel. Greg stared at a smear of red characters forming a message that rolled across the panel's digital display: *Completing phase II of deep-sleep cycle.* Greg read the words aloud in a hoarse whisper and then glanced down at Heinrich's pale skin. Deep sleep wasn't death, but it certainly failed to resemble life. Questions poured into mind. A voice inside him demanded to know why Heinrich had activated deep sleep. Greg could not remember the mission director ordering his crew to use the system for the sleep shifts. It was understood that each bunk was equipped with the device, but only for emergency circumstances—when life-support systems failed.

Greg's thoughts crept toward conspiracy. Had someone squealed to Halverson, who then confronted Heinrich about hacking into sensitive files? This was the best explanation Greg could conjure up, considering Heinrich had mentioned that ISS missions were now controlled by military money, people at the Pentagon. With hesitation the professor had hinted that under NSA doings, NASA scientists had lost much of their say over rules and legal rights aboard the station. Was it really true? What did this mean for interns?

Greg knelt down at the bulkhead's organizer. Inside the small compartment where Heinrich kept personal items was his phone. Greg had seen Heinrich copy Vashon's communication codes into it. He peered through the airlock, on down the linkway. Things were quiet, even inside the galley.

Slipping into the privacy of his bunk, he quickly located the file attached to Europa Command. Dr. Mann's phone was a fancy high-end device; a German branded android that had been custom programmed to communicate at ultra-low frequencies. Heinrich had talked about calling friends and colleagues around the world without the need for a conventional satellite link. The unit worked like a powerful two-way radio and had come in handy a time or two when he needed to contact the ozone observatory in Bonn while ISS was taking readings over Mexico.

Greg poked at the touch-sensitive screen and followed layers of inside screens that led him to Europa's coding. The name Rockwell appeared. But there were no codes in the file. Why hadn't Heinrich copied the communication codes before returning to his bunk, a procedure that would have taken less than a minute? Had someone or something stopped him?

*****

84

From the station's galley, Colonel Striker enjoyed a bird's eye view of the main corridor running past the astronomer's lab, to his private cabin.

In the opposite direction, the linkway accessed the main research labs, extending to the crew's sleeping modules. He noted the time as he watched Greg dart into one of the labs.

Sitting with one hand on his coffee he kept both eyes on the linkway. Perhaps it was the way the kid scurried in and out of the research labs that aroused his suspicion. After watching him for a third time disappear into another lab, Striker became curious.

With the civilian crew on a designated rest shift, Dr. Thompson was in the galley going over his notes before performing repairs on the station's main oxygen generator. Breathable oxygen levels were expected to drop significantly while the unit was out of service. As a result, Halverson had ordered the crew to lie down.

Striker kept a low volume that was intended for the confines of the galley. "Doctor, what's your take on that new kid we got on board?"

"Greg?" Thompson spoke with his eyes glued to his work. "Kid's okay by me. Well-liked by everyone."

"His work?" the colonel asked, fishing for faults.

"Hard worker, as I see it. Even Halverson agrees the young man's centered and focused on his learning. Puts in more hours than some of the other interns they've shot up here."

The colonel dropped two sugar cubes into his coffee and craned his neck for another look down the linkway. Turning back to Thompson he tapped a pair of fingers on his wristwatch. "Strange to see that kid wandering around. Didn't he get orders to observe a rest period?"

Thompson looked up and raised his eyebrows. "Who?"

"Ya know, that kid," the colonel hissed. "Didn't you hear a damn thing I said?"

"Kid's got a name, Colonel. Greg lost his circadian rhythms. Puked his guts for two days. He's just a little edgy, like the rest of us. With climate control down for just a couple hours, I doubt anybody will be choking to death. Besides, the exercise will do him good, maybe get him some shut-eye."

With a snort, William Striker directed a finger to his shoulder. "You see these stripes, Doctor? It's my job to be alert, watchful. To observe everything that goes on up here."

"How about what goes on down *there*?" Thompson responded, dropping a thumb toward the floor. "Isn't that where the troubles are?"

A rush of indignation fell over the colonel. "National security is my business. Just look at what's happening today inside North Korea, Syria, Iran ..."

"What *is* happening, Colonel?"

"That is none of your business!" Striker retorted.

Thompson laughed and redirected the conversation. "Sir, you weren't exactly Robinson Crusoe when you first arrived. Give the kid a break."

Striker bristled. "He's the first black kid to come through this program. All I'm saying is he'd better behave hisself on *my* watch."

*****

In the darkness and solitude that accompanied Heinrich's workstation, Greg waited for the terminal's login sign.

With closed eyes, he concentrated heavily on what he could remember of DeLong's distress signal. Fatigue had begun to make everything swirl in clouds of confusion. He pressed his thoughts on back to Pre-flight ... when Heinrich had helped him get through the survival courses, G-force training, all the way up to launch time. His personal mentor had done more than anyone else to help him adapt to this impossible environment. So why was Heinrich strapped to his bunk, under some sort of drug? Is this an arrest? One thing he was sure of: Dr. Heinrich Mann was no criminal! Greg paused and wondered if there was something he didn't know about the doctor. Something he should know?

Foolish thinking. That's what it was.

Greg glanced at the terminal before double-checking the linkway for unexpected company. There were no voices or sounds coming from the other research modules. He felt alone and vulnerable sitting in front of the terminal at Heinrich's workstation, waiting for it to finish a self-scan function before finally coming to life. Heinrich had logged on with a complex pattern of passwords that Greg couldn't dream of memorizing.

But Heinrich was the type to share his clever shortcuts to get the job done.

Pointing the doctor's android toward the terminal's infrared eye, Greg searched for a small icon; one that Heinrich had labeled *Mission*. Clueless of the password, he prayed the unit would automatically log him onto the network. He aimed and clicked. The terminal fluttered a moment until it revealed a menu screen. He was in.

"Yes!" Greg hissed in under his breath.

After locating Europa Command, he tapped at the keys and entered Rockwell's name. The screen went dark. Greg's knee bounced nervously as he waited. Soon the screen glowed a light purple behind a picture of the same Europa spacecraft he remembered seeing at the display inside the Mojave Space Center. Below the image, a full profile of Commander Rockwell rolled across the monitor.

In a hasty scan, his eyes descended to a line of communication codes in a shaded field at the bottom of the screen. Aiming Heinrich's android at the terminal, Greg quickly copied the codes electronically, machine-to-machine. Everything he needed to contact Rockwell quickly downloaded into the device's memory.

Logging off, he slipped out into the linkway and returned to his cabin where he sat on the floor against his bunk. There Greg began drafting a new message. The text was short and to the point, a choice of words that would have made his high school English teacher proud.

Emergency! Return to lunar orbit! Vashon's crew is alive!

Greg tapped the SEND tab. Suddenly the tension that had built up inside left him. He closed his eyes and exhaled. The reply he needed would take a few minutes from the time Rockwell was alerted to the message. It wouldn't be long now before the whole matter would be sitting on NASA's shoulders, where it belonged.

In the passage of a short interval, a vein of doubt crept into Greg's thoughts over the sheer boldness of what he was asking Rockwell to do. What if he and Dr. Mann were dead wrong about Vashon? Were there dangerous risks for Europa to suddenly change its course? If something terrible happened, the newspapers would destroy Heinrich Mann. NASA might even fire him. Would he go to prison?

Greg suppressed his worries for a moment when the phone's screen beeped and flickered. He slid his finger over the screen to view the message. A string of capitalized letters raced out to form neat little lines:

REPLY CODES AR-5430-OP
EUROPA CREW ENTERING SLEEP CYCLE
OVERRIDE CODE OC-9828473
NAVIGATION ID VMP-00451

Greg sat up straight and held the screen closer to his eyes. His jaw dropped as he read through the message again. The crew aboard Europa had set a three-day course for Earth. They were frickin' sleeping … while precious time was running out on Vashon!

Immediately Greg began to work with the fragments he remembered of DeLong's distress signal. He needed to draft a message that would present a set of believable facts to Rockwell.

At first this seemed easy. Europa's computer would process the override code and activate wake up commands. Rockwell, on the other hand, needed evidence that DeLong was alive. It was the only way to justify a course change. Realizing he would have to deal with that later, Greg reviewed the override codes and sent them. His thoughts returned to the doctor's arrest.

Was he a criminal because he'd been placed into someone's custody? Greg recalled knowing one of his friends whose dad was in custody for a weekend in Denver. Eventually the charges against him were dropped because he'd been mistaken for another man. Everything he knew about Mr. Mann was honest and caring. How could he be mixed up as a criminal? The whole thing was a mess, and it confused Greg the more he thought about it.

Did evil people ever think of themselves as evil? How did they rationalize their deeds? Could the doctor ever fit into that category? Feeling rather foolish, Greg shook away the notion. There were problems to solve, he reminded himself.

Inches above Heinrich's bunk, he watched a patchwork of green and red lights blink on and off. If one could activate the sleep cycle, there had to be a way to disable it. He focused on a small, lighted keypad affixed to the panel. His fingertips floated over the numbers and command keys, arranged in rows like buttons on a TV remote, until he came to the largest one. Its illuminated red letters spelled *LOCKOUT*. Hope evaporated with the sudden realization that unauthorized tampering might set off some alarm.

Breathing the station's expiring air had now begun to fatigue Greg. Earlier surges of adrenaline had postponed a creeping urge to lie down. But now with knowledge of the disastrous consequences of dozing, he felt a renewed sense of energy.

The device in Greg's hand chortled. An incoming signal activated the tiny screen.

REPLY CODES AR-5440-OP
INITIATING WAKE SEQUENCE
NAVIGATION ID VOP-00451

Greg raised a victory fist and swung it down. "Yes!" he whispered. Waves of vigor rippled through his muscles. Things were looking up for Vashon.

*****

89

Down the linkway, at the opposite end of the station, over the systems monitor in Striker's cabin, the distress beacon lit up every three seconds.

Having gone into the research module to cancel the distress icon at Heinrich's terminal, the colonel had transferred it to his own terminal. In the privacy of his cabin he estimated Vashon had no more than two, maybe up to four hours left.

He grinned into his glass of chilled vermouth.

Killing the satellite link had been little more than procedural housekeeping from the workstation inside his private cabin. By deploying robotic repair nodes in two government satellites, the colonel gave technicians in Florida and Arizona every reason to assume the malfunction originated elsewhere.

On the lunar surface the crew had conducted additional tests and managed to recover critical pieces of data that could be used to produce NASA's lost formula. Predictably, NASA's request to troubleshoot the system arrived on Striker's screen minutes after he had intercepted Vashon's uploading of files and data. Three hours after receiving his instructions from NASA, Striker submitted his report to ground technicians and confirmed that both satellites were functioning normally. Though, to his own benefit, he failed to mention that he had silenced all of Vashon's outbound communications, which resulted in an unforeseen complication that had thrust him into dangerous territory beyond his contractual duties with Rodney Panach. The manipulation of satellite communications had scrambled Vashon's ignition codes and prevented liftoff. This may have explained Dr. Mann dipping into classified documents. Nonetheless, the colonel made a personal vow nothing could be traced back to his own muddied work.

A handsome payoff from Admiral Petroleum, despite the fallen fate of DeLong's crew, Striker decided. Maybe he'd overlooked one dirty detail slipped into the cards. But it was now impossible to change things. Panach was hardly the type to abandon profits over the cost of a few lives. Though the heartless tyrant he'd become, little surpassed the man's generosity when it came to doling out cash rewards.

One annoying doubt still haunted the colonel. Vashon's distress beacon—initiated by DeLong—had found its way into Heinrich's terminal. Odd thing to know it had not been knocked out along with the satellite feed.

With help from a stiff drink, Striker tried to glean comfort from the fact that he had managed to eliminate records of DeLong's transmission aboard ISS. All that was left was the waiting game.

*****

According to Europa's computer, Rockwell was scheduled to be fully awake within one hour. While he waited, Greg considered the hierarchy of people on board ISS.

Colonel Striker, a khaki-clad military officer he rarely saw and never formally met, had not remained in his bunk like the others. Instead, he seemed to have his own functions aboard the station that had little to do with civilian research. Halverson had made a point not to speak about the colonel's work. This made it obvious to Greg that Striker was connected in some special way to unspoken military operations.

While the mission director slept, with no wish to be disturbed, Greg wondered if he should go to the colonel with his secret. Yes, he'd report only the distress message Heinrich received from the moon, and leave out the other stuff. The colonel would know what to do from there.

Greg grew confident over his resolve to take action. His fingers vigorously tapped on Heinrich's phone, laying out plans to go to the colonel and ask him to contact Commander Rockwell. Surely, DeLong and Striker were connected inside NASA's elite circle of officers and had probably both worked in the space program for years. Greg sent the message to Vashon—a quick word with the officer in charge of national security, living aboard ISS. Yes, Commander DeLong's troubles would soon be over.

Greg entered the galley and watched the colonel nursing a coffee at the crew's table.

"Uh, sir, I wanna report a problem ...a situation."

Striker eyed Greg with suspicion but then managed a smile. He leaned forward and laid one arm over the other on the table. A faded tattoo of a glaring eagle held its gaze on Greg.

"Sit down, son." Striker carefully watched Greg take a breath and slide into a chair across the table. "Okay, what's on your mind?"

"Um, it's about Heinrich."

"Dr. Mann, you mean."

"Uh, yessir. You see, he was working on some ozone mapping, and he got this message over his terminal."

Greg squirmed in the chair as an awkward pause fell over the table. Striker leaned back and crossed his arms. Swiveling to one side and then the other in the galley chair, he encouraged Greg to continue. "Okay son, so Dr. Mann received a message. Why don't you tell me all about it?"

"It was a distress call."

"A distress call, huh? From where was this call, young man?"

"A commander aboard a lunar spacecraft."

"The moon?" Striker's face flushed slightly, then turned to stone. "Are you sure about that?"

"Yessir. I guess the crew has been stranded since a failed liftoff. I just thought you should know," Greg disposed of a long breath and continued. "I mean, you would know the best person to contact ... to get them home safely. Right?"

Striker nodded approvingly. "That's a stretch for a manned mission, young man. Congress has postponed funding for space shots beyond this orbiting station. How can you say the message was authentic?"

"I don't know," Greg answered flatly. "Can't you check it out, anyway?"

"Of course."

Greg stood up to shake the colonel's hand, and then stepped into the linkway toward his cabin. A ton of bricks was off him. Certainly, he'd done his best. Mom would be proud.

By the time he entered his quarters, Heinrich's phone was lit up with a new message. Vashon had made contact! Greg was glowing as he entered the codes to access the message.

DeLong would surely be thrilled at his intentions of turning the rescue over to an authority aboard ISS. DeLong's words rolled across the screen.

Instantly, Greg's energy melted into nausea, his throat cramping up while a nervous twitch yanked at his right shoulder. He could hardly bear to look over the commander's text a second time. He couldn't believe what was happening. Not only was it charged with scandal, but it contained all the imperatives he could expect from another soul, helplessly depending on him.

DO NOT SPEAK A WORD ABOUT THIS MISSION TO COLONEL WILLIAM STRIKER!

There was more. Her text went on to explain why she suspected the colonel to be distrustful, and the possibility of him becoming involved in a plot to jeopardize her mission. DeLong ended with an urgent request to contact Rockwell for their rendezvous.

Time was running out. Greg pulled the device up close to his eyes and pecked at the screen. He hurried to copy the commander's message and paste it onto a new message screen where he began drafting a new sentence to Europa.

Rockwell would have to believe him.

Halfway through his line, Striker's broad-shouldered silhouette appeared in the airlock outside the cabin. Greg watched Striker pull the hatch closed behind him and in a surprising move, charge for Greg's bunk. In the darkened space between them, the colonel held out a small object, wagging it madly, then jabbing it toward Greg's face. The instrument's tip—shiny like stainless steel—was blunt, about a half inch wide. It was emitting a strange low-frequency buzz he'd never heard before.

Dropping the android onto the bunk, Greg could more carefully to track the weapon Striker was thrusting toward him. But with lightning speed its smooth tip swiped across one cheek, delivering a burning jolt through his face and neck. The shock penetrated downward and violently shook his torso. A million little ripples spread across his chest.

As quickly as the shock occurred, its furious presence faded, giving Greg the split-second opportunity he needed to recover his reflexes and focus on his task. Vashon was waiting!

One by one, Greg's fingers reclaimed the unit lying behind him on the bunk. But Striker was moving in again, this time in a tighter, closing arc. The buzz of the electrical gizmo fluttered and another jolt grazed his collarbone. Greg forced a swift recovery. Like a prize boxer at risk of losing his title, he remained agile and cool. With a last-second shift of his feet, he sidestepped the colonel's approach. Greg had mastered this while darting around his opponents on the basketball court. He angled left, rotating and crouching, until he'd worked his way into the center of the cabin. To his right the airlock was shut, but a narrow streak of light poured in from the linkway, suggesting that Striker hadn't secured it. A left hook or a straight-on blow to the colonel's chest would allow the second or two Greg needed to open the hatch before he could retreat down the linkway.

Striker advanced with more determination, his eyes locked on Heinrich's android. But Greg lightened himself over his feet and ducked under another swiping arc of the colonel's flailing stun gun. Greg circled the floor, threw a shoulder fake, and then landed a powerful blow below the colonel's left jawbone. The impact produced a muffled grunt that met his satisfaction as he watched the colonel struggle to stay on his feet.

Greg decided to use this moment to his advantage and reached for Striker's neck. Driven by a powerful thrust of his arm, Greg's young muscular fingers opened wide, searched, and closed over meaty flesh. He had the old geezer by the throat. Now what? He contemplated the possibilities of killing another man, but such a thought nauseated him.

But another voice screaming *self-defense* faded when his upper hand of the situation was suddenly cast away. The colonel had spun out from under his grip, leaving only the smell of blood as a trophy of successful in answering the colonel's aggression.

94

It had down little but slow the attack...and there was Vashon.

Again, Striker growled under his breath and lunged. Greg stepped out of the way and adjusted his grip on the smart phone. Clutching the device, he raked his thumb over its smooth screen, estimating the SEND spot and tapping it wildly. An audible sound emitted from the android.

The message was on its way!

Exploiting the distractions of triumph and glory, Striker recoiled, lunged, and throttled Greg in the throat. The buzzing noise intensified for several seconds. Greg's eyes flashed and his jaws chattered in traumatic fits. All attempts to shout into the linkway melted into silence. A hoarse whisper wheezed off his paralyzed tongue. His knees buckled and he collapsed to the floor, his arms still flailing with enough force to rocket the android toward the steel airlock where it shattered into pieces. Greg lay helpless, the colonel now straddled over him holding the device on him.

The simple task of breathing became a belabored task now. All remains of consciousness fading, everything Greg perceived of this crazy world was grinding down to a sluggish halt. His mind crumbled into cold darkness.

*****

A minute later Striker eased his battered old frame into a chair inside his private cabin.

Through his window a view of Earth produced a spectacular collage of blues and greens. He smiled at the distress beacon he had routed to a circuit at the top of his monitor. It said everything about life and death aboard Vashon. The moment had come. No doubt, Striker and Admiral had gotten more than they'd bargained for. The terminal's tracking beacon was dark. The colonel had snuffed out the lives of three highly trained scientists, along with NASA's initiative to control and manufacture *Aqualene*.

Striker counted silently, watching the darkened beacon: *one, two, three, four, five* .... Ambivalent of its crushing

95

tranquility, he counted on. At *ten* the beacon remained dark. Crossing his chest in the Catholic tradition, he pronounced the crew's death, uttered a prayer, and poured himself a drink.

The heel of his boot rested on top of the cabin's control panel as the colonel mentally began spending the money Admiral had contracted to pay in exchange for services. The liquor warmed him. And the troubled world turning below offered a panoramic glimpse of the best choices in real estate. He considered buying an island in some tropical latitude, maybe off the west coast of Central America where natives—unspoiled by unionized mainland resorts—were still serving Americans for pennies on the dollar.

Smiling to himself, the colonel re-opened the satellite channels between Vashon and NASA's frenzied ground control operations. The blockage—a simple aberration in software coding—had served its purpose, leaving half his problems behind.

Twelve

Earlier on Sunday, outside the gates of Admiral's newest plant, Panach's chest throbbed with exhilaration. Fresh business prospects were beating in rhythm with the V-12 engine idling behind him.

The push of a button on the McLaren's dashboard summoned guards at Crimson. Each appeared with automatic weapons slung over his shoulder. Two burley soldiers with buzz cuts, faded tattoos, and pursed lips—standard security issue at Admiral—marveled at the machine through mirrored sunglasses. A third waited near his post at the base of a brick tower.

With more patience than its master, the gleaming yellow McLaren panted eagerly as the gates swept inward toward manicured lawns and tree-studded gardens. Panach had renamed the property—a ninety-acre plot his father purchased cheap from an ailing San Francisco savings and loan in the 1980s—in honor of the widened reddish riverbed that passed through its west side border before cutting into an adjacent wooded lot still held in trust by the local farmer's grange. Admiral's political muscle had, in the span of two years, bulldozed fruit groves and rerouted local streams into one river to transform the valley into a grain-producing powerhouse. Regionally, with so much land at its disposal, Admiral had moved rapidly to adjust agriculture zoning to begin producing a steady quantity of ethanol, earning the company the cooperation it needed from a fervent grassroots community committed to derail conventional petroleum initiatives in its backyard. Meanwhile, increased threats of terrorism on U.S installations had weakened public trust, providing Admiral a reason to post a private security force at its Crimson facility.

Throttling the machine with punchy revs, Panach drove his car through the gates and paused inside, inspecting the guard units for defense flaws. In the shadow of a pair of snipers gazing down from the tower, the entrance guard sauntered forward toward the driver's side window.

"How's your golf game today, sir?"

97

Panach ignored the guard's attempts at conversation. "Just see that Wilson is sent to my office pronto."

The guard thrust his shoulders back and fisted a hip-mounted two-way radio as he watch the McLaren rumble on up the drive.

Gradually Panach backed off the throttle and the engine smoothed out to a pleasing roar. Fingering the custom handbrakes, he dropped the nose to a tire-skidding stop in front of the property's nineteenth century château—a two-story enchantment situated north of an expanse of lawns dotted with pines and spruces.

The car's gull-wing door swung open and Panach rolled out, hoisting himself into a wheelchair at the hands of an armed bodyguard who'd been waiting outside the estate. Wheeling over red brickwork past a Roman-styled fountain flanked by vintage rose gardens, he surveyed the business developments across the campus. Piles of dirt, assorted pipes, and heavy machinery still littered the site where he would be overseeing Admiral's newest brainchild.

Having acquired the aid of key individuals in government and industry, the venture was coming together in less time than he'd expected. But there were hurdles to clear before a marketable wonder fuel could be produced, an issue that kept him on edge. For one thing, his sources failed to thoroughly determine the progress of his chief competitor—the U.S. Government—and there was no telling how soon the markets would explode into a frenzy to buy federal bonds promising a sustainable replacement of crippled American gasoline markets.

As he rounded a bend in the garden, the pair of guards assigned to the main entrance of the chateau stiffened like infantry at roll call. Employing his usual scrutiny, Panach looked over the century-old brickwork. It sparkled behind exotic shrubs and languishing gardens that appeared to float up to beveled windows set in gold beading. Inside, craftsmen skilled in custom renovations had converted the valley's historic landmark into a network of upscale executive suites and a sophisticated surveillance post.

Entering the foyer, he nodded with tentative approval toward the double-guarded elevators. "You two will never know how much we hold at stake in this building. Security is imperative, gentlemen."

The guards gave a slight nod and resumed their guard duties.

Ken Burke, a former U.S. Army helicopter pilot, had eked out a dangerous living in arms smuggling between Karachi and a hidden seaport north of Mumbai before he was recruited by Admiral to perform nighttime surveillance operations at a cluster of drilling rigs along an oil rich peninsula along Eritrea's coastline. Eventually his piloting skills earned him a prestigious position closer to home, flying top executives between oil installations and key refineries in North America. Deemed best suited as Crimson's temporary site supervisor, Burke met his boss in the doorway of the control room on the second floor of the chateau. There technicians were scrambling to meet Panach's ambitious deadlines. Burke was a tough sinewy man with a blend of anger and mischief in his eyes. A deep scar angled down from his left temple to one corner of his mouth, revealing a history of situations he preferred to keep off the record.

"You can see, I've got things shaping up out here," he reported while scanning confidently over his crew's renovations of a large storage building on the property.

"Not fast enough," Panach grumbled, wheeling himself up to a bank of windows that had been refitted for the chair's height. From his vantage point he surveyed open holes and trenches at the foot of a mobile crane moving piles of building materials that cluttered the compound. He fixed his eyes on an electrical substation outside the new plant. "What in hell is going on down there? I ordered high-tension upgrades on that substation to be finished days ago. I don't need these son-of-a-bitch outsiders hanging around this place any longer than necessary."

"Sir, I'm shipping these guys out as fast as we can check off their work. The last electrical crew is slated to vacate the premises tomorrow." Burke tightened his posture and squinted into the phone he clutched awkwardly in one hand that was missing two fingers. Burke gestured the accompanying guard to wheel Panach into his private suite and up to the glossy new executive desk situated in front a giant wall screen.

Cecil T. Wilson, a contracted engineer in his forties, was sitting with his knees together on a sofa against the back wall. "Mr. Panach, I believe it's time to settle up. I've completed my—"

Ignoring Wilson, Burke scooped up a remote and stabbed at it. Activities on the main plant's floor lit up over the screen. "I arranged everything from the control room to be wired through this wall. You'll have complete access to the whole operation, in the privacy of your own suite."

"Like it ought to be," Panach grunted, offering a faint nod as he surveyed the layout of visual gadgetry around the room. "Fine, very fine. But what about security on the premises?"

"Our recruiter's website has netted us a diverse range of talent—mostly former CIA operatives and displaced mercenaries from the world's hot spots. These guys are showing up with stuff that'd make the local police wet the bed."

Deliberately turning his back on Wilson, Panach took advantage of the panoramic view he had of the compound, beginning with the ethanol plant. He checked its burn-off flame a mile from the chateau. His priorities shifted to the newly constructed plant—the facility that would change the course of Admiral's history. A cluster of small outbuildings and the company's dormitory on a small swath of landscaping separated the chateau from the west security wall. Beyond that the Crimson River flowed northward.

Panach held his westward gaze. "Those two buildings," he grumbled as he banged a knuckle on the glass. "See to it both are reinforced and guarded by tomorrow at this time."

"Sir, those are tool sheds we've set up for the gardeners."

Panach's muscular arms swiveled his wheelchair in a half circle. "Do you have a problem following a simple order?"

"Uh, of course not, sir." Burke pulled out his electronic notepad and scribbled down the information Panach began barking against the windowpane. He noted the arrival date of an important shipment and a litany of security demands to firm

100

up inside Crimson within twenty-four hours. Burke exhaled nervously. "There's one detail."

"Another problem?" Panach lit up a cigarette and watched the smoke stream out from his nose and turn into gray puffs wandering toward a ventilator in the ceiling. His voice bellowed: "Speak up, let's have it."

"It's the blue prints, sir."

"What about them?"

"The electricians don't have a complete set to refer to. According to documents obtained from Washington, we're short on a few technical details."

"Those were outside my—"

"The last man you hired let me down," Panach growled with a glare toward Wilson, then slid a hand over a shuffle of papers on his desk, scooping up what he was looking for. "This time I've located a more competent individual to take Wilson's place. A qualified engineer who will get this plant underway."

Burke produced a toothy grin. "A new employee, sir?"

Panach nodded. "Let's just say he's an independent, sweating over his reputation let alone his next meal. I've got an early meeting in Mexico City. Without raising suspicions, you'll hire him tomorrow morning at eleven."

Burke shot a vengeful grin at Wilson. "Anyone's a major upgrade over this one."

"Maybe, but I want you shadowing every move our new man makes out here. There's no time to lose, so you'd better get things right." Panach watched as Wilson's hands steadied and the tension in his face disappear as if he were somehow off the hook. Did he really believe the hour of liberation had come? As Admiral had learned in a few short weeks, Wilson was the type to hang out his shingle and secure a contract, only to siphon off pork barrel fat.

Burke popped open his electronic notepad and stood over Wilson. "Our expert from out of town has changed his mind on the manufacturing details at least three times. What's more, he's pretended to know less than what company records revealed during the month he spent as a big man in R & D."

Panach shook his head and snickered. "And to hear this fellow has the gall to demand a raise." Wheeling up behind his

101

desk, he lit a cigar while fingering a dossier with Wilson's name stenciled across the front. Panach rifled through its pages, grunting between dense brown clouds rising above his desk. "We're in the habit of cleaning house and moving forward here at Admiral. You've done nothing to advance my company's credo."

Wilson retreated deeper into the sofa's leather and rolled his eyes around the room. Panach watched him with festering indignation while privately affirming the man's ultimate destiny. "I have no use for your services," Panach barked. "What do you have to say for the record? Amuse me with a final statement."

"We could start with broken promises like the waterfront home ... and the sailing yacht," Wilson protested. "After everything I risk of my career and then my ass? You owe me *something* for that!"

Panach had turned back to the window. Silently he waved an authoritative hand through the smoke. His eyes wandered westward beyond the pump house. His diamond-clad fingers wagged toward the Crimson River. "Eliminate our dear Mr. Wilson. I don't wish to see him again."

Instantly the guard at the door swiveled, dropping his assault weapon into position. Burke motioned for Wilson to stand up.

At once Wilson burst into a panic. "You've got nerve to hire these x-con bastards," he snarled at Panach's back. "I'm warning you, if I don't leave this prison of yours alive, the FBI *and* the CIA will come crashing your gates down."

The CEO's words rumbled out a final time against the windowpane. "Leave no evidence Cecil T. Wilson ever came to work at Admiral. Erase his name from all government records, in the usual manner."

Panach smiled with satisfaction. Well-placed friends in DC afforded him the convenience of an occasional population adjustment.

*****

102

Early Monday morning, it was still dark about an hour south of Bellingham as two traveled Interstate-5 toward Seattle. Dell glanced again at Buford's fuel gauge.

The needle hadn't moved below the quarter mark at all since they'd poured just over three gallons of *Aqualene* into the gas tank. Adam surveyed their rear through the right side view mirror. He'd seen the same three sets of headlights behind them for several miles. With Buford cruising at seventy, he figured they would arrive in time for breakfast and check-in for his 7:53 flight to LAX.

Dell flicked on his right signal and began to slow down as the truck edged off the roadway. Up ahead a subcompact was parked with its hood up. The rear hazard lights were flashing dimly. The motorist had been waiting for hours.

"He's either out of gas or overheated," Dell suggested as he jumped out. Adam walked around to the passenger side. The driver, a young woman with a small child in the backseat, rolled down her window and promptly informed Dell that her boyfriend was on the way.

Dell pulled back onto the freeway. Suddenly a blinding light filled the truck's cab.

"What in—"

Dell mashed down on the accelerator. Buford roared up to speed, narrowly avoiding a rear-end collision. Adam twisted around and peered out the rear window past a rifle Dell kept in the gun rack. "This guy's barreling straight for your rear bumper."

The raised beams, belonging to a large truck or some sort of SUV, sank back a little ways as Buford shifted into high gear.

Dell breathed sighed relief and backed off on the gas. He swerved over to the left lane. Traffic was unusually light for that section of I-5. A couple of semis had slipped by them when Buford's dashboard lit up and reflected the same blue halogens again.

"Jerk's back on your tail," Adam commented, like a co-pilot reporting his flight bearings. The lights from oncoming cars revealed a black Escalade. "Why don't you move over? Get him out of our hair."

Dell jockeyed for the center lane. But the Escalade's beams moved over with them, then closer. "This bastard wants more than the fast lane," Dell complained, his eyes glaring into his mirrors. "Could it be your brains he's after, or that stuff sloshing around inside our fuel tank?"

Dell didn't give Adam a chance to answer. His face wrinkled as he yanked back on the custom floor shifter and dropped the transmission into passing gear. The engine wound up and thrust the truck forward again. Dell moved back into the left lane. With incredible luck, there were no trucks or taillights ahead of them for miles.

The Escalade's headlights fell back again. Adam began to worry about something else, and leaned over expecting to see the gas gauge drooping below near the quarter mark. The needle hadn't moved. Where the hell was the fuel going? How could the engine keep running without sucking it through? Aqualene was truly a miracle formula, and Adam could only begin to understand why it was so sought after by vested interests.

For a long and nervous minute, Dell held Buford at a steady hundred and ten—a speed that was bound to attract unwanted attention from the State Patrol. Adam cinched up his lap belt. The occasional flicker of freeway lighting ceased as they entered a darkened section of the roadway where Buford shot past a string of big rigs dressed in amber running lamps, each grinding along at a mere sixty in the right lane.

As they approached Everett—a city half the size of Seattle where Boeing had once assembled some of its biggest planes, a sea of red taillights suddenly illuminated Buford's windshield. Racing up from behind, the lights of the Escalade closed in and rapidly found Buford's bumper.

Adam positioned himself to search for lane openings on the right. "Now," he shouted over the back-rap of the engine, still in rapid deceleration. Dell jerked the wheel and dropped in behind a minivan. In a moment a space to their left showed up alongside the pickup. Dell swerved back into the left lane and stomped on the gas, taking them uncomfortably close to another rear bumper. The Escalade was back and approaching faster this time.

Dell glanced toward Adam, waiting for a safe opening.

"Not yet," Adam coughed just as the cab began shimmering with a blue tint of blinding halogen light.

This was enough for Dell to revert to a dangerous old habit of shoulder passing. Buford's motor wound up again, lurching the truck forward. Her tailpipes sang sweet baritones as Dell jerked her onto the left shoulder, allowing him to shoot the gap he'd been waiting for. Flipping the shifter up a notch sent them screaming past seven or eight cars before they dropped back into the legal fast lane. Adam's heart thumped with the nightmare of a multiple-car pile-up, and the risk of landing in jail for reckless driving tightened the knot in the back of his throat.

But when the Escalade's halogens were gone, things seemed to be looking up as they entered a stretch of sparsely lit roadway outside of Everett, past the point where much of the congestion had filed off at two adjacent exits. Dell had moved into one of two center lanes when a dull metallic thud hit the truck's cab. The Escalade was no more than fifty yards behind them. "The fucker's shooting at us!" Adam shouted, crouching lower against the bench seat. A second shot exploded Dell's side view mirror as the SUV slipped up closer on Buford's tailgate.

An open palm suddenly appeared in front of Adam. Dell was holding a large shotgun casing. He spoke in a no-nonsense tone Adam had never witnessed.

"Take down my gun. Put this in the chamber."

Adam gasped. "Look, man, I don't plan on murdering someone tonight ... even if it is in self-defense."

Dell's fingers slapped at a chrome latch to unlock the shotgun from the window rack. "Neither was I," Dell answered calmly. "We gotta scare this bastard off our tail, or it'll be an early grave for both of us."

In the annoying glare of the Escalade's headlights Adam paused to think about what was about to happen. Dell reached over his shoulder to release the second latch. The shotgun, similar to the one his dad kept around when he was a kid, straddled Adam's hands. With no more fuss Adam fed the shells into the chamber.

Dell adjusted his grip on the wheel and moved one hand to the shifter. "When I goose this old girl, that's yer cue to stick ole Bessy out the back window. That in itself may end things peacefully."

Adam couldn't recall ever pointing a gun at someone. He'd grown up around guns but was essentially a peace-seeking man. As a boy he'd learned to shoot moving targets. But this was different. This kind of shootin' was for keeps.

"You ready?" Dell shouted over the motor.

Adam gave no verbal reply just slid open the rear window. Next thing he knew the engine roared and Buford took her best leap, launching a curtain of black tire pitch that swirled past the tailgate. Adam shoved the gun's barrel out over the bed of the truck and tracked the Escalade over the V-shaped sight, watching the headlights fall back. A sudden rush of relief came over him. Dell's bluff seemed to be working. Then a hardening lump swelled up inside his throat. The Escalade was creeping up on them again. Adam boldly adjusted his hands on the gun and prepared to pull the trigger.

Dell's voice rang out. "If you gotta shoot that thing, get your head inside to save your ears.

Adam followed Dell's advice, and then squeezed the trigger back. The shot bellowed out and spat a long yellow flame. Instantly the Escalade's front end swerved violently side to side. Gradually the rig fell back, the driver fighting to stay on the pavement. The horrible screeching of rubber lasted several seconds until the fourth tire veered off the road into the unlit median. Adam watched the Cadillac's headlights bounce several times. The front-end dropped a final time before plowing into high grass growing from a depression. Leaning badly to one side, the Escalade gave in to soft ground and rolled over several times. Its lights disappeared. As Dell let his foot off the gas, Adam sat watching the median for any sign of a fire. Only darkness filled the night air behind them.

Trouble had abated as abruptly as it had appeared. Adam's exhilaration soon tapered off, replaced by post traumatic bouts of the jitters. Next to him Dell exhaled a long breath as he brought Buford back down to cruising speed. Accompanied by a long sigh he decided to break the awkward silence that had seeped into the cab. "That was damn too close for me," he sputtered. "Could use a stiff drink myself."

"Double that," Adam mumbled back. "Couldn't there have been some other way to deal with that guy?"

"Search me," Dell coughed. "We could call the highway patrol. Maybe get a squad car out there."

"That works for me," Adam nodded, "Sweetly anonymous."

Adam called the scene in as a blown out tire and hung up. The phone trembled in his hand as he shoved it back into his jacket and changed the subject. "How we doin on fuel? Old girl's gotta be runnin' dry after all that."

Dell glanced at the fuel gauge. He tapped it methodically with a knuckle. "Needle ain't budged one bit."

Adam grinned, his notepad trembling as he entered: *Compatible with conventional gasoline. Generous cruising range.*

Thirteen

At ten o'clock, Monday morning, the president and his Chinese counterparts reconvened.

The delegates and their interpreters entered the Oval Office, eager for positive developments. It was time for an official statement from NASA into the fate of Vashon and its three astronauts.

President Kirkpatrick entered the room and found his seat at the head of the table. He appeared exhausted, yet stirred and anxious. "My staff and I have been up all night on the telephone with NASA's communications center in Arizona. Ground technicians have attempted to contact Commander DeLong and her crew for several hours. All said, the effort remains fruitless at this point. Our space agency has declared this mission a devastating loss."

Despite Kirkpatrick's soft-spoken diplomacy, the tension in the room grew ugly.

Zhang stood up. His English was stubbornly awkward, but in this case he was determined to address Kirkpatrick through no interpreter. "Why we must sit here and dismiss lives of three astronauts, one of them belonging to us?"

The vice president picked up on Kirkpatrick's struggle to console the Chinese, and jumped in. He nodded at a wiry woman in a dark blue uniform and regalia appropriate during formal appearances, introducing her as a major from Houston's Mission Control. She'd led the navigation team during the Vashon's landing phase at the time radio communications were lost.

She rose to her feet and spoke about how hundreds of NASA personnel labored throughout the night to reestablish contact with Vashon, then admitted NASA hadn't been in contact with the astronauts for over thirty-two hours. This alone, she said, indicated a diminishing probability for the crew's survival. The major recapped Commander DeLong's earlier message reporting ignition coding had been scrambled and that she would try to reconfigure it.

After the lights in the room dimmed the major positioned herself alongside a plasma screen and pointed at the cut-a-way diagram of the lander, highlighting various components that could have failed. Her explanation included how each system may have caused the disruption of digitized communications. Hearing no questions from the delegation, she went on to describe how Europa had canvassed the landing site of a protected region at the base of a ridge that was difficult to photograph from orbit.

The level of interest among the Chinese soon escalated to the humming of Mandarin.

After a tense interlude, Zhang tapped his microphone. The chatter peeled away and the other members grew silent.

"My question is directed to the president," he announced in a heavy accent. Kirkpatrick nodded for him to continue. Zhang spoke through one of his interpreters: "If you would, sir, what has been done to eliminate the question of sabotage?"

Kirkpatrick drew in a breath that gave him the extra seconds he wanted to sort out his words. "We've been in constant contact with top surveillance officials around the world. This includes a highly trained officer at his post aboard the International Space Station. A decorated reconnaissance expert," Kirkpatrick said while glancing over a profile handed to him by an aide. "He currently serves as a diagnostic technician in government satellite communications. After running numerous tests on our relay systems, the colonel has assured us that NASA's satellite links are functioning properly."

The Chinese delegate listened to the last of the interpretation, pursed his lips, and returned his eyes to the keys of his laptop. He then spoke again through the interpreter. "Each of us eagerly awaits a report on what went wrong up there."

"Of course, plans for a retrieval mission are in the works."

"Thank you."

The president offered a hasty nod, then held up a new report just handed to him by one of his aides. "Ladies and gentlemen, according to the U.S. Navy's Fifth Airborne Division, the mineral shipments needed to produce *Aqualene* have left Johnston Island. Safely aboard a Lockheed C-130J transport plane, the shipment is scheduled to arrive later today at the Lemoore Naval Air Station in California. Arrangements for final delivery to our Nevada research facility are underway, as I speak. Let none of us overlook the milestones this alliance has achieved under Vashon's great minds and research, despite unforeseen and tragic losses. In the spirit of these heroic advances, our next summit shall take place at Lukefield, Nevada. It is there this remarkable formula will be initially prepared for manufacturing. An unveiling is planned in two days, at which time I assure renewed promise and hope to our coalition partners ... and the world."

*****

A dense fog rolled over Moi as she awakened, strapped to a chair in darkness.

Her hands ached. But worse was the tension of the cloth drawn tightly across her face and through the sides of her mouth. Focusing her energy on listening to the sounds in a nearby room, she struggled to take a full breath through the gag. Her memory began to account for the frightening events that prevented her from leaving town to see her father.

She had walked several meters across the gray expanse of the Seattle-Tacoma airport-parking garage when a van suddenly raced forward, its headlights blinding her. From flickering shadows the driver had come dangerously close until the tires screeched and the front end drifted to her left. Spinning around in a half circle, the rear bumper skidded to a stop inches from her knees. With no time for her to think, the rear cargo doors flew open. She could recall clearly how two large men jumping out in one swift motion grunted like hungry savages, then swept her up into the back of the van before slamming the doors closed. Immediately the vehicle was in motion, its floor shifting and jerking side to side under her as the screech of tires penetrated the steel around her.

When the van finally came to a stop after several minutes of driving, the rear doors flung open. Above her a woman's voice commanded the men to take Moi up the stairs into a room where she was secured to a chair. The blindfold stayed on. Like a nocturnal creature that relied on instincts to sense its surroundings, Moi picked up on the smallness of the room before falling unconscious.

Minutes passed until the air inside the space around her shifted. A dim wall of light filtered through the white blindfold, gradually revealing the outline of a tall woman. The doorknob clicked and the figure stepped out of view. Moi sensed the presence of the woman walking around her, as though to silently make careful examination of her.

The click of a switch above Moi's head illuminated the blindfold again. Before she could begin forming visual images, the cloth around her eyes was removed, prompting her eyes to adjust to the light.

"My name is Tobario," the woman said while circling Moi and tugging on the bungee cord that bound her wrists behind her. Tobario's fingers moved to the front and promptly searched for unnecessary slack in a leather belt that secured Moi's waist firmly to the straight-back chair.

Defiantly, Moi stared at a wall past Tobario.

Without looking directly at her she could make out that Tobario was a confident looking white woman with dark brown hair that was cut in a bob and curled inward toward her neckline. The gray suit she wore, along with the briefcase she carried, gave Moi the feeling Tobario had come strictly on matters of business.

The woman reached for a second chair in the corner of the room—an oversized walk-in closet with no window—and sat down. Then she began pulling papers out of the briefcase.

"I expect you'll be comfortable enough here until we decided what to do with you," Tobario finally spoke. "I am not here to hurt you, Miss Song. I can offer to contact your father. We don't want him to worry about you, now do we?"

The tension in Moi's body eased slightly as she allowed herself to breathe again.

Tobario pulled a notepad from her case.

"Give me your father's mobile telephone number," she whispered, tossing Moi a knowing smile as though Tobario was generous in offering her assistance.

Moi thought carefully. Quickly she decided it foolish to reveal clues of her father's whereabouts, given the few details she had received from her mother of his sudden defection from Beijing. He was in enough danger of being tracked by the Red Army. Instead, Moi wrote down her mother's home telephone number in China on the sheet of paper. She passed it back to Tobario avoiding eye contact. Her thoughts shifted to what had come to mind before Tobario had entered the room. If this group viewed her as ignorant, they might regard her as a liability and allow her to go free. She could play down her command of English. Make communication annoyingly difficult.

Tobario folded up the telephone number and smiled. She took a breath, leaned forward. "This is no good, young lady. I must contact your father in San Francisco."

Moi cocked her head and shrugged. "No unda-stand," she sputtered in a deceiving syntax.

Tobario ripped the paper into shreds and rose to her feet. She circled Moi's chair once and immediately began speaking in a nasal tone at a breakneck pace. Her words were now completely foreign to the man standing outside in the hallway.

Instantly Moi became mesmerized in the tonal rhythms of Mandarin Chinese that began flowing off Tobario's lips. Her choice of words, along with a clipped intonation revealed a childhood upbringing in the heart of Beijing—the same dialect her grandfather spoke when he moved in with her family outside the city ten years ago.

Tobario pushed on, her message penetrating Moi like a butcher's blade into lamb's flesh. "You are acquainted with Adam Harlow, a knowledgeable mineralogist caught in the middle of a dangerous rivalry between government and industry. Is that right?"

"I hardly know him," Moi said flatly in her native tongue. Her heart pounded madly once she began to comprehend the possibilities of whom she was dealing with. Aside from Tobario's command of the language and that the symbol of a nineteenth century highway robber—idolized by contemporary gangsters in Hong Kong—tattooed at the base of her right index finger, the woman exuded all that represented the

Chinese underworld: a deadly network of conflicting business interests that drew up its membership around the globe and tolerated no exit outside its customary funeral arrangements.

Tobario wasted no time as she continued at an accelerated pace.

"Mr. Harlow possesses manufacturing secrets, those which belong to a top level partnership between the United States and China. Such a commodity is worth trillions in annual revenues."

"So what do you want with me?" Moi snapped.

"You will have but one chance to convince Mr. Harlow to follow directions and fully submit to his superiors. He must do nothing to jeopardize operations. Do you understand?"

Moi nodded. A moment of respite hardly passed before Tobario demanded more about Adam.

"Tell me the whereabouts of Mr. Harlow's laboratory records."

Moi delivered a blank look.

"His files? Hardcopies? Documents?" Tobario suddenly grew impatient.

Moi stared through Tobario. Her pause dragged on for an uncomfortable stretch. Finally she lifted her eyes and spoke methodically. "I have nothing to offer you."

Moi possessed valuable information she could offer Tobario about *Aqualene*'s manufacturing formula, including what she had seen inside the lab ... and the broken vials in Adam's hands. Under the proper duress she could imagine the results her computer program had generated on the eve of Gamil's death.

"What do you know about the underground laboratory?" Tobario demanded.

"An innocent man was murdered there," Moi hissed. "Other than that, I know nothing."

"But your father has information that could get you both killed," Tobario blurted. "You had plans to see him this week, once Adam left town. Am I correct?"

Moi nodded faintly. Despite a swelling knot in her throat, she saw her father's smile. He had given up many days with his family, rarely home between flights and meetings with government officials. Yet when he was around, he had filled her in on just enough to see his destiny to exile. Now she believed he was trapped between conflicting alliances that depended on her loyalty. The question was to whom was his allegiance. Moi shuddered over giving in to an undeserving adversary.

Everything she'd suspected about her father's involvement with the United States clicked. Given all the secrecy, and the fact conservative factions sought to keep a lid on political liberals in Beijing, she realized the damage she might cause by knowing Adam. This helped explain why Tobario's group had prevented her from getting on a plane to San Francisco to see her father, a leader of a powerful group of liberals inside the Chinese government. He had teamed with a controversial press company to expose international arms deals the Communist Party was making with a terrorist network in exchange for oil shipments. For years her father had supported a dwarfed movement in Beijing that organized protests and pushed for air quality standards n city centers. But as the economy faltered, with the decline of oil supplies, her father began to expose government hardliners for profiting from scandalous trade with foreign despots.

Meanwhile, Moi had befriended Adam and allowed herself to become involved in research laden with secrecy and intrigue. Had her father, in the course of bringing truth to the masses, suggested Beijing could betray its Western partners? Highly probable, she realized. According to uncensored news reports published from underground press clubs operating at a number of national universities, China's top leaders had displayed a declining interest in American trade for two and a half years while the U.S. recession fell deeper into its dizzying descent. Eventually, funneling Chinese manufacturing interests into developing giants like India and South Africa made smart economic sense if the party was to maintain political stability among its countless factory workers, who were swiftly forming trade unions and demanding safe working conditions, free public education, and health care. Tobario obviously represented a powerful group standing somewhere in between labor and Chinese policy makers—a network of powerful

114

energy partners operating in Europe and the Americas who calculated the risks of losing more than just the flow of profits that came by selling petroleum. Everything under the sun attached to oil-based manufacturing remained at stake. Therefore, lying to this woman spelled out a deadly set of risks to her own life.

Straightening her posture, Tobario delivered a malicious sneer. Moi had not given her what she wanted: the key to Adam's formula that could potentially shift immense power back into the hands of those who stood at the threshold of an enormous power vacuum. Tobario touched a small electronic device at her hip, and then spoke aloud in a menacing tone. "It's time," she said in English with a knuckle to the door.

The guard entered the room. He carried with him a sheet of plastic film, which he held out taut near Moi's face. Tobario folded her arms and gestured him to continue. "Stretch it tightly over her forehead and bring it down past her chin."

A horrible fright rose up in Moi as the man's cold powerful fingers enveloped her face. Each one shook, as they had inside the airport-parking garage. His callused hands followed Tobario's orders as if he were merely wrapping leftovers onto a dinner plate.

With grinning satisfaction Tobario gazed at Moi. The woman's eyes seemed energized by the panic she observed in Moi's face, particularly the little shuttering spasms in her breath. Each one made it possible for her to feel the tension of a small bubble expanding and deflating between her lips, jutting outward and inward like a balloon.

Tobario drew her watch out from her starched white cuff. She turned to the guard. "Give this girl a minute or two. Then we'll see what she has to say."

Moi squirmed more desperately. The oxygen content in her lungs became painfully depleted. Solidly fixed around her mouth, the flexible membrane would eventually choke her. With the mask snuggly in place and her spent air becoming unfit to inhale, Moi's endurance melted into dreaded panic. Her shoulders tossed side to side, writhing and tugging at the cords that bound her body to the chair. The fire burning in her chest caused it to heave for several seconds until pulsating breaths diminished into feeble little gasps. Inside her head pounded with a searing pain as her bloodstream became increasingly fouled with carbon dioxide. The walls and furnishings in all their vivid colors blurred into bland grays behind a rain of starry little diamonds that pressed against her consciousness. Human shapes grew distant as her mind sped closer to total blackout.

By now, the guard had grown increasingly nervous, and stepped closer to observe her through the fogged membrane. His voice shuddered as he spoke. "Uh, I think that's enough time."

"Not by my watch," Tobario growled back.

"But she ain't breathing no more," the guard pointed out nervously.

Tobario glanced at her watch again, as though a predetermined number of seconds promised success in her efforts to exact the desired confession.

"Okay, sweetie, time's up," Tobario finally declared. She extended a painted index finger toward Moi's face.

Slowly—as if she were making up stoppage time in a football game—Tobario placed the tip of her nail onto the mask's surface. Moi felt it meander past her cold cheeks, twirling and teasing until it halted over the collapsed bubble in her mouth. Searing bouts of stabbing pain knifed through Moi's collapsing lungs, which demanded every nerve to hold on to her consciousness.

Screaming voices of her past exploded inside her head and a wash of strange colors flooded her mind, followed by the terror of asphyxiation that began shredding her sanity. The plunging of her faculties into a numbing coma was suddenly interrupted by the penetrating stab of Tobario's fingernail into the mask. Moi pulled in a rush of oxygen before the guard's clumsy fingers managed to peel back the mask over her cheekbones. Tobario's words were immediately discernible, filling Moi's ears with heightened authority.

"Now, Miss Song, what can you tell me?"

Fourteen

Adam's plane arrived in Los Angeles a few minutes before ten.

The section of concourse still open to commercial air travel was noisy and smelled of deep fried foods. Leaving the security zone, he worked his way outside to the cab line. Admiral's executive secretary had messaged Adam to confirm the company's request that he catch a taxi into town. There he would be ushered safely into the building. Outside the Power Building riots over fuel prices had swiftly turned violent. Admiral's private limousines were unable to leave the premises until the cops got things under control.

Adam got to the curb just as the last two cab drivers pulled away with fares.

He checked his watch. It was after ten, less than an hour before his interview. There was no time to guess when another taxi might show up. These days, most were too busy with cross-town business to service the airports.

An electronic kiosk nearby listed airport shuttle buses arriving every quarter hour, but a red flag on the screen indicated the next bus due was delayed by another eleven minutes. Adam scratched his jaw as a wave of panic hit him. The screen updated the delay again. The bus wouldn't arrive for another *eighteen* minutes!

He'd glanced up the drive when the front of a city bus was approaching. Adam gazed back at his watch. This would have to do, he thought, and climbed aboard the city bus.

Finally the airport was disappearing behind him. A few people were standing when the driver headed out onto a main arterial, toward the smoggy LA skyline. Down a barren boulevard, then another and another, mile after mile, Adam stared at burned out offices, crumbling apartments, and closed factories blanketed by graffiti. Along the curbs were stripped vehicles as far as the eye could see. Wooden fencing had all but vanished in a winter that brought unseasonably cold temperatures in the midst of severe shortages of heating fuels. Dogs left to stray could be seen rummaging through uncollected garbage cans stacked alongside streets and alleyways. Everything Adam saw from the bus window substantiated local and national news reports of how badly the gasoline crisis had marred American life.

The coach soon entered the heart of downtown. Passengers exited, others got on. At every stop, the clientele climbing on board worsened. Loud, belligerent toughs filled in the last empty seats toward the rear. The driver kept his eyes forward as the bus crawled past security checkpoints where city vehicles had their undercarriages examined for explosives. A moment later the driver pulled up at the next stop near an intersection where a traffic cop was directing pedestrians through a blockade.

Adam watched a chunky redheaded youth and two other kids wearing black bandanas get on board. A minute later the redhead moved from a forward seat back toward the middle where Adam was sitting. He had a stained t-shirt and jeans that stunk of sweat and weed. He looked over Adam's business attire, then dropped into the same seat, delivering an accidentally-on-purpose shoulder slam to Adam.

Trouble soon erupted inside the coach.

Adam turned his shoulder, cutting the kid a break and attempting to avert a violent confrontation. But the kid was obviously high and hastily persistent. He stuck his face in Adam's, grinning past broken front teeth and cussing in a threatening tone. The shrill of a teenage girl behind them cut up into laughter. Her antics spread like fire among the hoodlums.

Redhead apparently got enough of a charge out this and was planning an encore. Unfortunately, his reckless mischief had underestimated its target. In one swift motion Adam ejected a coiled elbow, smashing into the Red's throat to deprive him of his next breath. Adam followed up with his prized chokehold that folded his victim's torso into a twisted half nelson—a move he'd perfected on the high school wrestling team. Having ratcheted up his grip, he waited for the customary howl for mercy. It came in desperate muffled shrieks.

"Okay ... okay, man ... lemme up ... dude, I'm chillin'!"

A stir among the passengers raced toward the front, which alerted the driver who reacted with a stomped of the brakes while blowing a whistle he had looped around his neck. His huge frame came lumbering down the aisle toward the altercation. He shook both fists, threatening to call the police. An electronic device glimmering in his hand sent the toughs scattering out through the rear doors.

The bus was moving again and a strange normalcy returned to the crowd. Had this kind of incident become so commonplace in every big city?

Unfamiliar with LA, Adam listened attentively to the driver calling out stops by their street names. A couple stops later he heard the street on which Admiral Petroleum's office was located. After feeding four dollars into the driver's kiosk he stepped down to the curb. Adam was standing in front of a boarded up bank. A rusted sign advertised federally insured loans. Compressed air from the brakes blasted past his ankles and the bus pulled away.

He viewed the block in one slow, eye-absorbing circle. A crowd was clamoring madly on the next block. Adam crossed the street and established his bearings with the help of a map he'd printed at Dell's place. To his left were the Arco Towers that now belonged to Admiral Petroleum Incorporated. The police had pushed the protesters across the street and had cordoned off the sidewalk at the base of the building. Adam checked his watch and breathed a long sigh of relief. Pushing back his hair, he smoothed the wrinkles from his pants and approached the double guarded entrance to LA's mega footprint.

*****

The company aircraft, a luxury-class Cessna Citation capable of cruising over 600 miles per hour at thirty five thousand feet, began its descent over the northern reaches of Mexico's Baja.

In the plane's rear cabin the company president debriefed his progress after an early morning meeting with state energy officials in Mexico City. With much success he'd completed

119

his final leg of negotiations, renewing Admiral's contract to operate refineries in Mexican waters along with legal passage of company tankers along the Pacific coastline. Inside thirty minutes Panach would drop down onto a small airstrip northeast of the San Fernando Valley.

During the descent, a soft tone came over his earpiece. It identified audio communications were coming in from the International Space Station. Panach activated his usual security protocols and initiated the voice stream.

"What do you have to report, Colonel?"

The colonel announced he had taken care of NASA's communications link, as agreed in their deal.

"You're not going to spoil my day with traceable evidence … and a federal inquiry, are you, Colonel?"

Striker yawned into the link. "Relax, all fronts will be covered. You've got my word."

"You mean they're not yet covered? Is something wrong?"

The colonel was defensive. "I didn't say that. Only a few minor details to wrap up."

"Don't play games with me. Let's have it."

There was no reply, and after a pause Striker's voice streamed back to Panach.

"Alright, some Kraut researcher got into classified documents, the same material we've been—"

"I don't recall a German scientist on my payroll," Panach interrupted.

"He's not."

"So what gives? Why is this interloper digging into NASA files?"

Striker hesitated. "He knows about the mining mission."

Panach lost it. "That is highly classified. Give me a name, Colonel. The President of the AFL-CIO? Who the hell is this man?"

Through the audio link the colonel's indignation revealed a subtle resistance to give up information so quickly. After all, there were sub-deals to be made … at a price. But soon the colonel relented.

Panach considered his options. "What does Dr. Mann know about Vashon?"

"The astronauts attempted to contact someone aboard ISS, requesting a message be relayed to NASA. Mann intercepted the message through a private band established years ago for a preliminary Mars mission. However, I've taken—"

"Look Colonel, I'm paying you to make a few communication adjustments. I regret that means interfering with a manned lunar mission returning to Earth."

Striker cleared his throat and let go a heavy sigh. "Mr. Panach, tampering with communications is one thing. But killing astronauts? That was not in our arrangement."

"Neither of us can tolerate screw-ups that result in federal indictments, can we Colonel? At this point the outcome of this assignment takes precedent over petty moral issues. There simply can be no chance of that crew coming back to raise questions and suspicion. Factoring them out of the picture will become a credit and a legacy to both of us, should the details remain forever untold, Colonel. Do you understand?"

Striker paused a long painful moment before grunting his tentative agreement through the link.

"Furthermore," Panach added, "Kirkpatrick and his Beijing buddies must be compelled to declare the whole project impractical. A loss. Go do what is necessary to silence the German scientist, and you'll be a world closer to a very comfortable retirement."

Fifteen

Mammoth framed photos of Admiral's gas pipelines, offshore drilling platforms, and international refineries graced the towering walls leading Adam and two armed guards to the elevators inside the Power Building. The place was ominous but magnificent, too.

Handsome stainless panels jutting up from the floor assured visitors the firm's esteemed place in the energy industry. Covering them, in bright damson and deep indigo, illuminated digital readouts displayed company statistics, synchronized in real time.

Adam paused to comprehend the jittering digits, each one responding to every fluctuation of the global markets. The current numbers touted Admiral to be controlling 83% of petroleum sales and 76% of the natural gas distributed in North America. The figures included gasoline shares of nineteen smaller firms owned worldwide. According to an electronic map gracing the wall behind him, the majority of British and European concerns were now operating under the influence of Admiral. To think NASA had contracted business with this entity brought him mixed comforts.

The elevator doors parted. Reluctantly, Adam stepped on board, feeling like he'd purchased a ticket for a ride he wasn't going to easily forget. Racing upward, he envisioned layers of corporate tigers muscling supply markets, floating capital bonds, and driving prices at the pump. This conglomerate seemed to be fueling itself with all of the devices needed to become the dictator of giants, while fending off threats of savvy competition in its quest for global dominance.

Though Admiral appeared to be everything Adam had loathed of the industry, especially in light of the struggle American start-ups were making toward greener ways to fuel the nation, capital-funded projects at public institutions had been put on ice. Prospects of stable employment had dried up. Keeping one's head above a deluge of poverty took priority over wrangling in political ideologies. Besides, Adam had done what he could to help restore the government's role in developing affordable energy. Yet he'd grown increasingly doubtful the beleaguered energy department could actually pull off nationwide distribution of *Aqualene,* if not for several years. Enamored by personal debt and the risk of watching foreclosure proceedings take his mother down, he had promised himself to give private industry a fair chance. As the floor propelled him closer to his destination, Adam Harlow had to think this thing through, weigh the issues, and prepare to choose a course of action. His money was gone, and no other opportunities came close to what Admiral could offer.

So why was belief in whatever awaited him upstairs a matter of concern? The world is filled with believers...and the non-believers. At times matters of trust beckon one or the other. People who want to believe will always find a way. Inversely, those who wish not to believe will always find justification for doubt.

The opulence of Admiral's wealth robbed Adam of his breath the moment he stepped off the elevator. He was standing inside the most powerful oil company's top floor business hub, a place where some of the most influential decisions on the planet were made. Before him handcrafted windows framed of gold sparkled in chiseled crystal, tastefully accenting mahogany walls and plush furnishings. Rising out of the floors—hardwood inlaid with gems and mother-of-pearl—huge glass sculptures towered up to cathedral ceilings. Adam set eyes on the collections. Handmade miniatures of clipper ships and old world ocean liners, to scale World War I flying machines hung down over rare handmade automobiles, greeting Adam throughout a maze of polished and dusted inventions and artifacts ushering America through its Gilded Age. Chamber music tinkled from an invisible sound system overhead.

"Welcome to Admiral Petroleum." At first the woman's voice startled him, but he recognized the graceful inflections.

"Ms. Lopez?"

"Yes, Mr. Harlow," she answered softly. In a long cotton dress, she smiled and floated toward him from a large desk across the room. "How can I make you comfortable?"

"A glass of water, please."

Such an austere request under the circumstances. When she returned Adam drank it and finished surveying the cathedral-styled lobby. "It must be a real pleasure to work up here in the clouds, kind of like entering a heavenly museum each morning."

Ms. Lopez nodded politely but did not comment. She checked the electronic clipboard she carried and then escorted Adam into a small conference room along the perimeter of the lobby. "Our site supervisor will be interviewing you today, Mr. Harlow."

She turned and let herself out, pulling the door closed behind her.

Adam moved slowly through the room, studying the large photographs of Admiral's properties around the world attached to walls of delicately carved rare hardwoods. The number of refineries and oil drilling installations—many of them now mothballed—seemed endless. Still alone, he sat down at the oblong table in the middle of the room and pulled a two-page résumé from his attaché. A quick scan over the details, everything was in order. His college degrees and work experience qualified him for a number of geo-chemical based research teams in the industry.

Today's meeting, however, was more about personalities than technical savvy. Adam had e-mailed his credentials to Admiral the same day Chemtx let him go. He had considered it a provisional insurance policy that would yield him an interview, in spite of Chamberlain's efforts to discredit his name.

There was a knock at the door. Inside stepped a dark-haired man in his forties introducing himself as Ken Burke. He claimed to be a site operations manager at one of the Admiral's newer facilities.

Adam stood and shook hands, noting the long facial scar over his sturdy appearance—tall and fashionably dressed with an air of authority in his gait. His handshake was firm under penetrating, almost threatening eyes.

Burke motioned him into a different chair, directly across from the dossier that had Adam's name printed on it. As Burke checked his watch, the conference room door swung open. In

124

walked two suited gentlemen, each dressed to the tee with an oversized briefcase at his side. They seated themselves on either side of Burke, forming a trio that faced Adam like a team of high-powered negotiators. So far there was no sign of a NASA official; someone in charge of debriefing candidates on *Aqualene*'s successful recovery.

Burke introduced his two cohorts as company attorneys. Their presence was a legal procedure to validate any proprietary agreements between company and employee. Fair enough, Adam thought.

"Okay, Mr. Harlow, let us get down to the crude," he chuckled as he began thumbing through Adam's dossier. "I see that you contacted us for work back in January, after leaving a Seattle firm. Is that right?"

"Yes, sir, that is correct."

Burke reached into the envelope, expecting to draw out something he'd missed.

"Have I misplaced a letter from Chemtx referencing your performance?"

"No," Adam replied boldly. "That company's president hardly knew his employees."

"What can you say about your discharge?"

"Company leadership employed risky ambitions poorly aligned with my principles."

"I see. So you took a stand against the firm's business priorities."

Adam tried to shove aside a diminishing regard for Burke, interpreting the abrupt remark as a simple test of interpersonal relations skills. "Let's just say the firm was headed down a one-way street toward disaster. I wasn't going to take that ride."

Burke leaned back in his chair, tapping his fingertips on the table's glossy surface.

"Based on what I've read, Chemtx appears to be a big player in hydrogen-cell technology, and therefore, still a friend to petroleum," Burke noted. "We sell the product needed to process hydrogen. It's up to companies like Chemtx to engineer effective methods of harnessing it."

125

"Exactly my point. Chemtx has made some dreadful oversights, when you consider the growing number of fatal accidents on record."

"I see," Burke replied, glancing down at Adam's file. "Can you tell us what you have been doing in the interim; consulting, short-term projects ... lectures?"

"Research for the federal government, you know with NASA."

Burke nodded, his eyes exchanging something unclear with one of the lawyers before shifting back to Adam. "Yes, of course, Mr. Harlow. We try to anticipate professional gains that might come out of government-funded initiatives. Taxpayer's redemptions, sort of speak. Progressive insights that better qualify an employee to function effectively at Admiral."

Wondering if there had been a wire crossed in NASA's message, Adam paused to sort things out. Burke hadn't disclosed any details about disseminating data related to *Aqualene*, nor had he asked for definitive from his candidate. Clearly, Dell had been wise in urging Adam to take his research to the Propulsion Labs. Adam would avoid the subject until Admiral's people could prove a valid relationship with NASA.

Carefully he arranged his words, fully intent on staying within professional and ethical boundaries. "As has been the case for years, the federal government is exploring some of its own initiatives for developing synthetic fuel. A facsimile, I'm sure, of what every other energy firm is doing out there."

"An initiative to pull America out of a nation-wide energy slump?"

"You could put it in those terms."

"So tell us, in your opinion, has NASA been successful in accomplishing its goals?"

Adam crossed his arms and smiled back at Burke. "Let's just call it a work in progress. I fulfilled my assignment as one of many consultants. The rest is confidential."

One conclusion Adam was prepared to make was that Admiral had little interest in what the government was doing

126

in its high-powered labs. That seemed a little odd, but at the same time, it would be convenient.

"Thank you, Mr. Harlow," Burke nodded. "Is there any more you wish to state about your background?"

"I trust you've compiled the pertinent facts regarding my experience in the geo-chemical sciences. Should Admiral find my credentials useful, I prefer to serve in R & D, with an emphasis on alternative resources."

Burke produced a satisfied grin and turned to confer with his two attorneys. One of the men set an accordion file on the table and pulled out a bundle of legal documents. After a briefly whispered consultation Burke came to a conclusion. "Mr. Harlow," he coughed with elevated authority, "we'd like to offer you a position at our Crimson Plant—a newly constructed facility right here in California. Cutting edge technology with an emphasis on grain-based cellulites."

Now they were getting somewhere. "Advanced ethanol products? Bio diesel?"

"A helluva lot better grade than what consumers are grappling over at the pumps. We've been re-engineering biodegradable distillates in hopes of replacing diminishing returns on gasoline production. Primarily canola and wild grasses, mixed with genetically engineered corn—all under automated processing. This area may not be at the top of your resume, but it's the best I can offer you at the moment. That is, of course, until something more appropriate opens up."

Adam's heart raced with ecstasy. He'd kicked one foot through the crystal doors of mega-budget research. Grain-based diesels with their low emissions had been gaining momentum for years. At the least, ethanol sciences offered him moral solace against perpetuating the hydrocarbon binges that continued to drive the major energy markets.

Burke had picked up on Adam's elation and was now wagging a ballpoint pen between his fingers. "Mr. Harlow, does this sound like something you are prepared to accept today?"

Adam noticed Burke's eyes return to his diamond studded Rolex for the third time in one minute. "I can," he replied boldly. Given the job market this was no time to squabble over particulars. Compensation and medical benefits were a given. According to industry stats he'd perused while on the plane, Admiral had a grand reputation of doling out handsome salaries to its entry-level engineers. Their medical outdid banks and schools.

Adam stood up and shook hands with Burke.

The attorneys cracked patent smiles and nodded with outstretched hands. They followed Burke's lead by joining in a ceremonial applause before sitting back down.

Burke pulled out a small case and presented it to Adam. Inside was a solid gold fountain pen. He promised to have Adam's name engraved on it, sealing their mutual alliance. "We'll need to take care of business before going on," he added. "I'm going to turn you over to our in-house legal team to finish up. Now if you'll excuse me for just a few moments, Mr. Harlow."

Burke exited the room. The company attorneys leveled their eyes on Adam as they placed forms, one at a time, in front of him. Each document covered the usual formalities that were part-and-parcel to hiring an employee working in the capacity of generating and handling proprietary information.

*****

Burke hissed at the tech as he entered the dimmed lab down the hall. "Get him on visuals."

The tech adjusted the controls on his console. "Take a look."

Multiple images of Mr. Harlow appeared over the wall monitor in front of them. Each frame displayed a different angle from various points around the conference room.

In hushed volume through a speaker on the table, Panach's voice crackled. Speaking from his private jet, he demanded an infrared image be transmitted immediately to the aircraft. The tech fingered a joystick on the table, which could re-position a receptor from the ceiling in the conference room where Mr. Harlow was waiting. It panned over to his attaché on the floor beside him. Burke stared into the screen as he watched data begin streaming from the digital file inside the case, then spoke into the conference link that connected him to his boss inside the company jet.

"I can't make out much of anything," Burke complained. "It's all scrambled."

"Of course it is," Panach's voice rattled the speaker again, "which proves our communications with him have paid off. Obviously he's carrying the plans ... so I'm holding you responsible for gaining possession of the file. Send an imprint to the lab immediately."

Burke nodded obediently at the video lens, then put his attention onto a grid of photos that were popping up on the screen. "He expects to submit this stuff to the Propulsion Labs?"

"Only if he has a reason to believe he's in the wrong place. Therefore, we've got to be sure he's comfortable. Harlow's got to trust Admiral to handle everything from here. It's your job to get him out to the air field and ready to board my jet in forty-five minutes."

"Yes, of course, sir," Burke answered

The needle on the impulse meter in front of him began jumping.

The tech's face rippled as he shook his head and whispered: "First sign of nerves I've seen out of this guy."

Panach's voice grumbled from the speaker again. "Get back in there and finish the deal before we lose him."

*****

Adam read the print again, for the third time, then paused over one of Admiral's legal documents, the gold pen now twirling between his fingers.

Burke re-entered the conference room and sat down with crossed arms. A worried look stuck in his eyes.

"Is there a problem, Mr. Harlow?"

Fearful of conveying the wrong image, Adam's gaze jumped off the page and on to Burke. "I would like to be excused for a few hours; long enough to deliver some important materials to a lab in Pasadena."

"No worries," Burke said abruptly. In an instant he was on his feet. "Our security director lives in Pasadena. I'll have him drop it for you on his way home this afternoon."

Adam shook his head. "Pardon me, but that won't work. I'm expected in person."

"The Propulsion Laboratories?"

"Yes, that's correct. Would you be kind enough to call me a cab? I will return in a few hours to finish up hiring formalities. I'm prepared to report for work first thing in the morning."

Adam watched a level of anxiety flare up in Burke's eyes. The man was clearly compelled to follow some undisclosed company agenda—an itinerary that ran counter to the logistics Adam had carefully worked out on his flight from Seattle.

"I'm terribly sorry, Mr. Harlow, but we've got to board the company jet in thirty-five minutes." Burke was looking at his watch again. His hand fell to an intercom button on the table, "Sarah, get in here now," he commanded through the speaker, then spun on his polished loafers to face Adam again. "Ms. Lopez will arrange everything with our private courier. Your parcel will go out within the hour. Highest priority."

Adam pinched the pen's gold shank between his teeth. He clutched his jaw and held a breath for several painful seconds. Mailing the formula had its risks. Upon his acceptance of the assignment, Renee had given him clear instructions to show up at the Propulsion Lab to verify his identity, deposit his sample, and arrange for a demonstration of his findings.

It didn't help that Burke was growing increasingly edgy as he ratcheted up his case. "The cab fare to Pasadena would be horrific this time of day, not to mention the dangers of traveling east through such a depressed part of town. Why don't you relax, let us take care of everything. I'll personally cover all the costs and save you the trip."

"Impossible," Adam coughed. "I must—"

A knock at the open door cut him off. It was Ms. Lopez. The graceful Latino woman smiled at Adam and stepped inside the conference room. She held up three sizes of packing envelopes.

130

Burke shot an arm to Adam's shoulder and turned to the secretary.

"Ms. Lopez, please congratulate our newest addition to the company. Mr. Harlow needs to send an urgent parcel. Would you honor him with Admiral's finest hospitality?"

Adam found it excruciatingly difficult to refuse for risk of insulting his new employer along with the executive secretary. Ms. Lopez had been his first positive contact at Admiral, instilling in him an indelible sense of trust in her.

Ms. Lopez smiled at Adam. "This way, Mr. Harlow." Gently she guided him by the elbow out into the lobby. "Our driver is downstairs in Accounting. He's on his way up to pick up your package right now."

Something about doing business with Admiral's executive secretary made compliance with Burke a little bit more tolerable. Adam considered the violent protests around the city and quickly rationalized away Renee's conditions to show up in person. He would simply have to fabricate an exception to the rule. After all, NASA technicians could open his file and find pertinent details needed to complete most of its factory specifications. He would have to make time on a day off to catch a shuttle flight to Pasadena and meet with NASA technicians about the particulars of his interpretation of the formula. Thankfully, none of what he intended to share with the government would be considered a conflict of interest in Admiral's ethanol division.

Adam breathed a little easier after sealing his flash file into a padded envelope. His palms trembled as he cradled one remote, but plausible journey out of America's protracted fuel crisis.

Immediately Burke angled himself between Adam and the elevator. Behind him stood three security guards. Each seemed to verify the exchange that followed. Barring final hesitation, Adam placed the parcel into Ms. Lopez's hands. He trusted her, somehow, but harbored suspicions about the others. "Make sure this goes out today, please."

"I will send Mr. Burke the confirmation that NASA received it," Lopez assured him with a smile.

A softened grin filled Burke's face as he stepped forward and extended a firm hand to Adam's shoulder. "This world, so full of procedural muck, could use more pragmatic souls like you, Mr. Harlow. Let us now get under way. Our CEO will be traveling with us. You are among the few to meet directly with him. We are honored to have him along to inspect plant operations."

Ambivalence rode in Adam's gut during the twenty-five minutes it took the limo to wind its way past impoverished filth, before exiting the worst of LA's outer downtown section. The streets were littered with uncollected garbage, tossed about or trampled upon by young hoodlums if they weren't heaping broken furniture onto bonfires that belched black smoke skyward between condemned buildings. Admiral's car was a popular target for hurled bottles and other debris that could quickly be taken up as arms against a passing enemy of the downtrodden.

Soon the limo pulled onto a privately operated airstrip that catered only to the upper crust of LA. By the time he was ushered on board the private jet and seated in the main cabin, Adam felt like throwing up the airline food he'd eaten somewhere over Oregon that morning. Things were unraveling too quickly. He felt like a fighter pilot with his hands bound behind him, watching his life drop into a banking dive.

In a matter of minutes he was gazing over LA's expanse of depressed suburbia. The plane leveled off above a thin layer of charcoal brown cirrus. Adam found himself leafing hastily through a magazine showcasing exotic European cars and exclusive properties for sale. Why not? Nothing more intelligent or enlightening could be found in the rack.

"Our flight is less than two hundred miles, allowing you some time to meet with Mr. Panach," Burke announced from the cabin's aft door.

Adam struggled to make sense of everything that had transpired that day. He toweled his face and released his belt, all the while mentally preparing to come face to face with the country's most influential businessman. Burke motioned him through a secured bulkhead into a dimly lit private suite at the

132

rear of the plane that smelled of rich tobacco. Did he have a choice?

"Come in, Mr. Harlow," a guttural voice erupted over the whine of the engines. Unseen by anyone entering the cabin, Mr. Panach sat facing the opposite direction until his chair motored around to face Adam. "Let me mix you a drink."

Adam declined the liquor while he surveyed several fine furnishings and tasteful artifacts bolted to the aircraft's walls and floor. Mr. Panach stayed put as he stuck out a massive hand, imposing a grip that matched the resonant baritone that exploded off his tongue. Pinching the stout cigar lodged between his lips, he pulled it out and waved it at a leather recliner on the starboard side of the cabin. Then swiftly he gestured Burke away, demanding uninterrupted privacy with Adam.

"It is one of those rare pleasures I can indulge in," he said, "Making acquaintances with a new hire. You see, young blood flowing into my company usually possesses the brightest of talents ... and fewest of fears. Everything it takes for a young maverick to climb the ladder of corporate success."

"I hope to keep my fingers on the future of energy, rather than scaling the rungs of corporate management," Adam replied bluntly, keeping his tone neutral.

"Very well, indeed," Panach observed. "A man who knows his priorities deserves due respect. I had hoped to acquire you earlier, barring previous obligations that follow a man of your capacity."

"Just another one of those government projects," Adam commented. His thoughts returned briefly to his parcel, the one last seen in Ms. Lopez's delicate grasp.

Panach let go a barrel laugh. "Don't discount your talents, my good friend. Some of those little government deals can roll into something big enough to put a tall feather in a young fellow's cap. I'm sure you've earned your stripes."

Putting business aside while Panach sipped on brandy, Adam thought about his mother for the umpteenth time since leaving Seattle that morning. He had phoned to update her from LAX about his intentions to meet with NASA engineers, without mentioning the job interview at Admiral. Delighted by the news, she had encouraged him to seek any job he could find. Times were growing tough at home along with everywhere else. She didn't have to remind him of that.

He remembered the signing bonus that appeared in Admiral's email firming up his travel plans. Indeed, this was perfect timing for a much-needed transfer payment to the mortgage company holding the deed to his mother's place. He would surprise her with a lump sum payment to avert the foreclosure proceedings levied against her estate.

A smile punctuated Adam's face. "I would consider a spot in your R&D department," he told Mr. Panach. "Perhaps you'll see that's the best means to take my career to a new level … and better serve the company."

Adam broke his gaze from Panach's deep inset eyes. A host of amenities waited at the CEO's fingertips. Cognac, vodka and a menu of whiskeys crowded a gold-trimmed hardwood pantry at arm's reach. Evidenced by unprecedented wealth brought by his prevailing influence in the western hemisphere, Panach was a traveled man with a long acquired taste for expensive liquor, exotic hors d'oeuvres, and the pleasures of indulging in the finest tobaccos.

Inhaling deeply, Panach gleaned maximum pleasure from his cigar when Adam moved to direct the conversation back on topic. "Times are ripe for perpetuating the advancement of cellulosic research."

Panach nodded. "I'm rather impressed. You are obviously aware the sugars in our feedstocks, such as wild prairie grass and even sawdust, have been locked inside lignocellulose—a compound more complicated and expensive to break down than corn kernels.

"But recent developments have yielded the right enzyme to make it cost-effective to produce sizable quantities of ethanol. Our discovery of a microbe that converts organic matter directly into the fuel has eliminated costly steps by using plasma-torch technology to turn virtually any carbon-based material, including garbage, into a synthetic gas."

"That puts Admiral on sure-footing; a road to sustainability," Adam remarked with some renewed hope in Big Oil's resolve to move further away from hydrocarbons.

Knocking cigar ashes into a beveled silver tray, Panach motored his chair upright. As it turned out, he was considerably smaller than Adam had imagined. His broad golden face and close cropped hair—still black in places—complemented the Latin accent.

"Young man, this firm has made its share of forward leaps. But it doesn't come close to long-term survival. It's going to take some remarkable minds to save us from financial ruin."

Panach displayed a sincere look of forlorn humility as he spoke in depth about Middle East border wars and the continued sabotage of pipelines and refineries around the world. His oratory began to sound as if he and Adam were the last two men in the oil business, while the rest of humanity had taken flight in a massive exodus to a world that uses no energy. With a renewed sense this new boss was a mortal human being, Adam was conscious of a slight drop in his blood pressure. Was it a fatalistic helplessness he'd detected in the CEO's tone?

"Sir, if it's any consolation, despite the standard criticisms aimed at big firms, Admiral wins more headlines for diversified expansion than most of its competitors."

It was true. Admiral had enjoyed a series of syndicated print on its ability to out-produce other firms on ethanol and bio-diesel fuels. Considering the power and influence corporate entities had on the networks, Adam had to wonder how much the media been doctored.

Panach was smiling at this and seemed to take it as a matter of fact rather than a vein of patronage. "I respect a man of erudite observations. However, accolades of such are growing far and few between. From now into our next decade it's going to take a miracle to keep this industry alive. A miracle from people with specific knowledge of synthetics. Insights far beyond what corporate savvy has managed to perfect under this wretched economy."

The aircraft's engines suddenly dropped an octave. Adam could see they'd begun descending through wisps of cloud rushing past the porthole behind Panach. Darkening sky fluttered between the opaque clouds as tiny beads of moisture raked across the outside lens. He thought about Clarence

Riggs. Did Panach have any clue of Riggs's discovery and its magnitude? What was the impact on Big Oil?

Panach was speaking again, as much through his eyes that danced from beneath one long heavy brow like a long undulating caterpillar crawling across his forehead. Never mind the man's distinct physical features. What came next from Panach surprised Adam.

"Allow me to get to the point, Mr. Harlow. You demonstrated impressive influence at Chemtx, some of which got you into trouble under questionable leadership. Walking in your shoes, I would have handled it no other way. There's a time for each of us to step out of the ranks. Walk your talk.

"Furthermore, it's no surprise to me about your involvement with the government, given your exclusive knowledge of mineral synthetics and simultaneous catalysts. It is that kind of expertise that will get this country back on its feet."

Something inside Adam muted an urge to blurt out the fact that Riggs had beaten him to securing NASA's interest in sustainable energy. If Admiral wasn't disseminating data for the Propulsion Labs, what was it doing? Moreover, why was Adam the only candidate sitting on a company jet with the most influential man in the private energy sector? Had he missed some small detail along the way?

The cabin lights dimmed. Panach touched a button on his recliner. The screen on the wall lit up and began displaying a video presentation of exclusive homes with waterfront and mountain views. "Seizing property is seizing opportunity, my friend. This company owns hundreds of these luxury estates. One will be selected for you as a reward for committing your talents to Admiral."

There was no reply, and after an awkward interval Adam said, "Sir, I'm honored, but I don't see how I qualify for the grand tour ... the perks ... and the properties." His eyes fixed on the slideshow. "I'm curious, who owned these estates before you acquired them?"

Uneasy about how Panach might receive his question, Adam braced for the push back laced with mild indignation, followed by a lecture on macroeconomics in a world where the

136

circulation and flow of cash undermines moral-based theories on social solidarity. Panach was grinning, thoroughly caught up in his lavish conquests.

"Anyone who's ever made it in show business, professional sports, politics ... the like. Diversifying during hard times gives us an unprecedented edge against bankruptcy."

Dozens more foreclosures and takeovers, mostly mansions and exclusive view properties flashed over the screen before the cabin lights came on again. Panach pulled a large envelope from a worn leather satchel at his side. Carefully he extracted a document printed on fancy grained paper and placed it on Adam's lap. "I suggest you start simple, say Laguna, Palisades, or maybe Huntington Beach—a modest place in a cluster of luxury homes seized by our Properties Division."

The CEO was in full form, exercising bragging rights about his acquisitions. And now a feeling of disgust loomed over Adam, dousing the few aspirations he'd previously held of working for Admiral Petroleum. He smiled grimly into the gray skies turning to dusk outside the plane and recalled his father's battle against land barons who'd eventually poured into South Dakota to buy up and develop sacred spaces held desperately by small tribes living in the shadows of the Black Hills. In view of his mother's fate of losing her home, Adam wondered if he was about to rob Peter to pay Paul.

Again he rolled it over in his mind. You've been a damned fool before, he thought. But this tops all. He recalled being enticed by stock options at Chemtx, only to swim against the tide of unsustainable internal policy. In all his short-sightedness, he'd turned down a coveted research grant at MIT. Now, wait. Wasn't there another side? How was anyone to know the startup energy firm, with a mission to aggressively develop geo-thermal fusion, would falter its course, struggle financially, and eventually turn to hustling poorly monitored government subsidies? If only he'd accepted MIT's generous invitation! He wouldn't be falling deeper into the hands of Rodney Panach. Nor would he have to shoulder the headaches that came with knowing *Aqualene*. Damn!

Glancing stealthily at Panach, Adam shuddered. It was an involuntary response, brought on by a growing fear he could not describe or define. One way or another, something wasn't right about all this.

Good grief, Mr. Harlow, what in hell did you get yourself into?

Panach spoke again, cutting the silence that had descended over them. A brief slide show of elegant properties in sunny locales of lush gardens blinked over the screen. "Ah, here's one," he offered proudly. "Look at it, my friend, on Napoli Drive just north of the Riviera Country Club. I handpicked this one myself after we acquired it from a big name in Hollywood."

"Who was the unfortunate soul?"

"Sorry, it'll be another week before I can disclose that information, once the deal closes."

Adam gulped on a breath of cabin air and gingerly fingered the document. He felt tainted as if contracting a deadly virus. "This is not exactly the kind of signing bonus I had in mind," he confessed aloud. "Not for an entry position in ethanol research."

"Consider it my personal gratitude, Mr. Harlow—a thank-you in advance for contributing your knowledge and expertise … far greater than the conventions of the day. In this economy, one man's debt is another man's asset. I'm sure you understand what I am saying."

Adam's thoughts dashed back to the research data he had prepared in the digital file. In the course of minutes, Panach had referenced Adam's *exclusive knowledge* more than once. Was he more interested in what Adam had accomplished working on *Aqualene* rather than efficient methods Admiral could use to boost its production of ethanol?

Adam felt ensnared by the forces of Admiral's undertow drawing him deeper into trouble. "I don't believe your employees receive this sort of grooming unless—"

"A man in my position doesn't leave things to chance, Mr. Harlow. This company is going to need every bit of its hard-earned capital and your expertise in a young, uncharted field.

138

And for that, I am prepared to pay handsomely; say seven figures to start?"

"Quite the inducement for any man possessed by an appetite for luxury. But with all due respect, I cannot—"

"—consider disclosing proprietary secrets, supported by public tax dollars. Is that what you feel obliged to tell me, Mr. Harlow?"

"In defense of my integrity, I'd be lying to say otherwise."

Panach's smile turned into a deep belly laugh. "In these hard times, you're a rare bird, Mr. Harlow. Obviously the product of a small-town upbringing. Harbor no illusions; I'm going to enjoy knowing that about you. Admiral has always been purposeful in recruiting people of veracity, which takes us to our nationally renowned ethanol operation at Crimson."

Adam felt his eardrums flutter with the change of cabin pressure. Panach glanced at his speckled diamond watch. "We'll be landing in a few minutes. I want you to get some rest and be ready for a full day tomorrow. In the meantime, Mr. Harlow, ask yourself what you can do for this crippled industry. What you are willing to commit to our fledgling economy? I'm speaking of the blood, sweat, and brains it takes to make America stand proud once again."

As though the CEO had rung for room service, Burke appeared in the doorway. Adam felt empty, hollowed out. Completely lost for words, he was escorted out. The pieces of the puzzle had suddenly snapped into place in a deluge of unpleasant reality. The email he'd received at Dell's place, in all its apparent authenticity, was a setup. And who was Clarence Riggs? An alias? A clever guise to fool him into believing his business with NASA was at an end? Despite the verbal lashing he wished to unleash on Mr. Panach, Adam realized the less said to such a man the better. Careful *thinking* would have to see him through this nightmare.

*****

Three miles outside a town named Crimson for its red rock, discolored by copper mine tailings once dumped into an upper tributary draining to the South Fork American River, the

139

aircraft soon came to rest on a rural airfield. From what Adam could make of the shadowed landscape outside the jet's window, this was an isolated farming district, at least used to be. A narrow valley surrounded on three sides by jutting rock formations, their peaks streaked in orange in the final minutes of dusk. An odd locale for manufacturing fuels. One that made sense in light of Panach's desire to accomplish his ends under a cloak of undisputed political silence.

Followed by a burly crewman, Adam exited the cabin under charcoal skies and localized rain. A pungent odor of fermenting grains in the chilled ionized air filled his nostrils. The Cessna's mobile staircase corralled him into a nondescript white van idling on the tarmac. Inside the vehicle waited a pair of Admiral's staffers, each a facsimile of the mono-toughs he'd seen standing guard inside the Power Building. Both were company-issue, wearing identical blue-black, semi-formal attire—the type favorable to sustained physical activity. Through a side window, Adam kept an eye on the aircraft but failed to see Panach exit.

The ride to the Crimson plant afforded Adam time to fully digest what had transpired in just a few hours. The whole fabric of becoming a stooge for Admiral frightened him. He wanted more than anything to call someone. But that option had been negotiated away after signing a legal restriction against using mobile communications aboard company transportation and on company property. This sticky little detail came to light while attempting to contact Dell to thank him for accommodating him. Aboard the Citation, instead of linking up with its wireless provider, Adam's mobile phone had warned him he was in a restricted zone and was not permitted to place such a call. Burke had done little to disguise his pleasure of reminding Adam about company policy.

Ten minutes from the airstrip they passed a small section of clear-cut timberland. A mile of so farther he saw barren gravel deposits under sparse lighting, then a half dozen deserted farm plots, the darkened silhouettes of their buildings flattened. There was no sign of life or traffic for perhaps six or seven miles. As the van neared the Crimson facility the terrain resembled some sort of no-man's land.

Rural desolation! Was this the aftermath of nature? A flood?

More likely preparations to transform the land for mining and industry.

Something told Adam to turn his attention to the guard in the next seat forward. Over an open steel case he'd been toying with an oversized handgun. Admiring it like a pawnbroker, the guard cradled the weapon in his palms, stroking its brushed steel barrel. After several minutes of tinkering with its munitions clip and magazine, he carefully laid it back into the velvet-lined molding and clicked its case shut.

Dusk had faded into full on darkness. Large features of Crimson's lighted fortress could be seen in places but details were less visible to the eye. Adam heard thunder in the distance as the van pulled up to a set of tall steel gates. Instantly he heard shouting outside the vehicle as it came to rest. Voices, accompanied by heavy boot steps, drew near. The driver spoke to one of them through the window, supplying a pass code. After a relay of shouts over a rapid chain of command, the gates slowly motored open.

Its concrete mortar too high for the average man to scale, the wall outside the van obstructed a view of the property inside. If a man desperate enough should make it to the top, he would abruptly find himself tangled in barbed wire that hugged the footings, a few yards from the roadway. This was hardly the *country club* setting Burke had described during the limo ride through LA.

The van entered the drawn gates, up to a heavily guarded post connected with a stretch of cobblestone drive that angled toward the center of the property. Upon accepting the position at Crimson's ethanol plant, Adam had visualized a typical branch office buzzing with engineers and technicians inside a polished chrome edifice blanketed by tinted glass on the outskirts of a luxury housing tract, built exclusively for Admiral's privileged employees. How foolish he'd been to entertain such fantasy!

Reality hit Adam again, like a hurling brick.

The van rambled up a cobblestone drive, bringing into view the chateau. Within a half-mile radius armed mercenaries were everywhere, standing or pacing outside a number of tanks, towers, and various incomplete structures. All were under the spray of temporary industrial lighting. Each, Adam realized, was bent on protecting something clearly more vital than a grain-based fuel refinery in the middle of rural California.

Burke had bent Adam's ear on the process of procuring grain from local farmers in exchange for discounted ethanol. Though Adam had seen few operable farm sites on the trip to Crimson, Burke was touting the arrangement as glory for the consumer at the expense of an ailing oil industry, with Admiral paying more per metric ton than could any of the grassroots producers across the country. In turn, Admiral Petroleum could defray its costs by supplying kickbacks in the form of commercial and government fuel rations, therefore justify undercutting national markets. From Big Oil's point of view, a win-win for all. Eventually, the little guy would be relieved of his duties, his ambitions.

Burke pointed to a brick dormitory situated among dwarfed pines and newly laid lawns. "You'll be quite comfortable living here on our campus," he offered from the van's lower step. "The food is as good as the companionship out here; twenty-four hour attention, seven days a week."

Sixteen

Twilight had turned to darkness when the transport touched down at Lemoore after crossing the Pacific under clear blue skies and calm weather.

Inside a heavily guarded hangar it took several minutes for crews to load the cargo onto an oversized tractor-trailer. Three of the fifteen-by-twelve foot boxes, eighteen inches high, each weighing just over three tons, were strapped down to the truck's flatbed. The rig was fueled up and ready for immediate departure.

Destination: A classified secret NASA facility in a western Nevada desert. Expected arrival time: Just before midnight.

Under light rain that was expected to become heavy at times, Mason Transfer's driver eased the sixty-four ton tractor-trailer out of the base's cargo terminal, pulled onto Vanguard and headed east toward California State Route 198 through Lemoore and then onto Hanford. By the time the rig got to Highway 41 the skies had fully darkened. The pavement was awash in downpours.

The chopper, assigned by the Secret Service, escorted the rig at an elevation of fifteen hundred feet as both traveled north through Clovis and on to Yosemite National Park—the most direct route to the Nevada border.

The weather being unusually cold and wet for February, the driver turned up the defroster and reviewed his available pullover points in the event of flooding and washouts.

Forward the mighty Kenworth's cab growled a fully blown V-10 diesel, spinning a continuous variable transmission with multiple-lockup power converters programmed to harness optimum use of the engine's torque range. Capable of adjusting itself to a countless number of load and road conditions at sixteen hundred cycles per second, the Kenworth's computerized suspension gave its operator the sensation of maneuvering a hovercraft over peaceful waters.

When Mason's driver—a veteran employee with a celebrated driving record—had logged an hour and five minutes out of Lemoore, he was cruising north through

Yosemite on Wawona Road, skirting the west end of a section of burned-out forest land. The road flashed like a strobe as flashes of distant lightning sliced through the towering Sequoia trees that sheltered the highway in several sections. A glance at the video map confirmed he would be merging with an eastbound route from a small junction six or seven miles over the pass. From there he was to travel on Highway 120 to the vicinity of Mono Lake where the road doglegged south and then east again to rural State Route 6. Such would allow him a straight shot into Nevada toward the Lukefield Research Center. According to the map he was carrying, his destination was in the middle of a desert, under military surveillance, and classified top secret.

Federal agents had carefully plotted the route where traffic was sparse, making it an easy pass between the umbrellas of light that showered the populated lowlands. Before midnight the Pentagon would offload the three huge cartons, and the driver would swing back into California to a popular rest stop off Route 95 where big riggers preferred to bunk down during inclement weather.

With Mason truck making good time over Wawona Road, and the cruise computer set at an even seventy miles per hour, the driver occupied himself in a guessing game of what lay inside the mammoth cartons over his rumbling wheels. Was he transporting state-of-the-art military spyware—destined to hug the belly of a new secret-generation of surveillance jets? Perhaps it was part of a missile system designed to defend American cities against a grow threat of terror. Word had it Mason was moving more of that sort of cargo between factories and military bases nowadays.

His thoughts shifted into fear mode, with thoughts of transporting radioactive material that had failed to meet civil codes for interstate transport. The company had done it once before, explaining why Pentagon officials urgently classified the load as top secret, to save time and avoiding a devastating leak to the media. But the apprehension of a nuclear disaster soon faded as the truck entered a long steep upward grade. The cab lurched slightly on its downshift, revving the engine in preparation for demanding load conditions.

The rain pounded harder and blackness closed in on both sides of the narrow slice of roadway, bordered by the channels of light shooting off the Kenworth's twin halogens. Above him the dull throbbing of the Fed's chopper beat above the rain-washed cab, intent on keeping the rig in view at all times.

There hadn't been another motorist for miles, as if flash flooding had prompted the highway patrol to delay travel at designated intervals. More likely, with the Pentagon involved, the highway patrol would have received orders to restrict automobile traffic through a significant stretch of the mountain pass. No tail lights. No oncoming lights for several minutes.

A thick canopy of trees that had occasionally been arching over the road became denser now, blocking out the lights of the chopper, prompting the use of cab-mounted beams to navigate the darkened roadway. The overgrown canopy suddenly became solid, forming the likes of an unlit tunnel. The country music station's signal soon faded, causing the driver to fumble with its tuning. At that instant a rack of blinding red and blue strobe lights blanketed the windshield.

A hundred yards ahead a patrol car was stopped directly in the path of the mighty Kenworth, forcing Mason's driver to slam his foot down on the brake, sinking the engine's roar below the chatter of her mammoth tires skipping and hopping over the asphalt. The two loaded trailers whipped the Kenworth side-to-side like a weasel snapping the neck of a viper.

Cussing madly, the driver yanked the transmission lever into low and gingerly maneuvered the front bumper up to the patrol car; his headlights veering onto a U.S. marshal, feet spread wide, his arms stretched out with hands joined on the grip of a large bore revolver. Through the windshield the marshal motioned him to kill the lights but leave the motor running. He gestured the driver to step down onto the pavement.

Mason's driver complied, keeping his body language slow and predictable. Above him the chopper faded somewhere he guessed to be east of the scene. Instinctively, he raised his arms and walked toward the cruiser with caution. From the corner of his eye he noticed taillights of another big rig a half-mile up the highway pull away, traveling east as he had been. In the distance the blower whined and the trailer disappeared into darkness.

A sudden jab to his right kidney forced his attention to the officer. As the Kenworth panted restlessly at his back the driver was ordered to spread his legs and place his hands down on the hood of the patrol car. What the hell was this about? He'd been hired by the Feds for god sake. He had a schedule to keep and the weather wasn't getting any better.

"Look, there must be some kind of mis—"

"Shut up and head down!" the marshal ordered. He clicked the mic he'd pulled from inside the cruiser and spoke. "The cargo is now in our possession. Get moving."

Blinded by the obnoxious strobe lights atop the squad car, Mason's driver held out little hope of returning to his rig. The gravity of the situation fell upon him heavily. This was clearly not in the Feds' plan. All he could do was to await the mercy of this group of thieves. Wait for whatever fate was in store from the fake marshal.

Aside from the Kenworth's motor, the highway was deathly quiet now. No Secret Service chopper! No car traffic, or for that matter, no fellow truckers to rely on for help.

He heard the hollow thud of the Kenworth's door slam shut. A blast of compressed air echoed off the wet pavement and the truck's engine revved up. As quickly as this nightmare had begun, the rig pulled away, past the dancing strobe lights atop the cruiser.

Drawn up in knots of apprehension, the driver glanced toward the line of massive sequoias. He rehearsed hastily in his mind some crazy scheme of escape into the trees—a set of flailing punches that might delay the purveyor of this outrageous scandal before fleeing for his life into the darkness. A final replay of his scheme and a mumbled prayer, he managed a sideways glance at the uniformed imposter stepping around behind him.

That instant he spun around with a knuckled fist, but a dull pain had already begun to spread over his neck and shoulder. Some blunt object had struck him over the shoulder like a hammer. Before Mason's driver could gather his wits another

146

blow pummeled his skull, dousing the strobe lights and dropping him over the cruiser's hood onto the pavement.

*****

Under the watchful eyes of two security guards Adam poked at his dinner downstairs in the chateau. He was fatigued and hungry but somehow had lost his appetite.

Meanwhile, Burke had gone upstairs and was sitting in front of the plasma wall screen inside the CEO's office suite where Panach fingered a small panel on his desk. Virtual images of stainless steel plumbing, condensers, and fractioning tanks appeared in fully enhanced colors.

"What do you make of this?" Panach grunted.

Burke stared at the three dimensional CAD presentation for a long moment.

"Typical high-volume refinery," he shrugged. "Vacuum distillation, catalytic cracking, alkylation—"

"Open your eyes!" Panach growled. "It's a goddam copy of the file. The one Mr. Harlow was in such a hurry to take to Pasadena."

Burke slid his sunglasses over his forehead. Squinting at the screen again, he tilted his head to one side. "Seems hardly groundbreaking, if you ask me."

Panach grew impatient in his search for clear answers and picked up a laser pointer. Its little red arrow skittered down to a corner of the screen. "Boost that image. Right there, where vulcanizing stages take place."

Burke activated a programmable curser that maneuvered itself through a labyrinth of tubes and valves until halting abruptly, as though it had come to a roadblock. At the core of the plans was a patch of sophisticated circuitry entangled in a confusing weave of plumbing.

Panach wheeled himself up to the base of the screen. "I'm expecting an initial interpretation of Harlow's file from our labs within the hour. Take this section over to Reprographics. Get me enlargements and copies of it for our engineers."

"Yessir." Burke entered the boss's orders into his handheld tablet.

147

Panach was smiling again. He paused to read more of the text accompanying Adam's visuals. "Harlow has developed a mix-down process that extracts and rearranges hydrocarbons directly from the minerals, allowing us to crush, liquefy, and then process everything right here at Crimson."

We then fly the concentrate out to our ocean platforms for finishing stages. Storage and distribution will take place in international waters. The Mexican government has agreed to deploy a protective flotilla for security."

"Absolutely brilliant," Ken Burke replied tentatively, though privately he was struggling to keep up with the science. He was a veteran pilot with some rank at Admiral. It'd become a lot easier to delegate the thinking while appearing to be on top of it.

"Of course it is!" Panach barked as he waved a hand above his head. He glanced over an incoming e-mail. "We still have to get this fellow on board long enough to make it work."

Burke raised his eyebrows. "We've got the plans. Can't our boys just take it from here?"

Still reading the monitor at his desk, Panach pounded his armrest with a fist. "According to our lab techs in Memphis, Harlow's schematic presents a serious flaw. Intentionally or not, these plans are incomplete."

"He left something out?"

"An old trick," Panach growled. "A means to leverage his hand. Harlow's not as naive as I'd figured."

"Give me one hour alone with him," Burke replied, pounding a doubled fist to his palm.

"Don't be foolish! Harlow isn't the type to give in to a simple beating. We've got some time to bring him around. Let him get acclimated out here while we finish the groundwork. I'll have Mr. Harlow ready to assist us very soon."

*****

"It's time you met the crew that installed the electrical inside our newest chemicals plant." Burke escorted Adam into a small drafting room inside the chateau.

Wasting no time, he made formal introductions as though they were late to catch a plane. Adam took this opportunity to carefully observe each engineer. The lead man was Melvin Bates, a dark-haired man hardly a day over forty behind black plastic-rimmed glasses. He appeared outgoing and social in contrast to the others who looked too exhausted to engage in conversation.

"Sit down, partner." Bates had a slight drawl. His demeanor was too pleasant to fit Admiral's mold as a salaried employee. "You must be the expert they flew in from out of state," he said as he stuck out a hand. "Why, it's a real pleasure to know ya."

Bates fired off the nicknames of his crew. Each one slumped back in his chair with eyes darkly shaded by fatigue. In contrast, Bates glowed as if he were elected by the crew to lead them on their last trek. Or maybe he was overjoyed to meet a new incoming face at such a confined worksite.

Immediately he spread blue prints of Crimson's electrical outlay across the table.

"We've got the structure basically ready to go from here to there," he announced, running a finger along a solid blue line that represented the perimeter of the plant. Adam focused on the details and listened to Bates and his men take turns summarizing their work. It wasn't long before Adam picked up on conflicting opinions about wiring configurations and electrical loads. The conflicts ran deeper than a few minor deviations. This spoke subliminal volumes about the pressure these men had endured during what amounted to prison-styled, indentured servitude. He detected a gut level of anxiety in their eyes in the presence of Mr. Burke while he hovered, and monitored their conversation.

Bates and his crew had probably worked together for years—what with the nicknames and the way they seemed to complement one another's strengths. But now they were miffed, puzzled, even agitated over technical matters that would commonly be settled by referring to industry standards.

"I think we've run into some anomalies that will have to be worked out by someone who knows more of what this is all about," Bates lamented. "My crew returns to Oakland tonight,

149

so it looks like you'll be taking over ... with the help of Admiral's own talents."

Bates paused long enough to reveal some undefined puzzlement over the project before getting back to the blue prints. "The text calls for fitting miles of stainless steel tubing, running throughout the main building to complete a closed system of condensing and fractioning; an arrangement I've never quite seen in this industry before."

Adam nodded. He'd seen enough and dared not say what he knew of the plans in Burke's presence. The fine print at the bottom of the plans—a small section that had been overlooked when someone in the reprographics department hastily laundered the document—proved Adam's hunch that Admiral enjoyed a direct conduit into the U.S Energy Department. Unknowingly, Bates and his men were trying to exploit classified diagrams.

Within a few short minutes Bates and his crew climbed into a utility van parked outside the side entrance of the chateau. Under blustery night skies their taillights soon disappeared toward the eastern gates where Adam had entered the compound. Thunder rolled like a distant avalanche over the wastelands beyond the stone walls of Crimson.

Burke ushered Adam across the compound toward the dormitory. Following them was a guard wearing a pistol. At the dorm's entrance Burke punched a keypad and entered a hallway through a steel reinforced door. Overhead lights flicked on automatically. Adam noticed the smelled of new carpeting and fresh paint.

Burke pulled out a digital card and stopped in front of a single unit. "From now on, all other accesses will be accompanied by company security."

Adam scanned the hallway at the other doors. "Who else do you have locked up in here, the Energy Secretary?"

"With Bates and his crew gone, you've got the place to yourself."

Adam forced a smile. "Very well, I'll take the presidential suite."

Ken Burke waved the keycard toward Adam. "See for yourself."

Adam slid the card through the reader and pushed open the door to darkness. He stepped inside and bumped into a flimsy floor lamp. Behind him Burke clicked a wall switch and chuckled. The lamp illuminated a chest of drawers, a chair, and a single bed—a trio of cheap rental furniture.

"I'm touched by your hospitality. A six by eight cell with no bathroom."

Burke's long facial scar performed a somersault ending in a lopsided grin. "Think of yourself at college, Mr. Harlow. The facilities are down the hall. No visitors. I suggest you get plenty of sleep."

Adam did what he could to shove aside the rift growing between them and stepped toward the doorway. "My phone, please," he demanded. "I'd like to call my dad and tell him all about my fabulous new job."

Burke's cold hand maneuvered Adam back inside.

"Mr. Harlow, we both know that's impossible."

Seventeen

As he'd expected, Adam spent his first day in the ethanol plant under close guard and electronic surveillance.

Panach was flying somewhere across the continent on urgent corporate business. Meanwhile, the hours whizzed by at Crimson under a list of service tasks Burke went over in the drafting room after breakfast. Work began with mundane testing procedures of high-tension circuits that carried a 4160-volt rating; the standard feed used to power high volume pumps, compressors, and most other industrial scale components. Meals were basic—enough to sustain the mind and body before shipping off to the plant or the dormitory, cloaked by armed guards each day.

Adam's servitude went into its second night at which time he made the digital readout on the dresser clock the only visible light in the room. Vertical shades covering the small tinted window above his bed filtered out the low-voltage lighting that dotted the grounds, constantly patrolled by guards. Inside he was left to a shelf of tattered novels and assorted weapons magazines.

In the early morning hours Adam awakened to a faint disturbance in the distance. Though it was difficult to discern an exact direction, it appeared to be coming from the new processing plant—the one Bates and his crew had wired for Admiral's secret project.

At day break Adam was taken to the second floor of the chateau.

"Our Executive Suites," Burke announced proudly, pausing at the door long enough for Adam to soak up the control room and all its technical sophistication. Several technicians were busily keying in data and conversing in low tones through headsets. They occupied rows of video monitors and lighted control panels.

Through a side door that connected to the control room, Panach was staring into a screen that monitored Wall Street trading activities. "Mr. Harlow, I hear you're making some progress in our ethanol division. I never considered combining three mulching stages into one. I'll try to remember to pass that production savings on to the State of California." A flick of Panach's hand suggested Burke be gone and shut the door on his way out. The intensity in the man's eyes now lay solely on Adam, who immediately became wary of another such private conference between top and bottom.

It wasn't difficult to see Crimson's ethanol operation had been little more than a front to bigger operation. A secret operation unknown to all, including the government.

In a few short minutes Adam confirmed the company's true ambitions, explaining why Panach had sought more details about mineral synthetics—beyond the figures Adam had encrypted into his digital files. All came as no surprise, considering such expeditious hiring procedures, an extraordinary level of security at the site, restricted movement, and the blue prints he had viewed with Bates.

But there was something more compelling to Adam's presence there. Traces of crushed minerals had caught his eye along one of the pathways between the ethanol plant and the chateau. The previous day, after stopping abruptly outside the auxiliary plant, the guard escort had ordered him to move along before shoving him to the ground. In his haste to collect the scattered binders, Adam had slipped a specimen the size of a quarter into his pocket for later examination. Upon closer analysis, the minerals embedded in the sample had displayed a striking resemblance to those he and Gamil had been analyzing in the underground lab. In a shortage of finite answers, the sample at Crimson *did* explain how Admiral knew so much about the formula, confirming his worst suspicions: NASA would never receive his parcel. As he should expect, Admiral was attempting to glean *Aqualene*'s data but now encountered a roadblock.

Panach would be demanding clear answers and his unfettered cooperation.

Divided into multiple displays, the wall screen inside Panach's suite provided market valuations and international stock trading, the sort of informational amenities that were essential to chief executives who insist on micro-managing a

153

giant well-oiled machine. One that had to operate on a global scale.

The most shocking discovery about Admiral came to Adam over a single monitor sitting upright on Panach's desk that displayed a brightly lit room with an old-world fireplace. There were expensive paintings, tall windows, and well-dressed people shaking hands and conversing in front of the Seal of the United States of America. Damn! He was peering inside the Oval Office—a real-time broadcast over White House security's closed circuit network!

"You can't do this! You'll never get away with it," Adam protested. "Breaking and entering ... at the highest level of the law!"

Indulging himself over the shock erupting in Adam's eyes, Panach burst into laughter. "Mr. Harlow, I prefer to call it *political requisition*. Executive privileges work that way. Many great people have said it poignantly: the first casualty of war is truth. Yet, I'm not a man to wait around for the facts. Now sit down. Let us drink to a much grander occasion."

Adam elected to stay on his feet. That way maybe he could shake off some of his anxiety. In full view of the monitor he watched in horror as President Kirkpatrick shook hands with a departing cabinet member before turning to pick up one of several telephones ringing at his desk.

Panach muted the voice stream that came over the speakers. "Just old fashion American technology put to progressive use."

"You're not foolish ... you're scandalous! To be eavesdropping on the President of the United States!"

Being a fully entrenched opponent of cumbersome procedure, Panach cut loose one of his barrel laughs and directed his glare on Adam. "Sitting here before you is the most influential man on this continent, Mr. Harlow. Maybe the world. Do you think I hired you to putter around out here with low temperature hydrogenation, genetically altering organic combustibles? Horse shit. You're hardly the sort to be moon-shining ethanol in the middle of a protracted fuel shortage. No, Mr. Harlow, you're a much larger catch for whom I have a much bigger agenda."

"I told you once already, I'm not selling. There are plenty of rodents in Washington to do your bidding."

"One problem. No one alive on this planet knows quite what *you* do about a particular type of mineral synthetic. Believe me, we have our eyes on every engineer out there … and it turns out that *you* have the most to give back to industry, which under my direction will begin right here at Crimson. So, Mr. Harlow, it's time to get off your high horse and submit yourself to progress. Before it's too late. In the process, not only can I offer you unlimited wealth—a fair deal for a man days from pissing his life away in a gutter—but I can arrange full amnesty. After all, you *will* be scrutinized for jeopardizing government interests."

"Thanks! Life on a deserted island? Publicly scorned for selling the international community to Big Oil?" Adam inhaled and pursed his lips. "You can count me out."

Panach took the remarks as bravado and placed a crystal brandy snifter in front of Adam. He lifted his own glass. "To a bright a future for you and America. A toast to sharing intelligence and technology."

With the mind to fling his glass across the room, Adam gathered his wits and lowered himself into the chair opposite Panach's mammoth desk. The simultaneous thrill and tension of battling such a powerful figure rushed into him in exponential bites. "I'm flattered by your interest in me but—" His words suddenly dissolved into thought. Sitting across from the pillar of energy, Adam was forced to confront everything he loathed about the industry. After scoffing at Chamberlain for caving in to a profit-driven agenda over long-term stability and integrity, he questioned if he too had abandoned his own principles.

Panach shifted the weight of his upper half over crossed knuckles. "You want double what you're worth, is that it?"

Adam lowered his volume to drive home his message. "You'll just have to accept my resignation."

"Desperate problems demand desperate solutions," Panach replied, ignoring Adam's resolve to bow out. Instead he pointed at the Wall Street tick. "I can't tell you how pitiful … how ugly the markets are. Or how many of our banks have collapsed in the past two years. However, I *can* deal you in on an important development in this brutal world."

The air grew tense around him and Adam felt his tongue dry out the way it did the first time he met Panach. He braced himself for trouble. A major scandal. Something horrible that hung heavy in the room. A force that was potent enough to rip him apart inside.

"What could be uglier than to betray those who trusted me at NASA … my people … my honor? What can be more putrid than caving in to greed and conspiracy?"

Panach swooped down on him with vengeance. "How about that cute little China doll you had working for you in Seattle?"

Adam struggled to hide the worst of his fears. "She has nothing to offer you. Nothing to advance your dirty dealing."

"One itty biddy detail, Mr. Harlow. She has *you* … now doesn't she?"

"My use for her services expired the day I left town," Adam countered. He was betting on a small bluff that he hoped would divert some of Panach's deranged thinking.

"You'll pay the Devil to keep her safe, Mr. Harlow … because I just put her life up for sale. And bidding between two key rivals has skyrocketed in scarcely two hours. Only one person can halt the sale of Miss Song."

"How's that?"

"By fully cooperating, right here at Crimson."

Adam gasped for oxygen. The little energy left in him drained suddenly into his shoes. Panach's words squeezed him with a stranglehold.

"Now I've got your attention," he laughed like a mad ogre, scooping a document off his desk. "Montech Corporation, a longtime thorn in my side, wants her. I wonder why, Mr. Harlow. Besides her pretty face, what is it they find so precious about Miss Song? Perhaps it's because she knows the coding for obtaining classified state secrets—data the government fears it will lose control of if shared with private industry. Perhaps they can double their investment by demanding her ransom from Beijing. After all, they claim to be holding her father, a high-level diplomat laden with

156

incriminating secrets of his own while seeking asylum in the United States."

Adam thought it over for a moment. Everything Panach said was completely plausible. This may explain why Moi hadn't returned his calls. Adam was instantly curious about Moi's father and his role in the conspiracy to procure Adam's cooperation. On the other hand, it may be a pack of distorted lies.

"I don't see anything unusual about a Chinese official knowing a few things and then abandoning his Red Party. Thousands of others have done it."

Panach was quick to deliver the goods. "To escape a dangerous plot by a Shanghai-based energy cartel determined to nix China's partnership with Washington—an international pact that threatens to overshadow Asian black market oil interests?"

"So here you are, hiding in Ethanol Land holding the ingredients to control world markets ... with absolutely no accountability."

Panach let go of one of his barrel laughs. "You should have gone into tabloid journalism. There's a big market out there for such rubbish."

Adam sat riveted. His chest heaved. Nausea flooded him. While Moi's efforts could have paid him and NASA generous dividends, he had placed her in grave danger. Essentially, she had helped him and Gamil work a miracle. Now she sat helplessly waiting for her life to be auctioned off to the highest bidder, prepared to extract what they need before leaving her to the dead.

Panach let silence take command. With impeccable timing he laid out his offer bidding for Adam's cooperation, Admiral to prevent Moi from falling into competitor's hands. But there were no doubts that when Panach no longer needed her as bait to perfect *Aqualene*'s manufacturing operations, Moi would suffer either way.

"You won't accomplish much by dragging the girl into this," Adam snarled. He wasn't going to throw up his hands. Not yet. Moi knew little or nothing of the formula's design. She had simply written a program that had conceived it before

157

getting caught in the middle of a deadly crossfire. "And if neither of us talk?"

"Is that a threat or a foolish promise?" The confidence in Panach's tone indicated he had no intention of arguing over petty intercessions.

Adam decided to turn his energies to a logical debate. "I don't believe you can operate under the radar long enough to accomplish your ends," he said flatly. "At least not on American soil."

"That is where you're wrong, Mr. Harlow. The feds don't have a fool's clue to what we're really doing out here. Only that we are the *flagship* of ethanol producers in America—the only fortress this nation has against total economic ruin."

Again his words contained much truth. The man had done his homework in joining the dots. Admiral possessed enough of the plans to erect 95% of the manufacturing plant. And—by the greed of the devil—had gained possession of some portion of the minerals needed to begin producing the potent formula. By the same miracle, Panach harnessed the power and wealth to sweep the media clean out of his way.

Why hadn't there been news of the theft aired on TV news briefs he'd seen while watching pro basketball during dinner with the guards downstairs. Could Admiral really pull off a scandal of this proportion ... and without Adam's full technical disclosure?

Panach poured himself another brandy and knocked it back with a satisfied gulp. "Think of us as interdependent powers," he urged. "You want the girl back safely. I want to begin producing *Aqualene* at my earliest date. A level-headed fair trade if you ask any prudent businessman."

By now Adam saw no way of factoring Moi out of this deadly equation. He decided to approach Panach from a different angle. "Since I failed to show up in Pasadena, what's to keep NASA officials from snooping around out here for me...not to mention their tidy little mineral investment?"

Panach motored back his chair and fired up a fresh cigar. He drew in a generous lungful. "Don't confuse yourself," Panach advised. "NASA no longer holds any record of Adam

158

T. Harlow, born October 6, 1989, in Rapid City, North Dakota."

Adam drew in a breath and released it slowly. He thought about the events leading up to his boarding the aircraft at Seattle-Tacoma. "Before flying to LA, I messaged NASA's research pool. The out-sourcing office was expecting me to show on Monday."

"You would have received a personal reply confirming your arrival and a dispatched transport to get you from the airport," Panach grunted. "Standard procedure under today's security protocols."

Haunted by his recollection of an automated reply stating there was a problem with Adam's login name, a strangling knot grew in his throat. He had assumed the minor glitch would be easily resolved upon his arrival at the labs. Hadn't Ms. DeLong briefed him on the agency's email protocols? Still, NASA's lack of transportation arrangements at the airport seemed to validate Panach's position.

America's oil baron cradled an electronic calendar in his palms.

"We erased your name from all records linked to the federal registry four days ago. That means you were never born, leaving you completely at my disposal."

Adam labored to assemble some logic, angling back to his informal pact with NASA. Delong would have some independent record of him. Wouldn't she? Panach was blowing neat little rings of smoke with a pompous gleam in his eyes.

"Still planning to jump ship, Mr. Harlow?"

"I was never on board," Adam growled back at him through clenched teeth.

Panach's chair was buzzing. Wheeling alongside the desk, it tilted forward, low enough for the man's loafers to meet the floor. He puffed a cloud of rich brown smoke from his cigar and smiled across to Burke who had slipped unseen into the room. Panach's words rolled out snappy and crisp with a hint of impatience. He'd been hoping for a different turn of events. "Inform Montech that our deal is off. Dispose of the girl. I'll pay for the funeral."

Adam gasped for another breath. Morally strangled by Panach's insidious orders, he grappled with his fears as he got to his feet, twisting around toward the sofa to see if Burke was really going to expedite the command.

Burke sat cross-legged and grinning as he picked up the office extension from an end table. He waited for Adam's eyes before pressing a single button. Across the room the dial tone resonated from the speaker.

"Wait!" Adam begged. "Okay, okay, dammit! I'll do it. I'll cooperate. You can finish your fucking plant."

Burke intercepted a faint nod from Panach. Slowly he set down the receiver.

Panach was smiling again. "I'm happy to see good sense prevails. Perhaps Mr. Burke will be kind enough to make the necessary arrangements for you to speak with the girl ... after we've seen material progress out here at Crimson."

"Then what?" Adam growled.

"They say living gets easier when you're in love, Mr. Harlow. I could never put that kind of trust in a woman. But if you can, you'd better get everything right. I'm giving you *three* days to make Crimson fully operational so we can begin producing *Aqualene*."

Adam's chest pounded. He pulled himself up straight, his eyes locked with his most hated adversary. "First I need your personal guarantee. Promise me she will be set free ... and that I will see her safe again."

Panach was grinning. "Given that you are successful, I'll take into account the caveat of complete cooperation."

Later that day, Burke prepared a presentation to be projected onto a pull-down screen inside the new plant where Admiral would begin manufacturing *Aqualene*. He handed a pointer to Adam. "Needless to say, you'd be wise to elaborate on a few items."

A voice cut in behind them. "I'm looking for clean facts and clear details, Mr. Harlow. You lied about your degree, but that doesn't disqualify you from making me a wealthier man."

Panach had positioned his wheelchair just inside a huge rollup door that was lowered to block out daylight. He rolled himself closer and dimmed the lights from a control on his

160

armrest. The room lit up in a full spectrum of color. The presentation Adam had prepared and finalized on Moi's laptop appeared on the wall and began initiating a demo sequence.

Considering this to be his last line of defense, Adam reluctantly began his lecture. He described how three chief elements make up the target substance, including one that was to be carefully extracted from a low-level, radioactive mineral before producing the correct catalytic compound. His mind searched for every possible way to avoid critical details and soon found himself rambling on with generalities.

Panach rapped a hand on the top of his briefcase.

"This isn't Chemistry 101, Mr. Harlow. Get on with the presentation."

Adam pointed the laser device at the screen again, then launched into how three key minerals would be crushed, heated and vulcanized before entering their condensing stages. He began to take on a new tact in hopes of gaining an upper hand during the plant's construction phase by saturating the presentation with lavish technical terms, steeped in self-invented calculus. It was a gamble, but unless Admiral's geophysicists had specific knowledge of *Aqualene*'s mineral properties, they would have to rely heavily on Adam for the next three days.

"One important detail," Adam warned the salaried engineers carrying miniature laptops. "Contrary to standard fractioning, we're dealing with a slightly lower temperature range. However, operating under a closed roof could offset our specifications and generate an unyielding thermal factor. Therefore an adequate cooling apparatus for the primary condensers will be necessary. An external gravity tower should meet capacity demands."

Privately, Adam reasoned such a structure would extend the time on the project and increase his chances of getting picked up on aerial surveillance.

Burke took the recommendations seriously and now wore a puzzled look on his face as he poked the requirements out on his tablet. Panach's voice trumpeted across the plant. "No tower, Mr. Harlow. The river directly behind that wall will serve as our cooling agent. Mr. Burke will fly in a team of our own outfitters tonight and see that they install the system within twenty-four hours. That concludes today's presentation."

Burke peered at his organizer after hustling the engineers back to their work areas.

As Bates had indicated, his crew had hard-wired the plant for specialized machinery that was arriving around the clock from three different continents. Packages of sophisticated hardware for grinding and separating the minerals waited on pallets. Adam studied the furnace design and read its specifications carefully. It was time to make the necessary calculations and begin the assembly process.

Panach insisted on meeting with Adam each morning to go over the day's goals. To get the plant up and running in 72 hours meant setting an arduous schedule. Adam was now in charge of overseeing the entire production with absolutely no margin for errors.

Moi's life depended on it.

The first full day at the plant passed with hardly a moment to slip under the radar. Adam found himself thoroughly observed and scrutinized in all technical matters. The details outlining the government's version of *Aqualene*—procured by someone with adequate clearance and a palate for espionage—had given Admiral's engineering team a backup to Adam's documented work. As it turned out, some of his assigned subordinates behaved more like agents of verification, consuming much of his mental energy as he carefully considered his next step.

The next day ended in exhaustion, so much that Adam hardly ate dinner. Afterwards, Burke showed up at the chateau wearing a smug grin that did nothing to improve the cosmetic impact of the scar running down his face.

"You've earned some telephone time," he announced.

"I'll call my lawyer," Adam grunted under his breath.

"No, I was referring to the girl, lover boy."

"I wouldn't believe it if you told me she was still alive," Adam remarked with diminishing hopes of speaking to Moi privately.

"I'll give you one minute to find out." Burke's sneer approached the likes of a challenge instead of an invitation. "Privileges from the boss upstairs."

"Tell him I'm grateful," Adam said, doing a poor job of hiding his rising anticipation to hear Moi's voice again. He began crafting a fast-paced agenda and chided himself for never learning a little Mandarin. One stinkin' minute on the phone would hardly determine the playing field, nor would it be time to express a deepening regret for drawing her into this mess.

At a desk inside a small office near a guard post on the first floor of the chateau Adam watched him punch a speed dial button and then let one hand rest over the phone, prepared to cut the connection at will. Through a desk-mounted speaker, Moi identified herself and greeted Adam slowly. The pace of her words and a sluggish intonation suggested she was ill or under the influence of sedatives. Conversation was painfully awkward. Aside from a subtle attitude he recognized in her voice, Moi's headstrong character was completely absent. Clearly she was exhausted.

Fearful of losing valuable seconds, Adam took charge of the conversation. "Nice accommodations," he offered. Then an idea grew into action. "The company's got all the amenities of a haunted wonderland; freshly catered meals ... and the view of Robinson's loft from the Swiss—"

Suddenly Burke's face wrinkled with suspicion. "Time's up, pal."

His finger jabbed at the switch and cut the line.

Eighteen

Wednesday, President Kirkpatrick and his Chinese delegation touched down on a military airstrip inside the Lukefield Air Force Base in western Nevada.

The tour's purpose was to allow financiers of the project to view the minerals returned aboard two lunar mining probes nine months earlier.

A regiment of Marines in combat gear patrolled the perimeter of the logistics center where the cargo had arrived less than twenty-four hours earlier. AWAX equipped aircraft circled the base's perimeter in search of unauthorized aircraft within a fifty-mile radius. Sharpshooters held positions on rooftops and radar towers. Each combed the surrounding terrain through field glasses. Surveillance crews peered at closed circuit camera links. Inside the confines of the base during the formal luncheon, the president ordered the auditorium lights to be dimmed. A hush fell over the delegation as a painted fog of high-resolution graphics simulating *Aqualene*'s production sequence commenced in spectacular holography.

"Today you will witness marked progress in reconstructing many portions of the Aqualene formula," streamed a narrator's voice from the speakers. "In the coming weeks we hope to recover more of the lost data, and put what you are about to see in this presentation into full production around the world."

Impressive statistics about the fuel's promising qualities preceded synchronized animations of the plant's machinery, operating in the airspace above their tinted faces. Computer-enhanced images took the viewers on a dramatic journey along with the minerals through the inside of condensers and heat exchangers until simultaneous chemical reactions delivered a steady flow of blue liquid that dribbled out into a chemist's beaker. Moving on to a model of a huge basin of seawater, massive quantities of *Aqualene* were pumped into underground tanks and reservoirs.

The production ended with high profile clips describing how conveniently the fuel could be distributed and stored, the same way gasoline had been for decades. Upbeat music augmented shots of an American family casually driving away from a filling station in an emissions-free family car powered by *Aqualene*. Sign prices above the pumps advertised a fraction of the day's gasoline prices.

Dignitaries, their advisors, and interpreters looked eager to catch a glimpse of the minerals for which their governments had secretly spent billions to excavate from the moon. Outside the visitor's center, NASA officials scurried around and poked at electronic itineraries. The president's aides led the delegation toward the research complex where the ribbon-cutting ceremony was to take place. Mr. Kirkpatrick made a short speech about the unyielding stamina of the Vashon crew and how they had given their lives to deliver the world from the bondage of petroleum. With the snap of scissors, the shiny green band—a symbol of *Aqualene*'s clean answer to the energy crisis—sprang back and fell to the floor. The alliance members applauded and proceeded across the polished floor, admiring the chrome plumbing that snaked to and from large vats and boilers. Three massive hoppers of steel towered over state-of-the-art control panels, equipped with glowing plasma screens and video monitors. NASA technicians stood proudly next to each new apparatus for photographs. Each took turns disseminating complex properties or clarifying figures in response to questions raised by the delegation.

Realizing this agenda failed to hold their attention for long, Kirkpatrick picked up a wireless mic and announced the time had come to unveil the coalition's prize minerals. The rest was technical babble intended for scientists to transform into economic recovery.

Four Marines in full regalia stood at attention outside an adjacent hangar, the site housing three reinforced vaults. A formal sequence of shouts from a staff sergeant commanded the lockers be opened. All three doors swept open simultaneously like velvet curtains at a Broadway musical. A NASA spokesman stepped forward and invited the dignitaries to arrange themselves in a semi-circle, encompassing the spot where he wielded a large utility blade. Anticipating Kirkpatrick's nod, the spokesman made a long cut along the side of the carton. The audience hushed and adjusted their eyeglasses. All stared into the open vault. Someone mumbled nervously about being a part of history. Taking their cue from an officer standing to one side, two scientists walked into the circle and stripped away padded foam under the corrugated packaging.

Collectively, the delegation rested its gaze on the smooth gray surface of the quarry. Small stones appeared here and there in random formation. Kirkpatrick caught sight of the wavy lines, resembling wood grains streaking horizontally. Immediately he noticed puzzlement fall over the lead technician's face. He stepped in for a closer look, running a white-gloved finger over the cargo. He struggled to suppress a gasp the moment his finger arrived at the protruding edge of a timber knot. Privately he appeared to scrutinize the authenticity of this shipment. Enduring awkward seconds with members of his team he ruled the cargo couldn't possibly be shrouded in cement for any legitimate purpose.

A murmur of whispers escalated into babble among the guests. Shen Zhang was the first to display speculation. He had been watching the technicians and now turned to report his inferences to the others.

At Kirkpatrick's requested, a second NASA scientist stepped in to analyze the cargo, wielding a sharp instrument. A calculated sniff jolted her, but she was too late to compose herself. Something had gone terribly wrong. Despite the delegation's lack of technical savvy, there was no use in covering up the inevitable truth.

Sporadic mumbling erupted into heated chatter. Meanwhile, Kirkpatrick pulled the chief spokesman to the outside edge of the lockers. "Okay, this prank is getting stale. Where are the minerals?"

NASA's man swallowed hard. He turned a darker shade of red and his eyes flashed with anxiety. "This is it, sir. The same load we hoisted off the semi, only two days ago!"

Kirkpatrick took a breath. "Open the other cartons."

The spokesman shook his head. "We could have a look, but—"

Kirkpatrick turned to address his delegates. "Ladies and gentlemen, I'm positive we'll find everything in order. Now, if all of you would please step this way."

As the delegates shuffled on to the next locker, the German chancellor joked about the research facility being located too close to Hollywood. The humor of the Americans playing jokes of this sort was fitting. Soon the delegation was buzzing again, confident, eager.

Everyone watched for what looked like eternity as the same two representatives broke away the outer edges of the two remaining cartons. A chorus of gasps erupted. Both cartons contained the same identical dull gray mass. Without warning a team of scientists in bright yellow jumpsuits showed up and began pushing their way through the crowd. Carrying electronic equipment at their sides, each one stabbed at the gray substance with steel probes.

Seconds ticked into minutes. Collectively, the coalition was losing its patience. The German Chancellor—a longtime friend and close political ally to Washington—spoke up, directing his words toward the president and the delegation. "Quite possibly, could we be witnessing the results of a very sophisticated theft, Mr. President?"

Instantly this yielded some degree of consensus among the others. Zhang added his own commentary, viewing the dilemma from a conversely opposing perspective. "Or has NASA and Washington orchestrated a genius cover-up? American-styled scandal?"

The threat of running out to the media at the front gates with a full story boiled over when the Chinese began demanding Kirkpatrick's immediate explanation. Despite a heavy accent, Zhang spoke poignantly.

"We have bankrupted our treasuries in vain to fund your Vashon space mission, only to learn its crew is dead ... and our share of the minerals is nothing more than household cement!"

NASA's chief spokesperson assigned to the coalition cut in before Kirkpatrick could utter his rebuttal.

"Let me assure you, ladies and gentlemen, that a simple explanation will come of this. Until then, not a word can be

167

spoken to the media. Such a leak would surely hinder an FBI investigation—one that shall begin at this very moment."

"Certainly there is some kind of mistake," Kirkpatrick added. "A simple mix-up that can urgently be resolved with unyielding resourcefulness."

By now, Zhang and his envoy had stepped away from the group, engaged in hyper-speed chatter in Chinese. Turning the delegation back over to the NASA chief, Kirkpatrick took the opportunity to duck into a staff sergeant's office where the clerk nervously connected him to the Pentagon.

Kirkpatrick's voice quivered in frantic whispers. "What in the name of Christ is going on out here at Lukefield?" he growled. "In the presence of our esteemed allies, we have unveiled nothing, I repeat nothing but concrete!"

Kirkpatrick paused as he waited for an explanation. The line was silent. No answers. Then he lost his temper. "We've got an international crisis on our hands!" *Pause.* "No." *Pause.* "Of course it is. We'd better inform Central Intelligence, and get the FBI on this, pronto. We'll initiate an internal naval investigation and start tracking those minerals all the way back to Johnston Island." *Pause.* "That's right. And keep my aides informed of every detail, around the clock."

Kirkpatrick slammed down the receiver and furiously stormed out of the office. A gaggle of Marine colonels were poking at their androids when the president gathered his composure and approached in a nervous trot to the opened lockers. "Lukefield must be searched from end to end," he commanded. The officers nodded obediently and entered their notes. "That cargo didn't just vanish into thin air. It's either been misplaced or stolen. Fax the Oval Office a detailed report of the delivery from Lemoore Naval Station, by 6:00pm today."

Kirkpatrick drew a breath and faced his delegation. The limo drivers had pulled up and quickly ushered everyone in through rear doors. Inside the lead car, Kirkpatrick's voice cracked as he promised that federal agents would get to the bottom of things."

Still, he felt heavy with nausea, knowing his words meant nothing without the minerals. The dreaded but necessary task of sitting face to face with the Chinese delegates had arrived. A spirited forum on the mineral crisis was likely to come down to a string of diplomatic resolutions—demands Washington was unprepared to meet.

The chauffeurs sped to the airstrip, past the gates where cameras clicked. Zhang broke from a huddle with his interpreter and addressed Kirkpatrick directly. Aides on both sides furiously took notes.

"You expect my parliament to hold on to empty faith? Pledge our complete trust in America?" he shouted in broken English. "Without the endorsement the party and its people, our finance ministry wired billions into your space program ... then lost one of our best astronauts!"

Kirkpatrick drew a lengthy sigh. A mounting urge to crumble joined rising pains in his chest as he swallowed against the knot in his throat, nodding in despondent silence and double-checking his demeanor against the mood of the partnership's most vested member. He spoke in a humble tone, "Washington is forever grateful to China's contribution to this project. I speak for a nation when I say we deeply regret this tragedy."

Unmoved, Mr. Zhang began speaking through his interpreter again. The tone of the conversation hinted at a de facto ultimatum China would likely impose against the United States. After heated debate among the Chinese delegates, one of the interpreters leaned forward nervously. "Our government will decide on a period of days within which time Washington must verify full recovery of the minerals. Failure to account for China's share of the cargo will constitute a breach of obligation, according to the by-laws of this pact. Beijing's highest command will be notified of these unfortunate circumstances upon our return. Regretfully, China will be forced to consider military action should Washington fail to comply."

Kirkpatrick listened with astonishment. The words of the Chinese envoy threatened to drive a wedge through the partnership, and into future economic relations with the Asian giant.

The FBI had nothing material to offer the president that evening, and by early the next morning, the White House staff was humming in chaos. Upon returning to Beijing, Zhang had formalized China's resolve to hold Kirkpatrick accountable. The official communiqué offered Washington seventy-two hours to recover the minerals. In strongly worded text, the Premier of China asserted that complete and immediate repayment of Communist Party assets toward the Vashon Project be considered a prudent alternative to a military blockade against the United States and its naval bases defending oil shipments from intact alliances still operating in the Middle East.

Nineteen

By Adam's third night at Crimson, plant assembly operations had progressed reasonably well, allowing him to make a number of mental notes about the manufacturing process.

These he deemed useful to NASA, should he ever make it out of Crimson alive. Meanwhile, he had harvested new suspicions about the magnitude of Admiral's exploits.

From the first time he set eyes on his spartan quarters, he believed Burke and his henchmen were spying on him through some optical device. As a precaution, Adam had left the single lamp turned off while reentering the room each night after dinner. He theorized the company kept tabs on him through the digital readout on his dresser's clock. Its glowing numbers modulated for several seconds, then held steady. In a cyclic loop, Adam speculated, the device—cabled into the wall behind the dresser—was taking infrared shots in real-time photography, for intervals of nine seconds. In almost complete darkness, he had counted a 23-second period that lapsed before the next photo cycle began. From his bed he watched the pattern repeat itself each night before falling asleep.

Nightly he listened to a broadcast out of Fresno over a crude radio set strung together with eight-foot strands of small-gauge wire he had sneaked out of the plant. The geological specimen he'd found on the grounds contained a trace of galena—an ideal mineral for converting radio signals into minute electric audio signals that could be heard through his cheap pair of earphones Burke had mockingly tossed back at him after confiscating his cell phone the first day at work. Adam had perfected the crystal radio in the early morning hours following the unexplained rumble of heavy equipment that awakened him for three consecutive nights.

During tonight's broadcast of a basketball game in San Antonio, Adam stretched across the bed and studied the faint outline of the window above him. Counting through the clock's nine-second shoot before jumping to his feet on the mattress, he stood at chest level with the window frame.

Carefully he lifted the shade away from the glass and ran a fingertip along the perimeter of the sill. Lighting along the walkways leading to the processing plant dimly illuminated the ledge outside his window.

With six seconds to spare before the photo cycle would begin again, Adam fingered the tiny latch, rotated it, and bumped the window open. He was surprised to find the slider had not been bolted into place, causing him to debate whether it was a trap or a security oversight.

Burke was the type to provoke his opponents into undertaking costly risks.

Adam dropped back on the bed. A cold evening breeze whispered past the darkened laurel bushes outside. The night air soon cooled the beads of sweat running off his hairline as he gathered the blanket over him in mock sleep.

Evening security was making its rounds in larger numbers while the last engineers exited the plant. He would wait until after midnight when the skeleton nightshift took over. Adam reviewed his plans over again in his mind. His clothes and jacket hung on the chair, ready when the time came to move. The radio announcer chattered in his ear about a San Antonio win over the Trailblazers in overtime.

Soon Adam's eyes pinched into slits. An overwhelming temptation to sleep fell over him. He had eaten very little of the catered chipped beef and mashed potatoes the guards were devouring at the table earlier that evening. Now his stomach stabbed at him for sustenance.

The clock's LED cycled for several minutes. Adam detected a subtle change in the air. It was just after midnight when he heard the faint rumble of the diesel motor stirring across the compound. He listened closely and could identify the machinery being used on the compound. Its distance suggested activities near the courtyard's patio to match those he'd heard before. The radio program soon changed to music. A viola and a string bass took turns soloing through a popular jazz standard he'd heard a hundred times in his college dorm.

With the phones still in his ears, Adam took his cue from the clock's rest interval and climbed off the bed. Counting softly to himself, he slipped into his jeans and jacket. He pulled on a pair of sneakers he kept in his overnight bag for hands-on mechanical jobs. Seconds before time ran out he slipped under the covers for the nine second count. Again, Adam sprung to his feet and gripped the window shades to peer outside. The compound was clear. He'd prepared to pull out the phones and shinny up the wall when a woman's voice interrupted the music with a late-night news bulletin:

The White House is under fire for attempting to cover up a pending ultimatum from Beijing. The document, received late yesterday, demands the United States recover an undisclosed shipment of classified cargo, half of which is said to belong to the Chinese. The dispute between Washington and Beijing has resulted in the threat of economic, and possible military sanctions. At this point, details of the rift are still unclear. However, Pentagon sources confirm the presence of a blockade against American oil tankers in the Indian Ocean. Stay tuned for additional updates.

Adam was out of breath when he hit the mattress. The threat of a military confrontation with Beijing sent chills through him as he pondered what Kirkpatrick's administration had done to inflame the Chinese.

Following a string of late-night advertisements, the announcer's voice returned with instructions for tuning into the emergency-broadcasting system. The music was playing again. Adam rose to his feet and stared down at the window track. Light from a distant lamp across the compound glinted off a tiny white cord along the window frame's grooves. He held his breath while his heart thundered beneath his chin.

He should have suspected it. The frame was wired.

Referencing his limited knowledge of security devices, he tried to imagine what kind of switch would be used to monitor the slider. Most likely it was a trip switch, the kind that opened a circuit, and set off a lighted beacon or an alarm in a remote location. The goons inside the chateau would be alerted first ... if they hadn't been already.

It was a chance Adam had to take.

He rummaged through his pockets and found the receipt he got while buying a new polo shirt at the airport in Seattle. Dropping back down on the mattress again, he was counting as his hand worked inside the pocket to wad up the paper. Seconds later he was back on his feet, sliding the window along its track. Carefully Adam watched for the switch to appear. One inch, then two. No trip switch. He coaxed the window out further. Almost four inches brought something into view. Mounted beneath the frame's tracks, the flat spring-loaded lever pressed up against the window frame, armed and ready to be tripped.

Adam fingered the contacts and carefully wedged the paper wad down in between the frame's tracks and the lever. It wouldn't hold for long, he reasoned, dropping back down on the bed a final time. The next twenty-three seconds of liberty came. Adam jumped to his feet and stuffed the bed with his extra travel clothes before climbing through the window.

Behind him he drew the plastic shades and sat unseen on the cement ledge outside the window above two laurel bushes brushing up against the building. Instantly his attention turned to the hydraulic lift grunting and whining into view from his right. At fifty yards, Adam watched the driver maneuver the vehicle up the path from a secured storage shed. Over its steel forks rode a large utility box, bumping along toward the patio to his left.

Admiral's boys were up to something a lot more important than late-night landscaping.

*****

Eleven hours after Lieutenant Colonel Brigham arrived at the Mojave Space Center, he completed pre-flight briefing, slept for six hours, and prepared to board a five-man privately manufactured shuttlecraft known as Apex. The assignment: *Return with Colonel Striker and two detainees for questioning.*

The spacecraft was on loan to NASA after technicians ruled out timely preparations for launching the American space agency's only available Europa vehicle. Brigham, a British trained astronaut under a special commission with the European Space Agency, was among the few astronauts qualified to solo in the Apex cockpit. After negotiations with NASA he had agreed to the half-day mission, provided a three-way service link be established between ground communications and a flight engineer working for Apex's manufacturer in Houston. This provided Brigham a reasonable degree of technical support. At the same time, piloting the mission on his own would prove to Orbital's executives that the company's new cost-cutting program—an essential factor for expanding tourist-based launches—was a considerable success.

Shortly after dawn, Brigham piloted the forty-two ton spacecraft down the runway. Its nose rising toward the heavens, the seventeen-minute burn over the Pacific pushed Apex into its first layer of inner space. A secondary burn swung the craft into an orbit of 237 vertical miles, aligning Brigham on an orbital path with ISS.

From an economic standpoint, Apex closely resembled NASA's Europa vehicles in design, range, and takeoff configurations. It could handle most cargo jobs, and easily serviced personnel rotations to the space station. Both enjoyed hypersonic velocities at low altitudes, eliminating the need for vertical takeoffs. Ultimately, it was Apex's short turn-around time in maintenance—ideal for last minute trips to ISS—that made it a viable candidate for Brigham's mission.

Docking maneuvers occurred within an hour of takeoff, over the dark side of Earth. Once automated system checks were completed, the airlocks engaged and Brigham crawled through the standard portal that linked Apex to the space station.

The lieutenant colonel's face was a welcome sight to Skip Halverson and his crew. Brigham was a man who generally did things by the book, and was an ace with legal and military protocols. He was a pragmatic man who performed his duties objectively. In his judgment, difficult people were minor obstacles along the course of required duty. Minutes before leaving Mojave, he had carefully reviewed Striker's performance file. He noted the colonel's disillusionment with internal Pentagon policy after receiving reprimands for citing his superiors as blatantly tolerant of laissez-faire security procedures for the sake of weighted human rights doctrines. Brigham expected a chilly reception from Colonel Striker and

175

therefore expected to stay less than two hours aboard the station—enough time to carry out his assignment efficiently.

Striker had locked himself in his private cabin when Brigham showed up at the airlock and identified himself over an intercom system the crew used during docking. After an awkward delay, the airlock opened and Colonel Striker stepped out. The two saluted one another. Brigham wasted no time getting down to business about the two detainees. Colonel Striker, confident and eager to point out his edge in the case, escorted Brigham to Heinrich's cabin.

"Step into my brig, Lieutenant," Striker chuckled with a grin. "I think you'll be quite satisfied with the two packages I've wrapped up for you."

Brigham ignored the remarks and entered the cabin. He glanced down at Greg and then Heinrich, each white-faced and lifeless in their sealed bunks.

"Get these two ready for reentry," Brigham ordered. "We'll be pulling out in less than ninety minutes. You'll need to pack your bags, just the same, Colonel."

"Pack my what?" Striker was incredulous.

"Your personal belongings, sir. The Pentagon is pulling you off this post."

Striker paused. "And who in the name of security will man this surveillance post?"

"An automated service link will suffice until NASA can deploy your replacement. Now, Colonel, deactivate suspended sleep."

Brigham's British tongue had begun to visibly grate on Striker's Yankee sentiments. A bullish impulse compelled him to question the order for security reasons. "You're barely more than a lieutenant," Striker retorted. "What gives you the jurisdiction if not the authority to pull me off this post?"

Brigham reached into his breast pocket and pulled out a printed document. Carefully he unfolded it. "It hardly matters if I donned the colors of a corporal, sir. NASA demands your presence. A board of inquiry is set to convene late this afternoon."

Striker gave a snort and turned a cold glare on Brigham, snatching the summons to scan its pages. "Kind of strange,

Lieutenant, I see no mention of a Pentagon directive relieving me of my post."

"You are in international domain, sir. You'll have to file that appeal downstairs at the Mojave Space Center. These are NASA orders. They've cleared matters with your superiors in Washington."

Striker's eyes flashed with insubordination, but he pursed his lips and relented.

"You wait, Lieutenant, I've got a solid case against these two—breaking and entering, in the first degree. I'll see that both get jail time."

"Perhaps so, Colonel." Brigham met Striker's defensive sneer with a smile while his tone expressed calculated doubt. "That one is for the board to ascertain."

Growing more indignant, Striker shouldered up against Heinrich's bunk. He let go a mouthful of air and began poking at the keypad. "Any trouble from these two, it'll be on your watch, Lieutenant."

Brigham ignored the colonel's rants and waited for the readout to indicate the release of a waking stimulant. He watched Striker execute the same commands at Greg's bunk.

"If you will, Colonel, have these two reoriented and ready to board Apex in one hour."

*****

Eastward, toward the south wall of the chateau, the machine lumbered slowly as it seemed to take forever crossing the compound before stopping at the patio.

Adam surveyed the work party. Burke was operating the machine while two guards followed him on foot. A quick scan of the rooflines produced no guard units visible to the eye.

After streaking silently from the dormitory across the lawn, Adam paused behind a pickup truck. He was only fifty yards or so from the supply sheds where Burke and his men had loaded the stones. Upon reaching the patio, the pair of guards worked rapidly as if vital minutes were running out inside the ominous company hourglass.

177

The offloading process began immediately with the first guard pulling a large stone cube out of the box. He grunted audibly and grappled with a cube at waist level before passing it to the second guard. The high density of the material clearly exceeded ordinary stone. The second man carried each stone into an opening on the patio and disappeared below the surface. Beyond the pathway lighting Adam recognized the area; one day before he'd seen narrow cuts across the patio. Suddenly that piece began to make sense. Beneath the brickwork was a storage vault.

The guard reappeared a moment later for another cube. The off-loading process continued for several minutes until the box on the lift was empty and the two guards followed Burke again toward the sheds.

Seeing the chance to move closer, Adam rapidly estimated the number of stone cubes they would be loading before returning along the walkway. He based his calculations on the time it took to unload, coming up with four minutes. It was necessary to add an extra thirty seconds for the machine to turn around and approach the open vault.

Soon the two workers entered the shed. Adam detected no other guards in the area and bolted for the patio. Dropping to his hands and knees, he peered down into the two-by-six-foot hole. A single light bulb hung from the ceiling, which dimly lit an earthen floor below. He smelled old wine casks through the open hatch. Beneath him was a narrow cement staircase that dropped steeply, about seven feet. Crouching over the hole, Adam positioned his feet on the first step and worked his way down until he was standing eye level with the patio's brickwork. A glance toward the shed confirmed Burke was still in charge. His arms flailed around his head the way they always did when he was demanding a task to be done in a hurry.

Adam gasped at his own carelessness. He could feel adrenaline surging through him, much of it a product of fear transforming into a fight or flight state of mind. He'd overlooked the possibility of a third man, unseen below him in the vault, waiting for the next load of mineral cubes. Adam dropped his head down past the brickwork and listened for

178

signs of movement. Nothing. Only the loader's engine thumping from the sheds, he estimated at forty or fifty yards.

Adam eased himself down the lower steps and scanned the room for trouble. Nobody appeared in the musty darkness, lit only by the single bulb and the light of the moon filtering in through the open hatch. There, he feasted his eyes on stacks and more stacks of cubes. They were separated by gray tarpaulin partitions. Threads of light illuminated a band of speckles reflecting off one of the stacks.

Immediately, the iridescent hues of light caught Adam's attention. His eyes focused on the gray strands, occasioned by lines of deep blue, like a Montana sky. The moonlight slipped behind a cloud when his eyes finished analyzing the specimens—unlike any mineral he'd studied at university. These were unique indeed. They were more exacting than the minerals he had received from NASA, the ones he'd used to make a crude batch of *Aqualene* at Dell's place.

His wristwatch glowed in the dim light, cautioning him that he was running out of time. But his urge to go up top and disappear in the night was halted by another diversion—a circular hatchway inside the chamber, leading toward the main plant. He remembered the blue prints showing a labyrinth of connecting tunnels running underground. Burke had restricted discussion of the underground section, but had sent company engineers there to install the plant's cooling lines. Adam was standing inside one end of Crimson's underground tunnels. The patio above him served as a well, but not perfectly disguised access to the minerals Admiral would use to produce *Aqualene*.

On the front of the iron door was a wheel, the kind used to open an airtight hatch aboard a ship or submarine. The wheel was rusted in places and failed to budge when Adam tried it. According to his calculations, he had another minute—enough time to scratch for samples as proof of his find. Then he would climb out and run for the river.

While chipping off specimens from several cubes and jamming them into his coat pocket, Adam heard the rumbling of the loader again. The nearness of it plunged him into panic for the stairs. Carefully peering from the entrance, he watched

179

the bright lamps of the machine approaching him like a truck bearing down on a mouse over a dark mountain highway.

In the glare of the lights, Burke and his men were less than twenty yards down the path. Adam's chest pounded as he considered a roll-out-and-run strategy. But he quickly abandoned the scheme after sighting a large handgun holstered to Burke's hip. With the plant ready, and the minerals available in ample supply, Adam was no longer an asset for Admiral. His loyalty to NASA prohibited Panach from letting him out alive.

His panic was quickly conjoined with another terror-filled reality. From the vault's stairway, Adam stared at the line of dorm windows across the compound. All were dark except for the one he had crawled through minutes earlier. Admiral's surveillance goons would be on his trail in minutes.

From the edge of the hatch, Adam ducked low and squinted out toward the two guards walking alongside the loader. In seconds, the whites of their eyes were upon him. He scrambled below madly searching for cover. At the foot of the stairs the iron hatchway caught his eye again. But his desperate attempt to open the mechanism left him little hope. Instead of disappearing into the tunnels, he would have to blend in against the shadowy recesses of the chamber and stay put until the last cube was unloaded.

He could then sprint past the processing plant toward the river and scale a twelve-foot fence enclosing two electric cooling pumps. From there he would descend the rocky bank to the river, exiting the property in less than a minute. The strategy was quick and simple—an escape plan that would work … if he remained unseen.

From the darkest wall next to the iron door, Adam watched the handler appear on the steps with a heavy stone cube in his hands. With a string of primal grunts, he descended. His powerful arms hoisted the stone into place on the middle stack before he scaled the ladder and out through the open hatch. A moment later he returned, shoved one more cube into place, and ascended the stairs in a rush. Outside there were frantic whispers.

A low level commotion had begun.

Muffled shouting erupted over the patio and a parade of footsteps halted outside the opening. Burke began speaking to his men. Beneath them Adam listened and waited. Any moment he expected a flurry of Gestapo boot steps to pour into the vault and shoot him at close range. His chest pounded as he prepared for the worst. He'd never imagined a bloodied end to life. That was for soldiers and street gangs, not professional engineers, insulated from the perils of violent conflicts. But the voices suddenly disbursed. The loader's engine revved up again, and the subtle odor of combusted biodiesel wafted into the chamber. The light bulb hanging from the ceiling went dark.

Burke had probably ordered a full-scale lockdown with the search springing into high gear. Storage chores were clearly over when the overhead door appeared, swinging side to side over the entrance, and the boots of two guards jockeyed for footing around the hole as the men guided the cement lid down into its permanent resting spot.

Permanent. The mere thought of the word frightened Adam. Stale air closed in on him almost immediately, taking him to a higher level of panic than he'd known. And that sent him lunging up the stairs for the hatchway door.

Too late! The door hovered a final moment before thumping into place.

Adam was sealed in.

In a crush of darkness, he dug his hands into his pockets. Inside was a book of matches he'd picked up inside the lobby at the Power Building. As the little flame burned, Adam circled the chamber, searching its shadowy walls and corners for cracks; any evidence of ventilation. A way out. But the danger of burning up his oxygen compelled him to kill the hungry light.

Twenty

Despite the aviation pluses of dense air cloaking the Mojave basin, a plethora of sand storms churned over the desert floor, a condition that often put the best shuttle pilots through their paces during landing maneuvers.

A wicked convection had been brewing for hours, according to Brigham who had just navigated Apex through its fiery re-entry. Now, on a new front, weather conditions over the desert threatened to batter the spacecraft within moments of breaking through a thin layer of cirrus that typically insulated highflying aircraft from violent downdrafts.

However, the topic of weather conditions over the landing zone proved insubstantial against the human complications beginning to unravel aboard Apex.

Lieutenant Colonel Brigham had cleared the Pacific Coast and reported setting a due-east course over Mexico. The last of the ocean blue was out of sight when the mood shifted away from the lingering tensions of the crew's infernal ride, and onto an unexpected disaster in the cockpit. At the helm Brigham had just completed his final depressurization sequence. A private chat over his audio link with Heinrich—reclined and harnessed in the cabin's aft section—revealed changes in protocol regarding NASA's jurisdiction over foreign nationals working aboard ISS. The conversation was intended to offer a margin of comfort to the doctor despite Striker's pending charges against him. But that had deteriorated when Brigham complained of nausea and chest pain.

Now over the California Baja, the spacecraft banked hard and stripped more altitude in a northeast descent toward a mountainous ridge along the Rio Grande. Through a tentative audio connection Heinrich heard Brigham curse over pains in his chest. Abruptly the doctor glanced at his watch. Behind its sweeping secondhand he noted the altimeter's reading. Fifty-five thousand feet! It was too damn much airspace to shave off for an emergency landing in the sparsely populated Mexican valley below.

*****

Adjacent to Heinrich, in the aft section of the spacecraft, Greg adjusted his grip on the seat's handhold.

He had begun to feel the effects of acute dehydration, coupled with the horrendous G-forces he'd suffered once Apex had leapt out of orbit and slammed into Mother Earth's blistering atmosphere. Bracing for another violent wave of the dry heaves, his thumb hovered over the vacuum switch, tethered by one of many transparent rubber hoses running into the base of his helmet. Resisting the need to shift his body position for the ninth time in the collapsible jumpseat, Greg loosened his harness as much as Heinrich would allow.

Favoring his right shoulder, he could now maintain eye contact with Heinrich who was fully reclined between him and the starboard wall of the cabin. There, Striker was belted alongside a storage panel—a staggered configuration that put him slightly forward and right of Greg when facing the cockpit. Still silent—the result of an intolerance to menacing internal body pressures imposed on humans during re-entry—the colonel remained unconscious of the events about to occur along Apex's final approach.

"You gonna be okay?" the doctor inquired, his voice resonating inside Greg's helmet.

But he offered little more than a cough in reply. Greg had managed once and could manage again on his own, he decided. He busied himself in steadying his breathing in the midst of dealing with anger, melting into despair, over his failed role as intern aboard the station. His mind, still jangled from drugged sleep, had cleared enough for him to recall his inability to successfully contact Commander Rockwell. Adding to his anguish of losing Vashon was the incident of falling into Striker's trap. The consequences of letting three astronauts die while rummaging through sensitive data cut into him like a hot knife. "Look man," he grunted impulsively into the link, "I can't have any of this shit getting' in the news. It's gonna kill my mother."

183

There was an awkward space of silent in Greg's ear until Heinrich responded, "Look, young man, I've no doubt NASA will be too damn busy defending its own honor to hold a press conference on your behalf."

Dr. Mann's tone was icy and distant, sounding more like a lawyer than the scientist who'd orbited with Greg for several days. Where'd he come up with the nerve to stick the government's interest ahead of his, anyway? Greg's thoughts darted back on board ISS. Up there the crew had appreciated him for who he was, diligent and ambitious; treating him with a level of dignity and trust he was hard pressed to find back home. Now he felt stupid for playing along; for his timid, hushed behavior with the colonel. Why hadn't he taken action when the situation demanded action? For Greg's own indecisiveness, Brigham had ordered the crew to *refrain from contact*. Yeah, don't say nothin' to the beef, Greg had grumbled while shuffling off the platform like a sentenced con. Not even a thanks or a goodbye.

Humiliation only added to the rage that swiftly reached its boiling point.

"Damn all of you," Greg spat into his mic. "Call me a dumb ass for sucking up to this space business."

But Heinrich was above quarreling, like most intellectuals. Instead of ripping his head off for acting like a punk, the doctor was calm, humane … almost indifferent about it. "Don't bludgeon yourself," he crooned in his slow fatherly tone. "Plenty of others are ready to beat you down in this cruel world."

"Yes, I know. Some of them are disguised as friends aboard the fricken space station."

Heinrich lost his temper and went over the edge. "Dammit, kid, enough self-pity. We've all got to face a couple of bad crooks in the road. It's *me* they're going to grill over the fire, not some baby-faced high school kid. I'm the one who stands to lose everything … my career, a place in the professional community. Everything!"

Against the turbulence Greg strained to pull himself upright. "So, you do admit it's your—"

184

"Let it go!" Heinrich shot back. "We screwed up, you and me both. I'm sorry I ever—"

A sudden drop in altitude broke Heinrich's lecture into crackled static as the aisle lurched and the cabin twisted starboard. Greg stared forward while Heinrich toggled his link to the cockpit, opening a three-way audio connection. "Lieutenant, do you need assistance?"

Wrenching noises above the ceiling panels assured Apex of structural damage if Brigham didn't do something fast.

But he did not reply. Urgently, Heinrich repeated his question.

The link went dead silent until a violent wave of gasps exploded in Greg's ear. Heinrich's voice came on, rattling the earpiece in a crescendo of panic: "DO YOU NEED MY ASSISTANCE, LIEUTENANT?"

Their headsets squeaked with muffled gurgling sounds, followed by a string of shuddering gags. By now Apex had slumped into a deep starboard bank, twisting Greg harder against his belts toward the port wall. Heinrich's fingers fought to deflate his G-suit while he wrestled to release the chest belts at the same time.

"I should have recognized this earlier," he growled to himself. "The man's having a heart attack!"

Peering into the cockpit, Greg considered Heinrich's take on the situation. Sure enough, Brigham's legs were flopping around like a pair of hooked bass in the bottom of a rowboat, each foot randomly glancing off the lighted arrays. Next, everything Greg expected to happen did. The lieutenant's boot slammed against some important object in the cockpit, causing the cabin to shift and bellow. The floor creaked as it rotated before flipping to the port side. Outside Apex's engines whined and trembled. She began to drop like a rock. An odd sensation came over Greg. Weightlessness returned to the cabin, thrusting the unprepared doctor out of his recliner, and hurling him against the port wall. In a strangely suspended arc, his flailing body rebounded into a domed cavity directly above Greg.

"Throw me a tether," he shouted.

185

Greg yanked on one of three nylon-wrapped cables protruding from a spring-loaded reel attached to hidden sprockets between their seats. Struggling to grip the leader flopping about, Heinrich managed to secure it with a powerful hand and drew himself back down to the floor. Muscling his way down to a line of rubber grab loops running the length of the aisle, he pulled his sprawling legs toward the cockpit while ignoring the roar of environmental currents ripping past Apex's exterior skin. Inching closer toward the cockpit, Heinrich fought against the building G-forces, knowing how crucial it was to prevent his legs from flinging out from under him and colliding with a crosshatch of oxygen lines running sideways below the ceiling panels. His neck kinked inside his helmet to track Heinrich's progress, the doctor looked more like a mule on a string, with his back arching upward each time his feet slipped away to dangle into the air space at his heels. Hand-over-hand he grunted his way into the cockpit, maneuvering around to Brigham, now fully hunched over the master joystick.

Immediately the doctor's shout came over Greg's link. In a restless pant he explained that he was going to punch up a 32-degree heading and level out Apex at thirty-nine thousand feet. Greg ignored the details to watch him clutch the side of Brigham's jumpseat in a desperate effort to view the obstructed instruments. Whatever Heinrich did, worked. In seconds the craft began to level out. Clearly relieved, he spoke into the link, something about getting clearance into the Mojave, which, according to him, was about 280 miles from their present location. "Hold on back there," he said in staggered breaths, "while I get help on the ground."

Heinrich's fingers then danced over the controls on a panel that jutted out over his helmet. This, Greg estimated, had established the link to the flight control center because, with two hands on the master joystick, Heinrich began hollering into an external mic that snaked out from an array of computer screens under the front windshield.

"I've got a medical emergency," he repeated.

The radio crackled and a voice on the ground promptly acknowledged. The two exchanged some technical details about piloting Apex into the proper position for landing. Greg noticed there was a temporary sign-off. Now it was up to Heinrich to bring this mad kamikaze of a bird down without scattering their blood and bones all over the desert. The doctor's knowledge of flying—the little bit of cadet training he claimed to have received before leaving the Euro-Defense Ministry for a spot in atmospheric sciences—would have to get them home.

With Apex leveling out at his announced thirty-five thousand feet, Heinrich belted himself into the pilot's seat and summoned Greg over the helmet link. A parade of cuss words addressed to Striker was followed by a plea for help: "The lieutenant is on the brink of death, Colonel. I need your help."

Greg listened and waited for the colonel to respond. But he gave no reply over the link. Not a stir from him across the aisle. Nothing. Greg's eyes returned to Heinrich who was now narrating his moves, thinking aloud perhaps as he released the emergency rudder and switched the navigation mode to activate its use. One of his hands started moving it slightly, testing its response. Apex did so with a violent jerk, causing and the doctor's appeal for help to shift over to Greg.

"You'd better get yourself up here," he urged. "And make it fast or I'm going to lose Brigham, along with Apex."

By now most of Earth's gravity had returned to the cabin. Still, Greg was cautious as he released his harness and rolled onto the floor. "On my way," he coughed and began snaking his way forward in the same manner he'd seen Heinrich do it. The trip forward passed in seconds before Greg found himself inside the cockpit feeling ill. "Look man, I don't know much about dealing with a heart attack."

"C-P-R, Greg!" Heinrich insisted over the link. His tone had grown tense again, but this time Greg heard it differently. There was a charge of encouragement in the doctor's voice. "I watched you pass the procedure in Pre-Flight, Greg. And with good marks! I trust you."

Greg felt lost, hunched over the dying lieutenant. "It's the timing, I can't remember the—"

"Don't worry, I'll walk you through it."

Greg nodded and anchored himself on the opposite side of Brigham. Heinrich made an adjustment to the controls and then issued his first instruction. Greg followed it and loosened Brigham's harness, then rolled the lieutenant onto his back.

"Good. Now let's keep him from choking," Heinrich said. He then instructed Greg to turn the lieutenant's head to one side and wipe away a band of saliva sliding across Brigham's mouth. He had placed the heel of his hand on Brigham's chest to begin a forceful rhythm of heart massage when a violent down draft slammed into Apex.

Heinrich knuckled a wad of Greg's jumpsuit and glanced over the gauges. "We just lost four hundred meters," he reported, clutching the stick and banking hard to port. "Maybe we can slip out of the center of this convection zone."

As Heinrich eased off the throttles, Apex smoothed out and Greg got back to work.

"You got it, buddy. Press and hold...then release. Count to five and repeat," Heinrich sang over the howl of ice particles pounding the windshield. "At your next rest interval I want you to hang on to something tightly. I've got to chop us off some more altitude."

Nauseating seconds of rapid descent passed before Heinrich announced he was breaking into cirrus cloud layers, and with a little luck he'd swing Apex into the wind and begin his approach into the desert. "I've already put in for a clean bed and a hot meal for us down there."

Over the 3-way open link inside Greg's helmet, he listened as a female ground control officer took over the mic and began talking Heinrich down. He stared into Brigham's lifeless face. Despite the additional oxygen Heinrich was pumping into the lieutenant's helmet, and the steady work Greg had done for God knows how long, the man wasn't responding.

Heinrich exchanged final coordinates with ground operations and ordered Greg to return to his jumpseat in the aft section. "You've done all you can," he growled. "It's time to save ourselves...even if that includes Striker."

"Greg shook his head. "Give me more time."

"No good!" Heinrich shouted over the air convections buffeting the spacecraft. In a wild arc his hand gestured Greg back to the jumpseat. "Better strap yourself in tight. We're coming down hard." Greg cinched up Brigham's harness and did as he was told. Heinrich glanced back and waited for the thumbs-up sign, then pulled back on the stick. "With a pre-flare of the nose, I'm going for all the drag I can squeeze out of this bus."

Apex plowed into a steep, braking incline, shooting the nose high over the tail section. His stomach clawing its way up into his chest, Greg sunk into the recliner's molded cavity and locked his helmet into place, then rolled his fingers firmly over the padded handholds above his shoulders. The bird seemed to hang in mid-air when Heinrich hollered back at Mojave that the landing gear was down and locked. As the floor had nearly leveled out, a terrible thud wrenched his spine deep into the padding. Seconds passed before Heinrich's words echoed inside Greg's helmet. Radio noise filled in between each victorious phrase: "Main gear touchdown ... deploying drag chute ... nose gear down."

An awful blast erupted beneath Apex, but by some miracle of God failed to disintegrate the cabin.

"Contact!" Heinrich shouted over the link. "We're may lose our gear before this is over ... but we're down."

The reverse thrusters roared to life, threatening to bust out all port and starboard windows. Heinrich's body was tossing madly as he cussed out the throttles and stood on the brakes.

A brief moment of insidious noise passed before headwinds began factoring into deceleration. Heinrich shrieked with euphoria. He'd brought them down with what appeared as superficial damage to the craft's underbelly. Beneath them Apex bounced, skidded and fishtailed wildly as Heinrich jockeyed the craft between a fiery rollover and a triumphant finish.

Once the cabin came to a rest, Greg's helmet crackled with Heinrich's voice again. "You okay back there?"

But Greg failed to answer.

His mind had flashed back to Brigham, sprawled out less than six feet in front of him next to Heinrich. The man's legs hung limp off the seams of the black jumpseat. It would take a miracle to see him alive again. Anger stewed inside Greg as

189

Striker began to stir. It was as if he'd timed the whole nightmare to its convenient end.

Greg swallowed some of his despair when Mojave's fire crews arrived. Down the tarmac their vehicles raced from the space center. Soon firefighters in bright yellow flame-proof suits were busy spraying off the shuttle's underbelly, turning black smoke into plumes of gray steam.

Greg broke out of his harness and approached Heinrich, who had moved Brigham to the floor. Beneath the cockpit, the two heard fire crews shouting and their power equipment hammering on the fuselage. Heinrich and Greg took turns working on Brigham when Colonel Striker climbed out of his harness and removed his helmet. He stepped into the cockpit to levy his own assessment of the situation. Immediately he scoffed at Heinrich's willingness to beat desperately on a dead man's chest. "I had my doubts the lieutenant was fit for this mission."

Heinrich exploded. "Get yourself aft," he growled over the ringing of fire axes below the fuselage, "And stay out of my sight."

Under the circumstances and a lingering look of nausea in his face, Striker deemed it foolish to do otherwise. He stepped back to where power saws had begun ripping a gash up through the floor. Finally the damaged hatch behind the bulkhead gave way.

"We'll take it from here," a voice commanded from below.

Up climbed a large man in yellow and orange fire-resistant suit, followed by a pair of medics who stepped forward and squeezed into the cockpit.

"Welcome home," the fire crewman hollered as he pointed toward the opened hatch. "The transport is waiting."

*****

After undergoing a brief medical evaluation, Greg and Heinrich were checked into the quarantine ward inside the space center.

Their private rooms shared a common lounge area, attached to a dining area where they would live for the three-day observation period.

Greg holed himself up in his room and tried to contact his mother on his cell phone. Within minutes he came out complaining that a cell phone wasn't worth shit in the desert. Greg and Heinrich soon sprawled out over lounge chairs adjacent to a glass partition that separated them from the receiving room when a uniformed woman walked in. She was Emily Fazzoni, Second Lieutenant with the U.S. Air Force. She introduced herself as the appointed council assigned to their case and pulled out a chair opposite them.

She addressed Heinrich first.

"According to Colonel Striker, you had unlawfully accessed a classified government website. Can you explain what you were doing inside NASA files?" Fazzoni asked through an electronic intercom.

Heinrich described the distress message that had come over his monitor aboard the station. Then went on to explain the conditions which led him to follow up on the facts. "I was taking what I considered necessary action on a message that appeared authentic and needed immediate attention."

"Acting beyond your legal authority concerns me," Fazzoni remarked. Serious doubts now appeared in her eyes. Her silent references toward Greg sitting across the lobby indicated she was equally troubled about the outcome of his case. "Both of us," she whispered, "are quite familiar with the Pentagon's posture on sensitive material at an international level."

Heinrich nodded, but still felt justified in his actions. "As I see it, the antecedent leading to the colonel's interventions precipitates a blatant misuse of authority, which in the end may have prevented a rescue. That, in my estimation, will become the essence of our defense."

"Save the jargon for your defense," Fazzoni advised. "It appears Greg was simply following your lead, doing what he thought was prudent at the time. And in such case, he may be viewed with less accountability to the security breach." She paused to write something on her pad before her eyes returned

191

to Heinrich. "By the way, I got Halverson's report. It verifies everything Greg said about going to the colonel for assistance."

"Striker seems hardly shaken about all this," Heinrich remarked.

"Not surprising to me. In principle, the colonel was doing his job to intervene ... so it's going to be an uphill fight to implicate him on activating the deep sleep cycle as a means to detain you, barring the possibility of endangering your lives."

"A level of immunity he's got to be well aware of. What can you say about the man's history?"

"Not enough at this point," Fazzoni said, "other than some static he made after receiving orders to take a surveillance post in space, following a string of deadly misjudgments during his role as security advisor in Baghdad in the final days of the occupation. He was also suspected of altering intelligence on Iranian supply movements, resulting in a botched border raid last year. Embarrassing, yes, but viewed as simply procedural errors on foreign soil, according to Pentagon lawyers."

"Having read about it in the German press, I found it to be more than procedural. Quietly swept under the carpet after a smuggling ring possessing suitcase nukes turned up 175 miles inside Iraq. Consequently, no one bothered to look into the colonel's mistakes."

"I'll make a note of that, Doctor. Now, I must speak with Greg."

Heinrich turned to face a swath of the common area where his intern was slouched in a padded chair.

After Heinrich stepped away, Greg was peering through the glass at Fazzoni, who was smiling on the other side. Through the microphone she informed him she had already met with Colonel Striker and had requested a written report containing his formal charges against Greg for assisting Heinrich with the breaking and entering of classified material. The document included allegations to be filing against Heinrich as well. Shortly after reviewing the ISS report filed by Skip Halverson, Fazzoni had briefed the colonel of pending charges for abusing military authority in civilian jurisdiction, and delivered his rights under a military court-inquiry. NASA

192

had already assigned him a military defense counsel after the board reviewed the circumstances and then, as a matter of course, filed charges against Striker for procedural misconduct. The board would take over fact-finding to determine whether or not charges against Greg could ever stick.

Twenty-one

Adam Harlow's sudden disappearance inside Crimson had pushed Panach to his limits, prompting verbal threats from termination to execution if Burke failed to bring him back.

The crisis had thrown the chateau into pandemonium with Admiral mobilizing all of its security forces, each man armed with silenced pistols and a generous cache of highly regulated weaponry. Panach monitored the sweep from his office, demanding that Burke place guards along the inner walls of Crimson's property. He patted the holster strapped across his chest. "Dead or alive, I want Harlow in my office before sunrise. Our own engineering crews will handle the plant's startup operations."

Though nervous about Panach's personal threat, Burke was the type to thrive under pressure, taking pleasure in the task of rallying Crimson's marksmen—a cadre of dishonorable discharges, infantry misfits, and common fugitives who'd been recruited by Admiral under a policy of reciprocal tolerance. With a set of marching orders, they entered the processing plant in search of Mr. Harlow by fanning out through the plumbing, condensers, and every conceivable space invisible to the eye. The first one to flesh out a body awaited a handsome salary bonus.

Between the banks of monitors inside the control room, Panach paced his wheelchair up one side and down the other. He scanned the array of divided closed circuit screens connected to surveillance cameras hidden in every hallway, corridor, control booth, and electrical panel. The stakes mounted with haunting possibilities of Harlow sabotaging the operation ... if not the obvious risks of him running to the police.

*****

President Kirkpatrick reread his reply to Beijing and prepared to send it via electronic mail.

194

The White House
17 February
Dear Mr. Prime Minister:

Upon reading your letter of February 16, I was dismayed to learn that your government resolved to break off formal negotiations toward a just settlement among Energy Coalition partners. Further, it deeply troubles this administration and its cabinet members that Beijing had, with undue haste, considered a military-led interference of U.S. commerce as a solution to this crisis.

The facts remain that no immediate agreement is likely to be reached on this course of action until our Cabinets can adequately review further options. I regret to inform you that your resolve to hinder already crippled American trade relations has thwarted any viable means for diplomatic resolution.

At this juncture, it is impossible for me to calculate the consequences your actions are bound to have on public and congressional opinion. Regardless of the restraint in which our government handles this matter, I need hardly mention the dire consequences that will transpire from this turn of events. And that fact brings me serious regret to contemplate that the enterprise in which we share should seem destined to collapse in this manner.

It is with humbled dignity and concern for the future and security of our two nations that I implore you and your esteemed Cabinet to reconsider your nation's course of action, and return diplomatic negotiations to a state of normalcy.

Mr. Prime Minister, these thoughts I hope to impart to you on this fateful hour in our relations.

With assurances of my highest consideration.

Regards,

Wayne Kirkpatrick

Early the next day the president's conference call with delegation leaders ended in despair. Beijing had the audacity to affirm preparations for military action against the United

States. Through two diplomatic satellite channels, China's defense ministry confirmed deployment of a naval blockade against American oil shipments ... unless Washington agreed to expedite an immediate funds transfer of *nine hundred sixty five* billion dollars. Interpreters carefully repeated the details along with Beijing's demands to complete the transaction within forty-eight hours—a transaction that was completely out of the question, given the current state of the U.S. Treasury.

Following a tense exchange of official e-mails between Washington and Beijing, White House negotiators managed to affect little more than extending China's ultimatum another twelve hours.

Through intense shuttle diplomacy, Kirkpatrick persuaded the Kremlin to give the crisis more time. Europe's consortium, with much less of a stake in the project, had agreed to adopt a wait-and-see posture, throwing in an offer to assist in the investigation. Tokyo indicated it would delay pending demands from key members of the Diet for seventy percent of its original investment, followed by pressure on Washington to pay back Japan's share within two years.

Two days after the Lukefield debacle, the whereabouts of Vashon's mineral cargo eluded FBI officials. Little more could be said about the headway Interpol agencies were making overseas. To heighten matters, a devastating leak to the press now loomed on the horizon. With rumors of a Chinese blockade forming in the Indian Ocean, media sources demanded to know more details, beyond what had been disclosed as a fabricated trade dispute. The stage was set for a global chain-reaction of panic.

With less than half an hour before his emergency cabinet was due to return to the situation room, President Kirkpatrick stood alone. Inside the Oval Office the solitary glow of the tabletop map—mirrored by the strategies laid out of military advisors topping off plans down the hall— illuminated the room. It was here, in the privacy of his personal thinking suite where Kirkpatrick considered an immediate and forthright resignation from office. The vice president—a decorated general with an extensive career in redefining diplomatic policy in the Arab world—was expected, under these circumstances, to carry the baton competently. Kirkpatrick entertained a discreet declaration of failure in hopes of softening repercussions to the Administration, despite the long-term political consequences the crisis was expected to bring to the Democratic Party.

The president recited his lament and prepared to announce his plans. When he re-entered the situation room his cabinet of advisors was waiting. His chief of staff and vice president had gathered around the illuminated table, peering down at red and blue lighted icons representing Chinese and American naval movements around the world. The secretary of state ended a telephone call and joined the huddle. Kirkpatrick approached as each man listened intently to the defense secretary. The Chinese had already begun to reposition their naval assets. Washington's top war advisors now had less than twenty minutes to win over Kirkpatrick's cooperation before the window of opportunity would dangerously slip into uncertainty.

The White House's chief of staff gulped black coffee and loosened his rumpled tie.

"We can no longer stand here and ignore hard facts. The Chinese control a deadly fleet of Boomers well placed in the Indian Ocean, Mr. President. But, as you can see in this lighted display, most of them are antiquated."

He was referring to a disproportionate number of gray submarines, China's aging Cold War fleet, updated nearly two decades ago. Due to a major defect in their guidance systems, hundreds of newer units had been recalled for security reconfigurations. Models of the newer boats glowed orange and appeared dry-docked inside China's naval ports from Shanghai to Hong Kong.

"And quite noisy, I might add … making them easy to detect," the defense secretary said, grinning with pride to be on the side where silence proved to be a virtue at sea.

Kirkpatrick eyed the scatter of Chinese warships, most of them still positioned defensively in troubled spots throughout the Indian Ocean and along northern latitudes in the Pacific that correspond with the Korean peninsula and Japan.

197

"Do we know *positively* their current locations?"

"Indeed, sir," remarked the vice president who'd fired up a cigar and was watching its cloud of brown smoke collide in the glow of light splaying off the table. "The fact is America's fleet of attack subs has—and this has been the case for several years now—cataloged each and every nuclear-armed Chinese sub at sea; each precisely by its own individual propeller pattern."

"Amazing," Kirkpatrick remarked under his breath. Awe-struck by the wonders of military science, a renewed source of energy rushed through his body. He let his gaze rake over the table again, this time with valor he never experienced. An omnipotent chain of command stood ready at his beckoned call. The will of his mind and the wave of his fingers instructed the mightiest navy on Earth.

After exercising a strategic pause to give the president absorption time, his chief of staff pointed to a formation of American ships. "Mr. President, the naval intelligence maintains detailed reconnaissance on everything you see, as we speak, sir."

The commander in chief was panning the strategic map once again. His eyes bounced from one illuminated icon to another, straining to comprehend the firepower compressed into the hundreds of mechanized gunboats his naval operations had already deployed along key shipping lanes leaving the Indian Ocean.

As the icy realities of a war began to stack up against diplomatic obstinacy, Kirkpatrick released a heavy sigh. He shook his head and grimaced in silent deliberation.

"We simply have *no* alternative," advised the chief of staff. His voice shifted awkwardly to a grim cadence. With a glance at the defense secretary, he tucked his hands under each elbow. "At this point, Mr. President, we're better off to position ourselves for a pre-emptive strike; a move that will sustain far less damage in the event of a Chinese retaliation." His words produced decisive nods from the others, issuing him the privilege to join ranks with those who held a stake in boldly redefining America's military history. "Lest there be a rebuttal in the works, everything is in place, sir ... when you consider our standard maneuver coordinates."

Kirkpatrick had prepared to orchestrate the command of his tenure, but a wicked chill gripped him, piercing him deep the chest.

"For God's sake!" he suddenly protested. "Haven't we another option?"

With soaring blood pressure, he was suddenly too weak to stand up. His VP slipped up behind in time to shoved a chair under him. "Sir," he said with a palm to the president's shoulder, "it's the only option we have."

Desperately Kirkpatrick peered up into the decided eyes of his advisors, each a spin-doctor of persuasion in his own right.

It was the chief of staff who finally broke the unnerving void that served to only further delay the inevitable. "I'm sorry, Mr. President, but given the posture of these damned Boomers, knocking out the enemy first is clearly your most promising tactic, sir."

"Indeed, the chief of staff is correct," the vice president remarked with all the objectivity he could muster. "We must send a decisive message to Beijing. Keep the upper hand, before it's too late." He waited expectantly—glancing at his watch and growing eager for an executive decision, regardless of its consequences.

Still belaboring the matter, the president grimaced. Key members of his military council waited for a decision that challenged every precept of what he idealized for America, as a just republic committed to brokering world peace. Authorizing the first strike would, without fail, result in highly controversial fallout—a direct assault on his personal ethics. Moreover, he could be walking into a protracted war America could not afford to fight.

Equally compelling, a decisive, simultaneous strike against threatening Chinese Boomers promised to assure the United States several years of superiority. For America had given in to watching the Chinese military machine exceed her figures in hardware and nuclear armaments.

In one agonizing breath Kirkpatrick's answer exploded like a balloon.

"We'll just have to go with it," he announced in one instantaneous breath that left him distant and ill. Like a dark symphonic movement, taut dissonance spread from his chest to his extremities. His embattled conscience bucked and screamed its final discord. But soon an eerie calm came over him. America had but one choice. Take out those Boomers. Peace would be negotiable from there, he hoped.

Kirkpatrick threw back his rounded shoulders and drew in a shuttered breath. The situation room echoed with a growing transformation in a voice he hardly recognized. At the threshold of his first war, with debate falling behind him, he felt invigorated to decide on this national matter.

"Finalize deployment," exulted the president. Allowing his conscience no time to change his mind, he went on to order that a link to satellite reconnaissance be set up in the Oval Office at once. "I want minute-to-minute coverage on those boats."

"Yes, Commander!" the chief of staff replied with a patent salute. He was beaming at Kirkpatrick now, as though the president had joined a very exclusive fraternal circle of brass. "As I stated earlier, sir, I suggest we begin with the Indian Ocean, then move along the coast of Africa, and finally out to the Atlantic."

"Indeed, along these routes our foreign oil has trickled into port," chimed the vice president, in step with his closest cohort. "We've got a rotation of three airborne squadrons over those areas, on standby as we speak, sir."

"Very well," replied Kirkpatrick. "Let us reconvene in 30 minutes."

Feeling like the last civil man on Earth, the president watched his four advisors exit the Oval Office. He had acquiesced to the strike option. Then moved on to validate his authority by giving the necessary orders to follow through.

Alone behind secured doors, his back turned to the lit war table, the president fingered the contours of silvery etched muscovite. He slid the bottle of vodka over his palms. Its faded label revealed a pre-Soviet painting of the last Czar. It was a symbol of gratitude in a 1951 pact, sealing centralized cooperation and a gesture of goodwill toward Beijing from the

Kremlin at the eve of a new social order. The bottle traveled to Washington in 1998 with Chinese-U.S. relations steaming toward economic partnership.

Communism had once been the cornerstone of conflict between the free world and the Soviet-Sino pact. Could the hundreds of goodwill gestures since its collapse be shattered by a new era of aggression between East and West? Today, the rift ran deeper than mere ideologies. Decades of energy policies based on infinite supplies—the common denominator for modern economic stability—now threatened to tumble the world into pandemonium.

Clutching the neck of the bottle, the president raised its butt over his head. Tears welled up in his eyes. "To diplomacy and reconciliation," he whispered. "An incompatible truth."

The bottle began dropping in a resolute arc toward the floor when the intercom at his desk halted him.

"Mr. President, the Chinese have taken our embassy in Beijing."

*****

Television news channels around the world aired the crisis within minutes of the siege in the Chinese capitol, citing possible targets on two American tankers less than a day out of the only Persian Gulf port still open. U.S. Embassies in many parts of Asia abruptly closed their doors.

Families of military and official personnel scrambled for last-ditch flights home. Fuel prices edged higher, while sell-offs in all major financial sectors forced Wall Street to shut down early that day.

Politically, things were spinning out of control. Late that evening the president took an urgent call at his bedside from his defense secretary. Jolted by the news, Kirkpatrick sat up stunned. "You're telling me what?" Whispers turned to growls as the secretary's words reached critical mass. "How the hell did we lose track of *two* of their subs?" Kirkpatrick demanded. "The Pentagon assured me its best people were on this assignment."

"Yes, that's correct, Mr. President, but—"

"No buts, Secretary. You get back to me in one hour with progress! And one more thing, I want direct coverage from our reconnaissance operations in space. I'm told the International Space Station carries a manned link fully capable of staying on top of Chinese naval movements."

The secretary's voice cracked in Kirkpatrick's ear. "Yessir, but I'm afraid we've run into a small complication."

"A problem? Take minor issues to my chief of staff, and get back to me in one hour. Make sense?"

The defense secretary stammered: "Yessir, however I must beg to report a pressing detail that demands your attention."

"Hurry it up, then. I need some sleep."

"Our reconnaissance officer aboard ISS has been removed from his post, sir."

"Removed?"

"That's correct, sir. He's on the ground, at the Mojave Space Center."

Kirkpatrick lost what little composure remained of him. "What the hell for?"

By now the First Lady was sitting up in bed. She watched her husband jump to his feet and pace the floor while grilling the caller over the speakerphone. He paused nervously at the nightstand and splashed gin into a glass. His voice was soon growling into the phone. "Look here, this is no time to be pulling the plug on vital military reconnaissance. Unless this man is dying and unconscious, dammit, put him back up there!"

The receiver was silent as the defense secretary paused for unruly heart palpitations.

"That's an order!" Kirkpatrick added.

The defense secretary's voice shuddered into the phone. "I … I must apologize, sir … but NASA just informed me that Colonel William Striker, a high-ranking intelligence officer, has been detained."

"On what grounds?"

"Sabotage, sir."

Paralyzed by the news, Kirkpatrick sucked in a deep breath and gulped the last of the gin. He could hardly bear listening to his defense secretary fill in the gaps.

202

"Within hours of removing the colonel from his post our naval command lost the link that carries data on the two Chinese subs. I'm terribly sorry, sir."

Twenty-two

Next day, 8:15am, Pacific Coast Time, after playing back a recording of Greg's testimony, Second Lieutenant Fazzoni looked into filing criminal charges against William Striker.

Yet the wording of an international statute on jurisdiction indicated she had little on him in a case of abusing military authority. Yet testimonial and circumstantial evidence suggested two counts of *procedural negligence*, a motion that carried enough punch to detain the colonel for 3 days of questioning. After that he would be free on his own recognizance. In essence, Fazzoni had accomplished little beyond what quarantine had already imposed.

That morning Heinrich and Greg returned from a battery of post reentry evaluations. A pancake breakfast waited them at the dining table alongside the windows facing west.

Drenching his pancakes in hot syrup, Greg stared out at the runway and beyond into Mojave's vast emptiness. He anchored his elbows to the table and his fork swung over a lump of butter sliding onto the plate. "Hey, uh ... I'm sorry about the shit I laid on you aboard Apex. I guess things could be worse."

"Thanks, Greg. You know, things will turn out how they will. I have confidence in our defense."

"Does Fazzoni believe us?" Greg asked after a long silence.

"Either she does and she isn't saying much or—"

"Or what?"

"She's covering up for somebody." Heinrich gave a skeptical tilt of his head. The turned up lines on his face indicated a more-than-serious look, showing increasing concern that he may have jeopardized their own defense by talking about marooned astronauts. "I couldn't get a word from anyone around here about a manned lunar mission."

Privately, Greg persisted in his own cerebral mind game. He drew up mental images of DeLong and Rockwell, then placed them on the front page of every major newspaper and Internet news site around the world. With eroding hope, his eyes swept over the bare walls and across the vacant lobby. The receiving room and the main concourse beyond the transparent germs barrier were deserted beyond lonely. The only sign of life was outside a west window where an occasional service vehicle drove in and out of the huge hangar. Greg counted the hours and minutes before he could get on a plane bound for Denver.

His images of Europa gliding down over the sands faded when the TV in the lounge cut into updated news coverage of America's rift with China. The anchor's tone gave the story the usual political dissing. Only this time it was over the Chinese breaking economic sanctions after buying oil from Syria. Greg became notably agitated.

"How much you wanna bet the colonel skates free? You and me, we'll end up doin' *his* time?"

Heinrich shook his head. "I'll wager the little bit of faith I have left in humanity," he sighed. "Though it's going to take time for Fazzoni to connection him to a crime. We need more. Something to nail his ass for contributing to Brigham's death."

"You mean like the doctor's report has to establish the fact that Brigham wasn't ... uh, pre...posed to suffer a fatal heart attack."

"You mean *predisposed*, Greg? Yes, exactly my thoughts."

"That could take days!"

"Try weeks, maybe months," Heinrich snorted. "This whole thing is going to come down to a Pentagon colonel's word against ours. Striker will play the *hallucination* card, and try to roast us on the claim we fabricated the distress call in order to hack into secret government affairs."

Greg shook his head despairingly. "Without a witness we're dead meat."

"You're probably right, Greg. It's all going to depend on Stan Rockwell ... if such a name really exists."

*****

About 5:30 Pacific Time, the USS Powell led two other carriers steaming for tactical positions off the sea coast of China.

205

Every U.S. Air Force base in the eastern hemisphere found itself on high alert. Beneath the decks, flight squadrons readied themselves for instructions from the Pentagon.

Positioned in a strategic triangle between international shipping lanes, American coastlines, and island bases around the world, U.S. Navy attack submarines locked target coordinates on China's aging nuclear boomers. All but two. The Pentagon had devised a cunning multi-stage plan in which naval launches would take out all Chinese subs simultaneously—a strategy that promised to reduce the risks of a lethal counter attack over American soil. But with two bomb-laden vessels at large, the Pentagon and White House were forced into a desperate holding pattern.

*****

Painfully, Greg listened to his mother weep on the other end of the telephone.

He had been in space for less than a week before becoming ensnared by shame and dishonor. His legal fate was now up to a handful of NASA lawyers and a judge hammering things out inside a locked courtroom, closed to the public eye.

A knock at the door interrupted her sobs, but Greg did not get up to open it.

Between breathless pants behind the doorjamb, Heinrich's voice heightened with anxiety. "Ground crews are towing in something out there. I saw the big bird in the service bay lights!"

"Go away. I don't want no more of—" The receiver dangled at his side as he bounced to his feet. "Hold on, what did you see?"

"It sure ain't no Airbus rolling up out there!"

Heinrich's footsteps retreated down the hall. Greg apologized to his mother once more and pledged to call her back the next morning. He pulled open the door and peered into the hall. At the far end of the lounge Heinrich was leaning against the darkened windows, several steps from where Fazzoni had met with them the day before.

In bare feet Greg sprinted down the hall into the lounge. Past the glass partition toward of the receiving room he saw the doors were propped open. Through the windows to his right the tarmac reflected perimeter lighting. But he saw no spacecraft.

"You might as well wait it out," he told Greg while plopping down in a padded chair, slapping the vinyl cushion next to his. "Looked like another Europa class getting towed in. She's beneath us, I'd guess."

Aside from the pounding in each man's chest, the place was deathly quiet. Soon the faint sounds of voices somewhere down the main concourse grew louder, out of view from the quarantine lounge.

Without a word Heinrich jumped to his feet. Beyond the counsel's chambers the commotion began when several people in space-fatigues began entered through the open doors. Unfitting of the situation, they were laughing and visiting. Greg stood up and leaned against the glass. The voices were still too far to determine what they were saying. He cupped a hand around his ear and placed it on the glass.

"Who are they?" he whispered over to Heinrich.

"I don't know. One's got to be the crew's commander. Hard to tell without seeing any shoulder stripes."

"Where you suppose they're from?"

"Orbit. Satellite repairs, perhaps?" Heinrich offered dubiously.

Both strained to view the receiving area as two more astronauts walked in behind the first party. "What the ... looks like a double crew!" Heinrich was astonished. "They're dressed like no other astronauts I've seen come through here ... not even the Russians."

One of the crewmembers suddenly broke off from the group. He began pointing across the room to where Greg and Heinrich were standing in the quarantine unit.

The others stirred with excitement and turned their attention toward the quarantine section. Their chatter rose to a muffled clamor as they started toward the partition.

"It's them," one shouted. "The two from the station."

"What do they know about us?" Greg whispered.

"Beats me," answered with a keen eye on the group.

A male with a cluster of insignias on rumpled white lapels walked front and center between the others. He was escorting a tall dark-haired woman in a sleek blue and orange jumpsuit while repeatedly gesturing her toward the partition. The others—probably their crewmates—followed closely behind, hair frizzed by a static charge, until they halted up next to the glass.

Greg stepped back slightly. He was as puzzled as Heinrich seemed to be speechless.

Everyone stood spellbound, inspecting each other from opposite sides of the partition, like opposing troops who'd caught each other off guard. For a frightening moment no one spoke. Their eyes were glazed over in disbelief. Greg craned his neck to read the names sewn into the crew's fatigues. Directly in front of him stood *Stan Rockwell*, studded and badged with Air Force regalia. The way he'd watched over the others and kept them moving, he was clearly in charge of the group. Two other crewmembers stood silently behind him, both wearing Europa insignias on their sleeves.

Blowing out a hot stale breath, Greg turned to face Heinrich whose attention was fixed onto the woman in the forward group. Next to her was a tall Asian astronaut in green and black flight fatigues, with Chinese markings on his sleeve. Opposite the woman's other shoulder stood a dark-skinned astronaut who resembled Indian or Pakistani ancestry. For a prolonged moment the woman had locked eyes with Heinrich before turning to speak inaudibly to Rockwell, waiting directly behind her.

Greg noticed an uncommon grace about her as he read the embroidered name on her lapel: *Vashon Commander R. DeLong*.

"Oh dear, is that really her? Commander DeLong?" he choked. "It's the woman commander. She survived!"

Gradually, DeLong collapsed under her own weight, gasping and shuddering. Rockwell eased her down to the carpet. One of her own crewmen placed a hand to her shoulder. Bumping his nose into the glass, the Chinese crewman peered back through the partition at Greg and Heinrich. He spoke in a

208

hoarse whisper. "The two of you saved our lives," he said, raising a finger over his head to include the others. "If not for your decisive action, Vashon would be a lost mission. We'd have been left to die up there."

Heinrich knelt down to meet DeLong at eye level. She wiped her face. Meanwhile, a hundred questions flooded into Greg's mind. He pressed his fingers together and stared back at the others. Where was he to start? His most pressing thoughts dwelled on the hush-hush secrecy that had led to his arrest.

Finally, Rockwell broke the spell. He cleared his throat and positioned himself in front of the microphone affixed to the glass partition. "We've got a lot to flesh out together. I've glanced through Lieutenant Fazzoni's report. Each of us is grateful for the risks the two of you took in getting this crew home safely. Unfortunately there are some legal hurtles to iron out with NASA. Once our crews get moved into their quarters, we'll report back here for an emergency conference. I've arranged for legal counsel to be present. Any questions?" The others glanced at each other in agreement. Rockwell nodded. "Very well, see you back here in thirty minutes."

*****

By six thirty, NASA officials had entered the quarantine annex and seated themselves next to the glass partitions that separated Heinrich and Greg's area from Vashon and Europa crewmembers.

Colonel Striker entered from an adjacent quarantine room, filling in the fourth quadrant. He avoided eye contact with the others as he sat down no less than eighteen inches from his microphone. A tall wiry man was testing the audio as Heinrich and Greg came out from their rooms. The official introduced himself as Major Brender from NASA's classified division. He was in charge of handling logistics related to the Vashon Mission.

Brender wore a conservative gray suit. He removed his jacket and loosened his yellow necktie as he brought the meeting to order by summarizing a brief history of the mining venture. Quickly he covered the nature of the Chinese and

American partnership, which included an abbreviated blurb of the ongoing crisis over the stolen cargo following the crisis at Lukefield. Brender capped his summary with Beijing's military resolve to block American shipping lanes unless the minerals were recovered.

Dizzily horrified, Commander DeLong battled to steady herself. Even the Secret Service had lost track of NASA's first shipment of minerals. What's worse, she had committed to a last-minute decision to jettison a portion of the mined cargo aboard Vashon during her crippled lunar liftoff. In essence she had sacrificed the mining aspects of the mission in an effort to save her crew.

"We're completely at a loss here," Brender continued, "because there have been no demands for a ransom, nor any attempts to blackmail the United States for nuclear weapons in exchange for these stolen minerals. As you know, the shipment is useless without the complete manufacturing plans. So we must assume that a powerful entity has gained access to both. We have reason to believe this organization wants nothing less than to exploit energy markets worldwide, and do it under the guise of selling conventional fuel products."

Pondering the stakes, everyone in the room was stunned. Over a trillion dollars of international funding still lay on the lunar surface. The first cargo—a quantity that could satisfy a sizable share of petroleum demands for several years had fallen into the hands of thieves. The United States was suddenly powerless as a world leader, discredited for its inability to secure materials vital to energy independence.

The awful spell that had struck the meeting was broken. DeLong straightened her posture and spoke boldly into her mic: "What are federal and international law enforcement agencies doing to track the stolen minerals?"

"At this point, they're operating in the dark," Brender responded flatly. "Federal agents have focused surveillance efforts onto a few radical extremist groups ... but failed to uncover anything substantial. That is precisely why we need your help."

"How can *we* help?" inquired Heinrich.

The major cleared his lungs through flared nostrils. Carefully he met each pair of eyes before addressing the question. "Frankly, some of you may have valuable clues to this case. And since everyone here has been privy to Vashon in one way or another, we must put our heads together."

DeLong nodded and waited to hear out Brender.

"The FBI has been on the case day and night," he continued. "NORAD's surveillance team at their Rocky Mountain post has stepped up operations to a classified red alert. Meanwhile, Interpol has been sifting through hundreds of tips overseas. Our commander in chief—who, incidentally, has authorized a counter offensive against a Chinese blockade of foreign oil shipments—awaits the results of our discussion this very hour."

DeLong gasped. "What in heaven is going on out there?"

"Putting it bluntly, ma'am, this nation is in dire need of some damn straight answers."

Heinrich's hand shot up. "What about the Middle East war in all of this? Any clues there, Major?"

"Maybe, maybe not. New evidence uncovered by Saudi Arabia indicates the tragic bombing of an Iraqi pipeline by American forces was the result of a dreadful error in which covered up by a high-ranking general. The effects implicated a number of people in reconnaissance who may not have been responsible. In theory, there may have been an outsider's motive to shutdown oil shipments indefinitely by destroying a large part of the new Iraqi infrastructure. This might lead us to reasons for interfering with Vashon's mission. Still, there is too much speculation into the matter for me to discuss it. Yet, in light of circumstantial evidence, we're hoping for something to break in our favor. That is all I know at this time."

DeLong was nearly in tears when she interjected, "Major, we were just informed of the Lieutenant Colonel's tragic death aboard Apex. Is there something there that plays into all of this?"

"Hard to say, Commander. At this point, his heart attack appears purely coincidental. At any rate, we've all got our share of stones to uncover."

Brender called for a recess and stepped away to take an urgent phone call. Silently, Colonel Striker rose from his chair and disappeared into his quarters.

Greg saw the opportunity he and Heinrich had been waiting for and gestured for Commander DeLong's attention. "Ma'am, I don't get it," he whispered into the microphone. "Why didn't your distress message reach Europa?"

"Excellent question, Greg," the commander remarked with a smile. "We need thinkers like you in the space program. I discovered our communication codes were altered at some point during the mission, completely disabling our contact with NASA. That included our designated links with Europa. Eventually the beacon cancelled itself—an automatic procedure that occurs once docking maneuvers are completed.

Heinrich shot DeLong an inquisitive smile. She had covered the drama of lunar liftoff, which meant thinning out her crew's air supply to conserve oxygen before docking with Europa. But she hadn't said a word about any criminal factors.

"Commander, could someone inside NASA with intentions of interfering with the joint project between China and the U.S. be behind this?" Heinrich asked.

"You are every bit as brilliant as people say you are, Doctor."

*****

Later that evening Fazzoni showed up unannounced outside the quarantine unit.

Appearing to have nothing but business on her mind, she found Heinrich asleep in the lounge and requested that he return to his quarters after retrieving Greg. She promised she needed only fifteen confidential minutes with him before he could go back to bed.

Greg rubbed his eyes and sat down at the partition where he typed his name onto an electronic notepad. Fazzoni authenticated the document for court submission and tested the audio.

"Young man, first I need to preface our conversation with some news that directly affects you and Dr. Mann."

212

Greg waited with ambivalence. It was all he could do to listen to more complications dealing with his participation into Vashon's rescue. At the same time he welcomed anything good news Fazzoni might have to offer, though a quarter to midnight.

"Yes, ma'am," he yawned. "Go ahead."

"Your testimonies of certain events aboard the space station have been substantiated by two others through radio-telephone interviews," Fazzoni began. "I must disclose that I have doubts over Colonel Striker's future. At the very minimum, he is finished with ISS reconnaissance. NASA has issued a statement reauthorizing you aboard the station to finish out your internship. *Kids-in-Space* will arrange for your return trip up there. However, it could be several weeks before the next shuttle launch."

"What about Heinrich? What's going to happen to him?"

"Doctor Mann is prepared to shoulder any burden of guilt that might fall on you."

"Thank you, but he's no criminal," Greg shot back. "Heinrich acted to save three lives...until Colonel Striker jumped in."

"Still, he insists that you return to the station and finish your studies."

"Not without him. Besides, I've got basketball try—"

Fazzoni's palm shot up. "I'm not authorized to say anything other than the fact Striker's case against Heinrich may be shaky. If NASA drops the charges, Heinrich will have the discretion to return to ISS, too. As for you, young man, summer basketball try-outs are still a long way off. I've been informed you are the team's designated forward. Be sure to stay in shape ... and promise me you'll spend more time in the fitness module."

"Yes, ma'am."

The lieutenant folded her arms. "Those points covered; let's get back to the investigation. What can you tell me about Adam Harlow?"

Greg scratched his head and took several seconds to assemble fragments of his memory before he answered her.

"I've heard of him. I even saw one of his e-mails to Heinrich. By then Striker had already put the freeze on the doctor."

Fazzoni looked up from her notes through a pair of narrow reading glasses that hung low on her nose. "After going through federal surveillance data, Mr. Harlow's name came up in a few interesting places. A cross-reference shows him registered with an independent research database, that contracts record keeping with the government." She was waving a packet of printouts. "What I'm getting at is, he was working to recover a secret fuel formula, and may have made a crucial discovery. Therefore, it's imperative that we contact him."

"That could be the same guy. I mean, well ... he was asking Heinrich about some chemicals."

Fazzoni worked her pen on the paper without taking her eyes off Greg.

"Trouble is," she continued, "Mr. Harlow has encountered a few characters known to be dealing with organized crime...and his life might well be in danger."

Greg took a gulp of water and made the connection. The thought of Heinrich hanging out with the mob didn't fit. Counting the risks Heinrich had taken to help Vashon, Greg couldn't find a single way Heinrich's case connected to Adam Harlow or gangsters. Still, he considered it safer to play dumb. Greg could say nothing, and then leave it to Heinrich's testimony to satisfy Fazzoni. But what if Adam had made an important discovery, and really was in trouble? The detectives would eventually find a way to trace his electronic messages to ISS.

Fazzoni was now looking squarely at Greg.

"Describe the email you received when you were in possession of Heinrich's cell phone."

Greg shrugged. "Like I said, he was asking about chemicals, substances...some stuff unknown to Earth, I think."

"Can you tell me where Adam is living or working now?"

"Heinrich told me he was living in Seattle. Then got fired for slamming his boss, and started his own lab. A month later he was getting on a plane for LA. Honest, that's all I know."

"I see," Fazzoni replied. "One more question, do you mind?"

Greg yawned and shook his head.

"When did you last hear from Adam?"

"His message arrived an hour before Striker came for me."

"You've been most helpful. Now, I must apologize about your observation period here being extended. Sorry, doctor's orders."

Twenty-three

Adam felt like a Zen monk confined to a Himalayan cave. Only he'd been left for the dead without a prayer to utter.

Cloaked in darkness, the only progress he had made toward breaking out was to discover a sliver of light coming in above one column of stacked mineral cubes. This proved of little use other than to view the hands on his wristwatch. Daylight had come and gone, according to another paper-thin seam along the edge of the lid at the top of the steps. With shallow breaths and broadening ripples of fatigue pulsating against his bones, Adam waited for Admiral's loading operations to resume later that night.

Breathing itself had become a conscious task, intensifying a deeper sense of the cold damp ground that threatened to trim his body temperature as the earthen floor nipped at his flesh and penetrated his bones. Violent shivers interrupted the few short dozes he desperately needed, leaving him to bide his time with thoughts of preserving oxygen and body heat—a paradox that prohibited physical exertion or digging as a means of escape.

Adam began to arrange his thoughts, attempting to face his troubles and decide what was necessary. There was little use in stabbing at hasty suppositions. He must have a plan, one he could logically adjust to the circumstances. But what was logical? Only that which men knew, and they knew so little.

A shade of hope for escaping came to him when he considered Panach's deadline. For it had arrived. With the construction phase finished and the company in possession of his digital file as well as the minerals, the probability of Admiral dominating the energy markets with *Aqualene* becoming a most certain end game.

His thoughts of Moi came intermittently. He sat puzzled at himself and at her. He barely knew her. A yearning he could not define was growing inside him. No words of love had been spoken, no promises made. Yet something quiet and peaceful between them warmed him as he sat pondering his next breath

216

in darkness. These brief moments comforted Adam, until severed by the task of survival.

Guided by the pinch of light from the ceiling, Adam rose to his feet and felt his way to stacks of the cubes, behind which he had but no choice to relieve himself into a scraped out depression of earthen clay. His fingers ran along the surface of several stones now, bringing to mind the vivid colors of each group, as they had appeared the night he found them. Where did they arrive from? Who'd cut them so precisely?

Admiral had acquired a significant load of these minerals. Did the company excavate them from a mine? In what part of the world could this unique quarry be found? Could the minerals—resembling the specimens he'd received from Renee—belong to Admiral? Or for that matter, belong to another organization competing to for a major energy breakthrough?

Maybe NASA? Renee had spoken about a group of nations working jointly to produce *Aqualene*. Did this include such economic powerhouses as China?

Adam's mind returned to the business of formulating his escape. If Panach and Burke were to fire up the processing plant, sooner or later they would have to access the minerals in storage. He estimated that one cube from each stack could produce tons of *Aqualene*'s blue formula. The ratio of saltwater to formula was exponentially mind-boggling.

Based on the Crimson plant's blue prints, someone from would have to come through the tunnel network to access the mineral cubes. From the hatchway, fresh air would mix with the stale air currently occupying the space inside the vault. Being a visual thinker, Adam imagined himself negotiating a stretch of tunnel, exiting, and then dashing for the Crimson River.

The tunnel-to-the-river route! The most direct way out.

He returned to the floor and mentally rehearsed the steps. Each time the same sobering thought rattled him. The first of security to come through the hatchway for an armload of cubes would no doubt have to be subdued ... maybe worse.

*****

217

The sedan, a newer model by its smooth ride and factory odor, bumped along city streets and through controlled intersections for several minutes until it stopped and the driver shut off the motor. The two men working for Tobario mumbled something to each other as the front doors opened. A rush of cold salty air blew in where Moi sat in the back seat.

"Let's get this finished," one of them grunted back. The next moment a pair of hands clutched her arm above the elbow and tugged firmly. Outside, the cold winter air blowing steady against her face, stung regions unmasked by the cloth blindfold and gag. The wail of a boat's foghorn drifted into earshot, bringing to her mental images of fair weather strolls along the city's waterfront.

In one dizzied motion—bound at the ankles—her feet skidded the sidewalk as her body was hoisted up onto iron. Its frigid surface penetrated her jeans and blouse. The strangers answered her wrenching body and twisting arms with penetrating jabs to her delicate regions. Then, releasing their grip as if she'd been considered a deficient catch at sea, Moi was rolled over the edge and launched into a free fall. In a crush of anxiety, the horror of submerging into frigid water followed the explosive clap. The bay swallowed her instantly, forcing its salted flavor into her mouth and nostrils, streaks of panic raced out to her feet and fingers. In a mad wriggle to turn upward, glints of gray light penetrated her eyelids in the upsurge of currents, which helped to thrust off the blindfold.

Amongst streams of bubbles wrapped in kelp, Moi wrestled to free her hands. The duct tape tore the flesh around her wrists and refused to let go. Unable to determine top from bottom, her thoughts addressed the imminence of choking down water.

Thrashing wildly, her hands were the first to break into the night air. Indulgence came when her head cleared the surface. Short shallow gasps turned to long fortifying draws. And her lungs burned as she gulped the cold mist that embraced her.

Calmness descended upon her and she thought about Adam, and the possibility he had refused to give in to those demanding his knowledge? Doing so had imposed danger upon her life, yet... Suddenly these notions were pushed away.

Boney yet determined fingers clutched her bounded wrist, causing Moi to jerk and tug for freedom. But she failed to reclaim her arm. A second splay of fingers subdued her at the elbow and she shrieked for aid. But her cries only echoed back from the towering breakwater behind her.

Tenderly, an unfamiliar voice sounded over Moi's agitation. The woman repeated, "I won't hurt you. Now, give me your hand."

Moi managed to free one hand and wipe her eyes. Between the shadows of a street lamp, the face of a leathery woman shrouded in stringy hair appeared. She had been straddling a log, angled low in the water off a clutter of half-burned timbers lining the shore.

"This way," the woman wheezed in a slightly accented voice that revealed she was suffering from a respiratory condition. "Come here to me. I can help."

Moi judged quickly judged her to be harmless and reached out to grab the woman's hand. It was scaly and rough, but its warmth comforted her. The woman softened her grip and guided Moi into a shallow corner where she could climb up onto the same log. Moi's panting broke into trembling. She sat on the log staring at the place where the woman had made camp. A small lean-to, tucked back between dozens of pilings, sheltered a small boy sleeping under a blanket next to a smoldering campfire. Was this their home?

Under a chilled rain blowing in from the bay, the woman stood and gestured Moi to follow her inside amongst the timbers 30 feet beneath a roadway spanning the waterfront. She watched the woman build up the fire with scraps from cardboard boxes, then rummage for a blanket she draped around Moi's shoulders.

"Wait here," she whispered, nudging Moi closer to the fire.

The woman disappeared in the darkness of the pilings. Above them the rumble of a car passed into silence. The bay's lapping tides whispered beyond the shelter. The fire, which was devouring the paper scraps, warmed her. Piles of broken luggage and bulging plastic bags cast shadows against a stretched tarp wall.

Reappearing with dry pants and a sweatshirt, the woman pulled socks and a dry towel from a plastic shopping bag. She placed the heap into Moi's arms and returned to the boy's side. Moi changed into the dry clothes. The woman was now standing over her collection of bags and suitcases now, staring at them until she selected the one she wanted and then stepped toward the fire. The bay was still dark, as was the tiny camp. The flames had quickly turned to glowing embers. Erect on two knees, the woman carefully pulled a cereal box from the small suitcase. She jammed a hand inside and pulled out some rolled currency.

"I will get you a cab," she said in a low determined tone. "There's a kind man who sleeps in his car across the road. Come now." She picked up a vinyl handbag that had been drying by the fire and handed it to Moi. "This must be yours, I found it in the water."

After spreading a third blanket over her son the woman lit a candle and led Moi in among the pilings.

Moi gasped. "You saved me from drowning. I must repay you."

The woman offered no response. Instead, she kept walking, silently over a path that took them to a makeshift ladder where they climbed up to the street level. "Be the change you wish for," she muttered while glancing around for danger before giving Moi a gentle shove into the open door of the taxi. "The fare you need is inside your bag. Go while it is still dark."

Tearfully, Moi turned to clutch the woman's hand, but she'd pulled away and disappeared into the night.

The light of a gray dawn came when Moi showed up at Cindy Mollett's apartment. After a hot breakfast, Cindy insisted they go to Police Headquarters downtown.

The desk clerk ordered them to wait in a special lobby where a detective would call their names and conduct an interview.

Ten minutes passed before a weathered man in his forties wearing a brown suede jacket approached them. He invited them to come into his office.

"Coffee?"

Cindy nodded and took the paper cup he handed her.

"My name is Detective Larry Fischer," he said, handing both ladies his business card. "I'm with Homicide Investigations."

"There hasn't been a *murder*," Cindy exclaimed.

"I'm glad to hear that, ma'am. We're short on desk personnel right now, so I'll hear your case and pass it on to the appropriate section."

Fischer sat down against the window and picked up a memo pad. Behind him a hint of gray light seeped in through a narrow gap between two drawn curtains. Moi rubbed her eyes and peered at the man. She felt exposed and vulnerable to be sitting in a police station.

Moi nodded when Fischer informed her he was going to record their conversation.

After Moi told everything she could remember of being held by Tobario and the two men, Fischer turned to Cindy. "Ma'am, how does this case involve you?"

Cindy shook her head. "It doesn't, but I know the story. Moi is talking about a man she met while working at a small café in Pioneer Square. You see, he left town, so we don't know where he is, but the woman who was holding Moi demanded information about his work. Isn't that—?"

Fischer cut her off. "Whoa, ladies! Let's back up a little. This whole thing isn't making any sense. I need to know *who* in God's name you're talking about. Give me a name."

Picking up on how exhausted and confused Moi had become, Cindy took hold of her hand. "You can do it, sweetie. Tell the detective about Adam."

His notepad wagging between his fingers, Fischer spoke again. His words were slowly paced in a cop-talk monotone: "Adam who?"

Moi thought hard to remember how to pronounce Adam's last name. She repeated the full name, leaving out the *r*.

221

Fischer stood up and circled his office introspectively. "Ma'am, you mean Harlow. Adam Harlow?"

Moi nodded. Fischer's pen went to work. He paused.

"How do you know Harlow is missing or in danger?"

Moi stammered as she recalled the terrible experience, explaining how Ms. Tobario wanted to know about Adam's work. How she would come back every day and ask more questions.

Fischer stepped into the hall where he spoke to another detective. Tiring minutes passed. Cindy poured Moi a cup of water from a cooler in the office, then took her hand and reassured her the police would help. They would find Adam. Fischer entered the room again. His eyes moved off his smart phone and onto Moi.

"Ladies, this is not the first report of Mr. Harlow's disappearance. At this point, nobody on the side of the law knows his whereabouts...or even if he's still alive. You suspect Mr. Harlow is in trouble? Tell me, how would you know about his condition if you've been confined inside a locked room?

Moi told Fischer that Adam had spoken to her on the telephone on a previous evening.

Fischer's eyes lit up. "Okay, now tell me, do you recall any clues from Tobario that may give us his location?"

Moi thought hard about Tobario for several moments and then pieced her English together. "Tobario talked about California ... to the men outside my door."

"A city, a town? Any landmarks?"

"I am so sorry," Moi answered in a dismal tone. "Tobario was too clever."

"What about your conversation with Adam. Tell me about it."

"Adam said very strange thing over the phone. I don't understand."

"Tell me about it."

"Haunted park ... view of Robinson's place ... from mountain."

Cindy stood up to interject, "And they promised to kill him if he refused to obey their demands."

222

"Hold on a minute." Fischer ordered. "Back up a little. I want to know about this haunted park. And what about the mountain?"

"Some sort of clue," Cindy whispered.

"Of course it is!" Fischer remarked while returning his attention on Moi. The glare in his eyes searched for clearer answers now.

"Yes," Moi broken in. "I think Adam give clue to his location."

The detective considered her statement. "Possibly. Alright ... the mountain represents some vantage point; perhaps his own vantage point on a larger geographical scale."

"Maybe from a chalet or a ski lift." Cindy suggested. "There are several popular ski resorts in Utah and Colorado."

"And there's California." Fischer thought a long moment before shaking his head. "I'm thinking from a tall building. After all, the name *Robinson* has some part of this."

"Jackie Robinson grew up in Pasadena," Cindy added excitedly.

Moi was nodding along with her friend, trying to make sense of all this when a sudden thought came to her. Adam had been in her apartment where a map of Disneyland is tacked to the wall. Could this explain his odd reference to the amusement park in his phone call?

"Maybe he see map. My map!" she gasped in broken English.

Fischer rotated his chin toward Cindy and furrowed his brows. "Map? What's she talking about?"

"My Disney map ... inside my apartment!" Moi cried. Like most of her friends who'd visited America from Shanghai, she had made the customary trip to at least one theme park. Aside from New York City and Yellowstone, Disneyland was considered America's cultural Mecca for young people visiting from the Asia.

Fischer swiveled around to the computer monitor on his desk. He requested all references to the Disneyland site in Anaheim, California. In seconds he was scanning an interactive graphic of the park. "We may be onto something." His index finger tapped the screen. "Look, the Matterhorn is

223

here, representing Adam's location. The Robinson tree house is southwest, down here, in a direction that corresponds with his departure point. Perhaps the airport, or downtown, LA."

Fisher paused. Was this going somewhere? He scribbled onto a sheet of paper and stepped into the hallway again. Several minutes passed before he returned, shoving his phone back into a breast pocket. "Without a doubt, this case is more than a simple abduction. I'm turning it over to the Federal Bureau of Investigations."

Twenty-four

Jarring him from his brandy-induced nap, a voice from inside the processing plant erupted over Panach's phone link.

One of the company's DNA specialists—a former L.A.P.D. lab tech who was kicked off the force two years ago for tampering with evidence to exonerate a San Bernardino drug baron—was waving a tubular wand programmed to match samples of Mr. Harlow's hair and skin fibers with airborne particles inside the plant.

"Nothing fresh in here," he reported over the voice link. "I don't believe Harlow has been in the plant for two days."

As things stood now, the thought of Adam running to law enforcement officials infuriated Panach. Every aspect of Admiral's capital investment rested on manufacturing *Aqualene* in a cloak of secrecy. Had the use of coercion somehow undermined Crimson's intended outcome? Perhaps. Yet as a believer of raw, unforgiving fate, Panach was prepared to exercise his political capital. After all, the only empirical evidence against the company rested in its possession of NASA's cargo, which still remained brilliantly hidden.

With the world's eyes turned to a potentially explosive confrontation between Washington and Beijing, timing at Crimson had advanced from substantial to critical. Admiral's coastal operations had quietly outfitted a number of finishing plants aboard shut-down drilling rigs up and down the coast of Mexico and Central America—each one with a crew and ready to carry out the final mixing stages of *Aqualene*'s formula as soon as it arrived. From there, Admiral would deploy tankers under the Mexican flag and begin commanding the world's most powerful energy empire, all from international waters.

Success depended on transporting, by private aircraft, several hundred gallons of *Aqualene* each day to the submerged platforms. As long as Crimson kept operating, Admiral would control an endless supply of fuel at premium rates to oil-starved nations. The United States would be the most lucrative customer ahead of China and Western Europe.

225

Panach glued his attention on the monitor inside the control room that was linked to cameras operating at the west end of the property. He had finished assessing guard locations on the compound when there was a knock at the door. Exhaling smoke from a Haitian cigar, his finger tapped on his diamond-studded Rolex.

"You've kept me waiting," he growled at Burke standing in the doorway. "Where is Harlow?"

Burke wore a troubled expression. "We're still looking, sir. He will *not* escape, you have my word."

Panach's cheeks caved in slightly with each draw on the cigar as his eyes raked over the monitors again. "If Harlow gets out, the most logical exit will be at the river." He pointed at the video feed from a security camera behind the processing plant. Both men watched white water dash and plunge over dark angular boulders. "What troubles me most is that he'll head for that two-bit sheriff's office a mile this side of the airstrip. I suggest you find a way to keep those country cops busy."

Burke pulled out his two-way radio. "Yessir."

"Order the guards to shoot first and ask questions of the body, by tonight," Panach bellowed. "I won't accept any traces of him *outside* Crimson's walls."

Burke grinned with confidence. "Sir, this guy is hardly James Bond. If it's any consolation, early this morning we sprayed acres of underbrush surrounding the compound with chemical agents. I'll wager one month's salary that Harlow's out there lying in his own stench. It's just a matter of finding and plucking the body out."

Theories meant little to Panach, who was eyeballing a virtual production display of *Aqualene*. "I'm holding you personally responsible for Mr. Harlow's whereabouts. With or without the corpse, we fire up this plant at sundown."

*****

The catering chef drove hard the last few miles to Crimson's refinery.

226

The magnetic sign on the side of his van advertised the finest cuisine and best liquors available. An hour earlier, food fit for a king rolled off the line at the banquet kitchen and was carefully placed into hotboxes specially designed for long trips. Everything loaded in the van, the catering manager had checked his watch impatiently, as his banquet captain, the employee in charge of presenting the meal to the company's largest and most affluent client, fifty-five minutes east failed to show up for work.

Moments after receiving a call indicating the captain was ill, a well-informed temporary from a nearby hotel had shown up at the loading dock with a handwritten note verifying he was taking over that evening. Credentials in hand, he began preparing for an immediate departure. The catering manager was astonished at how efficient the arrangements had been made as he finished looking over the papers. Latching the rear cargo doors, he beamed at the sight of his best sirloin and finest champagne pulling out on time. "Follow the GPS," he told the chef through the window. "And be sure to present this bottle to the gate patrol once you arrive. Good luck."

Now, over an hour out of Fresno, the chef was within minutes of Admiral Petroleum's Crimson Site, according to the van's GPS. He turned onto a highway heading east. Upon accessing satellite images of a half dozen refineries owned by the nation's mammoth energy giant, he had quickly narrowed his choices down to Crimson, a relatively small installation surrounded by hundreds of acres of canola farmland. Admiral Petroleum had catered its meals from the well-known culinary artist, who tonight had conveniently provided him full access to the company's most-guarded facility. While tucked amongst the state's most remote farmland, the compound was said to enjoy the strictest private surveillance. This, according to certain individuals in the business of procuring classified information, was where Admiral sought to quietly launch an all-out assault on its industry competitors, and capture an unprecedented market share of the world's fuel energy.

After going over some basic tips of banqueting in his mind, the chef nervously squinted at a roadblock up ahead, less than two miles from the refinery.

227

Dusk occurred around 5:30 that afternoon. Central California weather channels forecasted a cooled air mass drifting in from the coast, bringing a chance of blustery weather mixed with rain.

Meanwhile, Crimson's inner core buzzed with activity. The senior engineers inside the plant ran final tests on crushers, evaporators, condensers, fractionators, and the support systems used to control temperatures and pressures throughout various phases of the manufacturing operation.

Holding the reins on compound security, Burke rushed to reconfigure Admiral's para-military. Panach had stipulated things clearly: all plant personnel be prepared to combat the outbreak of fire—a risk that was greatest during the start-up phases when newly machined surfaces had to be superheated to burn away residue compounds and contaminants; substances that threatened to impair the proper catalytic reactions. Until the plant's hydro-treating unit would reach its normal operating temperature, Admiral had every available man ready to assist with an emergency shutdown. The job was part and parcel of maintaining company security while smoothly testing an unproven manufacturing operation.

Shortly after sundown, Panach's resolve to start up the plant glimmered over the array of video monitors that displayed every phase of this venture. Each team stood by proudly as its technicians completed last-minute inspections. The mood on the production floor was charged with anticipation the moment Panach wheeled himself into the main plant under bright lighting. His presence commanded absolute silence, prompting him to address his assembly of chief engineers.

"Pillars of the future, you stand ready to embark upon a new era of energy domination. Our first product of mineral synthetic fuel shall fill our condensers by midnight. Within two days, these shipments must begin leaving Crimson completely undetected. Each of you, under Admiral's leadership, will collaborate in taking charge of world markets through a line of manufacturing facilities disguised as the inconspicuous components of our ethanol division."

More personnel stepped away from their posts and gathered in the center of the floor where their superiors were standing. Surrounded by hundreds of loyal faces, Panach raised his glass of champagne and proposed a string of inspiring toasts. For several minutes he rambled on like a Soviet-era factory boss, lecturing his men on the precepts of obedience and egalitarianism as the embodiments of neo-corporate survival. "Each one of you makes up the handle that opens Admiral's door to supremacy. From tonight forward we shall accept nothing short of world energy domination!"

His speech ended in a triumph roar, which produced a thundering applause among Admiral's legion of uniformed technicians as they scrambled back to their workstations.

Panach wheeled himself up the walkway, over the courtyard's patio, and returned to the chateau. The burgeoning numbers on screens monitoring world market demands for fuel and the flow of brandy at his fingertips thoroughly intoxicated him. Chinese threats of a blockade on oil shipments to the United States had driven up Admiral's domestic energy stock skyward. Now, filling those demands would grant Rodney Panach the *Dominacion Global* he knew he was entitled.

Twenty-five

The last trace of twilight surrendered to a phantom gray moon, darting behind broken clouds blowing eastward.

Just after 8:00pm the catering chef rolled up to a lone flagman. The two exchanged barely a sentence before he was on his way again. Situated at the crest of the hill, utility crews were repairing a severed line and had detoured whatever scant traffic there was onto a farming tract to the east, then back around to an access road that rejoined the highway a quarter mile from the Crimson Ethanol Plant. The rural street lighting along the highway outside of the property walls had not yet come on. The imposing walls of the refinery cast long shadows across the road and onto the scrub brush that grew wild along the opposite shoulder.

The chef pulled off the highway onto a stretch of pavement that led up to a set of huge iron gates. Without haste, a guard dressed in black fatigues appeared from a side access door in the wall. His erect posture and the assault rifle slung over his shoulder meant business as he raised a commanding hand. Then, with a slow measured gait of a Gestapo officer he cautiously angled toward the driver's side of the van.

Releasing a nervous cough, the chef flexed his fingers on the wheel. This was standard routine at any high-security compound, he reminded himself; a lot of muscle flexing to deter protestors and infiltrators.

The guard pursed his lips and shouldered up to the driver's open window. His eyes—tiny slits in the flood lamps above—darted side to side in search of any outside threat, if nothing else, validating his role as gatekeeper. He recognized the driver as little more than an aging chef who'd come to serve dinner to the boss and a handful of company mucky-mucks. The van would also be stocked with grub for security and the work crews.

The beam of his flashlight illuminated the cab. His eyes met the chef and he spoke in a slow deep tone. "Yer late and da boss don't like no waitin' round!"

"Utility roadblock a mile or two back," the chef wheezed. "Delayed me a bit. I'm ready when you are."

The guard eyeballed the van a final time. The crumple of lines on his face faded. "Straight up da drive," he ordered. "Escort's waitin' at the chateau."

The chef cut a smile and shoved a bottle of Jack Daniels through the window. "I wouldn't forget you fellas out here on duty."

Attempting to conceal his delight, the guard raised the bottle up into the flood light of the guard tower. He shot a thumbs-up sign toward the gate operator. Immediately the hum of electric motors sounded. Heavy iron lurched into motion and the hinges creaked as the gates began their broad sweep.

Holding down the clutch with the shifter in gear, the chef's pulse quickened as the gates met the driveway's edge. Easing the van over the threshold, he lumbered up the drive. He backed the vehicle up to the chateau's service access, jumped out, and pulled on a smock hanging behind his door. The smell of marinated beef waft out through side vents of the van. The chef adjusted his garment and greeted the armed escort.

The chateau was much bigger and grander than what he'd imagined from the description he'd received. Several levels of European architecture elevated the stone mansion well above gardens of fruit trees and softly lit vintage street lanterns, erected along brick footpaths leading to front and side entrances.

The chef carefully draped a white towel over his forearm the way waiters in fine restaurants do. After a somewhat clumsy orchestration of securing the hot boxes below each cart, he navigated them behind the escort into a service entrance. Two more guards waiting there met him. The chef stood patiently while each guard performed a cursory visual inspection of him, their weapon's polished gray barrels at their sides. They hadn't frisked him when one of the guards waved the chef into the service elevator. The escort made discrete little sniffs aboard the elevator as it ascended to the 2nd level.

The large room at the end of a long hall hardly resembled a dining hall. The chef saw teams of engineers darting around in white lab coats between banks of electronic hardware and video screens. This floor of the chateau was clearly the heart and brains of Admiral's brightly lit refinery viewed through an enormous window to his right. Logistics and security inside the chateau rivaled the sophistication of any classified government installation.

A long dinner table was situated to his left toward the back of the room—all within view of the monitors and gadgetry that made Crimson's ethanol business tick. It was this operation the U.S. president, via a White House video link, was scheduled to commend Admiral for, along with other economic contributions. Evidenced by technicians cabling the staging area, the conference was to take place in a few short minutes. Admiral's record production of bio-fuels in the region had caught the attention of a number of alternative energy commissions around the country. According to the itinerary the chef carried in his breast pocket, that evening a dignitary from Washington DC was to make a virtual appearance. He would speak briefly on behalf of the oil crisis and laud Admiral's role in producing wild-grass based ethanol as a significant contributor toward economic recovery.

From the chef's vantage point, the site's ethanol operation—identifiable at one end of the room—began to appear insignificant in contrast to a heavily guarded area he noticed to his right. Ostensibly resembling a security post, he revised his interpretation, behind a blue tinted partition, as a highly sophisticated system monitoring something much greater than the manufacture of grain-based fuels.

Hunched in rows over computer screens, suited technicians spoke into headsets and clicked on keyboards. Others moved from station to station, appearing to distribute important data to pertinent checkpoints. Meanwhile, a team of engineers huddled around a table. Their fingers busily crisscrossing the surface of a huge blue print, each conferred with another on the master plan and each of its operating components. Never far away, stoic security faces shadowed the brains of the operation, occasionally stepping back to speak into a walkie-talkie while passing discerning glances.

The escort turned to admonish the chef: "Cut the gawking. You'd better remember who you're serving."

"Yes, of course!" The chef turned and got busy arranging the credenza for the feast.

Several minutes had passed before the first unexpected event took place. One of the technicians across the room received an alarm on his panel. His announcement came over the public address in a controlled shrill. "Intruder detected inside Storage Vault B!"

A squad of security guards yanked their radios off their hips and rushed toward the monitor. Then a tall muscular man in black attire, who seemed to appear out of nowhere, sliced his way through the group and glanced at the video monitor. Before the chef could get a good look at him the man disappeared through an exit at the far end of the room.

Suddenly a man in a wheelchair entered the room through a small inconspicuous door near the head of the table. Instantly the chef recognized the man rolling up to the head spot at the table. He locked the chair into position within six or seven feet of the credenza, leaving the chef a close-up view of the man atop Admiral's pyramid. Rodney Panach cleared his voice over a pencil-like microphone that hung near him over the white linens.

"The President of the United States has authorized the link," his voice announced over the sound system. "Wayne Kirkpatrick will be making his scheduled appearance at any moment. Prepare the staging."

A notable buzz among his subordinates spread through the room.

The chef's blood heated and pulsed throughout his body. From his serving station he watched with heightened interest. Everything was ready, and banquet dining became the least of his thoughts. A venerable force surged through him now. He was in the same room with the most powerful man in business today, though Mr. Panach had no clue as to his identity. So far everything seemed to be in his favor.

Now mere steps separated him from the belligerent bronze-skinned energy magnate—the man everyone in high places admired and feared, for his directives had ranged far beneath righteousness and integrity. Panach was the godfather

233

of the industrial world who at the flick of a finger commanded any whim that might advance his lot.

According to a reliable White House source, Wayne Kirkpatrick had decided to stick with this scheduled conference for little else than to polish Panach's ego under the obligation of doling out economic favors—incentives they were so discreetly labeled—in exchange for political insurance. Despite more urgent matters in Washington this event mandated the president cultivate the necessary business relations his nation depended on under the edicts of national energy policy. Given the crisis unfolding in the Pacific, the conference would remain brief.

*****

One ear pressed against the hatchway directly below the garden patio. Adam tried to make sense of the muffled footsteps above him. They faded for a brief interval, then returned to the immediate area. After several minutes he heard nothing.

With diminished hopes of escape, he retired to the cold ground between two of the mineral stacks where earlier he had located moisture in the soil. This discovery had come to him in the darkness while listening to a pair of tiny claws scratching in one corner of the vault. The rodent, he concluded, had become trapped sometime during the construction phases before Adam's arrival. The creature had sustained itself on what turned out to be a small but welcomed pocket of rainwater, one that yielded Adam a small but measurable quantity of water.

Almost two days had passed since his escape from the dormitory. Inside the vault, the runny-nose cold air had become notably thinner, making each shallow breath more belaboring. Sleep came to him in short weary dozes, which gradually proved increasingly risky as the lack of oxygen threatened to take thought and reasoning away from Adam.

In the frigid blackness he had debated which was worse— the agony of hunger and dehydration, which caused his dry and leathery tongue to stick to the roof of his mouth, or the layered

234

migraines that pounded the insides of his skull.   Both conditions had begun to impair his ability to think clearly with a mind for engineering escape. His hopes had rapidly begun to dissolve. In stride and spirit with millions of Americans living destitute and on the edge of madness, trapped by the treachery of energy withdrawals, Adam too had failed to overcome the oppression Mr. Panach imposed on his subjects.

With a weakened grunt he pulled himself upright and slid his fingers along the back of his overalls. Something had been jabbing at his lower back—a subtle bulge that rubbed and teased the base of his spine—until he could no longer ignore it. His fingers, numb and nearly oblivious to the cold dampness of the chamber, clutched the object in the cavity between the two side pockets.

Through a tear in his right pocket, he worked it around and extracted a tube-shaped article. He lit one of his remaining matches. Bursting to life, the flame brightened the vault. In his hand he held the vial—a forgotten sample of the formula he had capped off at Dell's place minutes before hastily stuffing a mineral probe, one file, three salt tablets, and assorted magnifiers into his overalls. Behind the withering flame Adam took inventory of the affects that lay before him. Immediately he pressed renewed hope into action.

The blast from the tiny vial shook the chamber like an old-fashioned bank job. Adam stepped from behind a stack of NASA's minerals and stumbled through blackness, pawing for the door's iron wheel. Its mechanism still intact, gears meshed and thumped. The wheel surrendered more slack, rotating until the thud of colliding metal bounced off the chamber's walls. Probing the hatch door, his fingers curled around the iron lip where the seam had severed from its airtight seal. The hatch gave way and cool air penetrated his nostrils.

Adam eased one foot through the hatchway. A bare light bulb splashed gray shadows over the walls of a narrow tunnel, large enough for a man to navigate. A fan hummed somewhere down the line. He filled his lungs repeatedly. A rebirth of energy ran through Adam. Cautiously he took a second step into the tunnel.

Cold steel touched the jawbone below his right ear.

"Bang, you're dead!" A familiar voice bounced off the gray cement walls. "Let's go, Mr. Harlow."

*****

Like rolling thunder Panach's voice boomed across the control room where the executive engineers were hunched over a broad steel table covered in blue prints.

The next moment they joined their boss at the table where he had been bragging about how efficiently Admiral had deployed scores of bureaucratic pawns in Washington to successfully marginalize two world powers in the race to control energy markets. Aside from deposing several key scientists, progress was now a matter of sorting out a few logistics.

The chef surveyed the configuration of security and sheathed his carving knife.

A technician stood up at his console near a hexagon stage that had been assembled minutes earlier. He shouted that President Kirkpatrick was fifteen seconds away from appearing in the holographic video feed, downloading directly from the Oval Office.

Panach's baritone trumpeted again. His eyes were wide and glassy over several empty brandy glasses. Cigar smoke wound upward past his v-shaped eyebrows. Abruptly the sparkle of diamond-clad knuckles crashed down on the white linens. "I shall keep this short, gentlemen. The president will perform his political rites ... then we'll close the link and break out the champagne."

The chef toweled his hands before releasing the latch on the first polished hardwood case of France's finest champagne, a lot reserved for the wealthiest. Overhead lighting dimmed and a broad light beam flickered over the stage in the center of the room. Immediately, Wayne Kirkpatrick's image appeared under a glittering shower of holographic light. At the head of the table Panach waited for the audio feed. It broke and crackled then began streaming. Everyone listened as the president greeted Mr. Panach in a dignified tone. On cue from a set director positioned behind the president's image, the engineers applauded dutifully.

Cradling a stout bottle in his fingers—its label gilded in bands of solid gold— Panach smiled back. "Mr. Wayne Kirkpatrick," he chortled, "is it fair to say your administration fully supports and validates our mission to supply this great nation with cheaper, more efficient energy?"

"Indeed it does," the president answered through an annoying audio delay. "I have no reservations about Admiral's unmatched capacity to develop an improved ethanol product. Mr. Panach, with your company's leadership and perseverance we shall deliver America from the tides of economic strife."

A few of the suited engineers hastily responded with a padded salute, accompanied by political well wishing. They shifted their attention back onto Panach. A wave of his hand demanded the champagne begin flowing. In the Oval Office the president was handed a glass of champagne.

The chef scurried around the table pouring champagne, then put his eyes back on Kirkpatrick's image, with curiosity. Revealing a troubled look and speaking inaudibly, the president was conversing with someone off camera. A moment later he returned with a reluctant grin and briefly proposed a toast to Admiral.

"To expeditious economic recovery!"

Glasses clinked and a lull came over the room. Despite his pale, sickly complexion, the president managed to carve out an optimistic smile before gulping his champagne on camera.

The engineers followed suit and waited for Kirkpatrick to begin speaking again. On cue from Panach, the room erupted into applause. Kirkpatrick had announced he was granting Admiral two hundred and eighty thousand acres of pristine forest land for oil exploration and development. He had barely finished when the doors at the other end of the room burst open.

In walked the tall man wearing dark attire. In his grip, the arm of a man in soiled overalls entered. Two guards were strolling up from the rear with automatic weapons held to the detainee's backside. After three or four steps into the room, he was shoved to his knees. Ken Burke, the tall man who'd

237

delegated the searched, stepped forward to address Panach. The chef took note of the man addressing Panach. His face was familiar. The scar confirmed his hunch of distance memories the chef had long preferred to leave behind.

"As promised, I found him. Mr. Harlow was hiding out in our underground storage vault, sir."

Adam Harlow appeared pale and weak in comparison to those flanking him.

Panach's eyes nervously returned to the holographic link. For a copious moment Kirkpatrick had turned his attention to matters transpiring off camera inside the Oval Office. This gave Panach the interval he needed.

Glaring at his top security man who stood over Adam like a prize fighter, Panach spoke in a controlled tone so as not to be heard through the White House link: "I have no more use for Mr. Harlow. Deliver evidence of his retirement to me in the usual manner."

Kirkpatrick's image reappeared in the holographic transmission. Unaware of events unfolding at Crimson, the president searched his bearings and collected his wits as he raised his glass to another toast. Beyond Kirkpatrick's view, two of Burke's guards motioned their quarry to his feet. Adam refused. Instead, he pivoted himself toward the cylindrical light beam that shimmered in the center of the room, raising a free arm in attempts to capture Kirkpatrick's attention.

At that moment the table of senior engineers delivered a hastily concocted toast. The guards and technicians looked on with amusement as the president surrendered his faith to manufactured nonsense.

"To the liberation of our great nation from the bondage of poverty and des—"

A hoarse voice cut them off, catching everyone in the room by surprise. In labored gasps Adam Harlow spoke in labored bursts. "The dust of Apollo ... *cough* ... lies hidden beneath ... my feet, aging like ... *cough* ... a forbidden wine to be drunk only by—"

One swift stroke of the guard's assault rifle left Adam sprawled onto the floor, silenced. By his feet he was pulled beyond all possible camera angles. The accompanying guard quickly deployed a chokehold.

"A toast to unyielding guidance from our leaders in Washington!" Panach roared into his mic, smiling gleefully at the president, who again had lifted his glass in unison and was gulping champagne. On cue the chime of crashing goblets filled the room. Panach tossed back his brandy and exchanged final nods with Kirkpatrick. With a flash of shimmering diamonds, Panach's hand gestured his AV technician. His other hand covered the mic. "Kill the link ... then kill Mr. Harlow." Deftly, Panach gestured a departing wave at Kirkpatrick before the image of the American president faded.

A wary look in Panach's eyes suggested complications. Not unlike the toss of a coin, there was a chance things could backfire. If Adam's words had been transmitted, there would be questions. But noise from the celebration had likely distorted the audio feed. The guards had stowed away their weapons. And the president hadn't displayed any concern or confusion. Clearly he'd been occupied with other matters in the White House and had not heard Mr. Harlow's muffled speech.

The chef watched with intrigue as the last bits of the lighted transmission vanished. Panach's attention had turned fully upon Adam, whose death was presently a foregone conclusion. With Kirkpatrick out of the picture Panach would reap some pleasure out of Adam's company-sponsored execution. It wouldn't be the first.

Among the executive engineers seated at the table, a troubled look passed from face to face. Each man exchanged a worried look at the other. For most it was evident that cold-blooded murder had not been a part of their professional repertoire at Admiral. Instead, these were subservient brains who had invested talents in cutting edge science—a vision that was increasingly detached from their privately held dreams.

For the chef, his defining moment had come. The purpose of his trip to Crimson would now manifest redemptions overdue. Stepping away from the credenza, he waited until all eyes were on Adam. Carefully he hoisted a stack of dinner plates. In one rehearsed motion the chef released them, producing a terrible crash while extracting a semi-automatic handgun from the flaps of his apron.

"Stand up, Mr. Harlow!" he commanded across the room. The chef stepped toward the head of the table fully prepared to dispel any misconceived notions by Panach or his goons. The cobalt barrel of the chef's pistol rested against Panach's temple.

Chin high and dead calm, the oil mogul's voice rumbled. "If you have something to add to this celebration, Mr. Chef, let us in on it."

The chef removed his hat and carefully scanned the room. His eyes paused long enough on the guards to deliver a terse warning against any misconceived shenanigans.

"I'll give Mr. Burke the honors of making introductions."

Cautiously Panach swiveled around to face his top man. "Okay. Who is this man?"

Burke's eyes met the chef with ambivalence. "I know him as a CIA operative, sir. Showed up during a lockdown following a major security breach in Baghdad. The Green Zone ... too many years ago. I recognize the snake now. The name is *Striker*, sir. Colonel William Striker."

Panach spat through a gust of breath, visibly rejecting the notion as a prank. Malevolence dripped from his voice. "Never met him face-to-face, but I know the name. Continue please."

Burke swallowed dryly. "At the time I was employed with Atlas Security, a private firm in charge of certifying and transporting munitions. It was a hot afternoon when the colonel walks up and informs me that we were in possession of defective ammo—all part of a sting operation against a suspected arms ring operating in our platoon, right under our noses. So he whispers to a couple of us about somebody selling out American troops to terrorist infiltrators. To prove his point, he calls the brass out and urges one of my men to inspect a box of our munitions. Next thing I know the colonel walks back to me and shoves a wireless detonator he'd found in our barracks into my hand. He orders me to activate it ... right there in front of American and Iraqi brass." Burke lifted a hand to his face and pulled two fingers across the scar running from his left eye down to his neck. "I was among the fortunate that day."

Striker squared his shoulders toward the engineers. "Gentlemen, everything your Mr. Burke says is accurate. The results of a clever device designed to smear Western military presence. Rout American troop placements. Drive up the price of gasoline markets around the world. Bogus intelligence manufactured and exported by Admiral Petroleum."

The colonel eyeballed the guards as he shifted the gun over Panach's curly sideburn. "In the years since, your boss has pulled long strings in Washington to secure contracts for Atlas to handle international security operations in the most sensitive sites. As diplomatic ties disintegrated throughout the Gulf Region, the company fell under political and industry scrutiny, prompting legitimate personnel to resign and go elsewhere. This, as you might imagine, left Atlas to a handful of thugs operating under a clandestine code of conduct; chiefly cutting deals with the region's top gun runners."

"When did you become a crusading activist ... engrossed in the good of humanity?"

Striker ignored Mr. Panach's remark and continued. "Atlas's sole intent: Broker the spoils left by evacuated American troops—your own brothers and sisters. A rather significant component to the economic mess we're in today."

"Propaganda!" sneered Panach. "I sold off my share of Atlas a decade ago. I have no control of whatever became of that outfit. Admiral will never stand trial for the CIA's fumbled—"

Rodney Panach had just begun to ramp up his defense when a technician from the control room interrupted him. He carried a printed message to Burke. Nervously, the tech turned to address the CEO: "Uh, sir, our first analysis. I believe everything is ready."

"Read it aloud," Striker shouted with an expectant glare toward Burke.

Burke's eyes glanced at the document before shifting back on Panach, who now sat erect. The lines on his face twisted in mixed anticipation. Panach nodded his approval.

"Just now coming off the main service line, our initial product matches the combustible properties dictated by NASA. However, sir, it is 27 percent *more* volatile, which has caused an abnormal thermal factor. Soon we'll approach peak temperature tolerances."

The engineers were poised to respond to what translated into a potential emergency. Panach displayed no concern, however and ordered plant operations to continue. "We have only Mr. Harlow to thank for his design of a superior product. Therefore, I see no reason to hear out your rhetoric spoken by our saintly colonel. Clearly we have developed a better product, one that is patent-ready, which completely validates our alliances with one of NASA's contracted engineers. In such case, Admiral Petroleum shall again prevail. Kill me and you'll be answering to a higher authority ... once again, Colonel."

The dining room's nerve energy heightened immediately. A buzz of chatter spread into the control room. William Striker adjusted his posture, anchoring the gun more firmly against Panach's ear. "As I see it, you have nothing to celebrate. Not if I have a hand in this."

The colonel quickly surveyed the room and was relieved to find the main doorway clear. This helped press his thoughts onto the next phase of the mission. The colonel's eyes glared down at Adam who'd been taking in all of this from his knees.

"Get on your feet, Mr. Harlow!"

Adam paused to glance again at the company engineers who were staring at him from inside the control room. This proved to be a pointless hesitation, which thoroughly irritated the colonel.

"That's a *direct* order, Adam Harlow. Stand up and *move*! Anyone who tries to stop you will condemn his boss to a very untimely trip to the grave." Striker found himself in full form, barking in his drill-sergeant register that commanded respect and obedience.

Adam slowly rose to his feet, keeping an eye on three guards engaged in the mental standoff with the colonel. After gaining his balance he staggered past them through the main doors.

In a simultaneous overture, Panach boiled over. A powerful twist of his arm slammed Striker's gun against a wall directly behind them, causing it to discharge a round. The slug passed through the champagne locker and into the shoulder of a nearby guard. Startled by the blow, the guard leveled his AK-47 and spun full circle, spraying the room with lead in an arc that took out light fixtures and shattered the massive window overlooking the refinery. Any attempt to stop the colonel had plunged the command center into mayhem. Two technicians drooped over their controls in a pool of blood. Those who remained at the controls scrambled face down on the floor.

As suddenly as it had started the incident appeared to be over. Yet Adam was no longer present, and the colonel left to his own devices for escape. Emergency lighting began to flicker on in a far corner of the room when a ruptured fuel chamber monitoring device burst into flames. Fire would quickly spread.

Postponing his concern over Adam's escape, Burke doled out orders to the guards to stow their weapons and get busy extinguishing the flames. Panach was shouting at his senior engineers to secure the blueprints. Crouched unseen beneath the linen-skirted tables, Striker's mind clicked rapidly. Only a few seconds remained before Adam would be difficult to track down. The fire was spreading at an accelerated clip and building security with hoses were preparing to flood the control room. Confusion mounted. Behind all the panic, Striker enjoyed a narrow window of time for a prized opportunity to decommission Panach, once and for all.

Out of view, he rolled up his right pant leg and slid out the small Derringer he'd packed against his shin inside a knee-high sock. In the dark he oriented himself. Panach's chair swiveled and shook as he barked orders from the head of the table. The colonel crept closer. Consistent with CIA training tasks, his plan was simple and required no rehearsal.

Never had William Striker been more eager to engage a man of so much power and station. Careful to remain invisible, he found a parted section of linen and positioned the Derringer up through it. He would shoot through darkness at one end of the long table to the other, approximating a line toward Panach's gut.

A single shot rang out.

Wholly prepared to view one more grisly corpse in a lengthy career of covert encounters, Striker rose to his feet to examine his handy work.

The space at the head of the table was vacant.

Panach had somehow slipped away!

Twenty-six

Thoroughly agitated by the disruptions that had just occurred, Panach cursed his errors as he secured the door into his private suite behind him.

He knew Crimson's cement walls and electrically charged fences were treacherous for an ordinary man to pass. Adam Harlow had proved to be no ordinary man, but a deliberate menace, capable of jeopardizing company business operations. Joining him was the two-faced traitor who had most certainly sold out to Montech, and now he'd showed up to pilfer the same secrets Adam was willing to exchange for a Chinese girl and a free ride out of Admiral's hands. Colonel Striker was a dangerous adversary. The sort who could burn his bridges, breach security, and cause irrevocable damage.

At the same time, Panach confessed he'd been fool hardy and vain for initiating a virtual conference with Kirkpatrick. Even with political points to gain and the need to dispel mounting suspicions against his petroleum company, too much at Crimson was open to exposure.

Beyond the walls of his suite the engineers had begun the task of inspecting the damage. The blaze had spread dangerously close to *Aqualene*'s control banks, causing the inductive collector—an automated unit inside the plant designed to carry out molecular fusion of two negative combining agents—to fail. Meanwhile, the plant's floor manager was advising a controlled shutdown, once the word came from the top to do so. Shutdown would take nearly an hour to conduct safely. The plant had to be manually cooled while pressure in the condensers brought down without overloading the pump circuits.

But Crimson's job was not finished, and so Panach ordered the operation to continue at a caffeinated clip, well into the night. Though its operations would be short-lived, the plant had served its purpose as a model template for finishing dozens of clone sites completely invisible to the public eye. Panach needed some *finished product* to duplicate at selected domestic and international locations.

Within eight hours ahead of a new day, Admiral's own ethanol tanker trucks would begin rolling out with several tons of *Aqualene*. Transporting it to regional locations, unknown to federal authorities. The cargo would then be placed on company transport jets destined for the coast. NASA's mineral shipments would leave Crimson disguised as heavy machinery. The plan was a stroke of genius. Rodney Panach had accounted for the need to create a diversion by destroying the north end of the property in hopes of minimizing staged damage at ethanol operations to the south. Operations there would cease, once handpicked energy safety officials arrived to order a full shutdown and determine the cause of the fires, which were likely be linked to a series of wiring defects traced to Admiral's in-house electricians. Publicly, the company would accept blame and pay state and federal fines. Admiral Petroleum would appear a victim of its own internal errors.

The way things were transpiring—though slightly askew from his original scheme—Panach would see the outcome he'd hoped for all along. Beyond the smoke and confusion surging through the control center, he'd summoned his second-in-command to the suite. There he spoke bluntly: "I trust you don't find credence in the colonel's story about Atlas."

Burke nodded in agreement. "True, Striker *was* involved in the incident ... but that's not to say he wasn't a part of its scheme."

"It pleases me to hear you share the same wisdom as I, Mr. Burke. With no more to be said on the matter, you'll prepare my helicopter for our timely departure."

"What about Harlow, sir? I can finish him off ... and with great pleasure."

"You had your chance," Panach barked with a clap of his hands. "Leave him to the dead with the others out there."

Burke disappeared into a hallway leading to the roof access. Panach turned to the monitor at his desk. A real-time graphic indicated that operations inside the *Aqualene* plant had been dialed up and his faithful engineers were busy minding the operation. From his suite window the plant's dome shimmered in the light of a rising moon under broken clouds. At the near side of the building one of Admiral's ethanol tankers had pulled into a loading bay. A crew was preparing to transfer Admiral's first shipment of formula. Everything appeared to be on schedule. Tomorrow millions of Americans would be watching morning news coverage of the burning of Crimson. At carefully-timed intervals, company aircraft would be taking off for floating installations in the Pacific, far beyond the two-hundred mile limit west of Mexico.

Panach hastened his departure, anticipating a nighttime journey southward through the bottom end of California before veering westward over the Baja coastline. By dawn his private jet would touch down in a small airfield. He'd waste no time boarding a company helicopter and then reach a command platform in the Pacific, in time for breakfast. He looked forward to his role as chief conductor, orchestrating his master plan to dominate world energy markets as *Aqualene* began filling huge depositories at sea.

He slipped a small remote device inside his breast pocket. Mr. Panach made a final check of the personal effects he elected to leave behind, as evidence this hadn't been a final departure with no plans to return. Ephemeral images of the ninety-some salaried engineers inside the plant passed through his mind. Some of his best company men were toiling there, dedicated to thrusting the fledgling petroleum industry into the future of water-based fuels. According to fuel analysis reports in the control room, Crimson was accomplishing its intended goal by proving that Admiral Petroleum possessed its own unique version of the formula and could legally manufacture *Aqualene* in remote locations across South America.

He pressed himself up out of his chair and rolled onto the sofa. A drawer below his stubs motored open. From it he removed two prosthetic limbs, both of which fit snuggly over the uneven stubs that remained of his thighs He then snapped together three electrical joints and powered up their servos. Pulling on wool insulated pants and a fur-lined parka, Rodney Panach was prepared for blustery weather that frequented the Pacific coast this time of year.

Pushing his wheelchair aside, he awkwardly teetered through a doorway, unseen by personnel battling two remaining blazes inside the control room. In the narrow arched

247

hallway leading to a private elevator to the roof, Mr. Panach dismissed the sight of Ken Burke's goggled eyes. For no person at Admiral had witnessed their crippled CEO walking on two artificial legs. It had been several years since Panach had privately attempted to employ prosthetic devices into daily life. He had found them awkward and painful, given the condition of his failing spine.

Under Panach's heated glare, Burke stifled himself and gestured his boss into the elevator. Panach briefed his pilot on the way up.

"Trunk line and wireless communications disabled?"

"Check, sir."

"Explosives set and ready to detonate, at my command?"

Burke's grin revealed a silver speckled tooth. "Ready on your orders, sir."

Anticipating a nap aboard the Cessna in route to the Baja coastline, Panach adjusted himself against the wall of the elevator. The ride was slow and tenuous. Standing erect caused him immediate fatigue and an annoying touch of vertigo. He pushed his discomforts aside and returned to business at hand. Leaving Crimson a charred wasteland had been a plausible backup plan for weeks, perfected by the firm's legal team as unavoidable; a procedural chore.

The elevator halted and rolled open.

Burke swiveled past his boss, pausing briefly to determine if he desired a physical escorted to the chopper. A cursory glance into the man's eyes quickly erased such notion, prompting Burke to rush ahead onto the circular tarmac. From a radio clip he'd activated on his belt, the helicopter began powering up. Burke climbed aboard under the lopping blades. Panach had begun making his way across the pad when the rooftop trembled beneath his feet. An explosion inside the chateau lit up a back section of the compound.

Beads of sweat now streaming down his face, Panach halted in his tracks. It was time to re-appraise the situation. Tremendous heat generated by flames leaping from a rooftop vent directly above the control room flanked him on the right. Though absent of viewing angle, he suspected this was connected to a new fire at the ethanol pumping station behind the chateau. The mechanical joints inside his prosthetic limbs began to hiss and whine, quickly propelling him through a curtain of smoke curling up over the roofline and across the heated tarmac.

*****

Adam had dashed from the control room and disappeared down a main hallway. The colonel quickly made his exit, pursuing Adam in a dead run that took him to a stairwell and into a darkened corridor where Adam paused. Standing over two unconscious men evoked memories of the horrible toxins that had killed his father—generated by the burning of synthetic building materials.

Had his intentions to deceive Admiral and all its menacing ambitions had some hand in taking human lives? He could only guess what lie ahead. What would come out of his resolve to alter the plant's chemical configuration? Was Crimson's demise threatening to create a local environmental disaster in the making?

By tweaking the specifications to propagate an overheating condition and force a premature plant shutdown, he'd hoped intelligence satellites might detect unusual hot spots. Investigation might even lead authorities to the rogue plant. Every passing minute suggested the mix had unleashed more than its share of danger, and that reversal was out of the question.

Fumes from a damaged monitoring unit in the control room had spread along the currents of a deadly draft blowing through the heating ducts and out the chateau's floor-mounted registers. The odor, combined with a lethal mix of burning plastics, nauseated Adam. Confusion crept over him as he stood staring at the two corpses sprawled out over the smoldering carpet. The colonel appeared suddenly at his side. He wasted no time stripping off their ventilator masks and tossing one to Adam with a command to pull it down over his face. Adam did so, not without an uneasy feeling of wearing a device that seemed less than effective for its previous user.

Adam gathered himself and determined they needed to put distance between them and the chateau. Otherwise they were destined to be captured, shot, or asphyxiated. They pressed on to haste to find their way into the subbasement. This route, Adam reasoned, would take them away from the chateau and across the compound, unseen.

Twenty steps from the entrance to the subterranean corridor two of Admiral's security were sprawled out on a smoking stretch of carpet. One was drifting in and out of consciousness. The other was coherent but not for long. The colonel positioned himself over him, then planted a boot to the man's chest.

"Where the hell is Mr. Panach?" he demanded through his mask. The burning hardwoods crackled louder as the fire ate up square footage behind them. Neither man produced a definitive answer. This irritated the colonel. He glanced back at the flames gaining on them, then weighted his boot onto the man's chest. "You ain't going nowhere til I get answers. Now, where's Rodney Panach?"

The man pinned under the colonel's boot spat. He'd resigned to a policy of *silence*. The other one hacked and wheezed. In between feeble gulps for air his eyes grew wide with fear, reflecting the dance of orange and yellow flames rapidly approaching them. He grunted and sat, pointing upward.

"Upstairs? The rooftop? Where?" The colonel was growing impatient.

"The company helicopter," Adam shouted, twirling finger over his head. "He's leaving!"

Striker shook his fist. "If I know Panach he's up to saving his own ass from something more than a little fire. We need to get out of here. Which way?"

Adam led the colonel through shattered glass into the entrance of the tunnel network. Striker's arm swung out from his hip, halting Adam in mid step. "Step back!" The colonel lifted his automatic pistol and discharged several rounds, each one ricocheting into the canopy of smoke that blanketed the path ahead of them.

"Okay, let's go," he ordered.

Both adjusted their masks and disappeared into the smoke. In the bowels of Crimson a bare light bulb lit the cement ductwork every ten yards or so. After silently maneuvering the shaft they reached a junction. Striker pulled a palm-sized military PDA from his breast pocket and handed it to Adam. "Where the hell are we in this tinderbox?"

Clutching the GPS unit, Adam quickly scanned its orange glowing screen. "Fifteen yards north-northeast of the plant." He pointed to a connecting tunnel sloping downward beneath the plant. "We'll pass under the main floor and follow the cooling lines to the river. It's not the most direct way out, but—"

"Hold on," Striker protested. "Panach is an evil man, the type to burn his bridges and blow this place to smithereens. I say we bypass the plant and get our asses straight down to the river."

Adam paused. "Not until I warn the others."

Striker was incredulous. "Those bastard thugs? Not on your life!"

"Many of the engineers in there are decent men—victims of the economy. Family men, desperate for work." Adam recalled his own road into Crimson. Something inside him suggested the colonel had little room to talk on the subject of righteousness. A man could be driven by his fears as readily as by his valor. "With or without you, sir, I'm going in to warn them."

The colonel hesitated then hastily turned his gun toward Adam. You're going with me. I have a duty to—"

"Then you'll have to carry my corpse out on your back," Adam growled.

The colonel surveyed the area again. He cocked his head. "You'd better make it damn snappy. We've got no time for hugs and formal goodbyes."

Boldly, Adam ran down the fork leading to the plant. The air cleared of smoke as he neared the guard station. The post was little more than a phone booth sized hut situated at the underground entrance to the plant. Adam peeled off his mask and immediately recognized the guard on duty. "Tell everyone to get out!"

"Hold it right there!" the guard barked. "Security's been lookin' for you. And I'll be the one to get credit for haulin' your ass in." His weapon swung around and settled on Adam's gut.

"Look, this whole place is going to blow, either on its own or at the hands of your beloved CEO."

"What'd ya mean by that?" The guard eyed Adam suspiciously then glanced back at the guard post. Inside his partner was sleeping on a stool against the window. Impulsively he turned his weapon onto Striker who'd caught up to Adam. "Both you guys'r comin' with me."

But Adam had discarded his fears and slowly started toward the plant's underground entrance. Beyond it lay the main production floor.

The guard swung his weapon toward Adam's back. "Halt ... or I'll shoot!"

Striker reached over and fisted the gun's barrel. "Listen, stupid. Can't you hear it?" He'd cupped one ear against a steel ventilator next to them. "You hear the chopper? That's your loyal boss pulling out, gonna miss his own fireworks!"

Panting in front of the doors leading onto the plant's main floor, Adam turned back toward the colonel. "You'd better warn the engineers to evacuate the plant, now!"

"She's gonna blow!" Striker remarked. He released his grip on the guard's gun barrel. "This won't be the first time your Mr. Panach has made these convenient little sacrifices."

The guard drew a confused look before electing to rush back to the guard post.

As Adam hurried Striker through the entrance the guard's voice could be heard rumbling over the public address system announcing, attempting to put evacuation orders into words. The engineers paused briefly before returning to their work. Few offered little attention to the blue alert. A redundant series of drills had lulled them into a routine of ignoring the announcements over the PA.

A sudden change of consensus ripped through the plant. The fusion unit on the west wall had been reaching a melting point within. Suddenly its plumbing points were in flames. Another fire broke out at the base of one of the main condensers, setting off alarm buzzers Strobe lights that hung down over the main floor blinked furiously.

The lead engineer ordered his crews to initiate emergency shutdown sequences. His commands eroded as panic erupted into chaos. Seconds later the two external exits were clogged with technicians clamoring to get out.

This was the type of mayhem Adam had suspected could occur at Crimson. He'd noticed faults about the exits leading out onto the compound. They were narrow and inadequate for an emergency exodus. A handful of engineers punched through before a new obstacle stood in the way of escape. The iron doors leading out of the plant slowly rolled shut. They'd been powered closed like a sliding bulkhead sealing water-tight compartments on a distressed ship that was taking on water. Impassable!

"We're sealed in," someone shouted behind a veil of thick smoke. "They've dead bolted us in!"

"By wireless remote, no doubt," Striker said to Adam as they scanned the room for any feasible escape route. "One of Panach's methods of getting results while covering up unwanted footprints."

"There *is* another way out," Adam answered in a tone chillingly calm to the colonel under the circumstances. "Auxiliary cooling passages! We never had time to plumb into the main cooling loop. I studied them in the blue prints."

"That explains the fires," Striker crowed, as if an expert in such matters. Adam ignored the colonel's gloating and turned to a scaffold towering over him. Several technicians had begun shouting and waving madly from the top level where they worked on two of the main fractioning towers. It was a point where the formula would enter its finishing stages. Impact from a minor blast at its base had resulted in a partial damage to the structure, prompting some of the workers to descend the iron grid, while others crowded onto a damaged steel ladder. Climbing down seemed as hazardous as jumping, given the outbreak of a new blaze fueled by spilled chemicals at the base of the structure.

Striker arrived at Adam's side. Both stared up at a lone technician trapped on the highest level of three catwalks.

Adam pulled on a pair of work gloves from a nearby tool station. He spoke with resolve and determination. "I'm going up."

"The hell you are!" Striker barked though the mask he'd pulled over his face. "We'll never get out of here in time. Panach has us locked in, he's sure to let the place blow at any—"

The colonel's words drifted into smoke. Adam quickly instructed him on how to access the cooling passages so the engineers could exit safely. Then pulled the mask over his face and fixed his sights on the welder he'd worked with three days earlier. Dangling from the edge of the catwalk, he struggled to hold on. A lighting panel gave way above him, missing Adam and careening to the cement floor. At this point alliances with Panach were no longer important to Adam. One way or another, everyone at Crimson had been coerced to serve Admiral's self-serving interests.

Adam climbed up within yards of the welder. Hand-over-hand he worked his way across the hot steel rungs burning through the canvas gloves. His fingers would have otherwise been ripped to shreds on the unfinished edges of angle iron supports. Adam pushed away the cries of those collapsing on the floor below him, letting it all fade into a jumbled buzz. Crews below had procured masks and were scavenging unused building materials. Others were attempting to pry open access doors that led into auxiliary cooling ports Adam knew would exit to the network of shafts beneath the plant.

The mask's oxygen supply would expire in minutes.

Agonizing pulls brought Adam to the steel surface of the catwalk. There he flopped himself onto its hot grating. Without contemplating the consequences to his health, he tore off his oxygen mask and applied it to Ted's face, who had dutifully repaired the fractioning tower that evening. Ted had been neutral in the mix of personalities, and a friend to Bates. He'd been responsible for monitoring variations in the fractioning shaft temperatures with duties to detect and repair leaks in the towers.

Adam steadied himself with one arm. The other hand held the mask over the man's colorless cheeks. Below him high-speed pumps and compressors were just beginning to power down. Dangerous minutes would pass before the equipment would come to a rest. Meanwhile the risk of new fires was high. Adam was instantly reminded of this as a powerful blast ripped through the electrical station at the opposite end of the scaffolding. The catwalk creaked and buckled. Adam watched men scatter below, each one attempting to escape raining debris from stacks of building materials on a mid-level of the scaffold. Emergency lighting flickered. Then a frightful moment of darkness consumed the smoky air space. Adam thought about the thousands of sailors who'd been trapped in the bottom of their burning warships, surrounded by heavy machinery operating faithfully at ear-piercing levels. Flames danced wildly at the base of the condensers and billowing toxins churned in the weighted air.

A small patch of emergency lighting flickered on. It hardly illuminated the chrome polished condenser piping that twisted and turned in the open spaces above the floor. Adam shook in horror. The structure beneath him groaned until one of the main trusses snapped apart in the middle, causing the catwalk to list. He could hear another engineer screaming as he fell to his death.

Mumbling a parade of choking groans, the welder fought to maintain consciousness. Adam exhaled and took another shot of oxygen before placing the mask over the man's face again. But the welder coughed and shoved it away. His eyes squinted into the smoke.

"Better get yer ass outta here, Mr. Harlow."

Adam protested. "Let me get you to the doc. He's gotta be around some—"

"No way! Ain't no prayer left … not for me," he wheezed. Adam could hardly argue his point. He grimaced at the man's contorted body. A deep gash traversed his lower back. Blood that had trickled past his lips was a steady flow. He was grunting again. "Take the … ventilation service port … cut through … motor pool. Watch it … Panach's car … d-down…on sub... *Cough* … armed guards … got … orders to—"

255

Adam swiveled around and surveyed what remained of the trellis below him. By some miracle of God it hadn't yet collapsed.

"Go now!" the welder garbled weakly. His eyes flickered with a hint of compassion. Signs of life in the man's face faded.

Adam offered a sympathetic squeeze to the welder's hand.

In the sand-colored haze that hovered near the plant's ceiling, Adam turned and crawled over an intact section of the catwalk. Gripping buckled braces that supported the hand railing, he flopped onto his belly and swung his feet over the side. Essentially he was descending a perforated wall over which the insertion of handheld pegs prevented him from plunging thirty feet to the cement floor. Adam muscled his way down three cross members until he reached the forth one. Without warning the structure's main joist gave way. It teetered forward, dangling him directly over a chemical fire twenty feet beyond the soles of his shoes. The threat of falling into the flames shot adrenaline through his blazing guts, which spread out to his taxed limbs. Drawing a lungful of metered oxygen, he watched through the mask's stained lens as a toxic plume of smoke rose up from the floor. With a reversed handgrip on the angle iron supports, Adam swung one leg up over a tangled rail, the way he'd learned to shift a wrestling opponent's offensive attack into a defensive retreat. Adam's other leg followed with just enough momentum to latch onto a vertical brace. Under the force of his body's rotation the other foot guided his body down a pair of crippled cross members.

His feet found the floor where several men lay before him. Each had inhaled toxic fumes and appeared to be losing life. Adam turned to survey the room, finding no sign of Striker. Adam paused for one final pass over the carnage.

"Over here!" It was the colonel's gruff voice coming from behind a large gray cylinder. Beyond his shadow the engineers had broken through one of the steel doors and had emptied out into the compound.

Striker was standing over an open hatchway. Adam knew where it led—down into the subterranean tunnel angling east.

"Wrong way," he said flatly. "Unless you plan to return to the chateau and serve dessert."

The colonel wore a confused but self-determined look. "You got a better plan?" he said impatiently. "We'll be cut down if we walk through that door." Dejected, he watched Adam yank off a damaged brace from the scaffolding and use it to pry off the ventilation screen mounted low on the wall behind the second of six condensing units.

Adam stepped into the ventilation shaft, pausing to get the GPS from Striker. "You'll have to trust me on this one. By now the tunnels will be crawling with goons. Many are still clueless to what's really going on out here." Adam zoomed out. "Look, the *Aqualene* plant is at the north end of the compound. The ethanol plant is here, a mile south—and the most logical way out if we want to avoid ambush." He pressed another button. A detailed map of the north section displayed. "Panach has positioned most of his security forces here. Though unseen at the moment, we're virtually surrounded."

Striker wasn't sold on Adam's plan to shimmy down into the ventilation ducts and run the mile to the ethanol gates. "I suppose we'll hitchhike … or hail a cab down there," he replied grimly. "We're not running a mile through enemy lines only to be assassinated at the gates of this hell hole."

Adam was silent as he climbed down into the vertical shaft. The welder atop the scaffold had implied that less than ten feet below them a separate passage angled south. The tunnel ran for a couple hundred yards before branching off into Crimson's underground motor pool.

When he reached the horizontal connector beneath the plant's floor, he was surprised to find it accommodated enough headroom for a man to stand up. Grumbling to himself, Striker climbed down to where Adam was surveying the dimly lit corridor. While vertical clearance allowed faster travel, lighting was poor and debris littered the pathway.

Adam held the screen out toward the colonel. It displayed graphics resembling a parking lot full of utility vehicles.

"Nice choice," Striker remarked sullenly. "A forklift and backhoe?" He shook his head. "We might get there by sunrise."

257

Adam was grinning now. "We'll do better, Colonel. Take a closer look. Mr. Panach promised me a new car when I signed on. That's one promise he's gonna keep!"

Suddenly Adam leapt into an accelerating trot. "How are you in the hundred yard dash?"

Minutes passed before Colonel Striker caught up, panting and flush to find Adam crouched against a steel grating at the end of the ventilator shaft. From there both men peered into a parking area with tiered floors. A small fleet of combat-ready Humvees sat parked against brightly lit cement walls. A guard was making his rounds as if nothing was happening above ground, suggesting communications among security was sketchy.

"Panach keeps a big chunk of his ego down here," Adam whispered. He gazed at the GPS screen. "The car is directly below us, on a ramp around that corner." His finger skimmed over the screen's menu. A light on the front of the unit glowed red as he pointed the viewfinder toward the ground. Adam set the device for penetrating cement and adjusted the backlight. The screen became brighter as the image of a low-slung, wide-track sports car appeared. "If we can subdue the guard, she's our ticket out of here."

Adam pulled a screwdriver from his breast pocket and silently jimmied the hinged grating. The job of taking out the guard went to the colonel. Kneeling at the first bulkhead, Adam waited for Striker's signal to move out. As the two men rounded the corner, Panach's car came into view, its nose angled out for a quick exit. Adam moved like a cat, sprinting past more black Humvees, each outfitted with a large-caliber gun mounted behind the driver's cab—a small piece of Admiral's cadre of mobile gunner/bunkers.

Behind him Striker admired each machine then removed a butcher's cleaver from his smock and took care of the tires. Adam heard the sidewalls burst as he studied Panach's car with appraising eyes. The car sat obediently beneath an expensive canvas. "Let's get the hell out of here!" Adam shouted to Striker who'd crawled onto one of the trucks to examine its weapons. Adam monkeyed with the car's door

258

release. After a brief interval of pushing and prodding, the gull-wing doors whooshed upward.

*****

A series of powerful blasts leveled what remained of the chateau. The whining chopper hovered a protracted moment over the smoldering rubble.

"Take one last loop around the compound," Panach barked. Burke pitched the blades and pulled up, resuming their search for Adam on the same course they had taken twice already along the perimeter walls. The aircraft was navigating south toward the ethanol refinery when Panach abruptly changed his tact. "Swing this damn thing around! Make a direct pass over the plant. I got a premonition he and the colonel are closer than we think."

Obsessed with taking care of vital business, Panach glared at his watch and renewed his vow to kill the two and then be on his way to the Pacific coast. As competent as Crimson's men were, Adam Harlow and Col. Striker were a dangerous combination that had to be eliminated. Unexpected developments left no room for doubts.

Burke veered away from the east wall and back toward the plant. As they circled it, he became preoccupied with the chore of dodging flying debris and toxins spewing from a burning ammonia propellant tank. Burke nearly missed it—a detail he was sure to regret later.

"Sir, uh … is that your car down there?" Burke exclaimed.

Panach pivoted around in his seat. The sight of the McLaren's headlights leading it out of the motor pool enraged him. "Who the hell—"

Fury exploded into rage.

With mild regrets he had prepared to accept the sacrifice—losing the darling of his vintage fleet of supercars in exchange for the comfort of maintaining company security and political survival. Chaos or not, the car goes up with the compound, he'd decided. He had approved the decision following company legal advice that destroying precious personal

259

property would deliver *authenticity of loss* upon which he could rely, once the authorities showed up to investigate.

Lifting a pair of night-vision field glasses to his eyes, he gripped his pistol in the other hand and demanded Burke drop down for a closer look. Panach gasped. "It's them! Harlow and that two-timing colonel, they've got my car! I'll get 'em, damn it. I'll kill both of them!"

Burke followed Panach's orders to maneuver the chopper down for a head-on assault. Deftly he manipulated the joystick and altered the rhythm of the blades, slipping the aircraft over the edge of the plant's domed roof and into the path of the McLaren, now racing in the direction of the ethanol complex.

Panach peered at the chopper's infrared screen and cursed at the sight of seeing a young punk behind the wheel of his car. Another unfolding complication—far beyond a mild deviation from his plans to leave the installation in full confidence—incensed him. By no means could NASA's missing wonder boy and the backstabbing judas colonel escape Crimson's walls. Invoking a bit of his own legislation, Panach wrapped his fingers around the 9 mm Lugar pistol holstered across his chest. He clutched the mic on the two-way radio in the other hand. His instructions, tied to the threat of death, demanded his ground forces to secure Crimson's gates and do whatever it takes to prevent the F-1 from escaping.

*****

With all due haste, impaired by confusion, Adam gripped the wheel of Panach's car. He had not expected to find the driver's seat situated in the center of the car's cockpit.

It was truly a one-man automobile with barely enough space on either side of the driver to stow a set of golf clubs.

Under formal protest the colonel had squeezed in, grunting and twisting his frame before handing Adam an electronic key card he'd procured from the guard station. Adam convinced himself he had acted prudently by taking the wheel under the assumption the colonel had no clue of operating paddle shifters.

260

A McLaren is no Sherman tank, nor is it a Humvee. When it came to who was driving the over-powered sports car, the task seemed a better fit for Adam. Though his working knowledge of the controls proved severely limited against those witty British stuntmen who'd made a jest of testing European muscle cars at the BBC.

This specimen he identified as an English handmade job, designed and built in the 1990s for speeds exceeding 200 miles per hour. Adam's baseline experience was enough to maneuver the machine out of the motor pool in first gear. The rest would be left to one's learn-as-you-go spirit.

Gradually the gear pattern clicked into place and the car shot them down the service road toward the ethanol plant. The colonel wheezed a sigh of relief, muttering another Hail Mary. Adam settled back into the plush leather and throttled the engine up to gain speed. The car surged like a famished cheetah—untamed, beastly. Living up to every accolade ever noted about the F-1 series.

The tachometer fluttered then rose in a clockwise motion, propelling the car up to speed. On the far side of unrelenting darkness through intermittent rain, the south gates of Crimson's massive compound came into view. He'd up-shifted and flicked away the clutch paddle when a concussive blast reverberated off the car's backside.

It had been all Adam could do to hold the road under the fury of such a powerful machine. Fighting to recover, he jerked the wheel and veered the car back onto the center of the pavement. In the left side view mirror, mostly cloaked in ash and smoke, the chateau had morphed into a smoldering cemetery. Add to the confusion: magnified in the breaking moonlight, the gray shadow of a low-flying aircraft appeared out of nowhere. This time yards off the car's grill. Had federal agents arrived? ...wishful expectations.

In case Adam had grossly misjudged things, he squeezed the clutch handle and flipped the paddle into third gear. The F-1's raspy engine wound up to a high pitch roar and sucked him back into body-molded padding. The colonel grappled with the G-forces to prevent his head from colliding with the engine's firewall, its surface plating resembling a gilded Japanese shrine.

"That chopper looks like one of ours, Striker declared, waving his pistol half-heartily. "I just hope our boys are trailing Panach out of here."

"How do *you* know so much about the old man?" Adam was shouting over the motor's furious acceleration.

"Sad to admit it, young man, but I've worked for him, too—unfortunately on the wrong side of justice."

"That puts two fools in one fast car!"

No sooner had Striker shot Adam a sardonic nod, his fingertips jammed up against the windshield. Two of Admiral's gunners were down in the brush on their bellies like jungle rats. A gunshot instantly rang off the McLaren's hood. But the way it failed to skidder off toward the windshield, Adam calculated the shot's origin to be from a higher angle. Fired from an aircraft? In his next breath the chopper dropped into view and another bullet slammed into the windshield, leaving a clean hole in the top of the dash.

"Ain't what I'd consider friendly fire!" Striker gasped. "They got us sandwiched in like pawns."

The only thing that stood between them and the grave was the car's lightning acceleration. By fourth gear and a full twist of the throttle bar, installed for hands-only driving, the car rocketed past the chopper's dangling skids, a move that sent the goons in the bushes scrambling. A moment later the front bumper's impact on a portable barricade hastily placed in the middle of the road shattered it into tiny plastic fragments. Adam pressed on toward the ethanol plant. Conditions ahead suddenly looked murky. Something had ignited or detonated a fire at two storage tanks. Crimson was burning at both ends!

Adam slammed his palms down against the wheel. "The bastard's flamed the whole damn place!"

A crescendo of pulsating air beat against his ears again. The chopper was trailing them closer this time, despite the McLaren topping a solid hundred and twenty, and rapidly running out of pavement. Adam glanced skyward through a break in the windshield. Above a curtain of pine tops flanking the access road, Panach was leaning out the door of the aircraft. His pistol waved madly. Next to him who else but Ken Burke would be working the stick!

Idle talk among Crimson's guards extolled Burke as a highly skilled pilot who'd notched more than his share of Taliban kills into his belt, before the days of drone dominated air offensives.

In seconds the car ate up another five hundred yards of service road. Beneath the F-1 the asphalt narrowed and weaved right, channeling them toward a lighted security checkpoint. Beyond it company fire crews had blocked its entrance. A crisscross of inflated hoses was pumping flame retardants onto the blaze at the east end of the ethanol plant. This posed a serious problem. Adam would have to abandon his plans to exit Crimson through the ethanol plant's service bay.

Gingerly he pinched the clutch paddle and toggled back on the throttle. Gut-level intuition commanded him to pull on the brake paddle and backtrack along a spur that angled northwest. The opposite direction of the service gates—a tactic he was most certain he would regret. Yet on the upside they were spreading Crimson's security forces more thinly over a larger area. Others were peeling off to fight blazes that were erupting along a crazy network of small gauge above-ground pipelines.

Ignoring the colonel's renewed sniveling demands to turn back and smash through the service gates, Adam squeezed the handbrake and jerked the steering around for a one-eighty power slide before cutting onto a darkened service road he'd nearly missed. The engine roared and the McLaren began rocketing alongside the river. This led them toward the north end of the property—a move that proved invigorating in a long straight away, yet ineffective in shaking off the chopper.

Panach and his steely-eyed flyboy teased at the McLaren's rear bumper all the way. Adam soon spotted the chateau on his right as they neared the main plant.

"We've doubled back!" Striker protested. "Did you forget your wallet?"

Concentrating less on the colonel's bellyaching and more on the road, flashbacks of the Escalade pumped fresh adrenaline into Adam. His moderate personality could unleash a level of aggression necessary for battle against hostile elements. Where was Dell's shotgun when he needed it?

His resolve hadn't come a moment too soon.

Shots from automatic weapons pelted the rear of the car and walked forward over the titanium steel top into the windshield space. The colonel buried his head in the folds of the leather padding as a fresh barrage of lead chimed off the car's high-grade metal shell. Adam forced mental faculties to stay with him and quickly deemed it smarter to kill the McLaren's headlights and weave beneath a strip of well-spaced pine trees. This move might keep Burke guessing. In shaved down seconds and one tire tracking the shoulder they would slip past the crippled plant, zigzag on past the chateau, and then rocket for the east gate—a seamless plan after considering a majority of Panach's men had obediently devoted themselves to extinguishing fires that were spreading rapidly at opposite ends of the compound.

Despite generous yardage gains, Adam grew increasingly nervous as the car neared the fiery *Aqualene* plant. He knew the intensity of the formula he'd programmed into the processing unit. It packed as much punch as a ton of dynamite pressed into the eye of a needle. Renee DeLong would be proud. While his alterations had the sole intent of prematurely shutting down Crimson, it would also delay Panach and spare as much of NASA's minerals as possible.

Adam however had not anticipated this level of meltdown. To make matters worse, the McLaren stood no chance of shielding them from the heated fallout. As the sulfate-filled conductors—a component used to accelerate internal catalytic reactions—came into contact with the raw fuel product inside the plant, there was considerable cause for the domed structure to erupt into a white-hot blazing inferno. Increasing evidence of this reality was now spreading rapidly to the roof of the plant. Evidence of it was clear from the windows of the McLaren as it sped along the river road.

Within a hundred yards of the distressed plant, Adam and the colonel saw firefighters leaving the charred chateau to assist others who'd tapped into the main cooling lines in hopes of pumping water from the cold side of the system onto the blazing building. This created a double risk! Adam had anticipated the overheating condition when the auxiliary cooling lines were postponed during the hurried construction phase, never anticipating the use of untreated water to extinguish a blaze of this chemical makeup.

For unnerving seconds the McLaren's engine faltered. Adam downshifted, giving the motor time to recover. Closer to the plant he deemed it a total loss. Unaware of metal debris in the road until it was too late, he swerved and lost control of the car. All four tires howled and skidded into a fully inflated fire hose, blowing out the right front and sending the car into perpetual spins. The car slammed into the pumping station and came to rest as a pitiful wreck.

The impact had shaken Adam but didn't prevent him from pulling together his senses. He detected the odor of a broken fuel line and ordered the colonel to get out before a fire ignited.

One of the doors gave in to a boot and Adam scrambled out. Striker followed, cutting his hands on jagged metal. A spotlight instantly swept the ground beneath them, trapping the two in full illumination. Adam darted left toward the riverbank. The colonel hesitated before taking the same flight. Shots followed them through the shadows cast by stacks of building material and heavy equipment. The throbbing blades rattled their bones. Burke had maneuvered the chopper within a few yards of the ground. Panach's amplified voice reverberated off the cement retaining wall at the top of the bolder-littered riverbank. With his pronounced roar both were commanded to halt face down and give themselves up.

Striker crouched on all fours then covered his head with one hand. "Keep a stiff upper lip, young man. I'll think of something."

Reading the colonel's behavior as a passive surrender signal when a white cloth is unavailable, Adam broke for the fence. Along the way he spotted a depression in the ground that had been compacted by heavy equipment where the cooling line supports had been installed. The chopper's light beam flicked off in a pool of darkness and trailed Adam who'd dropped into a narrow stretch of soil then wriggled under a cyclone fence. Strands of galvanized wire perforated his shirt and gouged his back. One shot rang out. A thud from Panach's round pummeled the dirt next to Adam. Hardly a warning shot! The CEO pinched off two more but the fencing deflected both in a shower of sparks.

"Let's go," Adam shouted behind him toward the colonel. "You can make it!"

Colonel Striker appeared disoriented in the dark but managed to skitter in the direction of Adam's voice. He grunted and wheezed as he slithered under the fence line. The chopper's light apprehended but soon lost Adam in a field of large boulders. The strategy worked. They couldn't ask for better cover at the moment plus the colonel managed to join Adam under a shroud of darkness. Burke had swung the aircraft away in a large arc over the river, giving them to catch their breath and view the river from the top of the embankment. Below a space of forty maybe fifty yards separated them from the river.

Adam gestured toward the shoreline. "Sir, there's our escape. How well can you swim?"

Twenty-seven

Like a stirred hornet's nest, the Oval Office buzzed with confusion.

White House media personnel were packing out the last cases of the equipment used to carry the holographic link between Kirkpatrick and the nation's energy mogul. Across the room the president's military advisors huddled over the latest data on Chinese naval placements while his chief of staff debriefed them. Reconnaissance buoys had pinpointed the location of the two missing Chinese subs, which provided the key development needed to persuade Kirkpatrick to authorize engagement procedures. This required him to move up the time on three preemptive strikes against the aging Boomers—one in the Indian Ocean, the other two flanking international shipping lanes in the Pacific. A three-ring circus such a crisis was considered in Pentagon circles.

Yet another crucial detail demanded Kirkpatrick's attention.

The media chief in charge of White House press conferences and industry relations stood on her toes and waved a memo just handed to her by the director of White House audio records. She had remained patient to wait for the right interval in which Kirkpatrick could divorce himself from the war table to speak with her privately. Finally she stepped in the midst of the president's military advisors to advance her agenda. But her boldness yielded her no results. Two telephone calls on hold from the Pentagon now further distanced her from communicating her department's findings when the First Lady appeared in the doorway of the Oval Office. The woman, underweight and in her fifties, was clearly distressed. She'd watched through glassy eyes her beloved husband struggle to comprehend one urgent matter after another.

Panting and wheezing, Kirkpatrick raised his eyes to the vaulted ceiling. He needed time … time to tune out. To step back away from all the insanity. Unnoticed in room, he found himself standing beside his her. He longed to indulge even a single minute alone with his wife. Few words came of either yet he managed to draw comfort from her smile. They'd slinked a few steps toward a vacant corner of the room when his media advisor appeared out of nowhere.

"Sir, at the risk of intrusion, I must inform you of an oddity we've—"

"Pardon me, but—" interrupted the First Lady. She held a graceful palm up between them, though her tone was curt and direct. "—clearly you can see my husband is overwhelmed with details at this moment. The news can wait."

"But madam, just give me one—"

"*That's an order!*" Kirkpatrick's wife replied sternly. She angled her body around in an effort to shield her husband. No business was more urgent than giving the nation's top man an overdue reprieve.

Getting nowhere, the media chief backed down, all the while cultivating a fierce determination to seek out the president at the nearest interval upon him sending his lady off to bed.

*****

The colonel's panting soon abated. In their temporary refuge behind the boulders he'd given no reply to his aquatic skills. Nor had he protested the notion of crossing the river. No better option seemed to await them. The chopper had circled twice. Panach had shot randomly among the rocky embankment, and no Burke climbed to a higher vantage point. The search light poked around the boulders desperately.

During his last debriefing session with the production engineers at the chateau, Adam had noticed the plant's blueprints to reflect Panach's orders to utilize the river as a primary cooling source.

Though it should have taken months of state review and a full blown environmental impact study to generate a go-ahead, the plant had begun disposing of its waste coolant into the Crimson River at a rate of several thousand gallons per hour. Outside the compound's west wall, the twelve-inch cooling lines sloped steeply down to the riverbank. Admiral had deployed its own construction crews to cast a large circular culvert and then position it in deep water, about thirty feet from the shore. Perhaps the culvert might serve as safe cover and a resting point until they could complete their crossing.

Undeveloped wooded property stood at the opposite shore. From the boulders, Adam gazed out at what was to be his original escape route two days earlier. He was certain an access road within a mile of the opposite shoreline would connect to a highway and on to civilization. He peered at the gray foliage, shadowed by breaking moonlight under misting skies. It was federal land, according to the blue prints and maps he'd studied days earlier.

Inside the plant airborne toxins had diminished his vision and given Adam brief dizzy spells. The fresh air and moisture wafting up from the river had revived him.

Now in their moment of complacency, gunfire clattered down amongst the boulders again. Each shot ricocheted off the dark morbid faces of the damp boulders. Warily, Adam and the colonel watched the rim of the chopper's light dart about in a mad attempt to locate them. By now Crimson's goons had begun trickling into the area through a break in the fence about seventy-five yards upstream.

They would soon be discovered and surrounded.

Burke was swinging the aircraft around for a better view of the embankment. Panach had pulled his gun back inside the cockpit. In that short interval Adam decided it was time to make a break for the river. Striker had agreed to follow, now steadying himself around jagged rocks. Adam angled onto a route that kept them beneath the overhead cooling lines. Random shots pinged off the steel piping above them.

Adam arrived at the shore careful to use the cover of the iron water lines. Thoroughly exhausted and dehydrated, his first impulse was to kneel down in the shadows and drink from the river. He realized the dangers and told himself to remain patient. He'd soon be in the currents, which he carefully studied now and felt confident about swimming the river's width. Adam could help but harbor reservations about the colonel—a man in his upper sixties—who'd struggled to keep up on foot. The swim no doubt would present its own dangers of hypothermia. They'd have to make it across within a few

269

minutes. Or they could work their way north and traverse the bank—a plan that would take them dangerously close to a stretch of prison-style barbed wire coils anchored from shore into shallow water as a means to discourage unwanted guests.

Sound reasoning left Adam wading straight across toward the culvert. He was immediately up to his knees, the currents littered with brush and dead limbs pulled with greater force. By the time the two men were waist-deep into the frigid black, a parade of gun shots sprayed over the shoreline where they'd entered the river. Panach's security forces were filling in around them, but holding off gunfire.

Adam cussed and leapt forward, face down in the cold water. He immediately surfaced in a patch of darkness. In the excess of false hopes, the colonel had lingered some distance back where he appeared to have taken a bullet. Striker paused. He gripped his left shoulder. Adam identified his position and called across the shifting currents: "You gonna make it?"

"I'll manage," Striker wheezed back. "Superficial ... grazed my shoulder."

Adam took the colonel's word and pushed on toward the cement culvert. A few strokes later he hooked one arm over its circular edge. Turning back toward the shoreline, he saw no sign of his partner. A sure thirty yards from shore, he scanned the river's swift currents in a menagerie of confusing shadows cast over eddies and rivulets. Had the colonel veered off course? Was he being pulled downstream? Adam searched in all directions, calculating the risks of backtracking the colonel. A pair of light beams came bobbing down toward the shoreline. Panach's men were closing off any options of returning to shore. A small boat would have made things a lot easier once they could get out into the faster currents. To make the entire crossing remained their only option.

Like a Gatling gun, the chopper blades pitched and shuddered overhead. In the glare of onboard flood lamps Panach's scowl appeared in the aircraft's open doorway. The old man gingerly stepped onto the skid and paused to adjust his weight awkwardly over what appeared to be prosthetics. His drawn pistol led him further out over the skids until he reached a perch above his target. Taking careful aim, Panach hammered off a well-placed round that zipped into the icy waters inches from Adam's ear. Swaying side to side overhead, the baron of oil invoked the luxury of an eagle's view of his prey. He'd adjusted himself for a best-angled shot—one capable of mutilating human flesh—but an unforeseen circumstance halted his war games.

Panach was banking on Burke's adroit reputation behind the stick. With great care he'd managed to jockey the aircraft between a pair of electrical power lines strung from the plant down to the culvert where a high-volume pump was still humming. It had been plumbed to relay cold water up to the distribution station and into to the *Aqualene* plant.

Under Panach's orders the chopper had dropped dangerously low. The steely eyes of his pilot were deftly aligning the landing skids with top of the culvert. Despite it being an impossible task from Adam's vantage point, every maneuver Burke imposed on the aircraft evidenced death-defying flight skills. Circumstances would suggest Burke privately reject the orders on the grounds of a pilot's sound judgment. No deal.

The chopper's elevation continued to erode, inch by inch.

Adam was relieved to see Striker's head surface nearby. He wondered about the colonel's role in all this. What sort of relationship had the colonel maintained with Panach? With Striker lay an odd piece of this cat & mouse puzzle, little of which Adam understood. Had Admiral's high-level government exploits been made possible with some assistance from the colonel? If so what incriminating evidence did Striker have on the company to compel Panach to risk his life on the flimsy tip of a chopper to kill him? Did the colonel know something that could bring Admiral Petroleum to its knees?

Panach steadied himself over the starboard landing skid and gingerly inched forward. Despite the lethal proximity between Panach and the two men in the water, Panach paused and holstered his pistol.

He stood teetering as he observed them with curiosity. Had some new thought changed his course of action? Striker hoisted himself over the lip of the culvert, panting in chilled

271

exhaustion. Feebly he twisted around and glared up at his foe. Adam remained in the water.

"Give it up, Rodney," the colonel said in a conciliatory tone. "The Feds will be here soon. It's no use killing us."

"Don't count on it, Billy Boy," Panach growled. Adam listened with heightened interest, intrigued by the first-name references. Clearly the two had known each other for some time and were struggling with some irreconcilable difference.

Panach spoke again. "I have no use for either of you, for you have given me what I need to duplicate the formula." As if undecided who to shoot first, his gun swung in Adam's direction, then back to Striker. Inside him an impulse to murder both at close range seemed to be battling against some higher level of reasoning. Was there an alternative to eliminating the colonel after he'd triggered the chaos that had burned the plant to the ground? Moreover, what could he gain by sparing Adam Harlow? Panach had extracted most of what he needed to manufacture *Aqualene* elsewhere. Could he not easily move on and turn his back on all that smoldered of Crimson?

Adam bit his lip. He peered up into Panach's eyes. "That's where you're mistaken, sir. A minor flaw in the design process caused the plant to overheat. You cannot produce *Aqualene* in a safely controlled environment. Little of Crimson will be left to sort through, to say nothing of the minerals you stole from NASA."

"Consider this, Mr. Harlow. We have other resources upon which to draw. Have you forgotten NASA's little contribution to our program?"

Little indeed it was, Adam figured. Renee DeLong had spoken about NASA's unsuccessful recovery efforts. A sudden explosion inside the plant interrupted them. Glowing matter broke through the huge domed roof and illuminated the night sky. A second blast launched fiery debris that began to rain down around them like little meteors that zipped and crackled before splashing into the river.

Striker adjusted himself on the edge of the culvert, folding himself into a squat position as if he were preparing to duel Panach atop the ramparts of his little fortress. In the midst of the raining debris the colonel raised his chin and shouted up into the chopper's flood lamps. "Go ahead, cut *me* down," he offered. "Don't kill Mr. Harlow. Turn yourself in … and preserve the future of this nation!"

Attempting to conceal tense puffs of breath, Panach glowered down at Adam. "Sage counsel from the colonel, Mr. Harlow. But it contains a serious flaw."

Adam refused to comment, electing to wait. Listen.

"China has blockaded U.S. oil shipments over a mutual property dispute; the minerals necessary to manufacture *Aqualene*. The White House is minutes away from launching a preemptive strike. In all the aftermath, it is me they will salute. I will enjoy the privilege of emerging as the king of new energy—the economic locomotive to sweeping economic recovery."

Panach signaled Burke to navigate the aircraft downward while teetered over the landing skid. If he'd been more experienced in his prosthetic limbs, he could have leaped onto the culvert wall and finished off the two of them at close range. Instead, he seemed to be possessed by an unprecedented option.

Burke's voice rang out through chopper's open door: "Sir, I can't hold 'er between these damn power lines much longer."

Panach ignored Burke's protests. Suddenly *Aqualene's* evasive details were more precious than the bitter taste of revenge.

"Mr. Harlow, your father proved to be some small amusement … as well as a menace to progress. As for you? I see some potential. I could use a good man at my side, a young fella looking for a secured life." An awkward pause held between them. "Climb on up, Adam Harlow." Panach waved his hand around toward the plant. "We can leave all this behind. We'll start new, far out at sea, in safe international waters. I have the power to make things right for you. I can insulate you from prosecution. Leave it to me to handle everything. What do you say to a business partnership? A skyward ride to a brand new life!"

Exhausted by the onset of hypothermia, Adam gazed at Panach, glassy-eyed and silent. His body shook, seeking warmth. His mind grew confused demanding a fight to think clearly. He'd give anything to be dry. Warm. Safe. To see Moi Song. What were the chances of that now?

"No deal!" Striker garbled between heaving breaths. It was all he could do to swivel around toward Adam below. "See here, young man, it ain't worth it! You'll never live it down. Just sit tight. The Feds, they're coming. Give 'em time, young man."

Panach watched Adam pull himself up onto the culvert. His teeth chattered wildly. The frigid currents had exhausted him. Now was as good a time as any to apply some fatherly persuasion. He knelt over the tip of the landing skid and extended a hand toward Adam.

"What do say to a truce? A clean start! Choose a city— anywhere in the world. Name it and you've got a warm dry place to live out the easy life you deserve."

Colonel Striker watched Panach's hand move closer toward Adam.

"Power not only corrupts he who wields it, but those who submit to that power." The colonel's words shook with each gasp of breath—just loud enough for Adam to make out his words under the hovering chopper. "So if this ... is ... what your father ... left behind ... for a son ... I have nothing more ...."

The colonel's words faded. One leg then the other slipped down into the icy currents.

Shivering atop the culvert, Adam remembered his father as a tireless soldier for truth and decency. Yes, a soldier he been of another sort ... and the same had been of his own blood. The colonel was right. Panach wielded far too much power and would be satisfied with nothing less than all of it.

Adam lifted his chin and locked eyes with Panach. His mind raced over the realities at stake. The authorities would be here, well ... maybe he gambled. He had missed Moi and wanted to see her again. And what came of Heinrich? Sharing his discoveries with Renee would—

His thoughts of real friendships warmed him inside. He could dismiss his chilled aching body. Remembering the trusted began to erode the gravity of his misery.

"I'm staying," Adam said with renewed conviction.

"You're doing what?"

"Staying ... here ... I'm staying with the colonel," Adam repeated methodically. It felt damn good to know his plans and to know he would stand by them. "I'll die in honor of my father before I surrender my soul to Rodney Panach."

For a brief moment Mr. Panach stood speechless. Shocked by what he'd heard. Silently he retreated. At the cockpit door he faced Adam a final time. "One saint and one fool at the river. I had hoped for so much more, Mr. Harlow."

Burke's voice came through the doorway, "Sir?"

"Take 'er up!"

Adam swiveled to steady the colonel, propping him up against the culvert. Adam had regained enough of his strength to hang on and wait ... for what? Were they really coming?

Out of the corner of his eye he watched Panach lingering outside the doorway of the aircraft. He had pulled something from his jacket. A small black device glinted in the light, lodged between his fingers. Like a mad man Panach marveled at it. A queer grin across his face, he gazed back up at the compound. As if to embolden one final task, he peered at his para-military, unknowing but waiting. Standing by obediently amongst the boulders and along the fence line for his next command.

Burke throttled the chopper higher now. An awful fear swelled up in Adam. His eyes tracked Panach, still clutching the device between his fingers. Was total destruction his end game for Crimson?

The chopper coughed and jockeyed side to side. Burke hovered tentatively between the high-tension power lines, struggling more now to control the aircraft.

The colonel suddenly grunted undiscernible words, his arms flailing. His trembling hands clawed for the culvert's edge, but his efforts became futile. Adam levered a leg against the surface of the cylindrical culvert, buying Striker more time above the black swallowing currents.

The colonel's resolve to return Adam home safely had been of bravery and valor. For all this, would his superiors ever know the truth? Shivering like marooned Russian sailors in the North Sea, Adam took stock: The toxic fires burning at the plant, the men still loyal enough to fight them, the deafening noise of the aircraft and the way its blades tilted and pitched. Something wasn't right.

Burke was battling the controls, working to coax the chopper up higher, with no success.

Would everything Adam knew about *Aqualene* be lost in a few minutes? Was this the end for NASA's precocious formula? Surely others were on it, but what if ...?

With gloomy thoughts of watching it all go down the river, a massive fireball exploded from what remained of the plant. A dreadful concussive blast reverberated across the river, hammering at Adam's eardrums and lighting up the sky for miles. In the shimmering light Adam glimpsed the chopper flip sideways and hurl into one of the power lines. Vivid blue light illuminated the splintering blades. The aircraft twisted and careened as it seemed to float toward the ground.

The heated bravado of those fiery seconds played on forever, forcing Adam and Striker beneath the surface to escape the intense heat. With amazing flame speed the combustion ended as abruptly as it had started. Burning light faded. Darkness fell over the land. Adam had surfaced long enough to fill his lungs and survey the damage. More falling debris forced them under the water again. Adam held a twenty-second count and surfaced.

He was searching for the colonel's arm when a band of strobe lights appeared in the night. Over the smoldering remains of Crimson they came. Out of California's coal-black skies to the east, thumping twin-bladed gunships came—one, then two ... three.

They had arrived.

Twenty-eight

Under the glare of sweeping searchlights Adam rolled out from a twisted tree stump and sprinted along the smoky riverfront.

A volley of shots peppered the air around his head, driving him into a canopy of charred foliage. From his right hand down to his thigh stinging pain eroded his gait to a labored hobble. Ignoring the gush of blood under his shirt, he pressed on. But a second shot penetrated his right ear. Numbing death cascaded down his spine, forcing Adam to collapse into a shallow sandy grave.

An unfamiliar voice met his ears: "It is time, Mr. Harlow."

"The colonel, where's the colonel," Adam mumbled, pulling himself up into a painful sitting position. A woman's voice at some undefined distance broke through the taunts of Crimson's guards who'd gathered round him, poking and kicking him where he lay. Adam fought for another breath and wrestled against the firm grip of a firm hand that clutched his neck. He pried open one eye ... then the other.

"Time to sit up and eat." Dressed in white cotton, the nurse smiled at him. She cradled his head and lifted him gently upright. Her other hand adjusted the tubing that crossed over his right arm and up past his shoulder. "Mr. Harlow, you must eat something," she announced with a smile. Her tone softened and she placed a tray of liquids in front of him. "A gentleman from Washington is waiting outside. He wishes to speak to you ... so long as you follow the doctor's orders to get your strength back."

"Where am I?" Adam whispered.

"Sacramento Public Health," she answered. "Now it's time you eat something."

She wiped beads of perspiration from his forehead and handed him a fork. Adam set it on the plate in front of him. His stomach rumbled beneath a white gown he was wearing.

"Okay, send him in."

A well-dressed black man in his fifties entered the recovery room. He introduced himself as Cedric Pitts, a

277

regional chief with the FBI. "Mr. Harlow, I'm documenting matters concerning your involvement with Admiral Petroleum, including the necessary details that will go into the court deposition against the criminally charged."

Adam slowly considered what Pitts was saying as he pulled the fork away from his mouth. "Criminally charged? Who might I ask are you talking about?"

"Any and all parties who can be linked to cooperating or assisting to exploit government property."

"Look, I need to see my attorney. You know, things aren't always what they appear to be."

"Perhaps, Mr. Harlow. But for now I thought you might be more interested in the outcome of events transpiring from the time your involvement ended at the Crimson plant ... two nights ago."

Adam's jaw dropped open. "Two nights, huh?"

"Yes. You're quite the sleeper, Mr. Harlow. This is my third attempt to speak with you here. You've been out the whole time, but the doctor assures me you can handle a little conversation. In fact, you'll be as good as new in a few days ... if you do as that nurse tells you."

Adam rubbed his eyes and stared at the steamed rice and over-cooked vegetables. "And I suppose you want to know what I was doing out there at one of Admiral's refineries."

"Could be helpful. I would think showing up in Pasadena could have made life a whole lot easier. Nonetheless, a few details from you might help us expedite the filing of a corporate injunction against Admiral Petroleum. In the meantime the IRS and the Justice Department are arranging to seize and divide up all of the firm's U.S. properties."

Adam shoveled limp peas from one side of the plate to the other. From the hospital bed he dictated his account of Admiral's conspiracy while the Bureau chief monitored the text generated by voice-recognition as it appeared over a handheld video display. Adam made some final conclusions and then signed an affidavit. Honesty would have to do.

"Very well," the chief said when the statement was complete. Pitts placed the tablet into a padded silver case. "Now it's my turn to bring your life up to the present." He hummed through his nostrils as he glanced over his notes. "Let me start by saying you are indeed lucky to be here today. Apparently the chopper broke up and you were knocked unconscious by the concussion of the crash. Minutes later Secret Service agents assisting us in this probe showed up in time to pluck two of you out of the river."

"Where's the man who was with me?" Adam inquired. He glanced at the curtain separating him from the other bed. "I've got to thank him for sticking his neck out for me."

Pitts cocked his head, then squinted at his screen. "The other survivor recovered in the river is no hero, at least not that I can see. More accurately put, he's a fugitive."

Adam stared at the ceiling in disbelief. Pitts paced the room as he read from an affidavit. "Says here Mr. Kenneth Burke, an interstate fugitive is wanted for weapons racketeering linked with a handful of suspicious murders. He was rescued several minutes after Adam Harlow was pulled from the Crimson River."

"To hell with Ken Burke, what happened to Colonel William Striker?" Adam demanded.

The Bureau chief picked up his notes. "The colonel was found dead almost a mile downstream from where you were airlifted. It was a shame to see his career end in such a troubled legacy."

"Troubled?" Adam was incredulous. "The colonel snatched me from Admiral's clutches, only to save me and what I know about NASA's formula. More than sufficient for a dignified memoir if you ask me."

"Perhaps another day, Mr. Harlow. The Pentagon is viewing the colonel's activities differently. His actions aboard the International Space Station jeopardized the lives of three astronauts, not to mention a pair of civilians. His presence on Admiral's property is being viewed as a last ditch effort to dampen a pending court martial."

Adam shook his head and sighed. "Okay, that covers two sketchy characters, but you left out the biggest fish. Who's paying for Mr. Panach's funeral arrangements?"

"Think again," the chief replied. "Rodney Panach has been blessed with resilient fortune. After his private helicopter struck a power line and dropped into the river, he apparently swam to safety. As we speak he remains at large."

"Along with NASA's minerals?"

Pitts was grinning. "To the contrary, Mr. Harlow. Despite local law enforcement's allegations that Admiral was trucking them out minutes before we arrived, agents found the material lying on a flatbed trailer at a county hydro pumping station, several miles from the plant. The positive side to it is that NASA has regained possession of its classified property, enabling Washington to restore diplomatic relations with China after they had accused the U.S. of—"

"—stealing their share of joint ownership?" Adam interjected. "I heard the news the night I made my escape. I trust you'll ask me to testify against Panach the minute your people haul him in."

"Don't hold your breath," the chief lamented. "It'll take a helluva lot of evidence to locate and convict a heavy like Rodney Panach."

"You mean guts. It takes guts," Adam insisted.

Pitts raised his eyebrows. "Perhaps, Mr. Harlow ... the very thing that got your father in trouble. But that's political, and it's out of my hands."

Adam shook his head. "Then where were the minerals headed when Panach detonated the plant?"

"I have no doubts they were destined to wherever he's holed up at this very moment, probably aboard one of his many shelf-drilling rigs off the coast of Mexico," the chief answered. "Amongst a handful of converted installations, poised to manufacture *Aqualene*."

"International waters, right?"

"A foolproof plan to control energy, which nearly unraveled into a lethal confrontation between Washington and Beijing."

Adam cocked his jaw. "So, how did your people locate us?"

"Easy. Aside from infrared imaging, which detected an unusually hot fire, White House audio technicians dissected a video-conference between Kirkpatrick and Panach. This revealed clues to substantiate what we already had suspected

280

of Admiral. I believe your own sound bites contributed to our timely arrival ... and perhaps give you more than a dog's chance in court."

"I'm comforted to hear that *something* I did out there went according to plan."

"Your clues helped sew up tensions abroad," the chief continued. "Upon locating the minerals, a videoconference link was established with Beijing immediately. Formal reconciliation from Chinese officials promptly arrived through diplomatic channels. As a result, you're likely to be at least partially excused from fraternizing with organized criminals."

"Thanks for the reassurance." Adam's tone grew derisive, almost rebellious. With each passing moment he cared less of what the chief thought. "Tell me one thing: given all the facts about the Chinese blockade of oil shipments to U.S. ports, would the Pentagon have really committed to a military strike?"

"Quite possible," the chief gravely replied. "The tensions and confrontational dialogue that transpired between our governments took relations right down to the wire."

"You mean down to the *button*?"

"I'm sorry, Mr. Harlow, I'm not at liberty to—"

Adam shot him a knowing look. "What does it matter? Both nations would be leveled to finished equals."

Pitts checked his watch. "Thanks to some good people, we're not. Any additional questions before I submit my report?"

His thoughts shifted back to NASA and his underground lab in Seattle. Adam choked on the knot growing in his throat. He had saved his most dreaded question for last.

The chief peered with interest into Adam's eyes. "Go ahead, what is it?"

Adam swallowed his nerves. "Tell me, uh ... what happened to the Chinese woman, the one who helped me pinpoint NASA's formula?"

The chief began scrolling through his notes but didn't get far when Adam interrupted him.

"Her name was Moi Song," Adam crushed his eyelids shut and braced for the details in cold cop jargon. He expected

Panach to keep his promise if it concerned taking an innocent life out of an already complex picture. "By now I expect the Chinese are demanding her body to be shipped back to the family."

After several taps on the screen, the chief smiled. "What the devil are you talking about? Miss Song is being held in a detention facility in Seattle. INS has filed criminal charges against her."

Adam stiffened. "What the hell for?"

"True, she did help us track you down, which, by the way, wasn't easy since your identity had disappeared from the national registry."

"Talk to Panach about that one," Adam snapped.

The chief shrugged. "Nonetheless, circumstantial evidence, swirling in a cloud of suspicion, has convinced the prosecution Miss Song tipped off Admiral just after you got involved in this mess."

"Go on."

"Detectives believe she maintained some sort of association, perhaps a business arrangement with the Chinese syndicate before she was dumped into Puget Sound. I'm afraid this evidence gives INS prosecutors a helluva case against Miss Song, on charges of collaboration. There's more. In exchange for asylum, her father agreed to turn over information about a sophisticated black market shipping network operating between North Korean ports and rogue interests operating in the Persian Gulf—concealed by conservative hardliners in Beijing."

Adam coughed. "Illegal weapons, plutonium ... traded for oil?"

"Something like that. Miss Song may have surrendered information to someone with clout. An industry player who holds heavy stakes in global energy—a group bent on spoiling any cushy new alliances her father had established with Washington."

Adam could see it now. Moi was boxed in. "How did you expect Miss Song to prevent her father from talking to the wrong people?"

"I didn't." The chief's answer was matter-of-fact. "Actually, her old man's defection had validated her innocence until he was found murdered. Could have been Panach's doings ... or someone at Montech, which incidentally had also maintained connections to the Chinese mob. We do know both organizations would do anything to narrow down the field of knowledge concerning the *Aqualene* formula—an increasingly common way to ensure proprietary security. Simply put, the girl is under investigation for collaboration, and lucky to be alive."

Adam wasn't about to concede with Pitts. "Look, man! She was abducted, then coerced ... much like I was."

"Look, we have no clear evidence of that as a mitigating circumstance, Mr. Harlow. For one thing, she's not talking. No scars or signs of bodily harm. Only some physical evidence and an eye-witness account that establishes a positive connection between you two, putting her inside your lab at one point or another, probably for reasons you are unwilling to admit. Fact is she hasn't shown an overt willingness to protect NASA's interest. She'll be incarcerated in a federal jail until deportation is finalized. I'm sorry."

Adam exploded. Pressing himself upright, he yanked the IV from his arm. "She's innocent! Don't you understand? They were using her as a stooge. An instrument to get their hands on *Aqualene*, and then ... corner world markets!"

Adam reached for anything he could get his hands on in the chief's direction, but the chief recoiled. "I'll say it again: Song could produce nothing that proves she was on your side ... or acted in the interest of NASA, or any other branch of the U.S. Government."

"Just ask the Seattle Police," Adam snarled. "They hauled away the evidence!" Anger spurred him to make a desperate grab for Pitts. But the man was light on his feet and jumped back toward the doorway causing Adam to lose his balance and slide off the bed to the floor.

His fingers probed for the chief's ankles. "You gotta do something," Adam begged. "Demand to see more evidence. For god sakes, you're FBI!"

283

By now a team of doctors in the hallway heard the commotion and came rushing in. Two of them pinned Adam to the floor. A third produced a large hypodermic needle. A stinging jab to the side of Adam's neck set the room in motion. The walls circled him as the faces above appraised the situation. Consciousness drifted into dulled emptiness. For a moment the Bureau chief hovered: "I'm sorry, Mr. Harlow," he said calmly. "Miss Song's case is outside of my jurisdiction."

*****

Within twenty-four hours of locating Adam Harlow, much had begun to transpire in Washington.

Under the protocols of shuttle diplomacy, President Kirkpatrick salvaged the international pact and launched a state of the union address, confessing the incident over nationwide television. He pushed for greater transparency and strived to put the *Aqualene* cover-up story behind him. Meanwhile, NASA and Pentagon officials scrambled to arrange global press releases, which attracted international attention as the full story unfolded.

All the while, NASA had worked furiously to recover its formula and determined that Adam possessed working knowledge needed to manufacture *Aqualene*. A detective in Seattle had run a thorough search over the Bureau's automated surveillance database, but found Adam's name nowhere in the national registry—a criminal offense traceable to Rodney Panach.

It wasn't until NASA could verify a cross-reference to the Agency's own archived media during a routine back-up procedure, that Adam's location could be narrowed down to one of several ethanol refineries in California, owned and operated by Admiral Petroleum.

According to Lieutenant Fazzoni and a team of internal investigations officers with the Air Force, an avalanche of suspicion was set to crash down on FBI higher-ups after the Seattle Police Department submitted a report containing a woman's testimony that Adam was in danger of giving up government property to a powerful corporate entity. The motives behind the abduction eventually fit like worn sneakers, as did the circumstances surrounding the lieutenant's allegations against Colonel William Striker. All was fully supported by Admiral Petroleum's recent financial transactions.

One serious dilemma remained.

The petrol giant—despite a history of generating an unprecedented volume of antitrust lawsuits—was a powerful and influential ally to the Energy Department under congressional accords designed to maintain price controls and fair rationing. According to Internet sources, the company was now the nation's biggest producer of bio-diesel and ethanol products, winning respect from a lenient congress, aggressively legislating in favor of resources other than conventional hydrocarbon-based fuels. Moreover, Admiral consistently brokered patchwork deals on more foreign oil shipments to North America than any other domestic producer. Panach's aggressive tactics had bought America the crucial economic window it needed. Meanwhile, federal initiatives to replace petroleum were plagued by errors and delays.

After the incident at Crimson, Rodney Panach's face and profile had been inked into front-page headlines around the world. Internet media streamed real time updates around the clock, revealing the intriguing story of Admiral's long history of concealed theft and international espionage. From the heist and murder at Yosemite down to manipulating policy in Washington, enterprising media companies linked the crisis in their own reality makeovers to the troubled economy and soaring price of fuel.

The public was utterly spellbound.

Hours after samples of the plant's first formula were analyzed, federal lab technicians determined that Admiral's CEO had little economic dominance to celebrate. Attempting to stem public criticism against the federal government's cover-up of *Aqualene*, the lab's spokesperson issued its own statement to the press: *Lacking proper control elements, the fuel samples recovered from Admiral's Crimson plant in central California yielded chemical properties dangerously*

285

corrosive and severely harmful to metals, which were the likely causes of the meltdown that rapidly destroyed the hastily constructed refinery.

*****

"Reduced inflammation. White blood cell count normal. Minimal scarring." The physician on duty dictated his notes into a recorded alongside Adam's bed.

He drew the sheet back over Adam's legs, then jotted something down onto a touch screen he'd rolled out over his shirt's cuff. "Aside from some residual numbness in your feet, you'll be as good as new in a couple days. As for the smoke you inhaled, there's no telling what the effects will be until you're my age."

A minute after the doctor stepped out, the nurse strolled into the room. "You look much better today, Mr. Harlow. And on that note, I have a call holding for you, a young lady identifying herself as Moi Song. Please wait while I transfer it to your bedside phone."

Adam toweled his face, ignoring the armed security guard standing in the corner by the window. He considered every doubt he'd ever concocted about the Chinese national: *Her expertise in writing computer algorithms, his notebook he'd entrusted to her the night of her disappearance in the underground, and her father's adversities with Beijing.* All of it passed through his thoughts with renewed suspicion. Perhaps the INS did have reasonable grounds to detain and prosecute her. Ambivalence left him feeling foolish. Remorse, for going off on the FBI chief.

With reservation he picked up the receiver.

After a short delay over the circuits, Moi's voice spilled into his ear. "Adam?" she said in her broken English, "It is you? Are you okay?"

She spoke clear and vibrant—in a tone much more cognizant than she had the night he'd spoken to her from inside the refinery—as though everything was well and good again. Helplessly, he listened to his voice fall into a cold and

286

flattened cadence: "Oh, it's you," he mumbled. "I heard the news. The prosecution ... yesterday."

He paused, dreading where this conversation might take him. Moi spoke again. "I worry every day. The danger, the—"

Adam listened with scrutiny, keeping his emotions in check. His thoughts drifted from her words as he struggled to find his own. He hated himself for his lack of expression in matters of a woman. His experience with the female kind was limited. He reminded himself to be ... objective in terms, to find closure.

"Thanks," he replied after she attempted to summarize their friendship. "We helping each other ... but I take care myself. A disgrace isn't it, what they're saying, about you ... giving in to them. How could you—"

A cold distance fell over them. Moi trudged on, her wavering tone colliding with his icy silence, "I am sorry," she choked. "My counsel forbid me to speak about this. I don't know English well."

"Let's not hide the truth," Adam replied in a lengthy exhale into the phone. His eyes watered. He appraised his lack of privacy, mindful of the guard across the room.

"I need help," Moi announced flatly. "Immigration want to deport me."

For an instant her plea for aid gripped him. It was a fight to stay grounded and resolute, basing more of his judgments now on the Bureau chief's facts. Everything Pitts had said the previous was falling into place, faster than he wished.

"Of course they do," Adam shuttered into the phone. His voice grew icy. Tears blurred his vision. "You compromised government data, for which I will be held responsible. I was darn sure we'd make a helluva good team, but ...."

Adam had said enough. The rest was up to courtroom saints in black robes. He retracted the receiver from his ear and lowered it until the line clicked dead.

Moi was gone, forever.

Adam spent the afternoon convincing himself he'd made the right choice, letting go of a bad thing. The nurse removed the second tube in his arm and urged him to drink more water. Still drowsy and weak by mid-day, his body functions were gradually returning to normal. Hospital life would be past him in a few days.

The sun was low behind pink evening skies of Sacramento when he awakened to hunger and despair. Twisting for the nurse's call switch, his eyes were drawn to a large bouquet of flowers on the windowsill.

"Mr. Harlow, those came for you an hour ago." The orderly's voice came from behind the cloth partition. "Would you like me to read you the card?"

Folding a blanket, he stepped around the end of the bed and plucked the greeting card from the tall glass vase. Adam stuck out his hand to receive the card. He flipped the sealed envelope between his fingers, waiting for the orderly to finish cleaning and exit the room. On the front of the card Adam's full name was printed. No sender's name. The message inside was brief. Its style and content hinted at the writer's identity before his eyes could reach the signature.

Adam,

Welcome back.

To our satisfaction, it appears you have accomplished your mission.

Renee.

Twenty-nine

Earlier the following morning thunderstorms raked across Sacramento.

Adam took a hot shower and returned to his bed. He'd finished a light breakfast when the sun broke through parting clouds. The guard on duty secured the straps doctors deemed necessary after his outburst the previous day, then exited for coffee. Adam picked up the TV remote and flipped on a morning talk show simmering over the week's events. The U.S. standoff with China had melded into diplomatic repairs over which every pundit in the nation voiced an opinion. The energy markets stirred toward a mild recovery, propped up by a string of encouraging statistics from the Federal Reserve in view of projections linked to the manufacture of a new and revolutionary fuel in the United States.

During breakfast there was a knock at the door. Before Adam could speak a woman in a gray business suit strolled in and angled up to his bedside.

"Mr. Adam Harlow?" she inquired.

"Yes, ma'am?" Adam was still swallowing a mouthful of hash browns.

"Look, I don't know who you think you are ... and what you stand for, but you've got some nerve to—"

"Whoa, lady. Hold on. Could we at least start with an introduction?" Things had been crazy enough around here. Adam pulled at the straps over his belly. He certainly could not afford another outburst.

"Of course," she replied. "If you insist, my name is Cindy Mollett, a close friend to Moi Song—apparently her *only* friend in this country if you get your way."

Adam furrowed his eyes. Sacramento was at least a thousand miles from Seattle. "How ... and why did you come all this way to bust in here and preach about the virtues of friendship?"

Miss Mollett turned and began orienting herself to the small recovery room. "I'm fortunate enough to be with the airlines. The scheduled stopover provides me just enough time

289

to speak my mind." With a disgusting snort her attention fell onto the several bouquets arranged along the windowsill. "You're a big man, a hero ... a celebrity," she sneered. "Do you know *where* my friend Moi is right now?"

"Not in Beijing, where she belongs," Adam snapped. His finger hovered near the nurse's call switch. Here was one moment he could welcome security back in the room.

Cindy let out a long sigh. "Now I see why Moi is so devastated. You're impossible, Adam Harlow. I was rather naïve to leave the airport ... to inform you that I located Moi's car, along with your notebook hidden under the spare tire. We had considered that to be sufficient ... oh, never mind!"

Cindy's voice trailed off as she stormed out and down the hallway.

Adam gulped hard and reached out a hand. He opened his mouth to call her back into the room but he choked on his words. Women! The clack of her heels rapidly faded into the hum of hallway traffic.

He was stuck! The bed straps anchoring him to the bed pressed his trembling shoulders back against the freshly starched pillow. Adam was stunned by the breadth of his own stupidity. For a protracted moment the confusion that came with sparring against Miss. Mollett completely muted him.

Twice he'd blown it—first with Moi and now with her envoy, leaving him to brood over his troubles, strapped to a damn mattress.

Of course! The car. His notes were safe in the trunk of Moi's car. How could he have reacted so foolishly? Tormented by his own suspicions, Adam's chest pounded with regret. Undoubtedly he had responded with negligence by assuming the FBI and Immigrations had the complete story.

Regret swiftly turned to gut-wrenching anger with Adam quickly assembling the jagged pieces of his own ignorance. Moi had contributed no more than he had to endangering the future of *Aqualene*. Instead of selling out to Admiral or to its rogue alliances for whatever personal gain, she had risked her life to protect what belonged to NASA.

Futile were his efforts to twist from the bed straps and chase after Cindy Mollett.

Lowering his head, his thoughts turned to the task of surmounting INS bureaucracy in hopes of locating Moi. Then a knock at the door. Adam brightened. Had Mollett reconsidered and returned to expedite matters in a civilized manner? Crouching over both knees, Adam breathed a sigh of relief. Methodically, he pasted on a smile and prepared to compensate for his lack of acumen, unaware his ideals would betray him.

Instead of coming face-to-face with Moi's friend, he was peering at someone who seemed only vaguely familiar. Accompanied by a tall dark-skinned youth, Dr. Mann stood at the foot of his bed.

"Uh, catching up on your prayers, Mr. Harlow?" Chuckling in his German accent, Heinrich stuck out a hand and congratulated Adam on his role in the recovery of international property. "By the way, meet Greg Walker, my intern."

Anxiety turning to anguish, Adam motioned the two around where he could shake hands. "Look, guys, thanks for dropping by, but I need—"

Heinrich bellied up to the foot of the bed and made eye contact. "You look like the world has come to its end."

The knot in Adam's throat swelled. "Guys, I need some help. You've gotta stop her."

Heinrich placed a hand on Adam's shoulder. "Somebody take your money?"

"Worse. A woman, her name is Mollett, Cindy Mollet, get her back in here."

Heinrich grinned at Greg, then shot an amused look at Adam. "Shaking things up around here with the ladies, huh?"

Adam's voice thundered back: "Hurry! I gotta speak with her ... before she leaves the building."

Immediately Greg picked up on Adam's seriousness. "Okay, tell us what she looks like."

"Short brown hair, gray power suit ... and frickin tap shoes!"

Heinrich laughed. "Tap shoes?"

"When you hear 'em you'll find her. Please hurry."

Heinrich turned to Greg. "You take the stairs at the other end of the hall. We'll meet up at the drive-through."

291

Adam's description of Cindy had yielded no results when Heinrich found Greg at the hospital's main entrance.

Seemed like every woman in Sacramento had brown hair. And nobody inside the lobby fit the clothing description. Feverishly, Greg darted outside, only to spy a pair of seniors climbing into a sedan. Beyond them a vender was off-loading boxes from the backside of a utility truck.

That was it, for the drive-through.

Against a fresh wave of foot traffic Greg slipped back through the automatic glass doors and found Heinrich watching a stream of visitors and hospital staff exiting the elevators. Overhead a polite female voice sounded over the hospital's public address system, ordering some doctor to intensive care. That was when Greg heard the shoes.

"Listen! Sounds like her over there." Greg pointed toward a busy hallway intersection. Of a dozen people trooping toward them before spilling into the main lobby, a young woman with a sassy gait and shoes pounding the tiles mounted the steps of the lobby toward the main doors. She wore a dark business jacket and a gray skirt.

"Pardon me, ma'am," Heinrich blurted out. "Could you possibly be Cindy Mollett?"

His German accent produced just enough of a pause for her to glance at him through blazing blue eyes. Her shoes were clacking again. "I am," she snorted. "State your business. You can see I'm in a hurry."

There were no doubts in Heinrich's mind Cindy had experience fending off solicitors and strangers. "Ur, the name is Heinrich, ma'am." He adjusted his stride to fall in step with her as they navigated double doors out to the parking lot. Greg listened at an inconspicuous distance.

Heinrich took another stab at the pulsating exchange. "Madam, you might say I am an acquaintance of Adam Harlow."

"Don't waste my time, Mr. Henridge."

"*Heinrich*, ma'am. You see, I am here to attest on behalf of Mr. Harlow."

"I'm happy we've established each other's agenda, but that doesn't fix things, Mr. Heinrich."

The woman's feet clicked into high gear over the sidewalk.

Greg sped up within two steps of them. Heinrich pressed on his awkward pursuit. "Miss Mollett," he pleaded, "I have little choice but to confess that I know nothing of what this quarrel entails. However, I did make note of the despair in Mr. Harlow's face. And I can honestly disclose to you that he is quite desperate about working this through with you."

Cindy Mollett's shoes were relentless, continuing at a breakneck clip. "Not on my life."

"Perhaps there has been some dreadful mistake," Heinrich pointed out.

"A major big one, I should say."

"Yes, of course, ma'am. A mishap you could perhaps explain to my colleague, Greg Walker and myself before we bid you farewell."

Mollett's shoes fell silent, her shoulders high and her head still tilted forward. "*Who* did you say is with you?"

"Greg Walker, ma'am."

Cindy swiveled around to find Greg standing several paces behind them.

Carefully sizing him up and down, she produced a hardy smile. "You're the kid on TV! The one everybody's been talking about in the news. Is it really *you* who helped get those astronauts home safely?"

Greg tilted his head and rubbed his jaw. "Um, well…yes, ma'am, I guess I helped a little."

Cindy stuck out her hand. "Look guys, I apologize for acting rude. It's just that Mr. Harlow is—"

Greg raised both eyebrows. He wore an expectant grin as he shook her hand. "Mr. Harlow did look pretty serious about settin' things right with you, ma'am."

Cindy rotated a half circle, observing the brightening skies and a freshness in the air, then gazed back at the rambling hospital complex. She blew away a strand of hair hanging in her face. "I *did* come an awful distance. If there's any chance

293

for an acquittal it's going to hinge on a darn good testimony from Mr. Harlow."

Thirty

After speaking long distance to Adam from the Space Center, Renee DeLong wired President Kirkpatrick and requested that he and Moi be pardoned from pending charges of espionage. Radio and television reports carried the story in detail.

Deliberations in a closed court room had all but ended when the notebook from the trunk of Moi's Toyota was recovered by police and introduced into evidence as proof she had honored and protected joint Chinese and American interests. Validated by a grand jury's statement the pair had acted in the *best of one's capacity*, the president invoked an executive decree declaring both be exonerated from all criminal charges against them. The panel extended visa privileges for Moi's father, whom the Chinese parliament agreed to pardon after determining his political motives had been based on exposing illegal trafficking for the purpose of preserving legitimate economic ties between Beijing and Washington.

Immigration prosecutors working with data gathered by the FBI determined Colonel William Striker had conspired with a Chinese syndicate operating inside the United States by agreeing with a competitor to obtain details of *Aqualene*, only to renege on the deal and approach Admiral Petroleum with intentions of brokering a bidding war between the two companies. In light of the material's content, and acts of sabotage, the Pentagon sealed the colonel's records and informed family members he had acted with patriotic valor in his final hours.

Coalition members arrived in Washington to finalize details for putting *Aqualene* on fast track production at Lukefield. The following day the president held a reception to honor the people who contributed to the formula's recovery. Adam, Heinrich, Greg and Moi, along with NASA's astronauts and other technical dignitaries from the Mojave Space Center were flown into Langley Air Force Base in Hampton, Virginia. Escorted aboard military helicopters, they were whisked directly to the White House for a scheduled press conference. Waiting there were the international delegates representing the International Energy Coalition.

From a podium in the Oval Office, Kirkpatrick opened with a joke about his last speech. "Symbolically speaking, addressing the nation in a snowstorm had resulted in *mistaken karma*," he admitted. Cameras were rolling. "I humbly thank our many heroic individuals and government personnel for the perilous risks each endured in the quest for world peace and economic stability. All of you contributed to the preservation of freedom and the restoration of brotherhood between our great nations."

Kirkpatrick went on to offer additional praise to the international delegates for their political patience while disclosing key events leading up to renewed international relations. A series of e-mail tracks obtained by the FBI determined that classified data had been ferried by a geo-physicist hired to infiltrate Admiral for the purpose of gleaning off stolen information from the U.S. Energy Department—secrets that turned out to be deceiving. Such had remained the case at Crimson until Mr. Adam Harlow was recruited to bridge the gap, making him a primary suspect in an attempt to sell classified government secrets. But when a composition of his experimental version of the *Aqualene*—determined by experts to be an authentic specimen against the inferior product engineered at Crimson—had arrived at NASA's Jet Propulsion Labs, elements of coercion was factored into the case. The sample of independent work accompanied a dramatic account of a farmer's pickup truck traveling over 200 miles on less than a gallon of the fuel, providing proof that Mr. Harlow had intended to guard the best interest of his government and its people. The president closed his speech by informing the American people that fuel prices were destined to come down and rationing would end not a day too soon.

It wasn't until TV crews packed up and vacated the Oval Office the Chinese ambassador to the UN stood up to address those in attendance. Referencing a note card, he spoke methodically: "It is with great compunction that I disclose my government's resolve to leverage the United States over a simple breach of security. For the bonds of faith between our nations can be regarded no less than a lasting trust among our peoples. In the words of Confucius, wisdom can only be attained through securing contact with the Great Spirit. I believe each of you have acquired such vision."

The ambassador insisted he present a medal to each of the guests connected with *Aqualene*'s recovery. He approached the group, now standing shoulder-to-shoulder, beginning with the wife and two children of Gamil Kabib. Breaking their gaze from the room's ornate ceilings, both children stood obediently as the Chinese official offered their mother a formal bow. She responded in kind and then wept, suspending the delegation in silence. A representative of the State Department came forward and presented her with a five-million dollar stipend for her husband's contribution to *Aqualene*, prompting a thundering applause.

Moving down the line the ambassador presented a sealed envelope to a modestly dressed woman. She had pulled Moi Song from Seattle's Elliot Bay. Upon receiving her gift, she and her son retreated shyly. When the ambassador and the president finished giving out money and metals, the formalities of compensation soon faded into a jubilant party atmosphere. In a corner of the room near Kirkpatrick's private wine cabinet, Heinrich bobbed with excitement. Renee had turned up her charm with a host of declassified tidbits. She could now elaborate on government plans to confiscate Admiral's refineries to undergo modifications for the manufacture of *Aqualene*. "Rodney Panach has saved us a lot of trouble by setting up shop in twenty two strategic locations," she announced. "Federal investigators have determined he ordered simultaneous duplication of everything Adam had engineered at the Crimson plant."

"Absolutely brilliant!" Heinrich trumpeted. "Given minor alterations to those refineries, at what date have we a plan to begin production?"

Renee smiled with satisfaction. "Almost immediately! Properties on U.S. soil shall become sites for development, and will begin the earliest phases of fuel production. Ultimately, the ownership of *Aqualene* becomes a tax-supported venture and will operate much like a publicly owned utility ... eventually to be phased back into the private sector."

The wait-staff cleared dishes and hopped around to top off champagne glasses. Everyone huddled up to the electronic display that was used to demonstrate the intricacies of the NASA's Vashon Mission. A third lunar mining mission was slated for October while scientists continued to determine where *Aqualene*'s minerals were best taken from earth's crust with minimal impact.

Renee saw her opportunity to retreat from the buzzing reception. In a small foyer Adam stood, admiring a 15th Century tapestry from Persia. She'd long anticipated a private chat with the *man of the hour*.

"I never imagined I'd see you again," she began. Her voice possessed a serious ring. "When our disabled spacecraft docked with Europa in a dangerously low orbit, we were within minutes of death by asphyxiation."

"Sounds like both of us could have taken out some extra hazard and medical before setting out on this venture," Adam mused.

"My apologies for you getting ensnared in Admiral's trap."

Adam smiled. "I've decided to view this as one long-overdue adventure in a non-descript life."

Renee folded her arms. "You carry yourself well for a young, unemployed engineer. With that in mind I've recommended you for a spot in the U.S. Energy Department. We'll need a director who is willing to travel."

"I accept ... but first I'll need a few days to bail my mother's home mortgage out of foreclosure, and then update my resume."

Renee smiled. "Save it, Adam. I hear you'll be given a substantial sum of money for your accomplishments. And you're being appointed to the position this afternoon ... by the president himself."

"Now there's government efficiency."

"Promise me you'll finish up your degree, Adam."

"With pleasure."

"There's more. The Chinese are talking about placing Moi on a team in charge of configuring multiple shipping arrangements between six continents. You two will be coordinating a number of administrative and scientific processes."

Adam's eyes furrowed. "And her resident status?"

"She'll be granted dual citizenship, making international travel easy."

Adam grinned. "A fair settlement with an honest salary. Okay, how about the perks—you know: Waterfront homes, ranches, sports cars, stocks ... all the amenities I was promised at Admiral?"

"Bribery!" Renee appreciated Adam's wit. "Looking back ... I'm not surprised that company had its fingers in this mess. Rodney Panach has had too many brushes with the law over proprietary theft, money laundering, and pending anti-trust cases. I suspected trouble long ago. Court records reveal a lengthy history of depression, bordering on insanity. The guy's been to hell and back, beginning at age nine when his mother was banished from the family after her brother exposed the Panach Clan's involvement in a Venezuelan drug war. Almost ten years later young Rodney found himself in court for manslaughter after killing his twin brother in a drunken boating accident, at which time he lost both of his legs."

Adam raised a pointed finger. "Providing him the perfect mindset for taking over his dad's company, capable of indiscriminate murder anytime someone got in his way."

"If you ask me, the tyrant got what he bargained for: marooned on a derelict drilling rig, somewhere in the Pacific."

"Maybe so," Adam admitted. "Still, Rodney Panach is not one to disappear into obscurity. He'll be back, and in disguise—a reincarnate of all the evil he never got around to execute." Adam elected to change the topic. "Renee, I have to be honest with you. More than once I considered dumping the formula into public domain—a full scale Internet blitz."

"Your day may be coming, Adam" she laughed. "In effect, you and this coalition will be doing it together. Your team will make sure *Aqualene* is properly produced worldwide. It's going to take innovation, persistence ... and the foresight to wade beyond politics to focus on the public good—another reason for my contacting you about the recovery project."

"Oh? How's that?"

"Your research ambitions at college. We recruit many of our candidates based on their personal ambitions and self-generated projects. Your accomplishments may have seemed inconsequential to you at the time, but they were no secret to certain faces inside NASA."

"Nothing in my life's been a secret once *you* came along."

"I did give you fair warning."

Adam blinked, averting his eyes from hers. "After losing my father to unimaginable fate ... and then walking blindly into Admiral's trap, the task of trusting others seems a tougher road to walk."

Renee extended her hand. "A painful awakening?"

Adam nodded. "No matter how dark the circumstances, or deep the risks, I guess we've got to believe in one another. Especially in rough times."

"Well said for the sake of tangible love. Can I quote you in my report?"

"No you can't," Adam chuckled, wiping dampness from his eyes. "But I do have something you *can* put into your report." He reached into his shirt pocket and pulled out a tiny capsule. "That blue fluid everyone's calling *Aqualene* doesn't have to be so darn complicated."

"Improved plans ... already?" Renee began squeezing the ends of the capsule like a child fondling a bright red crayon.

"Yes, ma'am. With time to think inside Admiral's prison walls, I pondered all of it. My formula will take us farther than rare minerals excavated off the moon."

"Beyond that *blue colored water* selling on the Internet?"

"Already?"

She rolled her eyes and urged Adam to go on.

"Thanks to nano-composites derived from magnesium, the fuel completes its finishing phases with hydrogen extraction from saltwater inside a small pressurized chamber. It all could feasibly be processed beneath the hood of your car."

Renee shook her head and gave Adam a look of admiration. "Detroit ought to reward you well for this, not to mention one huge thanks from our coalition partners. This whole project has yielded lasting research, and we've developed a fuel that produces no harmful emissions."

"Now it's your turn," Adam said, stuffing the capsule into his pocket. "How did you manage to contact Heinrich at the space station after the colonel wiped out NASA communications?"

Renee laughed smugly. "My early suspicions were correct. Striker had scrambled our codes for transmitting to Europa Command and NASA's ground control centers. However, years ago, I wrote the coding for a SETI-sponsored workstation aboard ISS. That's how I could get through to a civilian terminal, the same one Dr. Mann was using."

"Clever thinking … Did you just say you worked with *SETI*?"

"I did."

"Get out of town! You … an acclaimed astro-physicist, mineral scientist, and space corps commander … pondering extraterrestrial mumbo jumbo?"

Renee was grinning ear to ear. "It was precisely my fascination with *life beyond earth* that drove me to finish school and get on with NASA."

Adam folded his arms and paused. "It's time you got better acquainted with Dr. Mann. According to Greg, the guy spent a year at a SETI camp on a mountaintop in New Zealand. Uh, well, I'll leave it to him to tell you what happened up there."

"As a matter of fact, Adam, I plan to meet him for lunch, tomorrow."

"Lunch? Tomorrow?"

"Yes! Heinrich and Greg asked me to meet them at a quaint little Greek cafe along Pennsylvania Avenue. It's on the way to the Air and Space Museum. Will you and Moi join us?"

END

Discussion Points for Book Circles

How does Adam Harlow's perception of the petroleum industry influence his desire to help resurrect NASA's *Aqualene* formula?

Discuss personal and career experiences that made Adam better qualified to successfully find *Aqualene*'s complex formula?

Throughout much of the story Adam confides in Moi Song—but later falls into serious doubt about her loyalty. Identify turning points in the story that shed doubt about her integrity. What evidence later proves she is trustworthy?

Some readers say Dell Jackson is foolish to collaborate with Adam on his farm east of Bellingham. What scenario validates such a point?

Despite William Striker's contempt for members aboard ISS, how does the author convey a benevolent side of the colonel?

How can we account for the fact that Dr. Mann and Dr. Tanaka, both prominent scientists, are so different in character and likeability?

Greg Walker manages to play a significant role in bringing resolution to the rift between Adam and Moi. How does his character make him the right choice for this role?

A blend of geologic wonder and mass quantities of saltwater provide the compounds for producing a fuel superior to gasoline. How do the Apollo missions of the 1970s contribute to Aqualene's extraordinary breakthrough?

During his reign at Admiral Petroleum, Rodney Panach rejects any station in life short of absolute power. Discuss a range of circumstances that threaten to erode his grip on the energy industry, aside from *Aqualene* serving to replace gasoline.

Given the positives of producing a clean and efficient fuel like Aqualene, consider in your discussions any negative impacts of introducing a miracle fuel on the energy market today. What national and economic stakes are at risk? Why?

Additional Research Points

- How much refined gasoline is consumed each day in America?

- How will "fracking" contribute to our nation's supply of fuel?

- How much influence does *oil produced at home* reduce the retail price of gasoline sold in America?

- How does "fracking" impact Earth's ecology and underground water supplies?

- Who controls America's nation's energy policy today?

- How does the average American consumer impact oil production?

- Determine how EPA fuel efficiency standards affect both fuel consumption and carbon emissions in America.

- How should America participate on an international scale to influence the reduction of hydro-carbon emissions?